From the author whom Ro...

"the reigning queen of Americana romance"

LINDA LAEL MILLER

The three brothers who began it all

THE McKETTRICK COWBOYS

McKettrick land. McKettrick pride.
The foundation of a dynasty.

Rafe McKettrick

Proud, passionate, and hot-tempered, he's
determined to win his inheritance, but he never
dreamed that the cost would be his heart.

Kade McKettrick

He's determined not to lose to his
brother in the marriage stakes—but he
hadn't counted on falling in love.

Jeb McKettrick

He thought proposing marriage would be the
hardest thing he ever did. That was before his
new bride's secret past wounded his pride.

These titles are also available as eBooks.

And praise for more McKettrick stories by

LINDA LAEL MILLER

"Highly enjoyable. . . . Strong characterization and a vivid western setting make for a fine historical romance."

—*Publishers Weekly* on *McKettrick's Choice*

"Engrossing western romance. . . . Miller has created unforgettable characters and woven a many-faceted yet coherent and lovingly told tale."

—*Booklist* (starred review) on *McKettrick's Choice*

"There's just something about those McKettricks . . . that makes you want to jump right into the pages and stay for a while."

—*Romantic Times* on *McKettricks of Texas: Garrett*

"Fast-moving, emotional."

—*Booklist* on *McKettricks of Texas: Garrett*

"A passionate love too long denied drives the action in this multifaceted, emotionally rich reunion story that overflows with breathtaking sexual chemistry."

—*Library Journal* on *McKettricks of Texas: Tate*

"High drama, spiked with intense romance."

—*Publishers Weekly* on *McKettrick's Heart*

"Love and blazing sex ensue in this satisfying romance."

—*Booklist* on *McKettrick's Heart*

"Heartwarming and heartbreakingly poignant."

—*Romantic Times* on *McKettrick's Heart*

ALSO BY LINDA LAEL MILLER

Linda Lael Miller

Secondhand Bride

POCKET BOOKS

New York London Toronto Sydney New Delhi

Pocket Books
A Division of Simon & Schuster, Inc.
1230 Avenue of the Americas
New York, NY 10020

This book is a work of fiction. Names, characters, places and incidents are products of the author's imagination or are used fictitiously. Any resemblance to actual events or locales or persons, living or dead, is entirely coincidental.

An *Original* Publication of Pocket Books

First Pocket Books paperback edition December 2004

POCKET and colophon are registered trademarks of Simon & Schuster, Inc.

For information regarding special discounts for bulk purchases, please contact Simon & Schuster Special Sales at 1-800-506-1949 or business@simonandschuster.com.

The Simon & Schuster Speakers Bureau can bring authors to your live event. For more information or to book an event contact the Simon & Schuster Speakers Bureau at 1-866-248-3049 or visit our website at www.simonspeakers.com.

Cover illustration by Aleta Rafton

Manufactured in the United States of America

20   19   18   17   16   15   14   13   12   11

ISBN: 978-0-7434-2275-8
ISBN: 978-1-4165-1453-4 (ebook)

For Dr. Sam Walters,

with love, admiration, and gratitude.

You made the difference.

Secondhand Bride

1

There was no place to run to, no place to hide.

Jeb McKettrick, always careening recklessly from the core of his being to the circumference and back again, was caught between the bunkhouse wall and the manure pile, with all the rage of a woman scorned bearing down on him in redheaded, whip-wielding, chicken-scattering fury.

Chloe Wakefield had found him, as surely as the needle of a compass finds due north, and chased him all the way from Indian Rock. Pretty much kept up, too, even though he'd been on a fast horse.

He was dead meat.

The buggy she drove might have been a chariot, drawn by the four horses of the Apocalypse, instead of a battered conveyance and a single lathered and huffing nag, both hastily procured at the livery stable in town.

For the length of a heartbeat, Jeb actually believed she meant to run him down, grind him into a pulp under the wheels of that spindly, black-bonneted rig. For all his reckless love of life, he could not help but conclude that there would have been a certain mercy in oblivion. At least then he wouldn't have had to deal with the problem.

Clearly, he was not to be spared.

After a minute or two, his stepmother's chickens settled down a little, though, and went back to their ground-pecking and feather-shuffling. Maybe that was a good omen.

The only rooster in evidence, Jeb scrambled for his trademark grin, his one talisman, found a shaky semblance of it, and stuck it to his mouth. He put his hands out from his sides and made himself the picture of innocent affability, though on the inside, he was a tangle of contradictory emotions—sweet terror, bitter amusement, and anger, too, because, *dammit*, he was right, and she was wrong. And because he had never guessed, before that day, that among his many secret and interchangeable selves lurked a yellow-bellied chicken heart.

"Chloe," he said, making a plea of the word, as well as a smooth reprimand. A red hen tapped briefly at the toe of his right boot; he ankled it aside impatiently.

Standing up in the buggy now, drawing back on the reins with powerful, delicate hands, Chloe fixed him in a sapphire glare. "Don't you 'Chloe' *me*, Jeb McKettrick!"

she commanded. "You're a liar and a cheat and three kinds of devil—you've all but ruined my reputation *and* my life, you sorry excuse for a man, and I have half a mind to whip the hide off you right here and now!"

He rolled his shoulders once, within his brown corduroy jacket, pushed his hat to the back of his head. He had no defense, other than his charm and good looks, which did not seem to be having any noticeable effect. "May I suggest," he countered, with an ease that was wholly false, "that you consult the other half?"

She set the brake lever, snatched up the buggy whip, and clambered down; all of this happened so quickly that the separate motions seemed to tumble into one continuous whole. Her auburn hair, falling from its pins and combs, blazed like fire around her face, which was flushed with outrage, and she advanced. "Scoundrel!" she spat. "Rounder! Do you have any idea what I've been through because of you?"

"Chloe," he said again, with hopeless goodwill.

She took his measure with her eyes and plainly found him wanting, but she *was* a little calmer, it seemed to him. Or maybe she was merely winded by the mad rush from town. By some perverse twist of fate, he'd just come out of the Bloody Basin Saloon when she stepped down from the afternoon stage, and he'd been as surprised to see Chloe Wakefield as she'd been to see him. He'd made up his mind to face her, try to make peace, but when he'd registered the look of shock and indignation on her face, he'd panicked instead, mounted up, and ridden back to the ranch like a mouse bolting for a hole in the wall.

"If there was any justice in this world, you would have sprouted horns and cloven hooves by now," she burst out. Pink spots pulsed beneath her flawless cheekbones, and her lovely bosom rose and fell with the rapid, shallow rhythm of her breath.

He waited. It was that or dive into the manure pile and try to bury himself.

"Did you think I wouldn't find you someday?" she asked, and though her eyes were still snapping with conviction, her tone was softer than before. Was she settling down? He couldn't rightly guess, and didn't want to err on the side of optimism, which was his natural inclination.

"I guess it never occurred to me that you'd come looking," he replied, in all truth. He'd fled to Tombstone, stung by the discovery that half his father's life had been a lie, and therefore much of his own as well, and facing the probable loss of what he held most dear in all the world—the Triple M. By decree of the almighty Angus McKettrick, the ranch would go to the first of his three sons to marry and provide the old man with a grandchild, a contest his eldest brother Rafe had all but won by getting hitched to Emmeline. And now Kade was married, too, and still in the running.

His own prospects had seemed worse than dismal at the time—who'd have thought they could get worse?

Back then, Jeb's plan had been to carouse his troubles away, bedding as many dancing girls as possible, playing as much poker as he could, and consuming copious amounts of whiskey. Instead, he'd encountered the lively Miss Wakefield right out of the chute, and things had promptly gotten out of hand. Oh, yes, from the moment he'd collided with Chloe in front of a mercantile in Tombstone, chaos had been the order of the day.

Hell, he'd have been better off at the OK Corral, siding with the Clantons and McLaurys against Doc Holliday and the Earps. At least then he'd have had a fighting chance.

Was that the glimmer of tears he saw in her eyes? Please, God, anything but that. For all of it, he'd rather be flayed alive than see her cry.

"You and I are married," she said. She held up her left hand, his ring glinting in the crisp sunshine of that October afternoon. Fresh color flared in her face. "Or did that slip your mind?"

He took off his hat, put it on again, this time with the brim drawn down, to cast a shadow over his face. He'd been over this same terrain a dozen times, walking the landscape of his own conscience, raising all the unflattering arguments that could be made against him, and shooting each one down like a tin can tossed against the crisp autumn sky. And none of that had prepared him for this single, inevitable confrontation.

The manure pile was beginning to look downright inviting.

"Our getting married was a mistake," he said, in what he hoped was a reasonable tone of voice. For a moment, he was back in Tombstone, a happy bridegroom of less than an hour, with a honeymoon ahead of him, being stopped in the street by a stranger, presented with irrefutable proof that he'd just been crowned king of fools. "It should never have happened in the first place."

He saw her stiffen at his words, then commence building up a head of steam again. "At last," she said. "Something we can agree on. I should never have given you the time of day!"

"Go back to Tombstone, Chloe," he said flatly.

"I can't," she retorted, with an indignant little huff of a sigh. "Thanks to you, and that scene you made in the Broken Stirrup Saloon, I lost my teaching job. I'm a poor moral influence, according to the president of the school board. *That's* why I followed you out here—to tell you that *you've ruined my life!*"

"I might have overreacted a little, back there at the Broken Stirrup, I mean," he allowed, but grudgingly. There was more of the old man in him, he guessed, than he liked to think. He felt Angus McKettrick's pride and stubbornness right there, behind his heart, jostling for standing room next to the coward. Furious with himself for letting Chloe get him on the run in the first place—so many people in town had seen him run for his horse and bolt that he'd probably never live it down. And that wasn't counting the spectacle he'd made in front of his brothers just minutes before, riding up in a frenzy and yammering at Rafe and Kade to hide him—God knew what *they'd* told her, when she'd stopped to speak to them. He took a step toward her, gratified when she took a corresponding step back. "Anyway, we settled all this before I left Tombstone. Far as I'm concerned, you got what you had coming."

She had the lid-rattling look of a kettle coming to a high boil; he thought the top of her head was fixing to blow right off and braced himself for a steam burn. "*You* did most of the talking, if you'll remember," she accused. "You never gave me a chance to explain!"

He wrenched the buggy whip out of her right hand and hurled it aside. If she went after it, she'd find herself up to her pretty little nose in horse shit, literally as well as figuratively. "Once I saw your wedding picture, *Miss* Wakefield, and the man you were standing beside in that daguerreotype didn't happen to be *me*, no further explanations were required!"

Her eyes widened, as though he'd struck her, and her mouth tightened. She took back the scant inches of sod she'd given up moments before, standing toe-to-toe and nose to nose with him. "*Please* stop trying to portray yourself as the injured party," she snapped. "You didn't mean any of the things you said when we were courting, and you damn well know it, you—you—"

Guilt foamed up inside him, like the head on a mug of just-drawn beer, but he blew it aside. His jaw clamped down so hard that it hurt, and the challenge hissed through his teeth. "Yes?" he prompted.

She was utterly defiant, a petticoat-Texan, holding the Alamo all on her own. "*You used me*," she repeated. "You wanted a wife and a baby, so you could get this ranch!"

He indulged in an insolent shrug, though he was surprised that she knew about his father's unreasonable demand. "You seemed willing enough to me."

That was when she drew back her hand and slapped him hard enough to loosen his teeth. Rage sang through him, so pure and so intense that it was almost pleasurable. He gripped her wrists, to forestall another attack, though there wasn't much he could do about her feet. He'd be lucky if she didn't haul off and kick him in the shins with one of those pointy-toed shoes she was wearing.

"You bastard!" she breathed. "You unconscionable wretch!"

He tightened his grasp, taking care not to hurt her. "Is that what you came all this way to say?" he shot back. "Well, now you've said it. Get in your hired buggy, Chloe, and go home to your husband!"

She struggled to free herself, sputtering, too angry to speak coherently. He saw the intention to splinter his bones brewing in her eyes, clear as clouds gathering on a dark horizon, and sidestepped it, still holding her wrists.

Her eyes shimmered with tears, and she made no attempt to hide them. "I would dearly love to kill you right now," she informed him, and he knew she meant it. "Jack Barrett *is not* my husband—you are!"

"What the devil is going on here?"

At the intrusion of an all-too-familiar voice, Jeb turned his head, as did Chloe, and saw his pa standing a few feet away, hoary thumbs hooked under his belt. Angus McKettrick was a big man, well over six feet tall, rugged as the Texas plains that had spawned him, and just then, he looked stern enough to have stepped right out of the pages of the Old Testament.

Riled and chagrined, both at the same time, Jeb let go of Chloe with a flinging motion of his hands, not at all sure she wouldn't take advantage of the distraction to kick him where it would hurt most, which sure as hell wasn't his shins. He knew he ought to answer his father's terse if perfectly sensible question, but he couldn't think of a single sane explanation. When he and Chloe were together, they either fought like wildcats or made love like monkeys, and there didn't seem to be much middle ground between the two extremes.

Chloe visibly smoothed her disgruntled countenance, favored the meddlesome old coot with a wistful smile, and put out a hand, stepping toward Angus as cordially as if they'd met at a garden party instead of out behind the bunkhouse, next to the manure pile, surrounded by chickens. "How do you do?" she said brightly. "My name is Chloe McKettrick. I'm Jeb's wife."

Angus looked baffled for a moment, but then a beatific smile spread across his face. He took the hand she offered and squeezed it warmly. "Well, now," the big man said, "my youngest here has been claiming he'd taken himself a bride, but I confess I was doubtful, since I never saw any sign of you." After tossing Jeb a look that would sear the hide off a bear, he beamed at Chloe. "I'm Angus McKettrick, the head of this outfit. Come on inside. The family will be pleased to make your acquaintance at long last."

Jeb tried to intercede. "Pa—" Sure, he'd let his father and brothers believe he was married, mostly to nettle them, to shake Kade's and Rafe's confidence a little, since they'd been so all-fired sure that one or the other of them would win control of the Triple M, leaving him out in the cold, but it had all been so much smoke and bullshit. Chloe was another man's wife, whatever her protests to the contrary, and that was the stark reality. "Pa, listen to me, I—she—"

Angus pointed a work-gnarled index finger in his direction. "Not another word," he warned, all glower, grit, and gravel.

Jeb seethed with indignation, but at the moment it didn't seem prudent to state his case. Besides, it meant saying straight out that he'd been bamboozled but good, and such an admission would have stuck in his throat like a wadded-up sock.

A regular ladies' man, Angus crooked his elbow at

Chloe, and she swept right around and linked her arm with his, leaving Jeb behind as surely as if he'd turned invisible. The two of them strolled off in the direction of the house, and neither one so much as flinched when Jeb threw back his head, about to split open in frustration, and gave a Rebel yell fit to rend the heavens.

It sure scared the chickens, though.

2

*C*hloe figured if she hadn't already dedicated her life and soul to the assiduous education of young minds, she could have been an actress. The performance she put on when Jeb's father squired her into that grand and rustic ranch house was a consummate one, worthy of the applause of heaven.

They entered through the kitchen, a well-used and oft-frequented place in that household, from all appearances: The two men she'd encountered outside, earlier, after crossing the creek like a she-demon, were there, seated at the long table, their sleeves rolled up to reveal powerful forearms, their faces alight with some private glee.

She knew the larger one, dark-haired and exuding a confidence that fell just short of out-and-out arrogance, was Rafe. He rose in her honor, but belatedly, after the other brother, Kade, had already gotten to his feet and nodded a greeting. He seemed sturdy and self-possessed, though his hair was a chestnut color, and his eyes were green, in contrast to Rafe's blue ones. They were breathtakingly handsome, both of them, but mere shadows, in Chloe's estimation, compared to Jeb.

The devil himself, posing as an angel of light. Damn his shiftless soul.

Chloe turned her attention to the two women in the room, one young, with golden brown hair and intelligent aquamarine eyes, the other middle-aged, soft and small, and of Spanish extraction. With booming pride, Angus presented Chloe as Jeb's bride, then introduced the first woman as Kade's wife, Mandy, and the second as his own, Concepcion.

Both women greeted her warmly, with smiles and curious looks that made her blush, though not as fiercely as she had before, during the altercation with Jeb. She probably looked like a hoyden to them, with her tumbling-down hair and smudged traveling clothes, and it was an embarrassing certainty that they'd heard all about her rousing arrival from Kade and Rafe. Standing in the yard, they'd witnessed her descent upon the Triple M and kindly directed her to their younger brother.

"Please, sit down," Concepcion said, getting a mug down from a shelf and hoisting a huge enamel coffeepot off the stove to pour. It was then that Chloe noticed the older woman's protruding midsection; she was carrying a child.

Chloe felt a stab of envy even as she nodded, taking the place Angus indicated, the chair just to the right of the one he'd drawn back for himself.

"Are you hungry?" Mandy asked, quietly gracious. "Concepcion and I have been baking pies—we have cherry and peach and dried apple."

Chloe realized, with a start, that she *was* hungry. She hadn't eaten a bite, in fact, since before she left Tombstone, the day before, to ride a northbound stage, never dreaming she'd run into the man who had courted, married, and abandoned her, all in less than a month. She swallowed, nodded. "Please," she said. "Cherry sounds good."

Concepcion presented her with a steaming cup of coffee and refilled the one Angus had apparently left behind when he'd gone out to intercede between her and Jeb. Mandy cut a generous slice of cherry pie and served it on a pretty china plate, brought her a fork.

"Thank you," Chloe said, wishing she'd taken the time to bathe, change clothes, and attend to her hair at the hotel in town, but she'd spotted Jeb right away, and she'd been so stung that she'd forgotten her original reasons for making the journey in the first place—the long-delayed telegram crumpled inside her purse, informing her that her uncle, John Lewis, was ailing. In addition, she'd read in the *Epitaph* that there was a teaching job to be had in Indian Rock.

One glimpse of Jeb McKettrick strolling out of the Bloody Basin Saloon had driven those worthy objectives straight out of her mind, and she'd traveled all this way in a white-hot dither of a rage, wanting his scalp, or, at the very least, an abject apology.

During their brief but fiery alliance, Jeb had told her he lived outside of Stockton, California, the lying skunk. He'd said he loved her. Bought her flowers and candy. Won her over, despite his patently reckless nature. On more than one occasion, he'd risked his neck to impress her, riding horses Satan himself wouldn't dare to mount, and he'd very nearly gotten into a gunfight with a man who'd spoken disrespectfully to her. Worst of all, he'd lured her into his bed, not once, but several times, and brought out a side of her nature that, in retrospect, appalled and astonished her.

Now, in the spacious, ordinary kitchen of the Triple M ranch house, she burned, recalling her wanton responses.

She glanced at the back door, which was firmly shut, and wondered, quite against her will, if her runaway bridegroom would put in an appearance, or if he'd already taken to his heels, as he was so disposed to do. The latter seemed more likely, given recent history, and though she would have preferred to feel just about anything else, an incomprehensible sadness all but overwhelmed her.

Angus's mouth being full of dried apple pie, it was Rafe who gave voice to what they were all surely thinking. "Seems to me you and my little brother aren't on the best of terms," he said, carefully polite. "Will you be staying here at the Triple M, or moving on?"

The last thing Chloe intended to do was take up residence in a house where she would be purely unwelcome, at least from Jeb's point of view. Even though he had told her a little about each of his family members, neatly transporting them to a ranch called the Double L, these people were essentially strangers, and she couldn't bring herself to roll out the whole shoddy story, right on top of the first howdy-do.

"I'll probably check into the Arizona Hotel for a few days," she said moderately. "You see, I came to Indian Rock to see my uncle and inquire about a teaching position. I did not expect to run into Jeb."

The curve of Rafe's mouth looked suspiciously like a smirk. "Evidently, he was pretty surprised, too."

Chloe drew a deep, bracing breath, released it slowly. The damage had been done, but her dignity was about all she had left. "John Lewis is my biggest concern right now," she said, just as the back door swung open, and Jeb stepped over the threshold, glaring at her. "My uncle is the dearest person in the world to me."

Jeb's face changed instantly when he registered what she'd said, and a weighted silence descended over the whole room. Angus cleared his throat, and Rafe and Kade stared down at their plates, all signs of their previous amusement gone. Concepcion's brown eyes brimmed with tears, and Mandy put a hand to her throat.

The pit of Chloe's stomach dropped like the trapdoor on a gallows. "What's wrong?" she asked.

Angus's gaze sliced to Jeb, who stood as if he'd been

frozen, just inside the kitchen. "You'd better take your wife into the study," he said gravely, "and tell her what happened."

Chloe's hand trembled as she laid down her fork. Jeb nodded grimly in response to his father's statement, took off his hat, and hung it on the peg next to the door with the others. "This way," he said, indicating a direction with a slight movement of his head.

Chloe's knees wobbled as she stood. "What—?"

Jeb said nothing, but extended a hand to her, and she made her way around the end of the table to take it. He gave her fingers an almost imperceptible squeeze.

Swamped with dread, Chloe let Jeb lead her out of the kitchen, along a hallway, and finally into a spacious room at the front of the house. There, he gestured toward a chair, and Chloe sank into it.

Jeb closed the double doors softly, then came over to her, drew up a chair of his own, facing hers, and took both her hands into his.

"Chloe," he began, his voice gruff. He stopped, started again. "Chloe, John Lewis is dead. His heart gave out."

The room, a bastion of masculinity, seemed to lurch at a sickening angle. "You're lying," she said, though she knew he wasn't. The wire she'd received in Tombstone—she remembered now, with dizzying clarity, that it had been sent by Kade McKettrick, in his capacity as town marshal—had been misplaced for weeks. She'd only gotten it yesterday, and she'd immediately packed up her belongings and purchased a stagecoach ticket. She'd written to the Indian Rock School Committee, in response to their advertisement, well before that, and had intended to wait for a response before making the arduous journey.

Jeb leaned in far enough to let his forehead rest against hers, and she did not pull away, as she might have done in any other circumstance save this one. "I wish I *were* lying, Chloe," he said. "But it's the truth."

She began to cry, softly and with sniffles, and Jeb drew her out of her chair and onto his lap. He put his arms around her, rock solid, and she let her head rest on his shoulder, breathing in the fresh-air-and-trail-dust scent of him. "*No*," she whispered. It was impossible for John to be dead, plain impossible. He was the only family she had, aside from her estranged mother and stepfather, who were in Europe, making the Grand Tour. John had been her dearest and most faithful friend—her *only* friend, it often seemed. She'd kept every one of his letters, along with the small presents he'd sent for birthdays and Christmas. Though his visits had been infrequent, he'd been a powerful influence, shoring up her confidence when it wavered, listening with interest to her sometimes outrageous opinions, assuring her that she could come to him with any problem, at any time, and count on his help . . .

And now he was gone.

She shivered, and Jeb's embrace tightened. "John was

a fine man," he said, against her temple. "He's been sorely missed."

Chloe gave a soft, plaintive wail.

"Go ahead and cry," Jeb said. "You've got the right."

Chloe Wakefield hadn't shed a tear since she was thirteen years old, when her uncle John told her he wouldn't be visiting her in Sacramento anymore, and by now she was out of practice. Peculiar how such things came back to a person. She sobbed into Jeb's shirt and clung to him, and he held her.

Presently, Chloe got hold of herself and lifted her head. Shadows slipped across the room, as if falling from the books on the shelves, the walls, the very ceiling above. She dashed at her wet face with the back of one hand and eased out of Jeb's arms. She had two feet, she reminded herself; she would stand on them.

She moved to the window and stood looking out, her back to Jeb. "He must have wondered why I didn't come," she mourned. The creek she'd crossed earlier, in such high dudgeon, sparkled with the last fierce rays of sunlight, while splotches of pink and gold and blue danced on its surface. "I should have been there."

"I reckon he knew you would have been if you could."

She turned, clutching at a swell of ire the way a drowning swimmer would a sturdy branch extended from shore. "You were acquainted with John," she accused. "Did you know all along that he was my uncle?"

Jeb got to his feet. "No," he said, and he seemed to be

telling the truth. Of course, that was no indication that he was—Jeb McKettrick was a trickster, lover, and poet one moment, womanizing, gun-toting, card-playing waster the next. He kept a store of masks behind that handsome face and donned the one that best served his devious purposes at the time.

Chloe searched her memory, but she couldn't recall mentioning John to Jeb; their association had been too brief, too breathless, and too full of passion for such an exchange. If Jeb had told her he was from Indian Rock, instead of Stockton, she would have made the connection and spoken of John.

"When?" she asked. "When did he die?"

Jeb looked as though he wanted to approach her, take her in his arms again, but, to her combined relief and dismay, he did not. He simply stood there, watching her. "Not long after I left Tombstone," he answered.

Chloe fought an urge to dissolve again, to put her hands to her face and weep uncontrollably. "Where is he buried?"

"In the churchyard, in town," Jeb said. "I'll take you there tomorrow."

Chloe stiffened. At the moment, stubborn pride was all she had left. No job, no husband, no cherished, always-understanding uncle. "No, thank you," she said. "You've done quite enough, it seems to me. I'll go on my own."

She saw his jaw harden, his hands clench momentarily into fists at his sides. "You're not doing this on your own," he ground out. "And that's the end of it, Chloe. I put that poor nag you drove out here in the barn for the night, but I'll hitch up another one, and we'll head into Indian Rock together. Do whatever you have to do to get ready—we're leaving in fifteen minutes."

Chloe opened her mouth, closed it again. Folded her arms. If she could have, she would have put down roots and wrapped them around the beams underneath the floor, just to keep from giving Jeb his way; but he was twice her size and had the look of a man who meant exactly what he said.

He made for the doors, worked the latches with both hands, and looked back at her over one shoulder. He was a lean man, smaller than his brothers, but agile, and with his blue eyes flashing and his fair hair catching the last of the daylight, he looked for all the world like a young and rebellious god just come from Olympus.

"I'm sorry," he said. "About John. About everything."

Chloe didn't dare answer aloud, not knowing what would pour out of her if she risked opening the emotional floodgates—frenzied fury? Avowals of love? She spared him a sharp nod and turned away again, back to the window, back to the fading scenery.

He went out, and if he closed the doors behind him, she didn't hear it.

Perhaps five minutes had gone by when Mandy came to stand next to her. The silence was companionable, a consolation to Chloe's wounded spirit, though it didn't last long.

"I've put some water on to heat," Mandy said, "in case you'd like to wash before you go back to town."

Chloe sniffled, though she'd long since stopped crying, on the outside, at least. "You're very kind," she said, without looking at the other woman.

Mandy touched her arm. "You won't rush away, will you?" she asked gently. "It would be a shame if you left too soon, if you didn't give things a proper chance."

At last, Chloe met Mandy's gaze. She'd been thinking what an unhappy accident it was that she'd ever crossed paths with Jeb in the first place, let alone seen him again in Indian Rock and pursued him through the countryside like some enraged harridan.

"Why do you say that?"

Mandy smiled a little, looking wistful. "I almost did that myself," she said. "Kicked over the traces and ran away, I mean. And it would have been the worst mistake I ever made."

3

A silver wash of moonlight illuminated John Lewis's resting place, and a chilly breeze ruffled the loose tendrils of Chloe's hair as she stood looking down at the headstone. JOHN LEWIS, it read, BELOVED FRIEND AND HONORABLE MAN. Beneath were the dates—he'd lived only fifty-four years.

She brushed at her cheek with the heel of one palm and, standing just behind her, Jeb laid a tentative hand on her shoulder.

"It's cold out here, Chloe," he said gruffly. "Maybe it would be better to do this in the morning."

She shook her head and, at the same time, wrapped her arms around her middle. Since the chill came from inside, rather than out, the gesture was of little avail. "That's a fancy marker," she said, with a lift of her chin.

"Becky sent all the way to New York for it," Jeb told her, without removing his hand. She felt some of his vitality pouring into her, and she was grateful, though she would have spurned it if she could. Just the way Jeb had spurned her.

Chloe turned slightly in order to look up at him. "Becky? Who's that?"

Jeb let out a breath. "Didn't he mention her in his letters?"

"No," Chloe said, strangely stricken. She'd have remembered if John had ever mentioned a woman. And surely he wouldn't have kept something so important from her, even if it was highly personal.

Then the twinge came, in a quiet, hidden region of her heart. She'd never told John about Jeb, let alone Jack Barrett. She'd been ashamed to admit she'd been so foolish, not once, but twice.

Jeb drew Chloe's shawl more closely around her shoulders. He'd offered her his coat, during the long buggy ride from the Triple M, but she'd refused, partly because she was stubborn and partly because she knew wearing something of his would bring back too many poignant recollections. They'd made love in his Tombstone hotel room several times, and she'd worn his shirt afterwards, while they laughed and played gin rummy in the middle of the rumpled bed.

"They were planning to be married," Jeb said quietly, his gaze catching and holding hers, pulling her back from that other place and time. "Becky—some folks call her Mrs. Fairmont, and some call her Mrs. Harding, depending—well, she owns the Arizona Hotel. They were in love, planning to be married."

"I wish he'd told me." Chloe felt utterly adrift.

"Did you tell him about us?"

"No," she answered. "Of course not."

Jeb shook his head, mildly exasperated. "You didn't say anything because you were playing a game, and he would have known you already had a husband. His reasons for not mentioning Becky were probably a little more admirable."

The words bruised Chloe, as they were surely meant to do, and she would have fought back vigorously if she'd been anywhere but at the foot of John Lewis's grave. "It wasn't like that at all," she insisted. "I intended to write to him, but you left, and I lost my job—"

She saw disbelief in Jeb's eyes. He thought she was lying.

Well, she wasn't. She *would* have told John everything if she'd arrived in time. She'd have explained about Jack, too, eventually. Told her uncle how Jack had courted her in Sacramento, convinced her he was a respectable banker, persuaded her to follow him all the way to Tombstone, over her mother's and Mr. Wakefield's strenuous objections, and marry him there. Less than half an hour after the ceremony, far from home and in disgrace, she'd learned the dreadful truth: that Jack Barrett was nothing but a common gunslinger. Most likely, he'd been after the Wakefield money—none of which was hers.

Jeb's jaw muscles, tight a moment before, relaxed, but by obvious effort.

"And maybe he never intended to marry her," she said

crisply, and started to move around him. Jeb stayed her by taking a firm hold on one of her elbows.

"Just a minute," he said, none too graciously. "Becky Fairmont is a fine woman. Rafe's wife, Emmeline, is her daughter, so she's kin to the McKettricks. If you're fixing to light into her for some reason, you'd best give the idea a bit more thought."

Chloe wrenched her elbow free. "I don't need *you*, of all people, to tell me how to behave," she said. Then she picked up her skirts and started hiking purposefully toward the gate leading out of the churchyard.

Jeb kept pace. "Don't you?" he countered hastily. "I'm probably never going to hear the end of how you rode me down like a rabbit, then laid into me with your tongue. In my estimation, Miss Chloe, that is not the way a lady generally comports herself."

"As if you'd know a lady if you met one!" Chloe huffed, and kept right on walking. Secretly, she regretted her vengeful descent on the Triple M, though she was damned if she'd admit it to the likes of Jeb McKettrick.

"It so happens that *Becky* is a lady," Jeb insisted. "So are Emmeline, Mandy, and Concepcion. You'd do well to follow their example!"

They'd left the graveyard and gained the main street of town, though all the light, noise, and activity seemed to be at the other end. Chloe strode toward it, ignoring the hired buggy and the patient horse Jeb had hitched to it, back at the ranch. "You can take your sanctimonious attitude, Mr. Lying, Cheating Sneak, and—"

"*You're* calling *me* a lying, cheating sneak?" He wheeled his arms, but stayed right with her, instead of getting into the rig and driving away, like she'd hoped he'd do. "Oh, now, *that's* a laugh!"

"I didn't lie," she said breathlessly, marching onward, "and I didn't sneak or cheat, either. *You're* the one who claimed to be from Stockton!"

"I guess your definition of deceit is a mite different from mine," Jeb growled, wrenching off his hat and slapping it against his thigh before jamming it onto his head again. "To my way of thinking, having one too many husbands takes the prize when it comes to deception!"

"Jack Barrett and I were divorced two years ago!"

The sidewalk began, and they stepped up onto it. Folks turned to watch them speculatively as they made their inharmonious way toward the Arizona Hotel, and Chloe didn't give a hang what any of them thought, though she reckoned she might regret that sentiment if any of them were on the school committee. As far as she could tell, Jeb was no more concerned with possible scandal than she was.

"Strange you didn't mention that—or mention him at all, for that matter—until you'd roped me in right and proper!" Jeb yelled. Fortunately, he lowered his voice before going on, because Chloe would have torn off strips of his skin if he hadn't. "When I took you to bed the first time, you pretended to be a virgin, Chloe."

She was everlastingly glad that it was dark, for she blushed heatedly at the reminder. Her blood sang under her skin and rushed to the places where he'd touched her, to throb there. "I wasn't pretending," she hissed. "Jack and I never—"

He took her arm again and stopped her, right there on the sidewalk. "Never what?" he demanded dangerously.

Chloe bit her lip. "What's the use? You won't believe me anyway."

He released her brusquely. "You're damn right I won't," he said. "How you could be any kin to an honest, hardworking man like John Lewis is beyond me!"

Chloe struggled, but Jeb held her fast. "*Damn* you," she blurted, "let me go! I've had enough of your insults!"

"Believe me, lady, I haven't *begun* to run through the list!" he snapped, but he released her. "Come on. Let's get you checked into the hotel so I can get back to the ranch. Where are your bags?"

"I suppose the stagecoach driver left them in front of the general store," Chloe said, deflating a little and perilously near tears. It was one thing, letting Jeb see her cry over John's death and quite another to allow herself to be provoked into it by his self-serving accusations. "I had other things on my mind once I saw you coming out of that saloon today."

He gave a long-suffering sigh. "I'll go back and get the

rig and pick up your things. *After* I see you to the hotel, that is."

"I can see myself to the hotel. Good grief, it's right there!" She pointed, in case he was too stupid to notice that they were almost upon the place.

"I'm going to make sure you get there," Jeb informed her, "and see that you're civil to Becky."

She swung her small handbag at his head, but he'd clearly had a lot of practice at dodging such attacks. In this case, it was a good thing, since she remembered only after the fact that there was a steel-handled derringer tucked away in the bottom, sure to split even *his* skull.

A tall man, just about to mount a fine gelding in front of the Bloody Basin Saloon, left his horse and ambled toward them. Chloe took note of his broad shoulders and rugged features and wondered at the sense of familiarity he roused in her.

He touched the brim of his hat and, out of the side of her eye, Chloe noted, with satisfaction, that Jeb was glaring holes through the man.

That made her decide to be friendly.

"Is my little brother giving you trouble, ma'am?" the stranger asked.

Jeb took a step toward him, then stopped. "Stay out of this, Holt."

Holt? Jeb had told her, albeit briefly, about Rafe and Kade, but he'd never mentioned a third brother. Clearly, there was some bad blood here.

Chloe dredged up her most fetching smile.

Holt, raising an eyebrow at Jeb's words, turned all his attention on her, and in that instant his resemblance to Angus McKettrick registered. Jeb's father must have looked almost exactly like this when he was young; no wonder he'd produced four handsome, strapping sons.

"Is everything all right, ma'am?" Holt asked, rephrasing his original question and patently ignoring Jeb, who was seething by then, fit to shoot flames from his nostrils.

"Your brother has been bothering me, sir," Chloe said, with a toss of her head. She felt waves of angry heat coming off Jeb, and she was wickedly pleased. "I would appreciate it if you would give him a thorough trouncing."

The corner of Holt's mouth twitched, and his gaze swung to Jeb's face, then back to Chloe's. "Is that so?" he asked genially. Then he heaved a great, regretful sigh, turning his hat in his hands. "Well, ma'am, as much as I'd enjoy accommodating you, I can't, in good conscience, humiliate my own flesh and blood that way."

"Why, you—" Jeb erupted, lunging at Holt.

Chloe stepped between them, though she couldn't have explained her action, given that she'd been sincere in her previous request. Maybe she'd understand it later, after a cup of tea and some quiet reflection.

She laid her hand on Holt's strong forearm. "If you wouldn't mind escorting me into the Arizona Hotel," she said formally, "I should be very grateful for the company.

It would seem that there are unsavory elements on the streets of Indian Rock tonight."

Holt cut another glance in Jeb's direction, as wry as the one before. "Yes," he agreed, expansively. "I've noticed at least one hothead."

Even though Jeb wasn't actually touching Chloe, she felt him stiffen just the same. "Go ahead, take her," he snapped. "And God help you." With that, he stepped off the sidewalk and stalked back toward the cemetery, probably intending to collect the abandoned horse and buggy and return to the ranch.

"Surly little bugger," Holt observed, watching Jeb's departure.

"I wouldn't call him little," Chloe reflected.

"I don't imagine you would," was Holt's reply. Clearly a gentleman, he squired her to the threshold of the Arizona Hotel and opened one of the double doors for her.

"Jeb never mentioned you," Chloe said, stepping through.

"He wouldn't," Holt answered dryly.

Chloe's interest was piqued, but she was, after all, grieving over her uncle and fresh from yet another round with Mr. McKettrick, and she decided to conserve her energy in case there were more battles ahead. She wasn't naive enough to think she'd gotten rid of her husband so easily; he wouldn't be happy until he'd put her on a stagecoach out of town.

Inside the lobby of the hotel, Chloe's attention was

immediately drawn to the beautiful dark-haired woman standing behind the registration desk, and she looked up as Holt and Chloe entered. Her eyes widened, and it seemed to Chloe that her lips trembled, despite her quick smile.

"Becky," Holt said, still holding his hat in one hand, "I've brought you a customer. Unfortunately, I don't know her name."

So this was John's intended bride—the woman her uncle hadn't troubled himself to mention. Chloe was oddly stricken, knowing he'd kept such a secret from her. Had he been ashamed, as she'd been ashamed of Jack Barrett?

Becky moved gracefully, rounding one end of the waist-high desk and approaching. She seemed elegant and self-possessed, not the sort of woman a man would dally with. "You're Chloe, aren't you?" the vision asked, her voice slightly husky. A hint of tears shimmered in her eyes. "John's girl."

"He was my uncle," Chloe heard herself say.

"Yes," Becky said, with what sounded like resignation. She looked questioningly up at Holt. "You brought her here?" she asked, puzzled.

He shook his head. "All I did was rescue her from the clutches of my youngest brother," he said. "Unless I miss my guess, Jeb'll be along soon. For the sake of the peace, I'd best get back to the Circle C before he gets here."

"Thank you for saving me," Chloe said.

Holt smiled at her earnest gratitude, more amused than cordial. "Any time," he said, and left her in Becky's charge.

"Don't you have any baggage?" Becky asked, after staring at her for a long time. She was still holding Chloe's hands in a too-tight grip.

As if in answer to her question, the first of Chloe's valises crashed through the doorway leading in from the street, soon followed by a small trunk.

Chloe felt her cheeks heat up. "It's just arrived," she said.

Frowning, Becky let go of Chloe's hands and swept grandly over to the door, nearly getting herself bowled over by a large hatbox bound tightly with grocer's string.

Chloe closed her eyes for a moment, bracing herself, but Jeb did not come inside. Becky asked him what he thought he was doing, and his answer was indecipherable. He hurled the rest of Chloe's belongings into the lobby, and that, apparently, was that.

"Great Scot," Becky said, closing the door after the last reticule. "I've never seen Jeb in such a state. He's usually so easygoing. What on earth happened?"

Chloe sighed. "It's a very long story," she replied, "and, frankly, I haven't the stamina to recount it just now. I'm perishing for a room, a cup of tea, and a hot bath."

Becky smiled, and this time there was nothing shaky about the effort, though her eyes betrayed a variety of misgivings. "You've come to the right place, then," she said. "We have a great deal to talk about, Chloe, but it can certainly wait until morning."

Chloe was full of questions, but, thanks to the most recent round with Jeb McKettrick, she was almost totally spent. She simply nodded.

Becky showed her to a small but pretty room at the top of the stairs, and presently a Chinese man brought her bags up, one by one. While Chloe was unpacking, Becky appeared with a tea tray, set it on the small table under the window, and studied her newest guest with thoughtful eyes.

"We've been renovating the hotel," she said, at last. "There's a bathtub, with hot and cold running water, just down the hall."

Not since she'd sneaked out of Sacramento had Chloe availed herself of such a luxury. Before her ignoble dismissal from her teaching position in Tombstone, courtesy of Jeb, she'd lived in a cheap rooming house, where she'd employed a sponge and basin for purposes of personal hygiene, after carrying and heating her own water.

"That sounds lovely," she said.

Becky was still watching her intently, and a frown had formed between her perfect eyebrows. "Chloe—"

"Yes?" Chloe prompted, suppressing a sigh.

"You know that John passed away a few months ago, don't you?" The question was gently put and held a degree of dread.

Chloe's throat seemed to swell shut. She blinked back tears and nodded. "Jeb told me," she managed.

"You didn't get the telegram Kade sent?"

Chloe stopped, with a nightgown in her hands, and faced Becky directly. "It was delayed," she said. "Someone at the telegraph office found it and brought it to me, just yesterday. I came immediately."

"That explains it, then," Becky said softly, and her eyes glistened again. Then, seemingly by force of will, she rallied. "Sit down and have your tea, dear. I'll go and see that the bathroom is ready." She crossed to the door, put one hand on the knob.

"Becky?" Chloe ventured.

Becky stopped, without turning around.

"I'd give anything to have been here to say good-bye."

"I know," Becky said, and went out, closing the door behind her.

4

When Chloe made her way downstairs the next morning, rested and ravenous, and thus in search of breakfast, she was disconcerted to find Jeb dozing on one of the leather-covered settees in the lobby. His hat rested over his eyes, cowboy-style, and he was fully dressed. He hadn't even bothered to remove his boots, which extended some distance beyond the arm of the sofa.

Chloe resisted an unseemly but compelling urge to bat both his feet to the floor, but she was half-afraid he'd think he was being set upon by brigands and come up shooting. She'd seen, in Tombstone, how fast that .45 of his could spring into his hand, and the memory gave her chills. She doubted it had ever occurred to him that, fast as he was, there surely must be someone out there who was faster.

She put the thought aside, touched her hair, now washed and brushed and bound into a tidy chignon, and smoothed her black sateen skirt with both hands. She was wearing her best white shirtwaist, with her grandmother's cameo pinned at the throat, and wanted to be perceived as a lady when she met with Becky again.

"Jeb McKettrick," she said primly, "wake up. Immediately."

He groped for the hat with one hand and lifted it just high enough to uncover an eye. "You," he said, almost accusingly.

As if *she* were the one out of place, not him. "What are you doing here?"

He took the time to yawn and stretch, and the combination was so damnably sensual that Chloe's body got to remembering again, with no prompting at all from her mind. He swung his legs down off the sofa and sat up. "I told you last night I meant to protect Becky," he said, but there was a twinkle in his azure eyes.

She considered snatching up a sofa pillow and whacking him with it, but she needed the teaching job, having spent most of her savings since being ousted in Tombstone, which meant a degree of decorum was called for, lest word get back to the committee. Assuming she hadn't already ruined her chances by creating a spectacle the day before, of course. "From what I've seen of Becky," she said, "she is quite capable of looking after herself."

Jeb grinned, intensifying the lingering effects of the stretching and yawning, which brought Chloe's temper to a slow, steady simmer. "That she is," he agreed. "You've found me out, Miss Chloe. I reckon the truth is, I'm here to aggravate you as much as possible."

"That's probably the first honest thing you've said since we met," Chloe retorted. "Well, you can go now, because you've aggravated me plenty."

He let his gaze drift over her before rising languidly to his feet. "You cleaned up pretty well," he observed.

Chloe folded her arms and tapped one foot.

He chuckled and shook his head. "You little hellion," he said. Then he leaned in slightly and lowered his voice. "I considered pressing my rights as a husband last night, but I figured you'd scratch my eyes out if I crawled into your bed."

"You're d—darned right I would have," Chloe said, though secretly she wasn't so sure. She tended to lose all good sense when he kissed her and when they made love . . .

She gave herself a mental shake. They had *never* "made love," they'd only torn each other's clothes off and coupled, always in a sweaty tangle of arms and legs.

Chloe fanned herself with one hand. Jeb grinned, as if he knew exactly what was going on in her mind.

She would have killed him, school committee be damned, if Becky hadn't come down the stairs just then.

"Well," said that worthy woman, "if it isn't Mr. McKettrick. I would have thought you'd be in jail by now, given the state of your temper when I saw you last." She smiled. "Join us for breakfast?"

"I wouldn't think of refusing," he said, looking at Chloe while he spoke.

She tried to singe him with her eyes. "I can't think why you'd want to sit down to a meal with a lying, sneaking cheat like me," she said.

"Oh, dear," Becky objected, though mildly. "You didn't really say that, did you, Jeb?"

He smiled endearingly. "Yes, ma'am," he said. "I surely did. And I meant every word."

Chloe had to stay herself forcibly from picking up a sofa pillow. What had she ever seen in this man? Her body answered the question quickly enough, but her heart was less forthcoming. "Go away," she whispered, though she had no real hope that Becky wouldn't hear. She was standing too near and listening too intently.

"It would be rude to turn down such a generous invitation," he said, with a slight nod in Becky's direction. "Besides, I could eat a bull elk." His eyes gleamed with mockery as he looked down into Chloe's flushed face. "Thanks to you, Mrs. McKettrick, I missed supper last night."

"It's your own fault," Chloe snapped. "You could have stayed at the ranch, where you belong."

"Mrs. McKettrick?" Becky asked.

"My name is Wakefield," Chloe said.

"That isn't what you told my father yesterday, out behind the bunkhouse," Jeb pointed out affably.

Chloe felt her cheeks catch fire; it was the curse of a redheaded woman, this blushing so easily. If only she'd been a blonde.

"Let's have breakfast," Becky reiterated. Plainly, she'd had considerable experience at keeping the peace, though the hotel didn't look like the kind of place that would attract rowdies. Boasting a porcelain bathtub and hot and cold running water as it did, not to mention a sink and a commode that flushed, it would have been considered well-appointed, even in Sacramento.

"I couldn't eat a bite," Chloe protested, with a searing glance at Jeb. It was a lie, of course. She had awakened several times in the night with her stomach gnawing at her backbone, and once or twice she'd been desperate enough to consider sneaking down to the kitchen to raid the pantry. Only the fear of being thought a thief had kept her in her room.

"Guess that's your choice," Jeb said, and headed for what must have been the dining room.

Becky waited, smiling a little, for Chloe to swallow her damnable pride and join them. She did so, with a gulp, and when she caught the scents of fresh coffee and frying bacon wafting from the kitchen, she was completely lost. Pride, after all, makes for a poor breakfast.

Jeb had chosen a table next to the window, and he stood until both Becky and Chloe were seated, then sat down opposite them. A small woman bustled through the far doorway, carrying a heavy coffeepot in one hand and three mugs in the other, a finger hooked deftly through the handles.

"Good morning, Sarah," Becky said cheerfully. "This is Chloe—er—Wakefield. Chloe, my friend, Sarah Fee. I couldn't run this place without her."

Sarah beamed, obviously valuing the compliment, and nodded a greeting to Chloe as she set the mugs on the table and poured coffee for the three of them. It was still quite early, so there were no other customers in the dining room. "Howdy," Sarah said. "The special is bacon and eggs, with fried potatoes."

"Sounds good," Jeb said. It was a mystery to Chloe how he was so nice to other people, especially women, and so odious with her. Not that he'd *always* treated her badly. Oh, no. When he'd wanted something—specifically the Triple M—he'd been charm itself.

"Don't you have work to do?" Chloe asked Jeb, when Becky left the table briefly, a few minutes later, to speak to someone waiting at the registration desk.

"No," Jeb answered, after taking and savoring a sip of coffee. "As a matter of fact, I'm mostly an irritant around the ranch these days."

"I can believe that," Chloe said.

"Always generous with a compliment," Jeb replied smoothly.

"*I despise* you."

"I know."

Chloe, having raised her coffee halfway to her mouth, had to set it down again, lest she spill it. "Just go away.

Please. I promise to divorce you as soon as I possibly can."

"Why go to all the trouble of a divorce?" Jeb asked blithely. "Since we're not married anyway."

"We *are* married, more's the pity!"

He raised an eyebrow. "Prove it."

"Dammit, Jeb, you were there. We stood up before a preacher. We exchanged vows. What a joke *that* was."

"Especially the part where you promised to love, honor, and obey."

Chloe narrowed her eyes. "Suppose I'm expecting?" she asked, in a whisper, just to nettle him. Actually, she knew for certain that she wasn't, but the tactic worked nicely anyway.

Jeb set his coffee cup down on the red-and-white-checked oilcloth covering the table with a resounding thump, spilling some of the contents and burning his thumb.

"*What?*" he hissed.

She smiled coyly while he cursed under his breath and shook his hand, though she felt unaccountably stung. It wasn't as if she hadn't known what he'd been up to in Tombstone; Jeb wanted a wife and a child—Jack had taken pleasure in telling her that, after that humiliating debacle of a wedding night—and he'd have taken any-body who applied. "You heard me," she said. He was a poker player; if he didn't know a bluff when he saw one, well, that was his problem, not hers.

"Dammit, Chloe, if this is another one of your tricks—"

"What tricks would those be?" she asked sweetly, as Becky returned. Sarah was back, too, carrying their plates on a tray.

Jeb was pale; she'd gotten under his skin for sure. Interest and hostility glinted in his eyes, and Chloe almost wished she *was* carrying his child. It would have served him right, after what he'd put her through, to see her make a grand exit on an outbound stagecoach, to bear and raise the baby elsewhere.

"Are Sarah and I interrupting something?" Becky asked lightly.

"No," Jeb said, uncharitably.

The food was delicious, and Chloe didn't even try to pretend she wasn't hungry. She didn't say two words throughout the meal, though, and Jeb probably didn't either, but Becky filled the space with chatter about the furniture she'd ordered for the new part of the hotel, a dress she'd bought for Emmeline, over at the mercantile, and the shameful price of bed linens.

They had barely finished eating when Rafe came striding in off the street, dressed for a long, cold ride and looking annoyed. His gaze sliced straight to Jeb.

"There you are," he said, without a trace of cordiality.

Jeb shifted in his chair, his face hardening. "Rafe," he said, by way of a greeting.

"Begging your pardon, Becky," Rafe said, and acknowledged Chloe with a terse nod, "but I'll have to deprive you of such genial company." He glowered at Jeb. "You see," he went on pointedly, "we've got a ranch to run, and with that new herd of cattle just in from Texas, we need every hand we can scrounge up. Even the slackers, like my little brother, here."

Jeb hesitated, plainly wanting to stare Rafe down, but in the end he pushed back his chair, with a loud scraping sound, and stood up.

Chloe smiled broadly.

Jeb paused beside her chair, leaned down, and spoke directly into her face. "Don't look so smug, Miss Chloe," he drawled. "I'm not through with you, by any means."

Having said that, he walked out.

"Sorry," Rafe said, though whether he was addressing Chloe herself, or Becky, there was no telling. He followed Jeb onto the street, spurs clanking.

"So there *are* people who can cow Jeb McKettrick," Chloe said, with some satisfaction.

"Rafe is foreman on the Triple M," Becky answered. "For the time being, he gives the orders." She smiled into her coffee cup, hesitated. "I can't say John didn't warn me," she said musingly. Then she moved to the chair Jeb had occupied, across from Chloe. Her expression, full of merriment only moments before, turned solemn, and a hint of tears shone in her eyes.

The change alarmed Chloe; something dreadfully important was about to be said, her instincts told her that, and suddenly she felt like fleeing or putting her hands over her ears. She did neither.

"What is it?" she asked, very quietly.

Becky pulled a lace-trimmed handkerchief from the sleeve of her dress and dabbed at her eyes. "It's about John," she said.

5

*H*is booted feet propped on a gaming table, Jack Barrett sat alone in the smoky back room of Tombstone's Broken Stirrup Saloon, pondering the divorce papers he'd taken from one of Chloe's hatboxes before her hasty departure for Indian Rock. This was all he meant to her, he reflected, a single document, signed by a lawyer and a judge. Resentment surged through him, but he quelled it quickly; a man in the grip of his emotions, he believed, was a man who could be taken by surprise.

He hated being taken by surprise.

With a slow smile, he pulled a wooden match from the inside pocket of his silk vest, struck it against the edge of the table, and set the decree aflame. When the fire got too hot, he turned in his chair and dropped the blazing sheets of vellum into a spittoon.

He watched idly as Chloe's personal declaration of independence burned, then lit a cheroot and settled back again to smoke and reflect on what he ought to do next.

He thought of Jeb McKettrick, the man who'd trespassed on his territory, and drew his .44 from the holster on his hip. Snapping it open, he spun the cylinder, frowning. The notches on the handle were a comfort to him— seventeen of them, one for each of the men he'd killed, some in fair fights, some by ambush, for a bounty.

With the pad of his thumb, he traced the small notches, counting them one by one, like the beads on a rosary, remembering, with a sense of accomplishment, each man's name and the place where he fell. McKettrick, he decided, would make number eighteen, and he'd strike the ground wherever Jack found him, though the circumstances had to be right. Chloe's lover had brothers, and from what Jack had heard, the McKettricks being well-known in Tombstone, they weren't the sort to be trifled with. Best catch the bridegroom alone, and off guard, though it would be a pure pleasure to kill him in front of Chloe. That would be a lesson to her, and a memorable one.

He felt a peculiar, quivering sensation in the pit of his stomach, thought briefly that it might be fear, and finally overruled the idea. He could avoid the brothers easily enough and, sure, he'd seen McKettrick use a gun, out behind the Broken Stirrup. He was fast, all right, but that had been a boy's game, shooting bottles out of the sky for money and fun. A way of showing off.

Jack shook his head at the memory. Where was the challenge in that? It was a waste of good bullets.

Dollars to dog turds, McKettrick had never put a slug

in a human being, and now he never would. Before the month was out, he'd be asleep in the arms of the Lord.

Giving a philosophical sigh, Barrett snapped his .44 shut and shoved it back into its holster. The way he saw it, he was saving McKettrick's soul, though he didn't reckon anybody would appreciate his effort, most especially Chloe.

His jaw hardened. The little trollop. McKettrick had made a fool of her in front of the whole of Tombstone, marrying her in the afternoon, then leaving her alone in their hotel room while he drank and gambled in this very room. As luck would have it, one of the other players in that night's game had been the head of the school board, and thus, Chloe's employer.

Recalling the scene settled Jack's nerves a little and brought a smile to his lips. He'd snagged McKettrick in the street, right after the ceremony, shown him the wedding portrait he, Jack, and Chloe had had taken two years before. The beaming husband had turned sullen in the space of an instant. Instead of confronting Chloe, Jeb had joined the poker game and proceeded to get royally drunk, and when Chloe had finally come looking for him, well after midnight, she'd found her fancy mister with cards in his hand and a girl on his lap.

She and McKettrick had had words, loud, public ones. She'd finally stormed out, but not before her gaze connected with Jack's. He'd been leaning against the wall the whole while, smoking and watching, and the look in her eyes went through him like a Mexican bayonet. He felt it again, even after all these weeks, and the pain, the insult of it, almost took his breath away.

He'd loved her so much, and it wasn't like he hadn't been patient with her flighty, fickle ways. A lot of men would have killed her for shaming him the way she had, divorcing him before the marriage ever got started, but he'd known she was young and had led a sheltered life up in Sacramento, with those rich folks of hers. He'd been willing to overlook her mistakes and take her back, even to hang up his gun for good, if that was what she wanted. Her folks hadn't approved of the union, but they'd have come around in time and put up the money for a ranch and some cattle.

They could have done all right, he and Chloe.

Was she grateful that he'd set matters straight where McKettrick was concerned? Hell, no. She'd turned on him, claws bared, said he'd spoiled everything, and that she wished she'd never had the misfortune to make his acquaintance in the first place.

Jack's chair creaked as he stood and stretched, the .44 a heavy reassurance against his right hip. Trying to comfort Chloe, after McKettrick hit the trail, he'd told her part of what he'd just learned from a drifter, down from Indian Rock: that her handsome lover was in need of a wife and a child, both of which he had to produce if he wanted to come into his inheritance, and that he was not particularly picky about where he dredged them

up—but she'd thrown his wise counsel back in his face
and threatened to shoot off his kneecaps with that derringer of hers if he didn't get out of her sight and stay
out.

It was partly his own doing, he supposed, that she was
so quick with that viperous little tongue of hers. He
should have straightened her out long ago. Taught her to
mind, like a woman ought to do.

The inside door creaked open, and he almost went for
his gun, but it was only one of the saloon girls, simpering
at him from behind a veil of war paint. He tried in vain to
recall her name, but it wasn't forthcoming.

"You feelin' lonely, Jack?" she cooed.

He was lonely, all right, but there was only one woman
in the world who could ease his yearning, and that was
Chloe. *His* wife. "Send the bartender's boy over to Car-
son's Livery," he said, ignoring the implicit invitation.
"Tell them to saddle my horse."

The tramp's rouged mouth formed a pout. "You leavin'
us, Jack?"

He snatched up his coat, from the back of one of the
scarred chairs, and reached for his hat, lying in the middle
of the table. "Yes," he answered flatly. "Do as I tell you."

"Where you goin'?"

He took a threatening step toward her, and she
backed out of the doorway, blinking, turned on her heel,
and ran to do his bidding.

That, he thought, was more like it. Chloe could take a

lesson or two from Little Miss No-name. He put on his hat, checked the .44 again, even though it was always loaded, and headed for the bar.

Half an hour later, with several shots of whiskey under his belt to fortify him for the journey, Jack Barrett rode out, traveling north toward the high country.

6

Sarah Fee came to take the dirty dishes away and wipe down the tablecloth, and cowboys and local businessmen began to wander into the hotel dining room, greeting Becky, tossing curious glances Chloe's way, and sitting down at other tables to order breakfast.

"My office would be a better place to talk," Becky said, looking and sounding distracted. She pushed back her chair and stood.

Chloe followed suit, still feeling unsettled. Whatever Becky was getting ready to tell her about her uncle was obviously weighing on her mind.

The small room behind the registration desk was neat and elegantly furnished, more suited to an Eastern parlor than an establishment like the Arizona Hotel.

"Sit down," Becky said, indicating a delicate chair covered in dark blue velvet. As Chloe complied, Becky settled herself behind the desk, with its beautifully turned legs. "Just before he died," the older woman went on, "John asked me to look after you."

Chloe felt an ache deep in the center of her chest, and a lump formed in her throat. "We were close," she said, "though we didn't see much of each other after I grew up." She'd barely reached her full growth the last time her uncle visited her stepfather's expensive house in Sacramento; he'd said good-bye that day, with a note of finality in his voice and sorrow in his eyes, and promised to write. He'd kept that promise, but the crack he'd left in Chloe's heart by going had never really healed.

Becky drew a deep breath, let it out slowly, and tried to smile. "He loved you very much," she said. "Up till now, I missed him for myself. Now, I miss him for you, too."

Chloe was on the edge of her seat, her hands clasping the arms of the fancy chair. Her eyes had gone so wide that they burned, and she could barely breathe. "Please," she whispered. "Tell me."

Becky sat up a little straighter, set her shoulders resolutely. "There's no easy way to say something like this—John Lewis wasn't your uncle, Chloe. He was your father."

"No," Chloe said, at once stricken and wildly hopeful. "He was my father's brother—he said—my mother told me—"

Becky simply waited.

Memories spun in Chloe's head, unwinding like a watch spring taken from its casing. *John Lewis is a bad influence,* she heard her mother say. *He puts wild ideas in your head.* Then her stepfather's voice joined in, cool and disapproving, like always. *I know you're fond of him, Chloe, but it's better if you don't see him again.*

"Why didn't they tell me?" Chloe demanded, still reeling. "Why didn't he?"

Becky leaned to take Chloe's hand and squeeze it once. "I can't speak for your mother. I know John kept it to himself because he thought you'd be ashamed of him."

"Ashamed? He was such a good man—"

"He was," Becky agreed, with quiet conviction. "But he made some mistakes when he was younger."

"What kind of mistakes?"

Becky hesitated, then got past whatever had held her back for those few seconds. "John was in prison," she said. "He was involved in a robbery."

Chloe thought she would be violently ill from the shock of it. Her gentle, unassuming uncle—*father*—committing a robbery, going to jail? Impossible. She put a hand over her mouth.

Becky rose, went to a cabinet on the other side of the room, and poured water from a carafe. She brought the glass to Chloe, who drank it in three swallows and longed for something stronger, even though she was a firm advocate of temperance.

"I could have used a father," she said weakly, when she'd set the empty glass aside. Her eyes burned, and her stomach roiled.

Becky remained beside Chloe's chair, a hand resting

lightly on her shoulder. "John thought highly of your stepfather," she said gently. "He said Mr. Wakefield took good care of you and of your mother. That was more important to him than anything else—knowing that you were all right."

Chloe realized her face was wet, but she made no move to wipe away the tears. "They must have sent him away," she fretted. "I'll never, ever forgive them."

"Shhh," Becky said. "You don't mean that. It couldn't have been easy for your mother, seeing John. And your stepfather, well, he was probably just trying to keep his family together."

"Yes, I do mean it!" Chloe argued, a flush stinging its way up her neck to blaze in her cheeks. "I was *so* lonely. Mother and Mr. Wakefield were always traveling, or giving grand parties, or going to them. But John was *there,* whenever he was with me—he made me laugh, and when he looked at me, I felt as if he was really seeing me. When I said something, he paid attention, instead of just waiting for me to be quiet—"

Becky had gotten snagged upstream in the conversation. "You call your stepfather 'Mr. Wakefield'?" she asked, pulling her chair around from behind the desk so she could sit beside Chloe. She pulled a handkerchief from her sleeve and handed it over.

Chloe dried her face. "Yes," she said. "So does Mother."

"Amazing," said Becky, shaking her head.

Chloe shot to her feet, too agitated to sit, and began to pace. "Someone should have told me!" she raged. "Dear *God*, how I hate being lied to!"

"People lie for all sorts of reasons, Chloe. In this case, it was to protect you."

"I didn't want to be protected—I wanted a father!"

"I'm sorry."

Chloe stopped. "For telling me the truth?"

"No," Becky answered, with a sigh. "I'm convinced it was the right thing to do. John would have done it himself if he'd lived. What I meant was, I'm sorry for all you went through, Chloe. I truly am."

"I lost my father without even knowing I had one," Chloe mourned.

Becky rose, put her arms around her, and Chloe let herself be held while she sobbed, just as she'd done the day before, with Jeb.

She'd best be careful, she thought, or this tendency toward weakness might get to be a habit.

"There's another thing John would do, if he were here," Becky said gently. "He'd ask about you and Jeb. What went wrong between you, Chloe?"

Chloe sniffled. "I was married before," she admitted. "To a man named Jack Barrett. It—it was a terrible mistake—I ran away from home to marry him, and my mother and Mr. Wakefield were furious with me. I sent them a wire, told them Jack had lied to me, that he was a gunslinger, an outlaw. They'd left on one of their trips by then, and their lawyer wired back that I'd made my bed and ought to sleep in it."

Becky made a clucking sound, motherly disapproval of a cruel fate, or, at least, that was the way Chloe chose to interpret it. She held Chloe at arm's length, searched her face. "Where does Jeb figure into all this?"

Chloe sighed, shook her head. "One day, I was minding my own business, coming out of a store, and I ran into him, dropped all my packages. He was so—I don't know—the way he smiled—"

Becky nodded encouragingly.

"I think I fell in love with him, right there on the sidewalk. We started seeing each other, and everything happened so fast—" She paused, blushed. She lamented Jeb's reckless nature, but she was impetuous herself. Hadn't she flouted propriety by leaving home to travel to one of the wildest towns in the West, and marry a highly unsuitable man? Hadn't she undone two years of hard work and common sense only to make the same grave error all over again, and all because Jeb McKettrick set her heart to racing whenever he looked at her?

She didn't want a man like Jeb. She wanted someone like Rafe or Kade. Someone settled and responsible.

Didn't she?

"Obviously, something went very wrong," Becky prompted.

Chloe bit her lower lip. "I should have told Jeb about Jack, and I didn't. I was—I was afraid he wouldn't want me. When he found out, there was no reasoning with him." She felt heat surge into her face. "I lied by omission, but Jeb lied outright. He said—he said he loved me. If he had, he would have been willing to listen. Instead, he spent our wedding night swilling whiskey, playing poker, and consorting with low women!"

Becky touched Chloe's hair, and it was a comforting gesture, the kind her mother had never made. "His pride was hurt," she said. "Men are silly that way. Give him some time, Chloe."

But Chloe was already shaking her head. "I've made a fool of myself twice already," she said, with vehemence. "I won't do it again!"

"Only twice?" Becky asked, smiling. "That's a pretty good record."

Chloe pulled away, pacing. "From now on," she vowed, to herself as well as Becky, "I mean to make my own way in the world. If I ever marry again, it won't be for love."

Becky raised an eyebrow, considering Chloe's words. Then she sighed, went to the door, and laid a graceful hand on the knob. "Let's hope you come to your senses before you get the opportunity," she said, and left Chloe alone to stew in furious regret.

$\mathcal{J}$eb worked shirtless in the afternoon sun, sweating and cursing occasionally, under his breath, while he dug post holes for the new fence line between Holt's place—the Circle C—and the Triple M. Rafe had made a big production of dragging him out of the Arizona Hotel, claiming he needed help with the cattle, but then he'd changed his mind. Next thing he knew, Jeb was breaking hard ground with a dull shovel. Being low man on the McKettrick totem pole, and having no desire to hit the trail again, he'd had no choice but to give in.

He was so caught up in his roiling thoughts that he didn't hear the horse approaching, didn't know he wasn't alone, with the buckboard and team, until a long, familiar shadow fell over him.

He stopped digging, let the shovel fall to the dirt, and dragged one arm across his forehead.

"Looks like you drew the shit detail, boy," Angus observed, swinging himself down from the saddle and hooking his thumbs under his gun belt. "Most likely, you deserve it though."

Jeb struggled to hold on to his temper. It wasn't smart to sass the old man; he might have given Rafe the foreman's job, with Kade second-in-command, but in reality Angus still ran the Triple M, and he used an iron hand to do it. "Thanks," Jeb said tersely. "That makes me feel *a lot* better."

Angus laughed, took his canteen from the saddle, and held it out. "Sorry it isn't whiskey," he said. "I reckon you could use some right about now."

Jeb took the canteen, though grudgingly, screwed off the lid, and drank deeply of the cold well water, tasting faintly of canvas and metal. He poured the rest over his back, chest, and shoulders, and handed the empty vessel back to Angus with a shoving motion. "You're right about that. Do you have some business with me, Pa, or did you just come out here to make everything worse?"

Angus looked a little less amused. "I've got business, all right," he drawled. "I want to know why Chloe is staying in town if she's really your wife."

"She isn't my wife," Jeb said, and spat. He realized he was standing just as Angus was, with his thumbs under his gun belt, and shifted his position.

The old man resettled his hat, plainly peevish. "Seems to me you ought to get your story straight, boy, and stick by it," he said. "For weeks, you've been claiming you were married. Then along comes one of the Furies, mad enough to snatch you baldheaded, and telling me she's your bride. What in the Sam Hill is going on here?"

Jeb thrust splayed fingers through his dusty, sweat-matted hair. "I wish I knew," he said, abjectly miserable.

"Might help if the two of us jaw about it a little," Angus offered, gruffly magnanimous. "Maybe we can work it through together."

"I married her all right," Jeb admitted. "Damn fool that I was."

"Well, then, that settles one question."

Jeb shook his head. "Not really," he said. "Right after the ceremony was over, Chloe and I, well, we were going to start our honeymoon." He stopped, cleared his throat, looked everywhere but at his father's face. "I saw her to the room, carried her over the threshold, and all that." He paused again, gave a bitter laugh. "I decided we ought to have some of that fancy French wine to celebrate with, so I went out to scout some up. I was on my way back when a fella came up to me outside the hotel and said he had something I ought to see. I was in a hurry, but I stopped. He showed me something, all right. It was a picture, framed and fancy—Chloe, all dressed up as a bride, standing right beside the man I was talking to in the street. He said she was *his* wife, and damned if he didn't have the proof."

Angus waited.

Jeb muttered a string of curses.

"Let's hear the rest," Angus prompted. His tone was

even; Jeb couldn't tell whether he thought the story was funny or downright sad. Hell, he wasn't sure of the distinction himself.

"I felt like I'd been kicked in the belly by a mule," Jeb said, still avoiding the old man's gaze, but he could feel it on him, just the same, steady and level. "I made for the nearest saloon, bought my way into a poker game, and drank up half the whiskey in the place."

"Some men would have gone right to Chloe and asked her straight out what was going on," Angus reasoned.

"I couldn't face her," Jeb confessed. "Anyway, she came and found me in a back room at the Broken Stirrup, and we had it out, in front of God and everybody. I spent the night in some cheap boardinghouse and steered clear of her until Kade showed up a week later and talked me into coming back here."

Now it was Angus who spat. "I don't reckon I need to tell you what I think of the way you treated her," he said.

Jeb picked up the shovel, jammed it into the hole, and flung out a spray of dirt. "No," he agreed, "you don't. But you probably will, anyhow. And what about the way she treated me?"

Angus didn't move, and he let the question pass unanswered. Out of the corner of his eye, Jeb could see that the old coot had his arms folded again, and the brim of his weather-beaten hat shadowed his face. "Chloe seemed pretty sure she was your wife," he said, "not that other fella's."

"She's a good liar and an even better actress." Jeb hit a rock with the end of the shovel, and the impact reverberated up both his arms to ache in his shoulders.

"One way or the other," Angus persisted quietly, "this isn't something you can run away from. You need to settle it, boy. For your own sake, and for hers."

Jeb gripped the shovel handle in both his blistered hands and sent it flying back over his head. It landed beyond the barbed-wire fence, on Circle C property, with a resounding clank. "I'm not running away!" he yelled.

"That isn't the way I heard it," Angus said.

Rafe and Kade. Damn them. They'd probably had a good time telling the old man how Chloe Wakefield chased their little brother all the way from town and finally cornered him behind the bunkhouse.

"Go and talk to her," Angus said.

"It's no damn use!" Jeb raged. "Chloe and I don't *talk*, we yell at each other!"

Angus smiled as he turned away. "That's encouraging," he said. "And fetch back that shovel before you head for town. Contrary to common opinion around this place, I'm not made of money."

8

*G*et back to the ranch. Go to town. Jeb wished Rafe and Angus would get together and agree on what the hell he was supposed to do. If this was a taste of what it was going to be like when either Rafe or Kade took full control of the ranch, he might as well shoot himself.

Angrily, he collected his tools, including the shovel, and threw them into the bed of the buckboard. After shrugging back into his shirt, he climbed up, took the reins, released the brake lever, and drove the horses hard for home. Mandy was in the barn when he got there, brushing down a fine pinto gelding—she'd made Kade give her fifty head of good horseflesh and most of the money in his bank account after they were married, because of some agreement between them—and for the first time in recent memory, Jeb got some sympathy.

Mandy smiled. "Aren't you in a state?" she asked lightly, coming out of the stall to talk. She was wearing pants, boots, and a chambray shirt from the trunks of outgrown clothes Concepcion kept in the springhouse.

"I've been in better moods," Jeb admitted.

She laughed. "It's Chloe, I suppose."

"Chloe, and Rafe, and my bullheaded old polecat of a father—"

"Poor Jeb," Mandy said, but her eyes were dancing. She looked him over thoughtfully. "If you're going to pay a call on Chloe, you'd better clean up first. You're a sight." She waved him in the direction of the house. "Go on," she shooed. "I'll unhitch the wagon and put the team away."

"There'll be no end to the grief if Kade finds out I let you do a man's work," Jeb said. He wanted a bath and a shave, though, now that she'd brought the possibilities to mind. He felt like he was wearing half the territory on his hide.

"I'll handle Kade," Mandy said, with well-founded confidence. Every cowhand on the ranch jumped when Kade whistled, but with Mandy, he was a different man.

Jeb hesitated another moment, then shrugged, left the team to Mandy, and made for the house. After a session with the razor, one of Concepcion's savory meals, and a good soaping and sluicing in the creek, he felt better, and he was almost in a good mood when he reached the outskirts of Indian Rock, about sunset.

He stopped at the Bloody Basin for a shot of whiskey before squaring his shoulders and setting his course for the Arizona Hotel, where he figured he'd find Chloe. If she was pregnant, he'd decided on the way to town, he might be willing to live as a bigamist, at least for a while. He grinned, thinking of the looks on Rafe's and Kade's faces when he told them they'd be working for him in a few months' time. He'd see that they got their fill of digging post holes, rounding up strays, and stringing barbwire.

Oh, yes, revenge would be sweet.

He found his ladylove in the lobby, sipping tea from a china cup and reading a book. There were little spectacles perched on the end of her nose and, as he drew closer, he saw that her eyes were red-rimmed.

She closed the book with a snap and snatched off the glasses. "Well," she said imperiously, "you're back."

He exercised forbearance and did not point out the obviousness of that statement. He even took off his hat. "Have you been crying?" he asked, though he hadn't intended to voice that particular thought.

"No," she said.

"Liar."

"If you've come here to insult me, Jeb McKettrick, I will thank you to leave. I've had quite enough disturbing news in the past twenty-four hours."

He sighed, drew up another chair, and sat facing her so that their knees were almost touching. "I'm not here to bother you, Chloe," he said truthfully. "I was hoping we could talk. Without tearing into each other, I mean."

"Inconceivable," she said, but her mouth twitched a little at one corner and, in the next instant, she actually hauled off and smiled. "You look very handsome," she added.

It wasn't the first time Jeb had been told he was handsome—he'd been trading on it for years—but the effect was entirely new. He felt shy as a schoolboy all of a sudden, and oddly tongue-tied, and that unnerved him. "You don't look so bad yourself," he said.

She gave a pealing laugh.

He turned his hat between his fingers and searched for words that might be accepted in a peaceable spirit. "Chloe, you said there was a child—"

She looked away.

"Is there?" he pressed, but without rancor.

She met his gaze, shook her head. "No," she said, and he thought he heard a note of regret in her voice.

He hung his head for a moment, surprised by the depth of his disappointment.

"You want that ranch very badly, don't you?" Chloe asked. He might have expected recrimination, since she'd already accused him of using her as a means to an end; but she spoke gently, almost tenderly.

He looked up, searching her face. If he lived to be a thousand, he'd never figure this woman out, and that was part of her appeal. She was a mystery, a challenge, and a pure hellcat between the sheets. "Yes," he said.

"Why didn't you tell me the real reason you wanted to get married?" She reached for her teacup, but it rattled in the saucer, so she turned loose of it and folded her hands in her lap. "I thought it all happened awfully fast. Our courtship, I mean."

"I guess I figured you'd tell me to go to hell," he answered. "Say you were a woman, not a broodmare, or something along those lines."

Her smile was strangely fragile. "Well, I might have," she admitted. "But the truth is always best, don't you think?"

He considered the question and refrained from pointing out that she hadn't been such a believer in telling the straight story back in Tombstone. "Not always," he said, and left it at that. "Chloe, why were you crying? Was it because of John?"

She nodded. "Did you know he was my father?" she asked, almost meekly, as if she feared the answer.

He shook his head. "No." He reached out, took her hand. "Come on," he said, hoping she wouldn't balk. "Let's go for a walk."

She didn't try to pull away, which was encouraging, but as he ran the pad of his thumb across her fingers, he realized that the ring he'd given her was gone, which was *dis*couraging. Not that he'd worn his own; it was tucked away in his bureau drawer at home. He'd wanted to toss it in the creek more than once, but something had stopped him.

Damn, but it was a complicated business, this being a man. Women had it easy.

9

*I*t didn't escape Chloe's notice, for all her befuddlement of feelings, that when Jeb led her out of the hotel for their evening walk, he headed in the opposite direction from the cemetery. The street was quiet, the storefronts dark, though the Bloody Basin was doing a rousing business, with tinny piano music pouring past its swinging doors.

Perhaps thinking, as she was, that it would be better if they didn't talk about themselves, and thus their differences, Jeb pointed out various landmarks.

"That's the jailhouse, over there," he said, indicating a pockmarked facade with brick sidewalls and a single dimly lit window. "Looks like Sam Fee has a prisoner, or he'd be gone home by now." He stopped, surveying the place, and shook his head. "Kade was marshal for a while, after John took sick. Damn near got himself killed, but we'd have lost the Triple M for sure if it hadn't been for him and Mandy."

Chloe made her way past the mention of John, though

it brushed against her spirit like a shadow. "What happened?" She wasn't ready to talk about her father and all the years that had been wasted because she hadn't known who he really was. The resentment she felt toward her mother would need some time to heal, too, and she'd be demanding an explanation first chance she got, for sure and certain.

"It's complicated," Jeb said, taking her hand and moving on again. "What it boils down to is, there were some outlaws trying to start up a range war. They stole some gold that belonged to us, and Kade and Mandy got it back."

The next stop on the grand tour of Indian Rock was Mamie Sussex's rooming house. "Mamie has a flock of redheaded kids," Jeb said, with amused affection. "Harry's a special favorite of Kade's—used to help him with his marshaling sometimes. He made a fair deputy, for a ten-year-old."

Chloe smiled at the mention of children; as a teacher, she naturally had a special affinity for them. "They must keep their mother busy," she observed. She was trying not to think about how good it felt to be talking about ordinary things with Jeb, with her hand resting in his. Best not get too cozy, though.

"It would be a mercy to her and the whole town if they were in school," Jeb said, with a slight grin. "They're full of mischief. There isn't any teacher, though."

She supposed she should have told him she meant to

inquire about the job, but she didn't. She was enjoying the temporary cessation of hostilities a bit too much.

"The town council's been trying to hire a schoolmarm for a while now," he went on. "No luck. Indian Rock's pretty isolated, and the pay isn't much, so I guess the pickings are slim."

Chloe felt a little trill of excitement, but caution made her tamp it down. Yes, she was a qualified teacher, a damn good one, in fact, and yes, she most certainly needed work, since her funds were all but exhausted, but word of her ignoble dismissal in Tombstone would surely catch up to her, sooner or later. As desperate as they were, the committee might turn her down flat.

She'd have no choice then but to go crawling back to Sacramento and live alone in Mr. Wakefield's vast house. The prospect made her shudder, but with two divorces behind her, she'd be a pariah just about anywhere she went. "Tell me about Rafe and Emmeline," she said, when the gap of silence had widened too far for comfort.

Jeb smiled, a mite wistfully, Chloe thought, and they sat down on a bench in front of the closed mercantile, still holding hands. "Now there's a story," he said. "When Pa informed us, on his birthday, that the first one of us to get married and present him with a grandchild would run the ranch, Rafe sent away for a bride, and Emmeline came out from Kansas City. Things were pretty rocky between them for a while, so he wrote off for another bride, just in case Emmeline didn't work out." He paused, chuckled. "Kade did the same, once he found out. The agency got mixed up and sent six of them. When they got here and found out Rafe was taken, they all set their caps for Kade. That made for some merriment, but most of them are gone now. Abigail stayed—she and Mamie run the rooming house together, and Sue Ellen Caruthers keeps house for Holt Cavanagh. I imagine he'll marry her one of these days, just for something to do."

Chloe mused a while, enjoying the comical picture Jeb had painted in her mind. It was purely a relief, after all her heavy thoughts. "What about you?" she asked presently. "Didn't any of the brides fix their sights on you?"

He hesitated. "No," he said. In profile, he looked serious, and when he turned his gaze on Chloe, she saw sadness there. "I told them I was already married."

Chloe had spoken in haste; now, she could repent the impulse at leisure. "I see," she said, changing the subject, sensing that there would be another storm if she didn't. "Holt referred to you as his brother last night. Why does he call himself Cavanagh, and not McKettrick?"

Jeb's jaw tightened. "He's a *half* brother," he said, somewhat tersely. "Pa was married to his mother, back in Texas. When she died, Pa left Holt with relatives and came up here, with a herd of cattle, to settle the Triple M. He met Ma, they got married, and Rafe, Kade, and I were born. Somehow, Pa neglected to mention, to us anyway, that he had another son." He sighed, and the tension in his shoulders slackened a little. "Holt never forgave Pa for leaving him, I guess, and he took the name Cavanagh out of spite, most likely."

"You don't like him," Chloe said.

"I don't trust him," Jeb replied. "He doesn't have much to do with Pa, or any of us for that matter. He came here to make trouble, plain and simple, and it's hard to like a man for that."

"Maybe he just wants the rest of you to acknowledge him," Chloe suggested carefully. She'd only met Mr. Cavanagh once, but she'd liked him instinctively. He was a gentleman, she knew that much, and she sensed a bold and stalwart spirit in him. And, like his half brothers, he wasn't hard on the eye.

"It'll be a while," Jeb said grimly. He stared at the ground for a long time, and another silence settled between them. Chloe decided it would be a mistake to argue Holt's case, though she was sorely tempted. People like Jeb, with strong families and deeded ground under their feet, tended to take such things for granted. Most likely, they didn't know what it was to feel lonely.

It was Jeb who broke the impasse. "Guess I'd better get you back to the hotel," he said. "Winter or summer, the high country gets cold at night."

For her part, Chloe would have been glad to stay right there, close to Jeb, but it was a foolish notion, and she knew it. She'd built walls around her heart, after John Lewis left Sacramento that last time, and both Jack Barrett and Jeb McKettrick had breached them, taking her unawares. The result had been pain, humiliation, and the loss of a job she'd loved.

She wouldn't make the same mistake again.

Except that Jeb kissed her, without warning, right there on the street. As before, her bones melted, and her blood thundered through her veins.

She pushed him away.

He caught her chin in his hand, made her look at him. "Remember how it was with us, Chloe?" he asked, his voice raspy and gruff.

She twisted free. "Are you willing to acknowledge me as your wife?" she demanded.

He didn't answer.

Chloe turned away and headed for the hotel, hoping he would call her back, hoping he wouldn't.

He didn't.

10

*T*he stagecoach was just too much of a temptation, stopped alongside the moonlit trail the way it was, and Jack Barrett couldn't resist a chance to line his empty pockets. He reined in when he saw the rig from a tree-lined ridge, pulled his bandanna up to hide the lower part of his face, and yanked his rifle from its scabbard.

Besides the driver, who was squatting next to the coach, cursing a broken axle, there seemed to be only two passengers, a woman and a little girl, both of them wearing calico and bonnets. No telling who might be inside, though—Jack proceeded with caution. He'd been on a losing streak lately, and he wanted money, not trouble.

The driver wasn't carrying a sidearm, Jack made sure of that first thing. As he rode up, he leaned in the saddle to look through the coach window: empty. He smiled behind his bandanna.

The woman and child stared at him in curious alarm, while the driver straightened and tried to bluff his way through the hopeless hand he'd been dealt.

"There's no money on this stage, mister," he said. "You're taking a hell of a risk, and it won't pay you."

The little girl stepped forward, evading the woman's grasping reach, and turned her face up to Jack, bold as you please. He figured she was seven or eight years old, ten at the most. He hoped he wouldn't have to shoot her; he'd never gunned down a kid before, and he didn't know how it would set with him.

"Are you a bandit?" she asked.

"Lizzie," the woman said, sounding scared and angry. "Get back here. *Now.*" She was a good-looking lady, but shrill. Jack didn't reckon he'd mind putting a bullet or two into her; he'd be doing a service to some man.

Lizzie didn't move. "Answer my question," she said, the brazen little snippet.

Out of the corner of his eye, Jack saw the driver make a move toward the step leading into the box of the coach. No doubt he had a rifle or a pistol tucked away under the seat.

Jack turned the rifle on him and pulled the trigger, watching with satisfaction as the old codger fell, bleeding, to the ground. "That answer enough, little girl?" he asked.

The woman caught the child by both shoulders and drew her back against her skirts. "Please," she said. "Don't hurt us. I've got some jewelry, and some money, too. Take it and ride out."

"Get it," Jack said shortly, "and don't do anything stupid, because, begging your pardon, ma'am, I'd as soon shoot you as spit."

Her face was snow-pale, even shadowed by the brim of her bonnet. "I won't. Just, please—"

The little girl was too young for good sense, it seemed, for she stood her ground. "You did a bad thing," she said. "When my papa finds out, he'll hunt you down and lynch you for sure."

Jack chuckled. The kid was an irritant, but he got a kick out of her brass. "That so?" he countered, keeping a close eye on the woman while she fetched her reticule from inside the coach. "What's your papa's name? I'll be sure and look him up."

"Don't you dare say a word, Lizzie Cavanagh," the woman warned, and then bit her lip, realizing, too late, that she'd betrayed the very thing she'd wanted the kid to keep quiet about. She cast a worried glance in the direction of the inert driver, then handed up a drawstring bag, a fancy thing, made of velvet, and heavy.

While Jack was fumbling to open the purse, the woman drew a derringer from the pocket of her skirt and pointed it at him, her aim true. He barely dodged the bullet, heard it tear a chunk out of the coach, and retaliated with the rifle. The woman fell, the girl screamed and ran to her, and Jack jammed his gun back into its scabbard and swung down from the saddle.

"Aunt Geneva!" the child cried, shaking the woman with her small hands.

Jack retrieved the derringer, dropped it into his coat pocket, and scrambled up into the driver's seat, in search of the strongbox. He broke the lock with the butt of his .44, lifted the lid, and congratulated himself for taking the trouble. There must have been a couple of thousand dollars in there, neatly stacked and tied with string. He cast a contemptuous glance at the lying driver, dead for his sins, shoved it all into his pockets, and whistled for his horse. The animal drew up alongside the stage, and he eased himself into the saddle.

The little girl looked up at him, her small face streaked with tears, her eyes defiant. The woman was bleeding from the throat, staring sightlessly at the sky.

Jack tugged at the brim of his hat. "You tell your papa, when you see him, that he owes me a favor," he said.

She jutted out her obstinate little chin. "What for?" she demanded.

"Not killing you," he answered. With that, he rode off into the night, wondering if he was doing the right thing, leaving a witness to tell the tale. He almost turned back, at one point, but in the end he decided against it. If the cold didn't finish the kid off, the cougars would.

He was miles away before he remembered that he hadn't checked under the stagecoach seat for a gun.

Maybe she had a chance after all.

11

$\mathcal{U}$nable to face the long ride back to the ranch, Jeb spent the night at the Arizona Hotel, though, regrettably, not in Chloe's bed, and he didn't sleep well. He was on the way to the livery stable, to collect his horse and go home, when he ran into Sam Fee, the marshal.

"Sam," he said, with a cordial nod. He would have gone on past, but for the look of consternation on the lawman's face. "Something wrong?"

"Stagecoach didn't come in yesterday afternoon," Sam said. "I figured they were just running late, but they should have been here by now."

Jeb felt a pinch in the pit of his belly. "You heading out to find them?"

Sam was already moving toward the stables. "Yup," he said. "I reckon I'd better. Could be they threw a wheel or ran into some other kind of trouble."

"I'll ride with you," Jeb said, matching his stride to Sam's.

"Obliged," Sam said. There'd been some trouble between him and the McKettricks, specifically Rafe, when

Gig Curry burned the Fee homestead to the ground and left the Triple M brand on a tree for a kind of calling card, but that was behind them now.

They were a couple of hours south of town when they found the coach and team of six fretful horses just off the trail, and there were two bodies on the ground.

Jeb cursed and jumped down from the saddle, with Sam only a step behind him. He crouched beside the woman, but he knew before he touched her that there would be no pulse. She'd been shot through the throat, and the ground was awash in blood.

Sam, in the meantime, squatted by the driver. "Dead," he said.

"Son of a bitch," Jeb muttered, and just as he was about to stand up, he spotted the barrel of a pistol, probably a Colt .45, gleaming in the window of the coach.

"Don't you try anything," a small voice warned. "I'll shoot you dead if you do."

Jeb squinted, hardly trusting his eyes. The speaker was a little girl, wearing a calico bonnet, and he figured she meant business.

He put his hands out from his sides. "It's all right," he said quietly. "Sam here is the marshal. We're not going to hurt you."

"You might be an outlaw," the kid insisted. Her eyes were big with fear and red-rimmed from crying, but she was a brave one, for sure, and meant to stand her ground.

"Sam," Jeb said easily, "let her see your badge."

Sam stepped into view, the nickel star gleaming on his coat. "He's telling the truth, child," he said, in his taciturn way. "Put down that gun, now, before you hurt yourself."

She took her time deciding the matter, but she finally lowered the .45—she'd needed both hands to hold it—and worked the latch on the door. "If you hurt me, my papa will skin you," she said, climbing down the steps.

"What happened here?" Sam wanted to know.

"What's your name?" Jeb asked, talking right over the marshal.

"Lizzie," she said, and her gaze dropped to the dead woman on the ground, then shot back to Jeb's face. "What's yours?"

"Jeb McKettrick. This is Sam Fee."

"He shot my aunt," Lizzie said. A tear trickled down her cheek.

"Who?" Sam asked.

"The outlaw, of course," Lizzie answered, a little testily. "He took all our money, too."

Sam and Jeb exchanged glances.

"We're going to look after you," Jeb said. "Find your papa. Everything will be all right."

She didn't look convinced and kept her distance. Little wonder, after what she'd been through.

"You must be cold and hungry," Jeb went on.

"Scared, mostly," the child answered.

"How old are you?" Jeb asked, while Sam went to unhitch the team from the stagecoach.

"Ten," Lizzie answered, with a sniffle, squaring her small shoulders. "How old are you?"

Under any other circumstances, he would have laughed, but there were two people dead, and a little girl had seen the whole thing. She'd spent the night by herself, most likely expecting the gunman to come back. "Twenty-eight," he said, and took a careful step toward her.

She looked him up and down, but when he fetched a lap robe from inside the coach, she let him put it around her. Sam, leaving the freed horses to forage for grass alongside the road, took the bedroll from behind his saddle and covered the woman's body with it.

"I've got some jerky in my saddlebags," Jeb said, to distract her from the process. "You want some?"

"I reckon I do," Lizzie allowed. "I wouldn't mind a little water, either, if you've got it."

Jeb fetched the jerky, along with his canteen, and brought them to her. "You mentioned your papa a little while ago," he said, sitting on the running board of the stagecoach beside her. "We're going to need his name."

She had a mouthful of jerky and chewed it thoroughly before swallowing. Washed it down with some water, too. Finally, she replied. "Holt Cavanagh."

Jeb's mouth dropped open. He closed it again. Waited.

Tears welled in the child's eyes, and he was hard put not to lay an arm around her shoulders, but she was a bristly little thing, full of pride, and he didn't want to scare her, either. "He didn't know we were coming," she said staunchly. "He might not even want me."

Jeb felt his gut grind. "Where's your mama?" he asked, after a quiet interval had passed. Now that he was getting over the shock, he noticed her resemblance to Holt.

"She's dead," Lizzie said, without looking at him. "She caught a fever last winter, in San Antonio. Aunt Geneva brought me here, soon as she could."

"You've had a hard time," Jeb said, but his brain was reeling. If Cavanagh was Lizzie's father, then she was flesh and blood, a niece. A McKettrick. Damned if the old man hadn't gotten his grandchild after all, and God knew what the ramifications of that would be.

She gave him a disdainful look. Of *course* she'd had a hard time, her expression said. She'd lost her mother and seen her aunt and the stagecoach driver shot down. She'd spent the night hiding in the stagecoach, cold, hungry, and scared.

"If you saw the man—the outlaw—again, could you recognize him?"

Her expression was doubtful, and her lower lip wobbled forlornly. "It was nighttime, and he had a bandanna over his face."

Sam had rolled the bodies up in blankets. "We'd best get the child and these poor folks to town," he said.

Jeb nodded, rose with a sigh, and he and Sam caught a couple of the team horses. They rigged halters and lead ropes from the stagecoach reins, laid the bodies over the animals' backs, and secured them with rope from their own saddles.

"Mister?" Lizzie said.

Jeb turned to see the child standing close by, waited for her to go on.

"Can I ride with you?"

He smiled, for the first time in what seemed like days. "Sure," he said. He scooped her up and set her in his saddle, then climbed up behind her and took the reins in one hand. Sam handed him one end of a lead rope, mounted his own horse, and they started back toward Indian Rock, the two team horses trotting behind them, bearing their grim burdens.

Lizzie turned in the saddle. "Do I have to call you Mr. McKettrick?" she asked.

He shook his head. "Uncle Jeb will do," he replied.

12

Naturally, their arrival in town drew a lot of attention.

Chloe, Becky, and Emmeline were among the first to approach them.

"Good heavens," Becky blurted. "What happened?"

"Stagecoach was robbed," Sam answered. "Two people shot to death. This little girl here, she saw it all."

Becky stepped forward, extended her arms to the child. Lizzie stiffened, took a grip on Jeb's coat sleeve, and wouldn't let go.

"Poor little thing," Emmeline whispered, shading her eyes from the sun as she looked up. "You must be frightened half to death."

Jeb's gaze met Chloe's and locked with it. "She's a brave one," he said. "And she's a McKettrick."

"I'm *not* a McKettrick," Lizzie said, turning a challenging look on him, even as she clutched his coat for dear life. "My name is Cavanagh."

"Land sakes," Becky exclaimed.

"Holt's?" Emmeline wanted to know.

"Evidently so," Jeb said, tearing his gaze from Chloe. "You'd better send somebody to fetch him."

Emmeline nodded and turned away to recruit a bystander for the job, and Becky stepped forward again, speaking quietly to the child.

"Come along now, sweetheart. Nobody's going to hurt you."

Lizzie consulted Jeb with another glance, and, "Is she a straight shooter?"

Jeb chuckled. "Yes," he said.

She deliberated, then let go of his arm and allowed Becky to help her down from the horse. They were already inside the hotel, with Emmeline right behind them, having dispatched her messenger, before it came to Jeb that he ought to dismount himself. When he did, he just stood there, feeling sad for Lizzie and envious of Holt.

Chloe laid a tentative hand to his cheek, and it scared him, how good it felt. "Was it bad?" she asked.

"Worse than bad," he admitted. He didn't want to leave her, but the work wasn't finished. "I've got to help Sam get these bodies over to Doc Boylen's office," he said.

She nodded, studied his face for a long moment, and turned to follow the others into the hotel.

Word traveled fast in a place like Indian Rock, and by noon, Angus and Concepcion rolled into town in a buckboard, driving the horses hard. They'd barely stepped into the hotel when Holt rode in at a gallop and left his gelding with its reins dangling.

Jeb, seeing the whole show from the bench out front, got to his feet and went inside.

"Where," Angus demanded, in a Zeus-like voice, "is my grandchild?"

"She's upstairs, sleeping," Becky said calmly, stationed like a sentry at the foot of the stairs, "and you will not disturb her, Angus McKettrick."

Holt, it appeared, would not be so easy to dissuade. He strode right over to Becky and stood toe-to-toe with her. "Which room?"

To everybody's surprise, Becky stepped aside. "Number seven," she said. "But don't wake her up. She's been through enough for one day."

Holt took the stairs two at a time. Angus looked like he wanted to follow, but Concepcion gripped his arm, and he let himself be restrained.

Five minutes passed, then ten. The only sound in the room, as far as Jeb noticed, was the ticking of the long-case clock on the lower landing.

Finally, Holt appeared at the top of the stairs, looking like a man who'd just been dragged over rough ground behind a fast horse.

"Well?" Angus half bellowed.

Holt gripped the rail with one hand as he came down the steps. He was pale, and there was a fevered light in his eyes.

"I didn't know," he said, without looking straight at any of them. "Goddammit, *I didn't know.*"

"She's yours, then?" Angus pressed.

Holt shook his head, a man in a daze, but he finally looked the old man in the eye. "Yes," he said. "She's mine, all right."

13

*C*hloe was drawn to the schoolhouse, against her better judgment, and made her way there soon after little Lizzie Cavanagh, attended by Becky and Emmeline, had been fed, soothed, and tucked into bed at the Arizona Hotel. Had she stayed, Chloe feared she would have been sucked into a whirlpool of caring, and that was an indulgence she couldn't afford. Whatever the words on her marriage license, she was *not* a McKettrick, and could have no real part in the drama.

The school was small, a one-room affair, perhaps twenty-by-twenty, with log walls and a sturdy shingle roof. The windows were new, and there were two swings affixed to the limbs of a giant oak tree in the grassy yard. The fence was picketed, and freshly whitewashed.

Chloe walked around the perimeter once, noting the raw-lumber privy and the small shed where horses could be stabled during the schoolday. There was also a tiny cottage, covered in white clapboard, and someone had planted rosebushes on either side of the small porch. A few valiant, bright red blooms still clung to the stems.

Leave Indian Rock, Chloe warned herself. *Go back to Sacramento.*

But she couldn't do it.

She tried the cottage door and found it unlatched. Inside were a gleaming brass bedstead, a potbellied stove with a supply of mesquite wood laid in beside it, a washstand, boasting a pretty pitcher and bowl and damask towels. There was a bookshelf, too, bare and waiting, it seemed, for her treasured volumes, and a hooked rug graced the floor. The furnishings were completed by a sturdy table, so new that it still smelled of pine sap.

The people of Indian Rock might not have snared themselves a teacher, just yet, but they obviously intended to do so, and they expected to make him or her welcome.

Chloe ached to live there, to unpack her treasures and settle in. She glanced at the bed, imagined herself there, with Jeb, and looked away quickly.

Fool, she thought. *He doesn't trust you. He doesn't want you. Put him out of your mind, or you'll go insane.*

She let herself out of the cottage, closing the door almost reverently, and proceeded across the yard to the front of the schoolhouse itself. Since she'd already trespassed, she might as well go the whole way.

The main building, like the cottage, was open to anyone who might choose to step inside, and Chloe's heart raced when she saw the interior. There were two blackboards, three long tables with benches for the students, a whole stack of textbooks, unused, their spines gleaming with newness. A globe stood beside the teacher's desk, promising worlds to explore, and the supply cabinet was stocked with drawing paper, pencils, bottles of India ink and nibbed pens, chalk and slates. If Chloe had been enamored of the cottage, she was transported now.

She sat down in the chair behind the desk, reached out to give the globe a spin. *Don't get your hopes up,* insisted a voice in her head, even as she dreamed of conducting lively classes in this cozy space, opening little minds to the vast vistas of the written word, of mathematics and science. Perhaps she might send to Sacramento for her telescope, gathering dust in the attic of her stepfather's home.

Her doubts brought her up short. *You were involved in a scandal. Besides, this is McKettrick territory. If there are sides to be taken, and there always are, the townspeople will line up behind Jeb.*

With a sigh, Chloe stood and smoothed her skirts. Maybe she would be hired, and maybe she wouldn't. All she could do was try, and keep her expectations as modest as possible.

She went to the door, stepped out onto the porch, and came face-to-face with a small, red-haired boy in clean but ragged clothes. He sported a constellation of freckles and an eager smile.

"Are you the new teacher?" he asked, almost breathless with suspense.

Chloe couldn't be sure what he hoped her answer would be. "No," she said honestly, putting out a hand. There was no sense in putting the cart before the horse. "My name is Chloe Wakefield. What's yours?"

The boy's exuberant expression collapsed into disappointment, but he took her hand in his grubby one and gave it a shake. "Harry Sussex," he said, in a deflated tone. "You *sure* you're not the teacher?"

"Fairly certain, yes," Chloe said, wanting to ruffle his thick hair and forbearing to do so. She sat down on the front step, and Harry took a place beside her.

"That's a shame," Harry sighed companionably. "The way things are going around here, it'll be a wonder if I ever learn anything."

Chloe suppressed a smile. "You are an unusual boy, Harry Sussex," she said. "I should think you'd rather be fishing or catching frogs or playing kickball than ciphering and reading lessons."

His thin shoulders were stooped with discouragement. "I want to be like Kade McKettrick when I grow up," he said disconsolately. "He's real smart. He reads books, and he can add up all kinds of numbers in his head. He knows the names of all the stars, too. Says there are probably people out there, living on other worlds, some of them just like ours."

"He must be quite a Renaissance man," Chloe observed. She'd had very little time to form an impression of Jeb's older brother, but Harry's description had raised her estimation of him by several notches. Where Jeb's whole credo seemed to be a resounding *Yippee!*, Kade obviously lived from his intellect.

Harry screwed up his face, puzzled. "*What* kind of man?"

"A smart one," Chloe clarified.

"I already said that," Harry pointed out, quite justly. His attention was deflected by a movement at the schoolyard gate, and his smile was instantaneous.

Following his gaze, Chloe saw a middle-aged man with a crop of messy hair, wearing a rumpled suit and carrying a battered medical kit in one hand.

The doctor opened the gate, smiling, and came toward them.

"This is Doc Boylen," Harry told Chloe. She recognized the name immediately, from the advertisement for a teacher in the *Epitaph*. "Doc, this here's Miss Chloe Wakefield, but she says she ain't the schoolmarm."

Doc favored Chloe with a cordial nod and a discerning once-over. "I received a letter from you," he said mildly. She wondered if he'd contacted the school in Tombstone, or heard about her disputed marriage to Jeb.

Chloe wanted to sigh, but she didn't. "I'm a good teacher," she said; she had confidence in that much, at least. "But I've got a history."

Doc chuckled. "Don't we all?" he said.

Chloe glanced uncomfortably at Harry; she didn't want to go into details about her past in front of him.

"The school is certainly wonderful," she said carefully. "And so is the cottage."

"Then I don't see the problem," Doc said easily. "As the head of the school board, I have the authority to offer you the position, here and now. The pay is downright pitiful—thirty dollars a month and meals. I'm afraid we spent most of our money on the buildings and the books."

Chloe's heart started beating its wings, wanting her to say yes, to run the risk, and devil take the consequences. "You might change your mind when you know the whole truth," she said carefully, trying hard not to care too much and failing miserably. She was filled with yearning.

Doc's smile remained steady. "Harry, why don't you run on home and ask your mother what's for supper?" he said, without looking away from Chloe's face.

Reluctantly, Harry rose to obey. He'd clearly taken in every word of the conversation up until then, and his eagerness to secure an education, and thus become more like Kade, had been mounting visibly the whole while. "It'll probably be beans again," he warned, with a note of stalwart pragmatism.

"I certainly hope not," Doc replied smoothly. "I'm in the mood for corned beef hash." He took a few coins from his pocket and gave them to the boy. "Stop by the mercantile on the way and see if they've got any canned meat. There ought to be enough for a piece of penny candy, too."

His enthusiasm renewed, Harry leaped off the porch and raced to the gate, pausing there to look back at Chloe, all bright countenance and good cheer. "You won't go anywhere, will you, Miss Wakefield? Before I learn the names of some stars, I mean, and how to add numbers in my head?"

Chloe couldn't bring herself to answer; a lump of longing had risen in her throat. Her gaze shifted back to Doc Boylen's kindly face, and Harry went on about his business.

"I'm married," she said straightforwardly, "and not for the first time." Most female teachers were single; working wives were frowned upon. Any hint of scandal was cause for prompt dismissal. "My references may be less than glowing, as well."

Doc Boylen set one foot on the step Harry had vacated and rested a forearm on his knee. "Are you a good teacher, Chloe Wakefield?" he asked.

"Yes," she said. "I certainly am."

A mischievous light danced in his eyes. "Just how many husbands do you have?"

She smiled, albeit sadly. "I've had two. I divorced the first one when I found out he was a paid gunslinger, and the second one isn't too sure he wants to claim me."

"Why's that?"

She sighed. "He didn't know about the first one."

"Ah," said Doc, with a sage nod of his head. "I see. And where is this confused fellow now?"

"Down at the Arizona Hotel, last time I looked," she answered. "Jeb McKettrick and I are—separated."

"I see," Doc said, taking a few moments to consider. Then he smiled and shook his head at some amusing thought. "So you're the wife he kept bragging about. Most of us didn't believe you existed—Jeb's been known to play fast and loose with the truth on occasion."

Chloe spread her hands. "Here I am," she said, somewhat ruefully. "In the flesh."

Doc mused a while. "He's likely to carry you off to that ranch sooner or later," he went on presently. "Probably sooner, if he's anything like Rafe and Kade, and obviously, he is."

Chloe straightened her spine, vertebra by vertebra. "I don't think there's any danger of that," she said. "We've got some serious differences."

"I won't ask what those differences are, but I daresay the two of you must have agreed on something, if you tied the knot in the first place. Just the same, if you can promise me a full year of service, I'll hire you right now."

Chloe tried to speak, failed, and tried again. "Thank you," she managed.

Doc took out his pocket watch, flipped open the case, and frowned at what he saw there. "Thirty dollars a month, the cottage, and meals. You agree to that, Mrs. McKettrick?"

"Yes," Chloe said, praying she would not come to regret the decision. "My answer is yes."

14

*H*olt had known, the moment he looked at Lizzie, lying there sleeping, with her dark hair spilling over Becky's linen pillowcase, that she was his. He saw himself in her and, more importantly, he saw Olivia. It had been all he could do not to awaken the child and demand to know where her mother was, but compassion had stayed his hand. She was a fragile little thing, and even though he had yet to learn the details, he knew she'd been through hell.

There would be time enough to question her later, when she'd awakened, and the two of them had been properly introduced.

Now, he stood on the back stoop of the Arizona Hotel, his hands gripping the rail, white-knuckled, his stomach churning, his mind spinning. He stiffened when he heard the door creak open behind him, knew before a word was spoken that if he turned, he'd see Angus standing there.

"You all right?" the old man asked.

Holt gave a bitter laugh. "Nope," he said, without turning around.

Angus stepped up beside him, moved to lay a hand on his shoulder, then evidently thought better of the idea and let it fall back to his side. This was a relief to Holt; he didn't think he could have borne to be touched—at present, his nerves were all on the outside of his skin. "I take it you didn't know about this child," Angus said.

Holt shook his head. "I had no idea," he admitted. He spared his father a brief, sidelong glance. "If I had, I sure as hell wouldn't have left Texas without a backward look." It was a gibe, and Angus grimaced as it struck its mark.

"That's what you think I did, I reckon," Angus said, with a sigh.

"That's what I *know* you did, old man," Holt replied.

"I thought you were better off with your mother's folks. What would I have done with a babe in arms? Hell, you couldn't even talk, let alone ride."

Holt thrust out a hard breath. "I watched the road for you," he said, without intending to reveal that much.

"I wish I'd gone back," Angus allowed. "But I had a ranch, and a new wife, and sons. There was no money back then, and no time. I had my back to the wall for years."

"I didn't care about money," Holt replied, consciously releasing his grasp on the porch rail, lest he snap it in two. "I wanted a father. Not an uncle who wished I'd never landed on his doorstep."

"Dill was hard on you, I reckon." To his credit, Angus sounded sincerely regretful. Trouble was, it was too little, too late. "I guess he and the missus never had any children of their own."

"I was curse enough," Holt answered.

"I'm sorry," Angus said.

"Your remorse doesn't amount to a pitcher of warm spit, old man, and there's no sense talking about it now anyway. Too much water under the bridge."

Angus shifted beside him, turned to lean against the rail with his arms folded. "I might believe that, except for one thing. You had an outfit of your own, down in Texas. Becky told me all about it, said the two of you were acquainted back in Kansas City. You could be any of a hundred places, but the fact is, you're right here in the Arizona Territory. That tells me there are things you want settled."

"I wanted a look at you," he said. "You and those boys you cared enough about to raise up under your own roof."

"You're mighty jealous of your brothers, aren't you?"

Holt tensed. "No," he said. "I'd just as soon forget all of you."

"Well, I reckon that's going to be difficult. Important thing is, what are you going to do now? You've got that little daughter in there, and she's most likely alone in the world, but for you. She wouldn't be here if she had other folks willing to take her in."

"I don't know what I mean to do about Lizzie," Holt confessed. "Maybe I'll put her in boarding school."

Angus turned his head and spat, a clear indication of his thoughts in that regard. "Well, hell, don't do her any favors. If you aren't willing to give that little girl a proper home, Concepcion and I would be happy to take her in."

"She's none of your concern."

"By God, she's my granddaughter, flesh of my flesh and bone of my bone. That *makes* her my concern. I won't see her handed over to strangers."

Holt's breath scraped at his throat, and his blood ran as hot and poisonous as venom. "If you think you're going to raise my daughter, you're full of sheep dip."

That statement seemed to please the old man, though it surely wasn't meant to. He gave a raspy laugh. "That's more like it," he said.

"I'm glad you approve," Holt scoffed.

"You go ahead and hate me all you want, boy," Angus went on. "I can take it, and I've gotten pretty well accustomed to it over the last year. But you mark my words: If you try to send that child off to some school, to be fetched up by strangers, I'll go there and bring her straight home to the Triple M." He paused. "I made one mistake with you. I don't intend to make another with her."

Holt turned to look into his father's face. "Why is she so important to you?"

Angus thrust himself away from the rail and let his arms fall to his sides. "Because she's yours," he said. And with that, he went back inside, leaving Holt to his own thoughts.

After five minutes or so, Holt left the back porch, getting only as far as the hotel kitchen before he ran smack into Jeb.

"What happened out there? On the trail, I mean?" Holt demanded. He knew Jeb and Sam had found the girl in a broken-down stagecoach, knew her name was Lizzie, but that was a mile shy of enough.

Jeb, sipping coffee from a mug, met his gaze squarely. "Somebody robbed the stage, shot the driver and Lizzie's aunt like squirrels. Lizzie said the woman's name was Geneva." He shook his head. "It was bad, Holt. Real bad. The kid will be a while getting over it, if she ever does."

Holt felt sick, because of the memories etched in Lizzie's mind, and because Geneva hadn't deserved to die like that. He was relieved, too, because it hadn't been Olivia found beside that stage. "Did Lizzie mention Olivia, her mama?"

He saw pity in Jeb's eyes and braced himself for what he knew was coming. "Not by name," Jeb said, with a shake of his head. His voice was hoarse. "She did say her mother had died in San Antonio, of a fever. Her aunt was bringing her here, as far as I can figure, to meet up with you."

Holt reeled inwardly. Olivia, dead. He couldn't imagine it; she'd been vibrant with life the last time he'd seen her, full of radiance and passion and spirit. Why hadn't she written him, at some point during the decade that had passed since their final parting, and told him they had a child?

The answer was pride, he supposed. She'd wanted to get married, he'd said he wasn't ready, and lit out with the Rangers. When he got back to Austin, six months later, she'd long since packed up and vanished. He'd visited her friends and Geneva, too, but they'd been tight-lipped, and said if she had anything to say to him, she'd find a way to do it on her own. He'd looked for her in every town he passed through, for years, before finally giving up.

He'd never dreamed, never imagined even once, in all his many speculations, that they might have conceived a baby. He'd simply decided that she'd married someone else, mourned his foolishness, and gone on with her life.

Jeb laid a hand on Holt's shoulder. "I'm sorry," he said.

Holt shook off the past. It was gone, and he had to think about the present and his daughter's future. "Thanks," he said, with some difficulty. "For looking after Lizzie, I mean."

Jeb shrugged, withdrew his hand. "I wasn't about to leave her out there," he answered. He smiled slightly. "She's a tough little kid. When we found her, she was holding a .45. Said she'd shoot us if we made a wrong move, and I believe she meant it, too."

Holt chuckled. "Damn," he marveled. "You'd think she was related to Angus McKettrick."

"Or you," Jeb said.

Holt nodded. "Or me," he agreed.

15

Jeb was just about to go looking for Chloe when she drew up in front of the hotel in a buckboard, with Old Billy, from the livery stable, at the reins. He stepped out onto the sidewalk, prepared to argue if she'd taken it into her head to leave town, though he supposed he should have been hoping for just that. Her going would certainly simplify matters, and complicate them at the same time.

He took off his hat to shove a hand through his hair, replaced it as he approached the wagon. When he reached up to help Chloe down, she hesitated for an instant, then took his hand.

"Where are you going?" he asked bluntly.

She took a few seconds to deliberate, probably working out how much she ought to say. "Dr. Boylen offered me a teaching position," she said. "There's a cottage included, and I'm here to get my things."

Jeb didn't know whether to object or be pleased. If she was telling the truth, and their marriage wasn't a fraud, he didn't want his wife working for a living. And though a part of him wished she'd never come to Indian Rock in the first place, the thought of her going elsewhere was no damn good, either.

Once, he reflected ruefully, he'd known exactly what he thought about everything. Since he'd met Chloe, life had become one big conundrum.

"Does Doc know you got fired from the last one?" he asked, then could have kicked himself for stirring up a hornets' nest.

Her face tightened, and she realigned her shoulders, as if bracing herself against him. "Yes," she said shortly. "So if you have any ideas about spoiling *this* job like you did the last one, you're too late."

Jeb rubbed the back of his neck with one hand, purely frustrated. "Chloe, I didn't mean to do that. It was just plain bad luck that the head of the school board happened to be in that poker game at the Broken Stirrup."

Old Billy waited, shifting from one foot to the other on the sidewalk in front of the hotel. "I ain't got all day," the smith complained. "Where do I find them bags?"

Chloe picked up her skirts and made to slip past Jeb and join Old Billy, but Jeb took hold of her arm.

"You're going to live in the cottage behind the schoolhouse, all by yourself?"

She answered in a brisk whisper. "Of *course* I'm going to live by myself."

She tugged, but Jeb didn't let her go. "Chloe, for all that there are good people here, this is still a wild town.

All sorts of cowboys and drifters come through. You ought to stay on at the hotel if you won't live at the ranch."

She blinked. "Live at the ranch?" she echoed. "Why would I do that? It's miles from town and, besides, according to you, we're not married."

"You'd be safer there," Jeb insisted. "You'd have a room of your own. As for this job—"

"*As for this job,*" she interrupted, "I've already accepted it. You needn't take any responsibility for me at all. I can take care of myself."

How did they always get into these snarls? He'd begun this conversation with the best of intentions, and right away it had gone down the wrong trail. "Chloe—"

She pulled free and swept past him. "I'll show you where to find my things," she said to Old Billy. Jeb might have vanished like smoke in a hard wind for all the notice she paid him after that.

Determined not to be put off so easily, he followed the pair through the lobby and up the stairs and helped Billy lug the trunks, valises, boxes, and reticules down to the waiting buckboard. Chloe supervised, taking care never to let her gaze connect with his, and made the final descent with them, a hatbox in each hand.

At the schoolhouse, they unloaded the whole shooting match again and carried it around back to the cottage. When everything was inside, Chloe thanked Old Billy and paid him a dollar. He hastened away, but Jeb lingered.

"You shouldn't be here," Chloe said. He wondered if she was as painfully conscious of the brass bed as he was. The thing seemed to dominate the room. "It isn't proper, and I don't need you wrecking my reputation all over again."

Jeb knew she was right—at least where propriety was concerned—but he couldn't bring himself to say so, or to leave, as he should have. "A lot of folks know we went through with a wedding ceremony, even if it was a sham. That'll cause just as much talk. They'll wonder why we're not living together." He paused, hat in hand. "I'm not your enemy, Chloe."

"You're not my friend, either," Chloe pointed out, busying herself with one of the trunks. "As for what people will think, I'm surprised you care. It's not as if you've ever acted like a husband."

He went to her, turned her to face him, catching sight of the contents of the trunks as he did so. Books. Piles of them. He looked into her eyes. "I could remedy that easily enough," he said. And then, before she could protest, he kissed her.

At first, she set her palms against his chest and tried to push him away, just as she'd done the night before, when he'd kissed her in the street, but then he felt a softening in her. She slid her arms around his neck and kissed him back in earnest.

"Chloe," he said, when they both came up for air.

She drew back, out of his embrace, smoothed her hair,

then her skirts. "Oh, no, you don't, Jeb McKettrick. You are *not* going to get me into that bed. And you are not going to cost me this job, either. I want you to leave, right now."

"If we're married," he reasoned, knowing he'd already lost this battle, "what's the harm?"

"You know damn well what the 'harm' is," she bristled. "You don't trust me any farther than you can throw me, and you're not willing to acknowledge me as your legal wife."

He grinned weakly. "I think I could throw you quite a ways," he said. "You don't weigh very much."

She didn't smile. In fact, she turned her back on him and started grabbing up books, setting them on the shelves with a lot of thrusting and thumping. "Go *away*, Jeb," she said, and he thought he heard tears in her voice. "I mean it. I want you to leave. Immediately."

He hesitated. "All right," he finally agreed. "I'll go. But I'll be back, Chloe. You can't hide out in this cottage forever."

"Go," she said, and that time he was sure she was crying.

He wanted to take her into his arms again, but he didn't dare. "I'll be at the Triple M," he said, pausing in the open doorway. "If you want me, send word."

"Don't watch the road for a messenger," she said.

He sighed and went out, leaving a part of himself behind.

*   *   *

Jack Barrett watched as McKettrick vaulted the school-yard fence and crossed the street, headed toward the main part of town. He itched to shoot the bastard, then and there, but he knew he couldn't indulge the impulse just yet. It was broad daylight, and he'd be caught for sure.

He turned his attention to the schoolhouse and smiled to himself. At least he knew where to find Chloe when he decided to pay his respects. In the meantime, he'd lie low. She wasn't the only one who'd landed a job that day; he'd just met the foreman from the Circle C, a man named Henry Farness, and he'd signed on to ride fence lines and punch cattle.

It would be a change from bounty hunting and playing cards for a living, but he was a good rider, and a hand with a gun, and he knew how to bide his time. He also knew that the ranch belonged to Holt Cavanagh and recalled the name from his conversation with the little girl, alongside the stagecoach the night before. If Cavanagh was her daddy, like she'd said, and she ended up living out there on his ranch, he might run into her. To his way of thinking, that merely added spice to the game, and, anyway, she probably wouldn't recognize him even if they met face-to-face.

He watched as McKettrick conferred with an old man and a very pregnant Mexican woman outside the Arizona Hotel, and wondered how many folks he'd have to kill before this thing was over.

Maybe he ought to go over to the schoolhouse, right now, and confront Chloe. Tell her the jig was up, and take her away. He had plenty of money, thanks to last night's enterprise, and they could start over somewhere new, live high on the hog. She was used to that, having been raised in a Sacramento mansion, and he'd enjoy buying her pretty presents and the like. He'd show her she'd been right to marry him in the first place.

He felt his face harden. Chloe was a wildcat, and she'd surely make a fuss, at least at first, when she found out he'd followed her to Indian Rock. Might even tell some-body that he was a gunslinger, and that wouldn't do. Folks in small towns tended to mistrust strangers, and he didn't want anyone wondering if he'd been the one to hold up that stagecoach and gun down the woman and the driver.

He'd have to stay out of Jeb McKettrick's way, too, for now at least. McKettrick would recognize him, after their meeting in Tombstone, and he'd get his back up for sure. That might precipitate events Jack wasn't ready to deal with just yet, much as he wanted to jump right in.

No, sir, the bridegroom wouldn't lay eyes on Jack Bar-rett until circumstances were exactly right and he was looking down the barrel of Jack's gun. By then, it would be too late.

Chloe would grieve a while, once McKettrick was dead, but that was all right. Jack meant to console her as only a loving husband could do.

A nudge to his ribs made him reach, by habit, for his

pistol, but fortunately, he realized it was only Farness, the Circle C foreman, and stayed his hand. Even forced a smile to his lips.

"You ready to ride?" Farness wanted to know. There was a look of consternation in his eyes, as though he might be trying to fit the pieces of something together in his mind.

This one's trouble, Jack thought, but he nodded, holding on to the smile. "Lead the way," he said.

16

Lizzie stood at the base of the stairs, her head tipped back so she could take Holt in with those changeling eyes of hers. She was clad in a ready-made dress from the mercantile, hastily purchased by Emmeline, since her belongings had been left behind with the stagecoach, and her dark hair, a legacy from her mother, gleamed around her face. The rest of her features were feminine versions of his own; he would have known that stubborn jaw and straight nose anywhere.

"Are you my papa?" she asked, in a matter-of-fact tone. She was pretending to be strong, he sensed that. Wished he knew how to go about comforting her, getting across that she'd be all right from then on, because he'd see to it.

"I reckon so," he replied awkwardly. He could feel Angus and Concepcion and Becky and Emmeline standing behind him, listening and watchful. What did they think he was going to do? Tell the kid she'd have to make her own way in the world, that he couldn't be bothered?

He cast a brief, scathing look back at his father. *I'm not like you, old man*, he thought. It wasn't entirely true, of course; his first impulse, after all, had been to pack Lizzie off to boarding school. What did he know about taking care of a child, especially a female? He might have followed through with his original idea, too, if it hadn't been for Angus's vow that he'd fetch her home to the Triple M if that happened.

The patriarch, stern as Moses on the slopes of the holy mountain, scowled right back at him and gestured impatiently toward Lizzie.

Holt drew a deep breath and faced his daughter again. "I'm real sorry about your aunt Geneva," he said. *And your mama,* he added silently. The news of Olivia's passing had left a hole in his insides; on some level, he'd always expected to see her again. Make things right somehow. Now it was too late.

Lizzie hoisted her chin. "Aunt Geneva wasn't going to stay on in Indian Rock after she got me settled," she said. "She told me you didn't like her, and she didn't like you much, either. She hoped you'd be nicer to me than you were to my mama."

Holt felt his pa's gaze burning into his backbone, but he wasn't fool enough to turn around again. "I loved your mother," he heard himself say.

Lizzie looked skeptical, and imperious into the bargain. She was going to be a handful, that much was clear, and he didn't have the first idea how to cope. If it hadn't been for his pride, he'd have let Angus and Concepcion take her to raise, but he knew they'd make a McKettrick out of her, and he'd wear an apron and a bonnet before he let that happen.

"Aunt Geneva said she'd rather eat poached snake eggs than hand me over to you, but she didn't have a choice."

Holt crouched, to put himself on the child's level, and he couldn't help grinning a little. "Poached snake eggs, is it?" he reflected, with a shake of his head. "Geneva was always definite in her opinions. But tell me—why did she think she didn't have a choice?"

Lizzie paused to consider her answer, but her expression revealed nothing of what she was thinking. He figured she'd make a hell of a poker player—it ran in the family. "The doctor said she was sick. There was a lump growing inside her, and she didn't reckon she had much time. She didn't want me to be left alone."

Holt's voice scraped at his throat as it came out. "And your mother was already gone."

Lizzie looked away, blinked, looked back, steady as a hangman. "Yes," she said. "A fever took her."

Holt wanted to touch Lizzie's hand then, maybe even draw her into his arms, but he hadn't earned the right to do that, and he knew she'd balk if he tried. "When was that?" he asked.

"Last winter." Lizzie studied him hard, frowning. "You've got a house, don't you?"

"Yes," Holt answered, thinking of that sprawling, lonesome place, out in the middle of nowhere. He'd bought it out of spite, because he knew Angus wanted the land surrounding it, and every acre had been an albatross around his neck ever since. Dammit all to hell, if he'd just stayed in Texas, where he belonged, he might have found Olivia in time, managed to change things somehow . . .

"Good," Lizzie answered. "Aunt Geneva said you mostly slept in places where you shouldn't have, back when she knew you." She paused. "I reckon she meant on the ground and in barns."

Behind him, Angus chuckled, then made a whooshing sound, as if Concepcion had elbowed him. Bless the woman.

"You'll have a roof over your head, a room and a bed and all you want to eat," Holt promised.

Lizzie tilted her head to one side, and then proceeded to negotiate. "How about a dog?"

Holt nearly grinned. "We can probably rustle one up someplace," he said.

"Old Blue just had a litter," Angus put in. "I'll bring one over as soon as they're weaned."

"Hush!" Concepcion said.

"And a pony," Lizzie pressed, probably drawing confidence from the support of her grandfather. "I want a pony, too."

"That depends on how well you ride," Holt said

firmly. He was determined not to lose control of this situation, assuming he hadn't already.

"I ride," Lizzie said, "like a Comanche."

Angus laughed again, and he must have dodged Concepcion's elbow because this time there was no loud expulsion of breath.

"We'll see," Holt said, as much for Angus's benefit as for hers. If that old man thought he was going to meddle in this, he had manure for brains.

Lizzie wasn't through with him yet. He wouldn't have been surprised if the kid had asked for references. "Do you have a wife?"

Holt considered his housekeeper, Sue Ellen Caruthers, who had already proposed herself for the position. A leftover bride, she'd come to Indian Rock to marry either Rafe or Kade, he couldn't remember which. The plan had come to naught, with Rafe already wed to Emmeline when she arrived, and Kade so besotted with Mandy that he couldn't think straight. Sue Ellen had been testy on the subject ever since.

He shook his head. "No wife," he said. Sue Ellen was a fair hand at the stove, and she kept the house clean enough, but she was possessed of a peevish and contrary nature. In point of fact, he'd sooner have hitched himself to a sow bear with a toothache.

Lizzie folded her arms, and it appeared that the negotiations had stalled. "A child needs a mother," she said, sounding more like a forty-year-old midget than a little girl.

Emmeline gave a soft burble of laughter.

"For the time being," Holt said firmly, and for the benefit of all who might take an interest in the matter, "you're going to have to settle for a father."

Lizzie huffed out a little sigh. "Well, all right," she said, with sobering reluctance. "I guess you'll do."

17

*O*nce Jeb had gone, Chloe sat down hard on the lid of her largest trunk and folded her hands. Within her bosom, the debate raged.

Go after him, said her heart.

Not a chance, her mind vowed.

Caught between the two, Chloe gave a sigh of frustration. She might have sat there wrangling with herself for the rest of the afternoon if a knock hadn't sounded at the cottage door.

He was back.

She was happy.

She would scratch his eyes out.

She stood up and promptly sat back down. "Who is it?" she called, taking care to sound busy, distracted, and completely unconcerned with Jeb McKettrick and his goings and comings.

"Emmeline McKettrick," was the cheerful reply.

Vastly relieved and incomprehensibly disappointed, Chloe got to her feet, smoothed her hair and her dusty skirts, and went to open the door, assembling a neighborly smile as she went.

Rafe's fair-haired wife stood smiling on the stoop, a covered dish in her hands. "I hope I'm not disturbing you," she said.

Chloe realized that she was exceedingly glad of company and stepped back. "Not at all," she said, though she knew she should have been putting away books and hanging up her clothes. There was no wardrobe, but the pegs on the wall would serve well enough. Compared to her accommodations in Tombstone, the cottage was a palace.

Emmeline stepped gracefully into the room, looking pleasantly harried. "We've had quite the drama over at the hotel," she confided, setting the dish on the table and taking in the cottage in a sweeping glance. Chloe would have bet that she hadn't missed a single detail, for all the subtle brevity of the inspection.

Chloe smiled. She liked Emmeline, as she had liked Mandy. They were obviously attractive, intelligent women, but they'd fallen for a McKettrick just the same. It made her feel a little better about her own lapse in judgment. "I wish I could offer you tea, but I haven't been to the mercantile for staples—"

"If I have one more cup of tea," Emmeline said, "I'll spring a leak."

Chloe laughed. "Sit down," she said, even as Emmeline, a step ahead of her, drew back a chair to do just that.

Emmeline beamed. "We finally roped in a teacher," she said. "What a relief. I was beginning to think we'd *never* find anybody."

Well aware that Emmeline was there as much out of curiosity as neighborliness, Chloe took care with her expression and manner as she appropriated the other chair. Most likely, word of her hiring had gotten around, and everybody in Indian Rock was full of questions about the new teacher. Emmeline had probably been appointed to scout the matter out and report back.

Chloe let Emmeline's comment pass. "Tell me, has Mr. Cavanagh made his daughter's acquaintance yet?" For all her own concerns, the child had been on her mind all day.

Emmeline looked pleased, and a little sad, too. "He's claimed her, and they're leaving for the Circle C first thing in the morning. The poor little thing—she's being very brave, but she *did* see two people murdered in front of her eyes. I hope Holt will be patient with her."

Chloe ached to think of the marks such an experience could leave on a little girl. Another problem occurred to her, too. She'd never been to the Circle C, but she knew it was a long way from town, farther even than the Triple M. "How will she go to school?"

Plainly, Emmeline had not thought of that. "I don't know," she admitted. "It's more than two hours to Holt's place, on a fast horse." Then, as quickly as it had disappeared, her smile was back, effervescent and inordinately reassuring. "Don't worry, Chloe. You'll have plenty of pupils. When do you intend to open the school?"

It was Thursday, and she had lesson plans to draw up. "Monday morning, I suppose," she said, cheered by the prospect. Then, musing, "Perhaps I should put up a notice somewhere."

"No need of that," Emmeline said. "It's already all over town that the school will be opening soon. Doc Boylen will have seen to that."

Chloe shifted in her chair, suddenly certain what the next topic of conversation would be: Jeb. "Good," she said, uneasy.

Emmeline regarded her frankly and confirmed Chloe's belated suspicions. "We haven't been able to get a straight answer out of Jeb," she said. "Are the two of you actually married, or not?"

Chloe sighed. "Yes," she said. "But Jeb doesn't believe it."

"How can he doubt a thing like that?" Emmeline asked practically, and with some impatience. "He was *there*, wasn't he?"

Chloe hesitated, biting her lower lip. She'd told Doc Boylen just about everything, so there didn't seem to be much point in beating around the proverbial bush. "There was—a misunderstanding," she said, stalling so she could choose the proper words. "I was—I was married once before, for exactly one day. My former husband showed Jeb our wedding portrait, and he decided he'd been duped." A flush climbed her neck, ached in her cheeks. "Instead of coming to me for an explanation, Jeb went straight to the Broken Stirrup Saloon and proceeded to drink, gamble, and cavort with low women."

"A true McKettrick," Emmeline commiserated. "The first time I met Rafe, he was in the middle of a fistfight. I almost tripped over him in the street."

Chloe's eyes widened. "What did you do?"

Emmeline heaved a sigh. "What *could* I do? I thought I was already married to the man and made up my mind to make the best of things." She smiled a little and shook her head. "We've had our trials, Rafe and I, but I'm awfully glad I didn't give up on him. Mandy would say the same thing about Kade."

Chloe withdrew a little. "It's different for Jeb and me."

"I doubt it," said Emmeline, bracing one elbow on the table and cupping her chin in her hand. "Why didn't you just show Jeb your divorce decree?" she asked, as a seeming afterthought. "That would convince him."

"He didn't give me the opportunity," Chloe said, irritated all over again, "and when I went looking for him, he made it plain he wasn't interested in anything I had to say."

"Pride," Emmeline said dismissively, though Chloe couldn't be sure whether she was referring to Jeb's pride or Chloe's own.

"Whatever the reason," Chloe went on, thrusting her shoulders back slightly and stiffening her backbone, "he left Tombstone with Kade, and I tried to pick up the pieces after he was gone."

"You were teaching school," Emmeline suggested, plainly fishing.

Chloe shook her head. "I lost my job the same night I lost my husband," she said. "I was living on my savings and trying to decide what to do next when I saw an advertisement in the newspaper. Indian Rock was in want of a teacher. So I wrote to Dr. Boylen to inquire about it. Then I—I got word that my uncle—" Suddenly, she choked up, and couldn't go on.

Emmeline touched her hand. "Becky told me," she said. "I'm so sorry, Chloe. John was a fine man."

Chloe drew a deep, steadying breath. "It was a terrible shock," she allowed. "But I'll come to terms with that, too."

"You have all of us," Emmeline said gently. "That's what I really came here to tell you. Rafe and me, Angus and Concepcion, Kade and Mandy, and certainly Becky. I know you probably feel very much alone right now, but you aren't—the McKettricks are a close-knit bunch, and until you say different, you're one of us."

Chloe's eyes burned. "But you don't even know me—"

"You're John Lewis's daughter, and Jeb cared enough to marry you. For right now, that's all we *need* to know." Emmeline pushed back her chair and stood. Her gaze fell, briefly, on the dish she'd placed on the table. "Don't feel obligated to sit here all by yourself and eat that stew," she said. "If you want to join the rest of the family for supper, over at the hotel, we'll be glad to have you."

The rest of the family. As if she was a part of the McKettrick clan. "I think I would like to be alone," she said softly, "just for tonight. It's not that I'm not grateful—"

Emmeline nodded her understanding. "Becky will be expecting you for breakfast, then." With that, she crossed the room and let herself out.

Chloe sat perfectly still for a long while after Emmeline had taken her leave, trying to make sense of all she felt. Then, seeing that for a hopeless cause, she lifted the lid on the dish and peered in at the stew. It looked and smelled delicious, but she had no appetite, so she covered it again and rose to her feet, on a mission.

Emmeline had asked her about her divorce papers. High time she got them out, she decided, though the jury was still out on whether or not she would show them to Jeb. It galled her that her word wasn't enough for him and, besides, it wasn't as if she wanted him back.

Did she? In point of fact, she hadn't expected ever to see him again, after their disastrous wedding night, and now that she'd landed practically in his backyard, she would have to come to terms with the matter, once and for all.

She found the hatbox where she'd kept every letter John Lewis had ever written to her, and they were all there, stacked according to years, and tied with ribbon. She'd have known if even one was missing, as surely as she would note the absence of a finger or a toe.

The divorce decree, tucked away at the bottom the day she received it, and never looked at again, was gone.

Fretful, Chloe rifled through the packets, certain she'd merely misplaced the document, but there was no sign of it. She went through another box, and another, and still another.

No papers.

Shadows were gathering at the windows of the cottage when she finally gave up the search, sank back into her chair, and laid her head on her arms.

Jack, she thought, too discouraged to fly into a temper. Of course it had been Jack who'd taken them, taken the only proof she had that she was legally married to one man, not two.

18

*J*eb had always liked his room well enough, modest though it was. As the youngest of three brothers, he was used to hand-me-downs, hind tit, and the last piece of chicken on the platter, and for the most part, it hadn't bothered him much. If being the last-born had its drawbacks, it also had its advantages—he'd done a lot of coasting in his time, gone his own way, with nothing much expected of him. No, Rafe and Kade had been the ones to carry that burden.

Now, with Chloe miles away, in the cottage behind the schoolhouse, and the kiss they'd shared still reverberating through his body, he was more conscious of being alone than ever before.

Rafe and Emmeline were across the creek, in their fine house, probably making love.

Kade and Mandy, down at the far end of the hall, in the big room that had been Angus's private domain until last spring, were most likely doing the same.

Hell, even Concepcion and the old man, having moved to Rafe's former quarters, had each other, and pretty soon, they'd have a baby, too.

And here he was, Jeb McKettrick, ladies' man, poker player, bronc buster, fast-talker and even-faster-gun, sprawled on top of his lonely bed with all his clothes on, staring at the ceiling and wondering exactly when the rest of the world had packed its saddlebags and gone right on without him.

He cupped his hands behind his head and crossed his feet. Concepcion would have his hide if she knew he was still wearing his boots, for she was a choosy housekeeper, and the thought brought a thin smile to his lips. It was a small comfort, this minor rebellion, but a comfort, nonetheless.

It didn't last.

Guilt rose up inside him, as surely as if Concepcion had been standing right there, with her arms folded and one foot tapping. He'd been young when his mother died, and Concepcion had filled the role admirably since then, cooking, cajoling, encouraging, and scolding, keeping them all going when it would have been a sight easier to give up. With a put-upon sigh, he heeled off one boot, then the other, letting them hit the floor with a thud. What he ought to do, he decided, was saddle up his horse and ride out. Never even look back.

Start fresh, somewhere else. Make something of himself.

He knew, even as he entertained the thought, that it was pure fancy, the leaving part, anyway. Hopeless as things seemed, given that Rafe or Kade would most likely inherit the lion's share, he loved the Triple M as much as his pa or either of his brothers did. Oh, he'd tried to break away a couple of times, riding for other outfits, as far away as Colorado and Montana, but he might as well have been tethered to a Joshua tree in the center of the ranch, for the place always drew him home again, calling to him in his sleep, howling through his soul like a storm.

His mind turned to Chloe. He wondered if she'd latched the cottage door, if she was troubled and wakeful, like he was.

He gave a mirthless laugh. Like as not, she was dreaming peacefully.

He rolled onto his side, turning his back to the wide, glowing moon intruding at his window, and purposefully closed his eyes. His body ached for sleep, but his mind was covering ground as fast as a wild stallion on a dead run.

Finally, with a muttered curse, he got up, opened his door, and made his way down the back stairs, into the kitchen. He lit a lamp, poured himself a cup of lukewarm coffee left over from supper, and sat down at the table to ponder the many and diverse ills of Creation.

He'd been there maybe five minutes when Kade joined him, shirtless and barefoot, with his pants misbuttoned and a look of silly satiation on his face.

Jeb scowled a greeting.

"Howdy, little brother," Kade said blithely, on his way to the pantry. He came out with half a cherry pie still in the pan, and rummaged in the silverware drawer for a fork.

"I guess love makes a man hungry," Jeb observed, somewhat testily.

Kade laughed and swung a leg over the bench at the far side of the table, intent on finishing off the pie. "You remember that much about it, do you?" he gibed.

Jeb took a sip of coffee and set the mug down with a thump. "Very funny," he said.

Kade chuckled, his mouth full, and gestured with the fork. "You know," he said, when he'd swallowed, "I could have told you this would happen."

Right, Jeb thought. Not so long ago, Kade had been in such a tangle over Mandy, he didn't know his ass from a gopher hole. Now, suddenly, he was wise counsel in the court of love. "Spare me," Jeb said, rolling his eyes.

Merry as a friar in Robin Hood's camp, Kade plunged his fork back into the pie, stopped with a chunk of cherry filling and crust halfway to his mouth. "You must not have been listening," he observed, "back when Ma used to read to us from the Good Book every Sunday. 'As you sow, so shall you reap.' "

"Now you're a preacher," Jeb grumbled. If he'd had anyplace to go, he would have left, right then.

"All those women you trifled with," Kade marveled, his eyes dancing with delight. "Old love-'em-and-leave-'em Jeb. You've met your match in Miss Chloe Wakefield, haven't you?"

"Is there a point to this," Jeb demanded, through his teeth, "or are you just amusing yourself?"

"That *is* the point," Kade said. "I think this is damn funny." He put the bite of pie into his mouth and commenced to waving the fork again, like a conductor in front of a band. "If I live to be a hundred," he went on, "I will never forget the sight of you hightailing it across that creek, wanting Rafe and me to hide you." He paused for a hoot of laughter. "Scared as you were, I half expected to see Geronimo and a few hundred Apaches after your scalp, instead of one redheaded woman with a buggy whip and fire in her eyes."

Jeb threw up his hands, then let his palms slap down hard on the table top. "All right," he said. "I made a fool of myself! I admit it. Are you satisfied?"

Kade was still shoveling in pie. "Yup," he said, ruminating on the memory with obvious pleasure.

Before Jeb could formulate a response to that, a commotion broke out upstairs, and Angus appeared on the upper landing, his white hair wild around his face, his eyes as big as cow pies.

Overhead, a lusty wail rent the air. Concepcion was getting down to business, and the old man looked horrified. Never mind that he'd had most of nine months to get used to the idea of a baby coming; he was in a panic.

"It's Concepcion!" he yelled. "Her time's come—she's never done this before—get the doc!"

"Sounds like it's too late for that," Kade decided, pushing the pie tin away.

"I suppose it's the same as with a cow," Jeb agreed, getting nervously to his feet and running his hands down his thighs.

Mandy showed up then, leaning around the upper railing, clad in a flannel nightgown. "One of you, go fetch Emmeline. The other, keep Angus out of the way. And somebody put some water on to boil!" With that, she vanished again.

"I'll get Emmeline," Jeb said, easing toward the door. Suddenly, he felt a powerful need for fresh air.

Concepcion let out another whoop. She was no coward, so it must hurt something awful, having a baby. Jeb shuddered.

"Land sakes," Angus boomed, "I've killed her!"

Kade took their father's arm and led him the rest of the way down the stairs. He was the practical one, and right then, Jeb was grateful.

"Sit, Pa," Kade said calmly.

There was another scream, and Jeb bolted.

When he came back, half an hour later, Rafe and Emmeline were with him. Emmeline, wearing a nightgown and shawl, rushed up the back stairs. Kade had made coffee, and there was a whiskey bottle in the middle of the table, already half-gone.

Concepcion shrieked, and swore in Spanish.

"Well, Pa," Rafe said, hitching up his suspenders and helping himself to coffee *and* whiskey, "are we going to have to wait for this one to grow up before you decide who gets the ranch?"

"It might be that long before any of you gives me a grandchild," Angus grumbled, adding a generous dollop of firewater to his mug. He paused, considered. He'd calmed down considerably in the time Jeb was gone from the house. "Of course, Holt's got a daughter. I reckon *that* puts the matter in a new light. I ought to give him the Triple M. Serve the rest of you yahoos right."

Jeb's gaze collided with Kade's and Rafe's.

Rafe recovered first. "Tell me that's a joke, old man," he said, in a dangerous undertone.

"He *is* my firstborn son," Angus said, drawing grim enjoyment from the situation.

"He wasn't part of the deal," Kade pointed out, unamused.

"Only because he wasn't around at the time," Angus countered calmly. "He's as much my flesh and blood as any of you."

Jeb's knees felt wobbly, so he sank onto the bench, next to the table. "Pa," he said, in what he hoped was a reasonable tone of voice, "in case it's escaped your notice, he hates your guts."

"Maybe he's got a right," Angus pontificated.

Emmeline sprouted on the landing. "Where's that hot water?" she cried.

Concepcion let loose with another scream, but the old man didn't turn a hair. He was on a roll, and he'd had plenty of hooch to calm his nerves. Jeb figured he'd be crowing like a rooster by the time that baby finally came.

"I'm getting it," Rafe told his wife, and slammed buckets around, emptying the pots of steaming water Kade had set on the stove to boil. "It's the whiskey talking," he said, to himself as much as anybody. If Angus *did* give the ranch to Holt, Rafe would take it the hardest, since he was foreman.

"Son of a bitch," Jeb fretted, glancing at the ceiling when Concepcion yelled again. Something about randy old men and the back acre of hell, he thought, though his Spanish was a little rusty.

"Holt is my son, and he did give me a grandchild," Angus reasoned.

Kade slapped a hand on the table, making the old coot start and nearly spill his doctored coffee down the front of his long johns. "But he isn't married," he said triumphantly. "That was part of the deal, Pa—remember?"

Angus frowned. "Damn," he said. "I did say that, didn't I?"

"Yes," Rafe, Kade, and Jeb replied, in one voice.

The room went silent after that, but then there was a new sound. A baby's insulted squall.

Angus forgot the argument and stood up, looking baffled and hopeful and scared to death, all of a piece.

Mandy's head popped around the railing again, but this time she was smiling. "It's a girl," she exulted. "Ten fingers, ten toes, and a healthy set of lungs!"

Rafe was partway up the stairs with the hot water, a bucket in each hand, when the old man blew by him like a gust of wind.

"Glory be!" he shouted. "A daughter!"

19

The sound, slight as it was, startled Chloe awake. She flailed against the sheets and quilt, entangled around her because of fitful dreams, and sat bolt upright in bed, blinking away sleep.

In the bright moonlight, she saw that the cottage was empty, the door still bolted, but the fine hairs on her arms and the back of her neck stood up, just the same.

It came again, and this time she identified it. Metal, tapping against glass.

She snatched the derringer off the little table next to the bed, scrambled into her wrapper, and went to the window.

Jeb McKettrick was standing in the grass, his hair lit with silver, just sliding his pistol back into the holster.

Chloe shoved up the sash and leaned out the window. "What are you doing here?" she demanded, in an affronted whisper. "Are you *trying* to get me sent away?"

He grinned foolishly, and she wondered if he was drunk. "I've got news," he said, too loudly. "Put away that derringer, will you? It would be a hell of a thing if you shot me."

Chloe set the gun aside, on top of the bookshelf. "For heaven's sake," she fussed, "it must be two in the morning!"

Jeb took a watch from his pants pocket and consulted it, swaying a little, as though even that small effort had upset his balance. "Three-fifteen," he said, plainly relishing the opportunity to correct her.

Chloe was building toward a boil, so she turned down the fire and put a lid on her temper. "What do you want?" she demanded, having second thoughts about the derringer.

"I told you," Jeb said, all long-suffering goodwill. "I have news."

"What could you possibly have to tell me at this hour?" She ought to slam down the window and ignore him, she knew that, but for some reason, she couldn't.

"I have a sister."

Chloe stared down at him, confounded. If she could have gotten hold of his hair, she'd have pulled out a handful. "What?"

"I have a sister," he repeated, very carefully, as though she were hard of hearing.

Chloe's mind, fogged by sleep and sudden alarm, finally cleared. She remembered meeting his obviously pregnant stepmother, Concepcion, soon after her arrival on the Triple M. "Oh," she said, taking a moment to envy the woman. She loved children, though with two failed marriages behind her, it didn't seem likely that she'd ever have any of her own. "Well—that's wonderful—"

"Her name is Katherine, for some saint," Jeb said, slurring his words ever so slightly.

"Have you been drinking?" Chloe inquired.

"Celebrating," he said, correcting her again.

"I'm very happy for you," Chloe said tersely. "Now, kindly go 'celebrate' somewhere else before you wake up the whole town!"

He didn't move, except to tilt his head to one side. "Do you ever get the feeling that the train's pulled out of the station and you're still standing on the platform?" he mused. The scent of whiskey rose on the night breeze, along with those of good grass and the last, late roses of the season.

The question touched a nerve, even though Chloe suspected that Jeb was talking about his own situation, not hers, and it made her testy. "I'll get the marshal if you don't leave," she warned, "and have you arrested. Don't you think I won't!"

He grinned. "You'd have to come outside to do that, wouldn't you? And then I'd take you in my arms and— have you ever made love in the grass, Chloe?"

Chloe slammed down the sash, and the glass panes rattled in their sturdy frames. Keeping well away from the window, she pulled on her clothes, then lit a lamp. There was no hope of sleeping, but neither did she intend to go outside, even though something elemental urged her to do just that. She would wait him out, get one of her books and read, right out loud if necessary, until he gave up and went away.

Jeb started to sing, softly at first, and then with escalating spirit. No serenade, this—it was a bawdy tune of the sort one might hear passing by a saloon. Not that she frequented such establishments. Except for her wedding night, when she'd gone looking for her stray bridegroom, she'd never set foot in one.

Chloe plunked down at the table, snapped open *Pilgrim's Progress*, and began to read, silently, but forming the shape of each word with her lips.

Jeb sang louder.

Chloe slammed the book shut and was assailed by dust. She went back to the window, yanked it open.

"Shut up, damn you!" she hissed. "People will hear!"

Jeb grinned. "I guess you'd better let me in, then," he said.

She was caught between a rock and a hard place. If she left him out there, he'd raise the dead with his catterwalling, and if she let him in, well, God knew what would happen. She reached for the pitcher on the washstand and flung its contents through the opening, dousing him.

He spread his hands, looking down at his drenched shirt and trousers in apparent disbelief. "Well," he said philosophically, "now you've *got* to open the door. I could catch my death out here." He favored her with another of his lethal grins. "Or, I could *really* start singing—"

"Don't!" Chloe pleaded. "I'll let you in. Just—*please*—stop carrying on!"

"Finally," he said, with a beleaguered sigh, "the woman sees reason."

She crossed the room in a few frustrated strides, worked the latch, and threw open the door. Jeb stood on the stoop, his eyes dancing, soaked to the skin. Up close, she could see that he wasn't nearly as drunk as he'd appeared—no doubt the sluicing had sobered him considerably.

"Bloody *hell*," Chloe muttered, stepping back to admit him, "you are half-again as much trouble as you're worth!"

He came in, shut the door, leaned against it. "It's been too long, Chloe," he said gravely.

She hated the surge of heat that rushed through her system, hated him for being able to arouse it. "Keep your distance," she ordered, though she couldn't have said whether she was talking to him or to herself.

He let his gaze drift over her, then went to the bedside table, where the lamp was burning, and blew it out. Chloe watched, in miserable anticipation, as he sat down on the edge of her bed, kicked off his boots, and began unbuttoning his shirt, starting at the cuffs. In all that time, he never looked away from her face.

She folded her arms, determined to stand her ground. Remembering the kiss they'd exchanged, on his earlier visit, she felt as though she were being sucked down into a patch of molten quicksand.

He pulled his shirttails out, dealt with the last of his buttons, worked the buckle on his gun belt, and all the while, she was a willing hostage, knowing she should look away and never even blinking her eyes.

Jeb shrugged out of the shirt, stood, and started with his trousers.

A hot flush bubbled up from Chloe's center, scalding its way toward her face. She felt herself opening to receive him, not just physically, but mentally and spiritually as well.

"What's the matter, Chloe?" he asked quietly, his expression serious now. "You say I'm your husband. Doesn't that give me a right to your bed?"

She swallowed. "No," she said, with consummate uncertainty.

He was naked, gloriously perfect, unabashedly male. He held out a hand to her; it was an invitation, not a command. She might have resisted the latter, but she had no chance against the former.

She had been rooted to the floor, but now she felt the twining tendrils of her determination snapping, one by one. She took a single step in his direction, but that was enough. In the next instant, she was in his arms.

He kissed her, deeply, slowly, as if they had all the time in the world, as if the morning, with all its recriminations and consequences, would never come.

And she responded, under no spell, but by her own choice.

Jeb divested her of her hastily donned clothes, a garment at a time, without lifting his mouth from hers. He found her breasts unerringly, weighing them in his hands, chafing the nipples with the sides of his thumbs.

She moaned, heard and felt the sound echo off the back of his throat. Her arms found their way around his neck, seemingly of their own accord.

Before their marriage, they'd made love often, and wildly, but this was the first time they'd been together as man and wife, and, for Chloe at least, that made the event sacred, despite her certainty that a wiser woman would have refrained.

Jeb came up for air, and his eyes smiled down into hers. He didn't ask if she wanted to change her mind; he knew her too well for that. Chloe never did anything she didn't want to do, on some level, and this was no exception. She was reeling with desire, and with a need to match Jeb's own, but she was under no illusion that she'd been coerced or even persuaded. For all her passion, her mind was clear as water from some hidden, sacred spring.

He wrapped a tendril of her hair around his finger. "I do believe you are the most beautiful woman I've ever seen," he said.

She laid her hands against his chest, lightly, and felt his nipples tighten under her palms. His arousal pressed against her belly, making her dizzy with promise. "Just how many have you seen," she asked softly, "since the last time we were together?" It was a dangerous question, put to a man like Jeb, but the answer was vital.

"None," he replied, without hesitation. And she believed him.

"That must have been difficult," she said.

He went to the bed, sat down on its edge, drawing her with him. His hands cupping her bottom, he leaned forward, touched her navel with the tip of his tongue. "Worse than difficult," he muttered.

Chloe trembled, let her head fall back in a sort of victorious surrender. "You surely had opportunities," she said, her breath catching. She felt his lips on her right hipbone, then her left, light and warm.

He chuckled against her, sent fire racing beneath her flesh. "A few," he admitted, "but my heart wasn't in it."

"I wasn't thinking about your heart," she replied. "Anyway, I'm not at all sure you even have one."

This time he laughed. Simultaneously, he pulled her down onto his lap, facing him, and eased inside her.

Sensation took her over, completely. She gasped in exultation, tangled her fingers in his hair.

He delved deeper. Groaned. It was a homecoming sort of sound, a seeking of sanction and solace, part relief, part anticipation.

Chloe gave a soft cry, trembling at the beginning of an ecstasy she knew would soon consume her, consume them both.

He found her breast with his mouth, took her nipple hungrily.

A muffled shout burst from her throat.

"Don't yell, Chloe," he teased, on his way to ravish the other breast. "It will draw more attention than my singing."

She bit down hard on her lower lip and made a desperate, soblike sound as he continued to enjoy her.

And then he began to move, raising her, lowering her, along the length of his shaft. Her eyes rolled back, she locked her thighs around his hips, and rode straight into the fire.

She lay askew on the bed, arms flung back, fingers still loosely curled around the rails of the headboard, hair blazing against the moon-washed white of the pillow. Spent, she slept, this angel temptress, and Jeb watched her for a long time, wishing he didn't have to leave.

The moon was already thinning, though, turning transparent, and dawn would not be long in coming. He had sung his way past Chloe's door, loved his way into her bed, but if his horse was still tied outside when the town woke up, somebody was sure to notice. The results would be disastrous for Chloe.

With a sigh of regret, Jeb stood, gathered his clothes off the floor, got into them. He was tucking in his shirt when Chloe opened her eyes.

"You're going," she said simply.

"Yes," he answered. "Get up and latch the door when I'm gone."

She stretched, made a little crooning sound that tightened his groin. "All right," she agreed sleepily.

If only she were always that compliant. In another few hours, though, she'd probably be cursing his name. He buckled on his gun belt. "I mean it, Chloe," he warned. "Don't go back to sleep until you've seen to the door."

She batted her lashes at him. "Yes, Mr. McKettrick," she said sweetly, and with a coyness that made him want to strip down and crawl right back into bed.

He went to the front window, drew aside the curtains. The street was empty. "It feels strange," he said, "sneaking out of here like we've done something wrong."

The bedsprings creaked, and when he turned, she was sitting up, propped against the pillows, the covers drawn to the upper curves of her breasts. She was brazenly beautiful, even in the predawn light, and might as easily have been a courtesan in some foreign palace instead of a schoolmarm in Indian Rock. "I need this job, Jeb," she said. "Right now, it's all I've got."

He wanted to contradict her, but the fact was, she was right. He had little to offer her, besides space in his room at the ranch and the pitiful wages he earned punching cattle and breaking horses to ride. No big house, like the one Rafe had built for Emmeline, across the creek from the home place. No horses or bank accounts to hand over, like Kade. They'd gotten those things by their own efforts, his brothers had, for the ways of Angus McKet-trick were old-fashioned ones. He believed in thrift and hard work.

It was ironic as hell, realizing he couldn't have Chloe, didn't deserve her, after what they'd shared in the night. Maybe that was why he said what he did, the way he did.

"Too bad we're not married," he told her. "You would have made a lively wife."

Silence buzzed behind him, and there was mayhem brewing in it.

He stepped out onto the small porch, smiled sadly when he heard something, probably a vase or a china plate, shatter against the door.

The ride back to the Triple M seemed longer than usual, and it was lonesome as hell.

20

Concepcion sat up in bed, holding the small, fitful bundle in both arms. She looked serene to Angus, if tired, a Spanish Madonna with her braid coming undone, her face and eyes glowing.

"How does it feel, Angus McKettrick," she asked quietly, "to be a new father again, after so many years?"

He hadn't slept a wink, and he needed to shave. "Damned odd," he admitted. He'd never had a way with words, and Concepcion knew it. She wouldn't expect him to spout poetry. He rubbed his chin and smiled. "But good."

She laughed softly. "It was an exciting night," she said.

He nodded his agreement. "You made sure of that." He glanced at the window, saw the dawn shining there, pink and gold and fresh as a new-minted coin. "While I was waiting for our little gal there to make her appearance," he reflected, "I put the fear of God into those boys of mine."

"Angus," Concepcion said warily, opening the bodice

of the nightgown to let the child suckle. Something stirred inside Angus, then resolved into weary contentment. "What have you done now?"

"Rafe made some smart remark about having to wait for little Kate to grow up before I made a decision about who would run the ranch, and I just couldn't let it pass. I told them I might give the place to Holt, lock, stock, and barrel, since he was the first one to give me a grandchild."

"You didn't," Concepcion scolded, but gently.

"I did," Angus replied, with relish. He chuckled at the memory. "You should have seen their faces. Like as not, all three of them sired a baby last night, soon as they got their women alone."

A pretty flush lit Concepcion's flawless complexion. "*Angus,*" she protested.

"Kade and Mandy couldn't seem to see anything but each other, when they went back upstairs to their room. Same with Rafe and Emmeline—they practically ran out of here, making for their own place. And Jeb—" Angus paused, smiled again. "Jeb headed straight for the barn, saddled a horse, and rode out. Like as not, he spent the night in town, with Chloe."

Concepcion made a soft clucking sound with her tongue, stroking the baby's downy head with one tender hand. "You are impossible, Angus McKettrick. You think every man is like you."

"I wouldn't know about every man," Angus said. "But I do know my sons." He stopped, speculating. "It'd be a hell of a thing if all three of my daughters-in-law got pregnant at the same time, wouldn't it? Sure make the race to win the ranch more interesting."

Concepcion's dark eyes were troubled. "When will you learn, Angus? It is wrong to set your own children against each other. I will not let you do that with Kate."

His chair creaked as he rose, went to the window. The lamps were lit in the bunkhouse, and there was smoke curling from the chimney. The Triple M was stirring, getting ready for a new day. He felt the same quiet excitement at the prospect that he always had. "I had to do it, Concepcion," he said. "The three of them were too damned comfortable. Spoiled. Their mother never let me lay a hand on them, but they were prime candidates for the woodshed all the time they were growing up. If I'd taken the strap to them a few times, they'd have been fit to run this place long before now."

"Their mother was right," Concepcion maintained, as he'd known she would. They'd had similar conversations before. "They're fine men, Angus. All of them."

He nodded, but he had reservations. Rafe and Kade were well married, and they were a credit to the ranch. Ran it better than he ever had, if the truth be told. But Jeb, now—Jeb was still a worry. He'd found the right woman, but Angus wondered if he knew what to do with her, besides roll in the hay whenever he got the chance. One day, he claimed he was married. The next, he swore up and down he'd been hornswoggled. He wouldn't bring

Chloe to live at the ranch, where she belonged, but he couldn't seem to stay away from her, either.

She'd be the making of him, Chloe would. Or the breaking.

"I admit that I worry about them myself," Concepcion said. "I ask myself, what will happen next? They all want this ranch—it is their birthright. They did not know Holt existed until a year ago, and they do not trust him. He feels the same way about them. Rafe, Jeb, and Kade are all hot-tempered, and there is no telling what Holt might do if they push him into a corner."

Angus wasn't accustomed to being wrong about much of anything. Just then, though, looking out that window at the land he'd fought so hard to get and hold, he wondered if there wasn't a first time for everything.

21

Lizzie Cavanagh tried not to think too much about the shootings, when the bad man robbed the stagecoach, and the long night she'd spent being scared, but it crept into her mind if she didn't concentrate real hard. She cried when she was alone, and she had bad dreams even when she was awake.

She was certain of very few things, being only ten years old, after all, and in a new place, with a stranger for a father, but she knew for sure that she missed her mama, and her aunt Geneva, too. And she knew she didn't like the lady.

Her name was Sue Ellen, but she insisted on being called "Miss Caruthers," like she was a teacher or something. She had one of those sharp-edged faces, and quick little eyes, always watching for an offense, but that wasn't really why Lizzie disliked her. It was because she'd heard them talking in the kitchen at the Circle C, her papa and Miss Caruthers, not an hour after they arrived the night before.

"I agreed to keep house for you," Miss Caruthers had said, in a withering voice, "but I didn't bargain for a child getting underfoot."

Lizzie's heart had practically stopped, hearing that from her hiding place in the hallway. She was lonesome, and still scared, and she kept thinking about the blood all over the ground and worrying that the masked man would come after her, some dark night, and shoot her dead.

"Lizzie is my daughter," Holt had answered, his voice low and honed to a fine edge. "If you don't want to look after her, then I guess you'd better pack your bags. They'll have that stagecoach back on the road by tomorrow." That had made Lizzie feel a little better, but then Miss Caruthers spoke again.

"I thought we were getting married."

Lizzie felt the same chill she had when Roberto Vasquez spilled his lemonade down her back last summer at the church picnic. She wanted a mother, all right, but she'd hoped for a nice, pretty one. Somebody like Becky, at the hotel maybe, or Miss Emmeline.

"I never promised you that, Sue Ellen."

Right then, Miss Caruthers commenced to crying, and she was loud about it, too. "You McKettricks are all alike," she wailed. "Drag a woman halfway across the country, trifle with her feelings, then just turn her out."

Holt's reply was cold. "First of all, you asked for this job. Second, I am *not* a McKettrick, and third, I did not 'trifle' with you or anybody else."

Lizzie wondered at his tone, wondered if he'd turn *her* out one day, if she crossed him. She thought of Jeb, who'd smiled at her and let her ride in front of him on his horse, said she could call him "Uncle," and she wanted to ask her papa what was so bad about being a McKettrick. The big, white-haired man she'd met in town—Angus—he'd said he was her grandfather, and she ought to come straight to him if she ever had a problem. *He* was a McKettrick.

Where, exactly, was his house? Could she walk there, or would she have to get one of the cowboys to take her?

She'd been pondering those questions when suddenly the kitchen door had popped open, and Miss Caruthers was right there, her nose and eyes all red, her mouth pinched up like a tobacco sack with the string pulled tight.

"Well!" she'd crowed. "A little snoop!"

Horrified, Lizzie had pressed herself back against the wall of the corridor, wishing she could melt right into it. For one terrible moment, she thought Miss Caruthers meant to slap her. In the whole of Lizzie's life, nobody had ever laid a hand on her in anger.

But then her papa was there, big as her grandfather, and just as strong. "Leave her alone, Sue Ellen," he'd said.

Lizzie had been hard put not to slide right down the wall. She'd hurried away, locked herself in her room, and refused to come out even when her papa knocked on the door, later on, and asked if she was all right. She'd hardly slept that night, either, between listening for the outlaw and fearing that Miss Caruthers would come into her room, yank her right out of bed to box her ears, and tell her she'd spoiled all her plans.

Lizzie might have been a kid, but she knew when she'd gotten in the way of something.

Now, it was morning, and she hadn't seen the outlaw, but Miss Caruthers was on the porch, with all her bags and bundles, and there was a buckboard right in front of the house, hitched up and ready to go. A cowboy held the reins, staring straight ahead, with his hat pulled low over his eyes. Lizzie got a peculiar, trembly feeling in the pit of her stomach, just looking at him.

"You'll regret this, Holt Cavanagh," Miss Caruthers said stiffly, as Lizzie's papa helped her into the wagon.

"I doubt it," Holt replied, though he had his back to Lizzie, and she couldn't see his face. She wished she could have, because then she might know if Miss Caruthers was right. Regret was something she'd learned to recognize, having seen it in her mother's eyes so often.

Miss Caruthers squirmed on the wagon seat and looked like she wanted to clobber Lizzie's papa over the head with her parasol, but in the end, she didn't. She elbowed the cowboy driver, and he started the team going.

They hadn't even gotten to the big gate that said CIRCLE C across the top when a rider came in, from the other direction, tipped his hat to the travelers, and made for the house.

Lizzie's spirits rose when she recognized the man. "Uncle Jeb!" she cried, and bounded down the steps to run out and meet him.

He grinned at her, though he looked a little peaked. She hoped he wasn't sick or something. "Morning, Miss Lizzie," he said.

Holt walked up behind her, laid his hands on her shoulders. There was no friendliness in his voice when he greeted her uncle, and she didn't have to look back to know he wasn't smiling.

"*Now* what am I supposed to have done?" he asked. He sounded like a man who'd been falsely accused one too many times and held a sore grievance because of it.

Jeb's grin held steady. "I don't reckon you had anything whatsoever to do with this," he said, swinging a leg over the horse's neck and jumping to the ground. "Pa figured you ought to know, though I can't rightly say why." He patted Lizzie on the head, something she wouldn't have tolerated from anyone else; but he was looking straight into Holt's face, and even though he was still smiling with his mouth, his eyes were somber. "You've got a baby sister."

22

$\mathcal{H}$olt hooked his thumbs under his gun belt and shifted on his feet, holding Jeb's gaze with his own. There was a ruckus from the corral, but he didn't let it distract him from the subject at hand. "I suppose I'm expected to put in an appearance."

Jeb shrugged. "Your choice."

Holt tightened his grasp on Lizzie's shoulders, then let go, afraid he'd hurt her. "Concepcion's been good to me," he said, begrudging every word. "I'll be there."

Jeb's attention had strayed to the corral, and the demon spawn he saw there. "That's quite a horse," he said.

Holt sighed. Because of that paint stud, three of his best men were laid up with broken bones. If the animal hadn't been so valuable, practically perfect in its conformation, he'd have turned it out to run wild, like it was born to do. "He's first cousin to Lucifer himself," he admitted.

"That so?" Jeb said, still watching the fracas. He'd looked downcast when he rode up, for all his ready grin, but there was something different in his face now, a narrow-eyed speculation. "Anybody ride him yet?"

Holt would have lied if his daughter hadn't been standing right there, listening to everything like it was gospel. He reckoned the least he could do was set a decent example, whether it went against the grain or not.

"Nope," he said.

He felt the quickening in his half brother before he saw it play out in his features. "I can ride him," he declared.

"Fifty dollars says you can't," Holt replied.

"You're on," Jeb said, and started toward the corral, where there was already a whole lot of dust-raising and cussing going on. His own horse had wandered over to the nearest water trough, oblivious to everything but thirst.

Holt reached out, stopped Jeb. "Wait a minute, little brother," he drawled. "I don't trade in charm. I'm putting up fifty dollars here. Let's see your money."

Jeb's grin was audacious, as usual. He patted his pockets—his clothes looked like he'd kicked them around on the floor a while before putting them on—and spread his hands. "Seems like I left it at home," he said. "If I lose— which I won't—you'll just have to collect your winnings at the Triple M."

Holt looked down, saw that Lizzie was staring adoringly up at Jeb, and softened a little, despite another flash of resentment. He could barely get the kid to talk to him, but she seemed to think her uncle had wings on his feet.

"All right," he agreed. "Lizzie, you wait in the house."

The child's face, filled with hero worship a moment before, was transformed into a study in rebellion. "No, sir," she said, folding her arms. "You can whup me if you want to, but I'm not going to miss this!"

Jeb laughed. "She's a McKettrick, all right," he said.

"She's a Cavanagh," Holt insisted coldly. Then he turned an irritated scowl on his daughter. "And nobody's going to 'whup' you, anyhow, so just put that idea out of your head for good."

"Can I stay?" she pleaded.

Jeb arched an eyebrow, waiting.

"Oh, hell," Holt spat, that being as close as he could get to a yes, and the three of them headed for the corral.

The paint was in fine form that bright fall morning, red-eyed and snorting, looking for somebody to stomp the life out of. Lizzie scrambled onto the first rung of the fence; Holt warned her, with a glance, to go no farther.

Jeb rolled his shoulders, resettled his hat, watching the horse the whole while. The paint planted his hind legs, watching him back. The air felt charged to Holt, and heavy, like there was a storm brewing. A couple of cowboys meandered over, dust-coated and curious.

"You might as well shoot that sumbitch," one of them said, gesturing toward the paint. "He can't be rode."

Holt indicated his daughter's presence with a slight inclination of his head and glared the man back a step or two. "Get the gear," he said. "My brother is feeling lucky today."

A rope, saddle, and bridle were fetched from the barn.

Jeb, having walked around to the opposite side of the corral and climbed up onto the highest rail, took the rope, made a deft loop in one end, and lassoed that four-legged fury in one try. The horse, ready for a fight, shuddered and blew, but he didn't move.

It seemed to Holt that every cowpuncher on the ranch had drawn nigh to watch the spectacle—they lined the fence, silent and watchful.

Holt imagined himself carrying Angus's youngest pup back to the Triple M in bloody chunks, and laid a hand on Lizzie's small, stiff back, as though she were a touchstone.

After the rope came the bridle, made special for cussed broncs. Jeb walked right up to that horse, slipped the rigging over his head, set the bit. The stallion nickered and tossed his head, as if to say, *Bring it on, cowboy.*

"Careful," Holt breathed, and only realized that he'd spoken aloud when Lizzie turned to look at him.

The saddle came next. The brute hung his head, and another shudder, this one ominously rhythmic, flowed visibly through his powerful body, muscle by muscle. Nonetheless, he let Jeb tighten the cinch and buckle it fast.

"Whoa, now," somebody said, though Holt wasn't sure whether the words had come from another onlooker, Jeb, or his own mouth.

Jeb planted a foot in the stirrup, the horse sidestepped and quivered again. Everything was dead still, it seemed to Holt; even the birds had stopped singing.

In the next instant, Jeb was in the saddle, and all hell broke loose. Old Demon Spawn turned himself inside out, flinging out his hind legs, then going into a spin. Jeb let out a Rebel yell and held on.

The stallion tried to sunfish—turn his belly to the sky—but Jeb was still with him, one hand in the air, though whether he was trying to keep his balance or just showing off, Holt couldn't say. The kid went right on spurring with his bootheels, and the horse went right on bucking.

The spectators seemed to let out one and the same breath, and a few cackles of delight went up. Holt glanced down at Lizzie and saw that she was beaming with excitement. Damned if she *wasn't* a McKettrick, whether he liked it or not.

Jeb's hat sailed off on the breeze; his bright hair gleamed in the sunshine. He hollered again, a purely exuberant sound, but the horse wasn't ready to give up yet. He flattened himself out in midair, and came down in a wicked whirl of horseflesh and foam, this time in the opposite direction.

Jeb gave another shout—the damn fool, the rougher the ride got, the better he seemed to like it—and gripped that horse's sides with his thighs like a banker holding on to a dollar. The dust flew, the cowboys cheered, and the horse kicked and twisted and hurled himself at the sky.

The struggle went on for some ten minutes, by Holt's watch, ten of the longest minutes of his life. *You see, old man,* he heard himself telling Angus contritely, *this whole thing was Jeb's idea, God rest his soul. I tried to talk him out of it, I surely did. Oh, well, you've got other sons.*

"Ride him, Jeb!" Lizzie called out, her voice pure and sweet. Jesus, he should have made her go into the house, like he'd planned. She'd already experienced more tragedy, in her short life, than most people ever had to endure— she didn't need to see this. Besides, she was *his* daughter, and it didn't sit well that she was so taken with Jeb.

The devil's saint had one last trick in him, it turned out, and it was a dandy. The horse pitched forward onto his knees, and Holt closed his eyes. When he opened them, he fully expected to see his half brother either rolling end over end over the paint's head, or already sprawled in the dirt, fixing to get himself stomped to blood and splintered bone.

Instead, he was sitting there in the saddle, his body relaxed, waiting for more action. Holt was embarrassed to find himself on the top rail of the fence, ready to run for the center of the corral, if necessary, and drag the damn idiot clear of the stallion's hooves.

The paint shivered, nickered, and jostled to his feet. He stood stock-still then, and, once again, Holt held his breath. In the next instant, he knew the battle was over. Jeb's grin was a white flash of victory in his dirty, arrogant face.

"I'll be damned," Holt muttered.

Jeb reined the stallion to the right, then to the left, then around in a circle. If the demon had any bucking left in him, he was saving it for another day, and another cowboy. He'd conceded the contest to this one.

Jeb rode to the fence, a wrangler handed up his hat, and he replaced it with a decisive motion of one hand. "You owe me fifty dollars," he told Holt.

Holt's belly unclenched, but he couldn't quite bring himself to smile. His jaw was clamped down tight as a bear trap. He took out his wallet, extracted the money, and handed it over.

Jeb folded the bills with an air of satisfaction and tucked them into his pocket, standing in the stirrups to stretch his legs. "Thanks," he said affably. "It's a start."

"A start to what?" Holt asked, irritated. Life had been so much simpler before he'd known these brothers of his—they were nothing but trouble, all three of them.

"A bank account," Jeb replied. He leaned in the saddle to ruffle Lizzie's hair with one gloved hand. "Thanks for cheering for me, kid."

A crazy thought struck Holt, right out of the blue. "You want a job?"

Jeb chewed on the offer, one forearm resting on old Demon Spawn's sweaty neck. "Depends on how much it pays," he said, in his own good time.

In seven years with the Texas Rangers, Holt had never seen anybody ride like Jeb McKettrick, Comanches included, but there was no sense in inflating the kid's head by going on about it. "I think we can come to terms," he said moderately.

Jeb's grin flashed again. *Hide the women*, Holt thought. "It'll piss Pa off for sure."

At last, Holt smiled. "Yup," he said, with grim pleasure. "It surely will do that."

23

*F*ar as Lizzie was concerned, that baby was the ugliest little critter God ever put on the earth, but she didn't reckon it would be polite to say so. She glanced up at her grandfather, beaming beside the big bed at the Triple M, then met the Mexican woman's kindly eyes. She was conscious, all the while, of her papa, leaning one shoulder against the framework of the open door with his arms folded.

"What's her name?" she asked. For her, everything began with that. When she knew what to call a person, she felt properly acquainted.

"Katherine Angelina McKettrick," Concepcion replied, smiling, and it seemed like that smile reached into all the dark places inside Lizzie, warming them. "We'll call her Katie, though."

"Katie," Lizzie repeated. "Sounds all right to me."

Her grandfather chuckled at her response and put out his big, tree root of a hand to her. "Come on, Lizzie-beth," he said, making up his own name for her, just like that. "Let's go out to the barn and have a look at Old Blue's puppies. See how they're doing."

Lizzie glanced at her papa, trying to read his face. He'd shaved and changed his clothes before they drove down to the Triple M in a buggy, and his wavy hair gleamed in the light. He was solemn for a moment, but then he nodded.

Lizzie took Angus's hand, still outstretched, and her papa stepped back to let them pass.

Old Blue, to Lizzie's initial disappointment, wasn't blue at all. She was gray, with floppy ears and yellow eyes, and lay curled up in a bed of straw in an empty stall. Five puppies nuzzled at her belly, fat and sleek.

She touched one of them, tentatively, filled with an instant yearning, fierce enough to make her breath catch.

Angus crouched beside her. "You know something, Lizzie," he began awkwardly, in the tone of a question, though he didn't seem to be asking her anything. "That little Katie girl you just met, she's mighty precious to me, like a present from God, tied up with a bow, but there's one thing I want you to understand." He cleared his throat, and Lizzie didn't look at him, figuring he didn't want her to, just then. "You're just as important."

Lizzie was happy, but her eyes burned, and she couldn't swallow. She had to look at Angus then, whether he was ready or not. "Why?" she asked, stricken with a strange, sorrowful joy.

Angus picked up one of the puppies, dwarfing it with

his huge hands, and offered it to her. She knelt in the straw, holding the squirmy little dog in her lap. "Your papa was as little as Katie, once—about the size of that pup you're holding," he said, in a husky, remembering sort of voice. He smiled, though it seemed to Lizzie that his eyes were wet. "He was mine, and I loved him as much as I'd ever loved anything or anybody." He stopped, some struggle going on inside him. "His mama died, when he was just a few days old, and I had to leave him."

Lizzie took the images inside her, one by one, to sort through and set in their proper places. "Why?" she asked, again. Her mama used to say that was her favorite word, and she reckoned it was true enough.

Angus sighed, ran the back of one hand across his face. "Times were hard, and I was hurting real bad. I couldn't seem to stay put, back then. Bounced around like a drop of cold water on a hot griddle. Anyhow, I gave my son to his aunt and uncle, and I rode out." He paused, watching as Lizzie stroked the puppy. She could feel its tiny heart beating against her thigh. "I'd change it all, if I could go back. I'd bring your papa right here, to this ranch, and raise him with his brothers."

Lizzie wondered how that made her as important as Katie McKettrick, who was evidently *very* important, even if she did have a red face and patchy hair and a bad disposition, but she didn't figure it was the right time to ask, so she just waited.

Angus was silent for a long time, and it was a sad silence, if a peaceable one. When he finally spoke, though, he answered Lizzie's question as surely as she'd offered it aloud. "When I met you, I knew it all came right, whatever your papa might think to the contrary. If I hadn't left him to grow up in Texas, you might never have been born. You're my granddaughter, with my blood in your veins and McKettrick grit in your belly. I'll love you until the day I die, and beyond that. I'll be here for you, Lizzie, like I wasn't for Holt, and when I'm gone, you can be sure your aunts and uncles will stand by you, too."

A tear fell on the puppy's back, and it was Lizzie's. Her grandfather's words would take a lot of studying before she understood them, but the impact of them struck her to the heart. She knew they were true, sure as the sky was blue and the mama dog was gray.

Angus leaned over, kissed the top of her head, then stood, with a creaking and popping of bones.

"That was a fine speech, old man," Holt said, when Angus reeled out of the barn into the afternoon sunlight and found him waiting there. "I was hard put not to applaud."

Angus stopped, squared himself, stood his ground. "Thanks for coming to see the baby," he said.

Holt was shaken, had been since he'd gone to the barn to make sure Angus didn't give Lizzie every puppy on the place and overheard their conversation. And he'd have died before he let it show. "What are you going to do with a girl?" he asked lightly, and did his best to smile.

"Spoil her," Angus said, with a scratchy laugh. "I reckon she'll be a sight easier to bring up than her brothers were."

Holt thought of Jeb, on the back of that incorrigible stallion, grinning like a kid on a rocking horse. "I wouldn't count on that," he advised.

Angus hooked his thumbs in his belt and rested his weight on one side. He wasn't packing the usual .45; maybe being the father of a baby girl had mellowed him. "She's got four brothers to look after her, once I'm gone."

Holt didn't correct the old man's figures from four to three, though he wasn't sure why. "You'll outlive the lot of us," he said instead, and with an ease he didn't feel. "That baby, she's the good Lord's way of giving you your comeuppance, old man. Just you wait and see."

"Seems to me the good Lord's handing out comeuppance right and left these days," Angus allowed. He cocked a thumb toward the barn. "Have you talked to that child about her mother? Asked her where they've been all this time, and what it was like for her?"

Holt ran a hand through his hair and thrust out a breath. "I don't know where to start," he admitted.

"Did you love the woman, or just use her?"

A flash of anger went through Holt, but he waited it out. "I loved her, all right," he said. "Trouble was, I didn't figure that out until it was too late."

Angus studied him for a long moment, then nodded. Evidently, the conversation was over.

He watched, a thousand questions tangled in his throat,

as the old man walked away. He was about to collect Lizzie from the barn and head for the Circle C when he saw Emmeline and Rafe crossing the creek in a buckboard drawn by two horses, but they hadn't come from their place. They'd been to town, and they had Becky and Chloe Wakefield with them, riding in the second seat. The new schoolteacher looked pale and tight-lipped, as though she were a captive rather than a willing guest. Becky had a sociable, slightly smug air. Damn but Chloe was a pretty thing. Made Holt ache, deep down, just to look at her.

He waited, out of curiosity, he guessed, rather than good manners, until the wagon pulled up beside the house.

Rafe secured the brake lever, wrapped the reins around it, and got down to help Emmeline to the ground, then Becky, then Chloe. Emmeline tossed an anxious smile in Holt's direction, Becky waved, and Chloe seemed ready to bolt for the hills. Emmeline took Chloe by one elbow, and Becky got her by the other, and the two of them half dragged her toward the house.

Rafe stayed behind, watching Holt, standing still as Demon Spawn fixing to buck, his features cast into shadow by his hat brim, then broke through whatever was holding him back and walked toward him.

"Come to claim your inheritance?" he asked. There was a flush in his neck, and along his jaw.

Holt frowned, puzzled. He hadn't expected a warm welcome, but Rafe's mood intrigued him. "What do you mean by that?" he countered.

Rafe sighed, took his hat off, and wiped the band with his handkerchief before putting it on again. "Never mind," he said.

"Never mind, hell," Holt retorted. "You started this conversation, and you're going to finish it."

Rafe surprised him with a sheepish grin. "Soon as I figure out what to say," he said, "I'll say it."

Holt shook his head. "Is everybody in this outfit touched in the head?"

Rafe laughed. "Some more than others," he answered. He pondered a bit. "You have anybody in particular in mind when you asked that question?"

"Jeb, for one," Holt reflected. "You ever seen him bust a bronc?"

"A time or two," Rafe said, and laughed again. "Just don't let that cocky little bugger tell you he's never been thrown. For every bronc he's ridden to a standstill, ten others have made him eat dirt."

"He's good," Holt said, though he hated to part with the admission.

"Best I've ever run across," Rafe confirmed. "Not that I'd ever let him hear me say it."

Holt was pensive. "I offered him a job on the Circle C today," he said, with a reluctance he didn't understand. "And he took it."

Rafe's face changed instantly. Gone was the easygoing smile, the affable tone of voice, the friendly stance. Now he was coiled, ready to strike. "*What?*"

"You heard me," Holt said.

Rafe reddened up, jerked off his hat, slapped one thigh with it. "If that doesn't beat everything," he hissed. "Pa's gonna have a fit and fall in it." He glared at Holt. "And that was the point, wasn't it?"

"It's a side benefit," Holt allowed. He tried to sound nonchalant, but the truth was, he wished he'd just paid Jeb his fifty dollars and kept his mouth shut about the job.

Rafe bunched up his fist, then let it fall back to his side. "Just last night, Pa was talking about giving you this ranch," he said, then swore. Plainly, he regretted giving up that much, would have taken it all back if he could have.

"Now why the hell would he do that?" Holt demanded.

Rafe jabbed at Holt's chest with an index finger, never knowing that he had the distinction of being the first man who'd ever done that without getting a few of his teeth knocked down his throat. "Because you're his first-born son," he bit out. "Because you gave him what he wanted more than anything else in this world—a grandchild."

Holt steadied himself, braced for the punch he knew Rafe wanted to throw, but it didn't come. And even if it had, it couldn't have stunned him any more than what Rafe had just said. He was speechless.

"And what do you do?" Rafe rushed on, practically blowing steam. "You as good as spit in his face!"

"Papa?" It was Lizzie's voice but, for an instant, Holt couldn't think who she was talking to. She tugged at his sleeve, looking warily up at Rafe. "You're not going to get into a fight, are you?"

Holt put a hand on top of her head. "No," he said, still watching his brother's face. "Get your things, Lizzie. We'd better be heading back to our own place."

Rafe didn't miss the emphasis he put on the last few words of that statement, that was clear by the blue snap in his eyes, but some of the tension went out of him, and he shifted his gaze to Lizzie and smiled, albeit with an effort. "You tell your papa," he said pleasantly, if a little stiffly, "that you're a member of this family, and there's something to be celebrated, so you're staying. Your uncle Rafe will bring you home in the morning, if Mr. *Cavanagh* is so all-fired set on turning tail and running like a rabbit."

With his oration completed, Rafe turned and stalked toward the house without a backward glance. The kitchen door slammed hard behind him.

"Can't we stay, Papa?" Lizzie asked, squinting against the sun as she looked up at him. "Please?"

"Lizzie—"

"*Please?*"

He squatted, so he could meet her gaze. "We'll compromise," he said. "After supper, though, we're going home."

Lizzie looked concerned, and determined. "Grandpa said he left you, when you were little as a puppy," she said.

"He's sorry he did it, except that I got born. Why can't you get over being mad at him?"

Holt looked away. Couldn't answer.

"I'm going inside," Lizzie announced, into the silence. "I never had any uncles before, and only one aunt. Mama's folks died when I was a baby. Maybe you don't want a family, Papa, but I do." Having said her piece, she followed the fiery path Rafe had laid.

Holt stood, watching her disappear inside the house. At least, he consoled himself, she hadn't settled on a puppy.

24

$\mathcal{J}$ust about the last place on earth Chloe would have chosen to be, on that particular day, was the Triple M. Emmeline and Becky had practically kidnapped her, though, saying she oughtn't be alone. Which made her wonder if they knew that Jeb had broken her heart all over again, then walked blithely out of the cottage, leaving her in pieces.

She'd cried for a long time, after Jeb was gone, because she'd let him use her. Then she pulled herself together, splashed her face with cold water at the basin, and given herself a thorough sponge bath. She'd dressed, arranged her hair, and set out for the main part of the town, with a specific destination in mind: the office of Victor Terrell, attorney at law.

Mr. Terrell was new in town, and happy to have a client, though he made a pretense of sorrow when Chloe told her she wanted to file a petition of divorce against Jeb McKettrick. If she hadn't had the hastily prepared papers in her possession, no power on earth, including

Emmeline and Becky, who were formidable when they'd made up their minds, could have made her set foot on the same acre of ground as her soon-to-be-former husband.

She was going to hand him those papers and let him know in no uncertain terms that she never wanted to cross paths with him again. True, she had to finish out the year at Indian Rock School, since she'd given her word, and avoiding Jeb might prove next to impossible, given the size of the town, but if she was going to have any peace of mind or self-respect, she had to cut the ties, once and for all. She meant to save her money in the meantime and scour the many newspapers Becky subscribed to for a new position. When the year was over, she would have a job waiting, as far from the Arizona Territory as she could get, and if she had to lie to get it, she would.

For all her determination, she wasn't prepared for what she felt when she stepped into the McKettrick kitchen and practically collided with Jeb. He looked surprised to see her, to say the least, and stood there like a tree in the middle of a stream as Becky and Emmeline flowed past him, staring. He swallowed visibly, then found his voice.

"Well," he said, plainly flummoxed.

"I want to speak with you," Chloe informed him tightly. "Alone."

He recovered quickly. His old insolence came to the fore, and he raised his eyebrows as he gestured grandly toward the inside door of the kitchen. "Pa's study ought to be empty," he said.

Chloe looked neither right nor left as she swept in that direction. If she'd made eye contact with any of the McKettricks at that moment, she would have burst into tears.

The study brought back unhappy memories; it had been here, after all, that Jeb had told her John was dead. It had been here that he'd held and comforted her, acting as though he really cared. Which, of course, he hadn't.

She fumbled in her handbag for the papers while he closed the doors. Held them out wordlessly when he turned to face her.

He watched her warily for a long moment, then waxed cocky again. "For me?" he taunted, putting both hands to his chest. Chloe fought not to remember how those hands had felt on her body, the intimate responses they'd wrung from her in the night just past.

She waggled the document, too angry and too hurt to risk speaking again.

Jeb took the papers, unfolded them, and read them. Except for a slight stiffening in his shoulders, he seemed unmoved.

"This seems like a lot of trouble to go to, when we were never married in the first place," he said, when he'd finished. His tone was light, even flippant, but his eyes were cold. "Wouldn't it have made more sense to divorce your *real* husband?"

"I will not dignify that remark with a response," Chloe said, after taking several deep breaths.

He slapped the papers against one palm. "What's the point of this exercise, Chloe?"

Chloe was thankful for her temper in those moments, though it had always been her worst character flaw. Without it, she might have given in to tears. "I want to put this whole episode behind me for good," she said, with all the dignity she could manage. "I will thank you to sign your name in the appropriate place and leave me completely alone from this day forward."

He had the nerve to look exasperated. "All right, Chloe," he said, approaching Angus's desk, scrabbling about for a pen and a bottle of ink, spreading the petition out with a furious gesture of one hand. "This game seems to be important to you, so I'll play along." He dipped the pen and signed with a flourish, and Chloe felt as though he'd stabbed her through the heart.

She raised one hand to her chest, lowered it again, quickly, before he looked her way.

"What are you planning to do now?" he asked. He might have been a callous stranger, rather than the man who had made such sweet love to her mere hours before.

Spinning in an emotional whirlpool, Chloe said the first thing that came into her head. "Maybe I'll get married. For real, this time."

He looked as furious as if she'd rammed him in the midsection with one end of a fence post, but only for an instant. As before, in the kitchen, he rallied immediately. "Who is he?"

She was in over her head now, and if she didn't brazen it out, she would surely drown. "Holt," she said, because everybody else she knew around Indian Rock, except for Doc Boylen, was already married.

Jeb went pale. "*What?*"

Dear God, Chloe thought, *what have I done?* She barely knew Holt Cavanagh, and if Jeb confronted him, he'd probably go through the roof. Call her a liar. "Jeb—" she began, meaning to admit she'd spoken out of anger, but he cut her off.

"Don't say another word, Chloe. *Not another word.*"

Her eyes widened. She opened her mouth, closed it again.

Jeb handed her the papers, turned his back on her, wrenched open the study doors, and strode out. That was the last she saw of him.

The celebration of little Katie's birth was agony for Chloe. She couldn't meet Holt's gaze, she was too ashamed, and the food Mandy and Emmeline served tasted like sawdust.

Rafe had been glowering throughout the meal, and Angus finally demanded to know what was the matter.

"Why don't you ask him?" Rafe snapped, jabbing a thumb in Holt's direction. "Or maybe Jeb?"

"I think I'd like to go home," Chloe said, into the thundering silence that followed. Becky, who had been watching her closely all evening, took her hand, squeezed it.

Angus pushed back his chair with an ominous scraping sound. "Where *is* Jeb?" he asked, though his gaze was fixed on Holt.

"Probably hiding behind the bunkhouse again," Kade said. The joke fell flat; nobody laughed.

Mandy, having left the table, put a hand on Chloe's shoulder. "Kade and I will drive you and Becky back to Indian Rock," she said, in a tone that dared anyone to object.

"It's late," Kade protested. "They ought to stay the night."

"Hitch up a wagon," Mandy said.

Tension pulsed in the room. Angus went out, shutting the door hard behind him. Little Katie started to cry in her basket next to Concepcion's chair, and Becky gave Chloe's hand another squeeze.

"Never mind," Holt said, rising from his chair. "I'll take the ladies to town if Lizzie can spend the night."

Lizzie, glancing warily from one adult face to another during the exchange, looked pleased.

Which was how Chloe came to be riding two hours in a buggy seat beside a man she'd told a whopping lie about.

Angus found Jeb in the barn, saddling his horse by the light of a kerosene lantern. The boy looked as though he'd been set afire and stomped out, but that didn't salve Angus's irritation.

"I didn't raise my sons to be rude," he said. "What the devil were you thinking, leaving your wife to get through the evening alone?"

Jeb wrenched at the cinch strap. "She isn't my wife, and she wasn't alone. The whole damn family was with her."

Angus narrowed his eyes. Folded his arms. *Dammit, Georgia,* he told his late wife silently, *you should have let me whup these boys when the situation called for it. I've got half a mind to take a strop to this one anyway, right here and now. And don't think I couldn't do it.*

"If you're not heading out to make peace with Chloe, where are you going?" he asked, in what he figured was a reasonable tone, given the circumstances.

Jeb took hold of the horse's bridle and led him toward the barn doors. "To the Circle C," he said.

Angus took the time to put out the lantern before he followed his son outside. He was in a state, but fire was a serious matter, and he couldn't risk it.

"Why would you be heading up there at this time of night?" he demanded, even though he reckoned he knew. "If you want a word with your brother, he's right inside the house."

Jeb put his foot in the stirrup and swung up onto the gelding's back. "Holt offered me a job," he said. "And I took it." With that, he reined the horse around and rode out.

Angus was still standing in front of the barn, trying to deal with a lot of unfamiliar emotions, when Holt came up beside him.

"I guess he told you," he said.

Angus turned, met his eldest son's gaze head-on. A lot of words came to mind, but he didn't think he ought to say any of them out loud, feeling the way he did.

"I'll look after him," Holt said, whistling for the horse he'd unhitched from his buggy when he and Lizzie arrived and left to graze by the creek. The animal trotted toward them.

"See that you do," Angus warned, and walked away. He wasn't ready to go back in the house and face Concepcion, so he made his way to the front porch and sat down in the rocking chair, where he'd passed a lot of his time, back when he was ailing. Jeb had run off then, too, and he'd sent Kade to find him. Hadn't drawn a peaceful breath until the two of them rode in, either, safe and sound.

He saw Holt drive past the house a few minutes later, with Becky and Chloe next to him, and he still didn't move.

The front door creaked open, and Concepcion was there. He knew by the starched-cotton scent of her, by the quiet warmth of her presence. "Holt told me what happened," she said. "Jeb will be all right, Angus."

Angus was a long time answering.

"Will he?" he asked.

25

*C*hloe kept herself busy all the next day, in a futile attempt to hold a legion of memories at bay, leaving the cottage only when she could stand in front of the small mirror over the washstand and see a sensible woman looking back at her, instead of a brazen hussy, twice divorced.

She had breakfast at the hotel, with a circumspect and watchful Becky, chatting merrily about her lesson plans for the first week of school, as though nothing was wrong.

She returned the divorce papers to Mr. Terrell, so that he could file them properly. After leaving his office, which was housed in a stuffy little room above the Cattleman's Bank, she proceeded to the mercantile, opened an account, and stocked up on tea, sugar, and other staples. Back at the cottage, she put everything away in its proper place, made up the tangled, Jeb-scented bed, in which she had wept for the better part of the night, and paced.

At noon, she picked some fading wildflowers from the schoolyard and headed for the cemetery.

John's headstone seemed to glow in the crisp autumn sunlight, and a few golden leaves danced on his grave, as if putting on a show.

Chloe laid the flowers next to the stone, smoothed her skirts, and sat down in the grass with a sigh, folding her hands in her lap.

"I'm a damn fool, Uncle John," she said.

The wind played in the treetops.

"I've got no business staying in Indian Rock. No business at all. If I had any sense, I'd be on my way to Sacramento right now."

A tendril of hair tickled her cheek; she brushed at it. Tears sprang to her eyes, unbidden and wholly unexpected.

"You must have known Jeb McKettrick."

Birds twittered, as if in reply.

"He's handsome," Chloe went on. Wagons passed on the road, but she had the churchyard to herself, which was a good thing, since she was prattling to a grave marker and a mound of dirt. "He makes me so mad sometimes, I could spit, and nobody's ever hurt me the way he did. But he made me laugh, too. I should never have married him—he's probably never had a serious thought in his life."

She plucked a piece of grass, tore it apart between her

fingers. The scent of it rose to her nostrils, a sweet and singular solace. *I wither and die,* that smell seemed to say, *then I flourish, green again.*

"Now, I, on the other hand," she continued firmly, "have plenty of serious thoughts. One of us had to be practical, after all."

A bee droned slumberously by, not having noticed, apparently, that summer was over and all the other bees were gone.

"I'm sensible, even if I am a little impetuous. I know you remember that about me." Chloe's shoulders sagged, and she reached for another blade of grass, heaving a great, despondent sigh. "Except when it comes to men. I thought I was in love with Jack Barrett. He told me he was a banker, and I believed him. Turned out he was a gunslinger, instead. A bounty hunter. How do you like that? Well, I know you wouldn't have liked it at all, of course, because you were sworn to uphold the law, and Jack lives to break it. That's why I didn't tell you at the time. You see, I had no way of knowing that you might have understood, just a little, because you were my father and because you were in trouble yourself once." A lump formed in her throat, and she swallowed. "Why didn't you tell me you were my father?"

A chorus of children's voices blew her way, frolicking on the breeze.

"I guess it doesn't matter now, anyway," she said. "But I would have liked to know, just the same."

A flash of movement caught the edge of her vision; she saw Harry Sussex walking the churchyard fence, skinny arms outstretched, red hair brilliant in the daylight.

"Get down!" another child called to him. A girl, Chloe thought. "You'll break your neck! I'm going to tell Mama if you break your neck!"

Chloe smiled and, as if she'd touched him, Harry noticed her at precisely that moment, jumped gracefully off the fence, and sprinted toward her, grinning.

"Afternoon, Miss Wakefield," he said. "Doc says you're going to teach school, for sure. I'm real glad about that."

Chloe nodded, putting on a brave face. "I'll expect you and all the other children in class by eight o'clock Monday morning," she said.

Harry's eyes shone. "We'll be there," he promised. A frown elbowed his smile aside. "You got any rules about shoes and the like?"

Chloe's heart warmed, aching a little. "No," she said. "But when winter comes, I expect you'll want to wear some."

Harry looked profoundly relieved. Most likely, he didn't own a pair of shoes, and if he did, they were reserved for very special occasions. "Ma says you're going to have your hands full, with a pack of wild coyotes like us."

Chloe got to her feet, dusted off her skirts, said a

silent good-bye to John. She wasn't sure what the future would bring, she wasn't sure of Jeb McKettrick, or even of her own good sense, but there was one matter upon which she was absolutely, unequivocally, rock-solid certain.

"I can handle it," she said.

26

*J*ack Barrett had to change his plans, and it was an inconvenience he sorely resented. He hadn't worried overmuch about coming face-to-face with little Miss Cavanagh, but Jeb McKettrick was a different case. There'd be too many questions asked if they happened to meet up before time. When he'd seen Chloe's beau ride through the Circle C's gates the day before, he'd known the brief stay was at its end. It was good-bye to the soft bunk, easy work, and good grub. Unless, of course, Miss Sue Ellen Caruthers turned out to be a decent cook and cordial company. She'd been willing enough yesterday, when he'd been assigned to drive her to town to meet the stage, simmering with rage at Cavanagh's spurning. He'd inquired if she was inclined toward revenge, along the way, and she'd said she was.

Now, riding northeast, intending to make friendly with his new ally and bide his time until the day of reckoning arrived, it was his sorry luck to run straight into Henry Farness, the foreman of the Circle C. *Past his prime,*

Barrett reflected, as he reined in to greet the man with a tip of his hat and a reserved howdy.

Farness didn't smile. He narrowed his eyes as he regarded Jack, taking in the bedroll and loaded saddlebags. "Looks like you're movin' on," he observed. "Seems a trifle sudden, given that you just moved into the bunkhouse."

Jack's horse, like him, was eager for the trail. It danced beneath him, nickering and flinging its head from side to side, and he gave the reins a firm yank. "I've got a restless spirit," he said, and that was all the explanation he meant to give.

Farness turned his head, spat. "We have our hands full on this place, what with the new herd and all," he said. "Need every man we can get."

"Jeb McKettrick can take my place," Jack said, then wished he hadn't spoken the name out loud. The smallest slip could get a man remembered for all the wrong reasons; folks might start adding things up in their heads, making connections between one event and another.

Farness shook his head. "Since you ain't been around long," he remarked, still watchful, "there's no way you could know how it is with that Triple M outfit. Angus'll drag the kid home by the scruff if he has to, but home he'll go, you can bet your last nickel on that."

"I don't reckon that's my problem," Jack said, pushing back his coat to uncover the .44.

Farness's gaze went to the gun, as any man's would,

but he didn't look scared. Maybe he didn't have sense enough. "You wanted this job pretty bad," he observed, "until one of the McKettricks showed up on the Circle C. You got some reason to run from them?"

If only the old fool hadn't gone and said that, things might have gone better. "Just a coincidence," Jack said, thinking of the notches on his gun handle.

"Then why'd you show me that iron of yours just now?" He glanced past Jack's shoulder in the next moment, fixing his gaze on something, and by reflex, Jack turned to look. It wasn't a ruse; there was a rider approaching, still a fair distance away, but coming on fast.

Jack shifted, with a creak of saddle leather, and when he turned to Farness again, the coot was holding a six-gun on him, cocked and ready.

"One thing you might want to remember," Farness said evenly. "In the high country, a man don't ride alone if he can help it."

Jack made himself smile. "Put that piece away, you old codger," he said reasonably. "I didn't draw on you."

"I reckon it must have crossed your mind, nonetheless," Farness replied. "You'd just keep on headin' in the direction you was goin' when we met and don't show your face around the Circle C again."

Though he controlled his expression, Jack had no command over the flush of anger that gushed up his neck to throb in his face. "Now that was a downright unneighborly thing to say," he lamented. He had his .44 out and fired before the foreman could get off a shot; as the old man fell, Jack turned and shot the oncoming rider right out of the saddle.

Too bad it wasn't Jeb McKettrick, he thought. Once that was done, he could dust off his hands, collect Chloe, and move on for good.

With a sigh, he got down from his horse, rolled Farness over, felt the base of his throat for a pulse. Dead, he concluded calmly. Served him right for running off at the mouth.

He mounted up again, rode to the place where the other man had fallen. A kid—Jack had seen him around the bunkhouse, though he couldn't recall his name. Given that half his face was gone, he represented no threat, but Jack put another bullet in him anyway, for good measure.

That night, in the cabin where Sue Ellen waited, he carved two more notches into the handle of his .44.

27

Holt was at his desk, tallying the figures in a ledger, when a knock sounded at the front door. He glanced at the clock irritably, figuring he ought to leave for the Triple M to fetch Lizzie home, dreading the inevitable encounter with Angus. Maybe the old man would be out rounding up cattle or something.

"Keep your britches on," he barked. He pulled his .45 from the gun belt on the peg next to the door, as a precaution, and swung it open.

A ranch hand, name of Simmons, stood on the porch, his face grim. "Sorry to bother you, Mr. Cavanagh," he said, "but there's been a killing. Two of 'em, in fact."

Every muscle in Holt's body tensed. "Spit it out," he said.

"Mr. Farness went looking for some strays, up on the north range, first thing this morning," Simmons said uncomfortably. "Ted Gates went with him, figuring on shooting some rabbits for the stewpot. When they wasn't back to help with the horses, some of the men went looking for 'em. Found 'em dead."

Holt swore. He'd ridden with Farness while he was still with the Rangers; the man had been a close friend. "You're sure it wasn't an accident?"

"Yes, sir," Simmons replied. "It's plain it was murder." He paused to shake his head. "Poor Ted wasn't but seventeen. He's been sending most all his wages home to his sweetheart, down in Tucson. They was savin' up to get themselves hitched."

Unconsciously, Holt flicked open the .45, still in his hand, spun the cylinder with his thumb. "Where are they now?" he asked, stepping out onto the porch and closing the door behind him. "The bodies, I mean?"

"Still in the wagon," was the answer. "I reckon the doc will want to look them over, in town, and the marshal ought to be told."

Holt caught sight of the buckboard, stopped in front of the barn, when they rounded the side of the house. He stepped up to the rig and used his free hand to toss back the bloody tarp covering the two corpses.

Jeb appeared at his side; he'd spent the night in the main house, planning to move into the bunkhouse when the workday was through. Holt hadn't seen him since dawn, when they'd eaten a silent breakfast together, each thinking his own thoughts.

"Whoever shot them was riding alone," Jeb said. "I followed the trail as far as Settler's Creek. Lost him there."

Holt laid the tarp down, full of cold rage. Henry had had come to the Territory at his urging, to ride for the Circle C brand, and he was dead because he'd made that choice. And the boy had barely been old enough to shave.

"Anybody have any ideas about who did this?" Holt asked, addressing the grim assembly circling the wagon.

"There was a fella quit the place early this morning," someone said.

Holt scanned the crowd, looking for the speaker.

Danny Helgesen stepped forward. "Maybe it was nothin', but he just signed on day before yesterday. Seemed to like the setup well enough until this morning. Folks move on right along, but this feller seemed a mite anxious."

"Why this morning?" Holt asked.

Helgesen's gaze slid to Jeb. "I'm just guessin' here, but he was fine until McKettrick showed up."

"His name," Holt demanded.

"Jim Barry is what he put in the payroll book," said the other man.

Holt turned to Jeb. "That sound familiar to you?"

Jeb shook his head. "No," he said. "I didn't see anybody I recognized." He nodded toward the buckboard. Beneath it, drops of blood stained the ground. "Want me to take the bodies to town?"

"I'll do it myself," Holt answered. "You ride down to the Triple M and fetch Lizzie home."

Jeb ran the back of one hand across his mouth, sighed.

"All right," he said. He hadn't signed on to be a babysitter, but he had the decency not to say so. "Take somebody with you, though."

Holt nodded, gestured to Helgesen. "Hitch up a fresh team," he said. "We're leaving in twenty minutes. The rest of you, get back to work. I'm not paying you to stand around."

There was no muttering as the other men turned away. Helgesen went about unhitching the horses from the wagon, and Jeb helped. Holt went into the house for a rifle and a coat and a box of cartridges. When he came out again, ready to travel, Jeb was sitting on the porch steps, looking up at the cool blue sky.

"You really need a woman around here," he said. There was an odd, grudging note in his voice.

Holt moved past him. "Unfortunately," he replied, as he went by, "you're right."

28

*C*hloe was brewing midafternoon tea when the knock sounded at her door. Her heart gave a fearful, joyous little leap, for she expected to find Jeb there, ready to rant or apologize, there was no telling which, but when she turned the knob and pulled, she saw that her caller was Holt Cavanagh.

He looked gaunt. His clothes were bloodstained, and he held his hat in one hand. "Becky tells me you've hired on as the new teacher," he said.

Chloe blinked. Her first frenzied thought had been that Holt had come bearing bad news about Jeb, and the blood on his shirt and trousers bore out the theory, but his words indicated some other reason for the visit. She managed a nod and a whispered, "What happened?"

"There was some trouble on the Circle C," Holt said. "I don't reckon it would be proper for me to come in and talk, with you here alone."

Chloe caught up with herself, shook her head. "No, it

wouldn't," she agreed. "But we could sit here on the steps. Would you like a cup of tea?"

He looked mildly surprised, by the offer of tea, Chloe suspected, more than the seating arrangements. "No, thanks," he said. He waited politely for Chloe to sit, and then took his place beside her.

"I guess you know I've got a daughter," he went on, when they were settled.

Chloe nodded. "Yes. Lizzie," she said. "I met her at the hotel, after the stage robbery, when Jeb and Sam brought her in. Poor little thing. How is she doing?"

Holt gave a deep sigh, turning his hat in his hands. "She seems to be holding up pretty well." He paused. "I know you've got a job here, Miss Wakefield," he went on, "but I'm wondering if we could work something out. It's too far for Lizzie to travel, to come to school, but she needs an education and a woman's company, and I've got you in mind for that."

Chloe waited for him to outline the logistics, which eluded her at the moment. She was well aware that when he found out what she'd told Jeb, he might not want her help.

"I figured I could have somebody pick you up here in town on Friday night, and bring you back Sunday afternoon. In the time between, you could give Lizzie lessons and set her assignments to do during the week."

"I see," Chloe said. It was an odd world. He couldn't set foot in the cottage, even in the bright light of day, without stirring up a flurry of gossip, but most likely no one would think twice about her spending two days on the Circle C, as long as she was serving as Lizzie's teacher.

"It would be a temporary arrangement," Mr. Cavanagh clarified, as a nervous afterthought. "Just until I could round up a governess and a housekeeper. Becky Fairmont will vouch for me, if you've got any worries about my character. We're old friends, and we've had business dealings."

Chloe blushed. She couldn't put off telling him the truth for another moment. "Mr. Cavanagh, I—"

"Holt," he broke in, with a weary smile.

"Holt," she said, accommodatingly. "Before I agree to this, there's something I have to tell you." She drew a deep breath, let it out in a rush, with her hasty confession. "I did something terrible last night, at the Triple M. I told Jeb I might—I might—"

"Might what?" he prompted.

"Marry you," Chloe blurted, and waited for the explosion.

To her utter surprise, he laughed. "Why?"

"Because he's so all-fired sure of himself, I guess," Chloe said lamely.

Holt was grinning, shaking his head, maybe at her audacity. "All right," he said.

She looked at him in amazement. "All right?"

He laughed again, though something serious glittered in his eyes. "I'll go along with the story," he said. "For a while, anyhow."

"Why?" Chloe asked, marveling.

"The hell of it, I guess," Holt answered. "Truth is, I'm starting to like my little brother, but he is a mite on the cocky side. Now, are you going to look after Lizzie's schooling, or not?"

"I'll be ready and waiting next Friday afternoon, after school lets out," she said, with wonder.

Holt looked profoundly relieved, and when he smiled yet again, the few doubts Chloe had skittered into the shadows, like mice fleeing the light. Jeb was bound to hear of the arrangement, and he could draw whatever conclusions he liked.

"Thank you, Miss Wakefield," Holt said. "I'll make this well worth your time. Lizzie's a bright girl, if a bit headstrong, and she'll be a fine student."

"I have no doubt that she will," Chloe said. If it wouldn't have been too familiar a gesture, she would have patted his arm to let him know she liked and trusted him. Not that she didn't intend to bring her derringer along, just in case she was wrong. "How well does Lizzie read? Do you know how far she's gotten with her arithmetic?"

The smile faded. "I didn't think to ask her either of those things," he said.

Chloe suspected there were a great many things Holt Cavanagh had yet to ask his daughter, but since it was none of her business, she didn't comment. If he cared enough to engage a teacher, even for just two days out of the week, he had the makings of a good father. And he wasn't going to hold her up for a liar, even though he'd be perfectly justified in doing precisely that.

"I'll find out when Lizzie and I sit down to our lessons next Saturday morning," she decided.

He stood, his business almost complete, and put his hat back on. "I'd best get back to the ranch," he told her. "Is there anything I need to have on hand? Textbooks and the like?"

"I'll bring what's necessary to start out," Chloe said, still planted on the step. "We'll take it from there."

"Thank you," he said, and headed for the gate. She walked that far with him, saw that a team and buckboard waited across the road, with a tired-looking cowboy at the reins.

Chloe watched as Holt crossed the road, climbed up into the wagon box, and elbowed the cowboy aside to take over the horses. He lifted his hat to her and drove off.

She sat a while, thinking, then went back into the cottage to pour tea. She'd be busy, between conducting classes in the schoolhouse all week and seeing to Lizzie's education the rest of the time, but diligent enterprise would surely keep her mind off Jeb McKettrick.

She hoped.

29

$\mathcal{C}$hloe's fine intentions served her well, until she went to the Arizona Hotel for dinner that night, just after seven, and found Jeb in the dining room, having a cup of coffee with Becky and Sam Fee. There were other diners present, cowboys, mostly, but they all congealed into a murmuring blur.

Hungry as she was, Chloe would have turned right around and gone home if Jeb hadn't looked up and seen her. She froze like a squirrel facing a rattler when their eyes met, her nerves raising a sweet panic inside her, and he pushed back his chair, stood up, and ambled toward her.

He was all spruced up, she noticed helplessly, sporting Sunday clothes and polished boots. His hair was neatly brushed, and even though he wore his gun belt, he looked more like a Sacramento lawyer than a rancher.

"I was beginning to think I'd have to come looking for you," he said, just as if she hadn't presented him with divorce papers and told him she might marry his brother.

Heat spread into every part of her; she couldn't help remembering the way he'd held her, touched her, driven her crazy, the night he'd come to the cottage. "Why are you here?" she asked. "I expressly told you not—"

"It's a free country," he said easily, though there was an edge to his voice and a challenge in his eyes. He tilted his head toward her; she felt his breath on her face. Mercy, but it was warm for October. "Relax, Chloe," he teased, in an undertone as effective as a caress. "All I want to do is have supper with you. A sort of farewell dinner. Best we part friends, don't you think?"

Her temper, sometimes her downfall, sometimes her salvation, flared. "If you think for one minute that I'm going to let you back into that cottage," she whispered, "you've gone stark, raving mad."

He laughed. "I could always sing," he said.

"That won't work twice," Chloe shot back.

"Then I'll just have to think of something else," he answered glibly. He put out his arm. "Now, smooth your feathers and come have supper, before folks get the idea there's a scandal brewing."

If a twice-divorced schoolmarm wasn't a scandal, Chloe didn't know what was. She hesitated, then accepted his arm, knowing he'd make a scene if she didn't. She didn't trust herself to speak.

Still at the table, Becky greeted them with a discerning glance and a smile. Sam stood, and nodded a somber greeting.

"I'd best get back to the jailhouse," the marshal said. "Good to see you, Miss Chloe. Jeb."

Chloe acknowledged Sam pleasantly, as did Jeb, and he left the table.

As soon as Chloe had settled into a chair, having deliberately taken the one beside Becky's, and thus opposite Jeb's, the other woman rose. Chloe barely refrained from grasping at her skirts, to keep from being left alone with Jeb.

He looked on all the while, wearing an insufferably smug grin.

"I'm hungry," Chloe said, unsettled by his cheerful mood. Maybe he was up to something, and maybe he was just trying to confuse her.

"Good," he said. "I think I'm in the mood for meat loaf tonight. What about you, Teacher?"

Chloe snatched the menu out of his hands and hid behind it. Her stomach, rumbling before she stepped into this dining room, was now doing a Mexican hat dance. While she was trying to think of something to say, preferably acidic, a man in a suit and string tie stopped beside the table.

"I was sorry to hear about those murders on the range," the fellow said to Jeb. "First that poor woman and the stagecoach driver, and now Farness and that young cowboy. It's as if the same old trouble is starting up again."

Jeb's smirk vanished, replaced by a grim expression. He glanced warily at Chloe, who had come out from behind her menu to stare at him with horror-widened eyes, then shifted his gaze to his friend's face. "Whoever did it," he said quietly, "we'll find them, and they'll hang for it."

"Hanging's too good for them," the man said, and, with a nod to Chloe and a brief farewell to Jeb, headed for the lobby and the outside doors.

Chloe's memory caught on the crimson stains she'd seen on Holt's clothes when he came to the cottage behind the schoolhouse that morning. She'd been concerned then, but finally decided that he must have been doing bloody work on the ranch. "There were two more murders?"

Jeb nodded. "I wasn't going to mention it, for fear it would spoil your supper," he said, with a touch of sarcasm. "Somebody shot two men on the Circle C. In cold blood, evidently."

The fine hairs on the back of Chloe's neck rose like wire, and she gave an involuntary shiver. "Dear God," she said. Killings were, unfortunately, not all that uncommon in the more rustic parts of the West, and she was still reeling from what poor Lizzie must have suffered, seeing her aunt and an innocent stagecoach driver die. The news of this second incident struck her midsection like a ramrod.

"We'll find them," Jeb said, and his eyes seemed veiled, even though he was looking straight at her. "Sam will get up a posse, and we'll track them to hell if that's what we have to do."

Chloe was more terrified of the look on Jeb's face than she was of any murderer. She saw an image of him in her mind, dead and bloody, and she was sickened. "That would be very dangerous," she pointed out carefully.

"Around here," he said, "when there's a mad dog on the loose, we put him out of his misery."

Chloe's confused stomach churned. "But you could be killed!"

The smile was back, but it was so cold that Chloe would have welcomed the insolent grin he'd displayed previously, and heartily. "I won't be," he said. "But he might."

Chloe clutched the edges of the table. She imagined herself visiting not one grave, down at the churchyard, but two, and if the mere prospect was unbearable, the reality might destroy her completely. "What if there isn't just one man?" she demanded. "What if there's a whole gang? I know you're fast with a gun, but he—or they— might be faster!"

He leaned forward a little. "Worried about me, Chloe?"

"You are *impossible*," she accused, finding it harder and harder to keep her voice down. "This is not some game, Jeb—it's not shooting bottles out of the sky behind the Broken Stirrup Saloon!"

Becky swept over, a small pad and a pencil in her hands. "Would you two like to order?" she asked, with hasty good cheer.

"Meat loaf," Jeb said, glaring at Chloe.

"Chicken, please," Chloe said, glaring back.

Becky made notes, hesitated briefly, and went away.

"I don't need you to tell me what's dangerous," Jeb said, his jawline taut, when they were alone again. "I'm a man, not a boy—or at least, you seemed to think so the other night."

"That," Chloe said, fighting tears, "was a terrible thing to say!" She started to stand up, planning to flee, though it meant starving all night.

Jeb stayed her with a sigh, and, "Sit down, Chloe. Please."

Chloe sat, but supper, a tenuous affair to begin with, was completely spoiled, even though she choked down as much of it as she could, and so was her evening.

Thanks to Jeb, she would have another sleepless night.

30

*W*ell, Jeb thought miserably, as he mounted up to make the long ride back to Holt's place, where he was now an official resident of the bunkhouse, he'd sure fouled up with Chloe.

Again.

He'd intended to apologize for the way he'd acted at the ranch the night before, try to straighten things out a little, as hopeless as the task seemed, but he'd let his pride get the better of him, they'd had words, and she'd left the hotel, right after supper. Wouldn't even let him walk her back to the cottage. Oh, no. Doc Boylen had come along just in time to do that.

He sighed. He was a natural botcher, that was the plain and simple fact of it. It seemed that every time he made the effort to reason with Chloe, he said or did the wrong thing—and he hadn't done any better with his pa. He wasn't sure what he'd expected the old man to say or do when he told him he'd be riding for the Circle C for a while, it hadn't been the shock and pain he'd glimpsed in his father's eyes before he rode out.

The schoolhouse was dark as he passed it, but he caught a glimmer of light from the cottage in back, and imagined Chloe there, puttering with those thick and well-thumbed books of hers, or maybe making tea.

The moon, full for the last three nights, was waning, and thus the road was darker. He'd been over that trail so many times in his life that he didn't have to think about it, and neither did his horse.

He'd traveled maybe five miles when the crack of a rifle sounded from a nest of boulders somewhere on his left; he felt the bullet splinter the bone in his upper right arm before he had time to react.

The pain was a blazing affront, a white-hot flash, but his training was ingrained. He reached across his middle and drew his .45 with his left hand, even as he fell.

He spoke sharply to the panicked horse, to drive it out of the line of fire, and rolled into the shadows on the side of the road. Another shot struck, pinging off the rock not six inches above his head.

His right arm felt as though it had been stomped to a mash by a team of dray horses. He scrambled deeper into the brush, cursing the darkness, breathing deeply and slowly, in an effort to gather his scattered thoughts and govern the inevitable emotions—rage, and no small amount of fear.

This was no time to lose his head.

"McKettrick!" his attacker shouted, out of the gloom. "You're a dead man, so you might as well come out where I can see you!"

He knew that voice, but from where? His fitful mind tried to seize on a name, a face, anything, but the wildfire consuming his arm crowded out reason. "Who are you?" he yelled back, more out of reflex than because he thought there was a chance in hell the man would actually tell him. He was dealing with a bushwhacker; anybody but a coward would have confronted him in the open, in the broad light of day.

"Somebody with a powerful grudge," came the response.

"I figured that much out for myself!"

"I hit you, I know I did. Come on out, now, and I'll put you right out of your misery." The voice was closer now, an evil crooning. A black fog rose around Jeb, threatening to gulp him down whole.

"I'm not going to make it that easy," Jeb answered. His belly pitched; he gulped hard to keep from losing his supper—he couldn't afford the distraction. In the near distance, he heard his horse, the comforting jingle of bridle fittings. *Steady,* he told himself silently, fighting to stay conscious. If he blacked out, he wouldn't have a banker's chance in hell.

"Now, don't be a fool." Closer still.

Jeb squeezed his eyes shut, opened them again, tried

to breathe in rhythm with the pain. "That's good advice," he said. "You might want to take it."

A laugh. A familiar one.

Who, dammit? Why couldn't he catch hold of the name?

The ground vibrated slightly under Jeb's chest. Hooves. Someone had heard the shots. Someone was coming. Riding right into a bullet of their own, most likely.

He lifted the .45, fired the customary three-shot warning in the air.

The other man swore, whistled for a horse. Maybe he'd heard the riders for himself, and maybe he knew the signal for trouble.

Jeb raised himself far enough to see the road, sight in on the shadow he glimpsed there. He got off a shot, took a chunk out of the gunman's left leg as he mounted.

There was a muffled cry of pain, but his assailant gained the saddle all the same. Jeb ducked just as another bullet struck the rock next to him.

The hoofbeats were louder now, drawing closer, at a fast clip. Four horses, maybe five.

"This isn't over, McKettrick," the rider called in parting. "We'll meet again, I promise you that—whether it's on this side of the veil or in the heart of hell!"

Jeb didn't have the breath to answer. He laid his head down and let the darkness take him over.

31

*J*eb came to on the examining table in Doc Boylen's office, with the old sawbones breathing whiskey fumes in his face. The pain, blessedly absent while he was out there at the end of the tether, wrenched him hard back to center, and the impact took his breath away. He tried to sit up, get away from it, even as he knew there was no escape.

Doc pushed him back down. "Take it easy," he said. "You've lost a bucket of blood."

Jeb set his jaw, trying to resist the pain, and that only made it worse. "Christ," he gasped, unsure whether he was praying or cursing. Maybe it was a little of both.

Doc showed him a syringe. "Morphine," he said. "Lie still. I'm not too steady tonight."

"Oh, that's great," Jeb bit out. "I get shot, and the only doctor within fifty miles is a drunkard."

Boylen chuckled as he jammed the needle into Jeb's good arm. "I would think," he drawled, "that you'd be a little more charitable in your estimation, since I'm trying to save your miserable hide. If I didn't take a nip now and then, my lumbago would get the best of me for sure."

The effect of the morphine was immediate; Jeb let out his breath. He'd heard the riders approaching, out there on the road, but he hadn't seen them. "Who brought me here?"

"Some of the boys from the Triple M. Your good luck that they happened to be in town last night, whooping it up. Way they tell it, they were on their way back to the ranch when they heard shots up ahead, and decided they ought to look into the matter."

Jeb tried to touch his wounded arm, assess the true nature of his situation, but Boylen blocked the motion.

"How bad is it?" Jeb asked.

"Bad enough," Boylen answered. "I mean to operate, soon as I sober up a little." The twinkle in his eyes said he was kidding; Jeb sure as hell hoped that was the case. A moment later, Doc confirmed the matter. "That was a joke," Boylen said. "The part about sobering up, I mean."

Jeb was in no mood to laugh. "Well, it was a damn sorry one."

The doc chuckled again. "You'll be all right," he said. "Look on the cheerful side. You'll have women fussing over you, and Angus'll probably stay off your back, for a while, anyhow. In the meantime, Sam's outside, waiting to talk to you. You up to it?"

Jeb let himself float on the morphine, like a piece of driftwood riding the ocean. "Send him in—not that I've got much to tell him. And Doc? Don't tell Chloe about this just yet."

Doc nodded, patted Jeb's good shoulder. "You just lie still, now. Try to gain a little ground while you can. When that shot wears off, you're going to be hurting worse than before."

"You're just full of encouragement."

Doc laughed, stepped out of view. Jeb heard the surgery door open, and there was an exchange of murmured words. Then Sam was beside him.

"See anybody?" he asked, never one to mince words.

Jeb shook his head. "A shadow is all," he said. "Is my horse all right?"

"Your horse is fine," Sam said, in the manner of a man who would waste no more words on a minor subject. "I reckon it was an ambush?"

Jeb wet his dry lips with his tongue, wished mightily for water. His throat felt like sawdust. "Yep," he confirmed. "I need a drink."

Sam fetched a ladle of tepid water from somewhere nearby, helped Jeb lift his head, and held the rim to his mouth, waiting while he drank.

"Did he say anything?"

Jeb coughed, settled down again by force of will. "He knew my name. Said he had a grudge, and that he'd see me again. I shot him in the leg, but he rode out, so he couldn't have been hurt too badly."

Sam digested all this. "We'll pick up his trail in the morning."

Jeb thought of the killings on the Circle C range. He'd tried to track the lone rider, after Farness and that poor kid from Tucson were gunned down, but it had come to nothing. Whoever this son of a bitch was, he knew his business. "Good luck," he said.

"You recollect anything else?"

"I've heard his voice someplace before. I can't rightly remember where."

"Like as not, it'll come back to you," Sam said, without particular conviction. "Guess I'd better leave you be. Doc says he means to do surgery in the morning, and you need your rest to brace up for it."

"I'd like to see those riders from the Triple M. Tell them thanks."

Sam shook his head. "That'll have to wait. They've gone to tell your pa and brothers what happened."

The pain prodded at the edges of the drug's sweet influence, trying to find its way back in. "Nothing they can do," he said.

Sam was already out of Jeb's limited range of sight, though he must have paused in the doorway, because he answered. "They'll want to be here just the same, I reckon."

Jeb closed his eyes.

He heard the voice of his attacker. *Somebody with a grudge.*

Recognition teased his mind—for an instant, he knew who had shot him—but the impression was gone as soon as he slipped back into the darkness.

32

*J*ack Barrett rode overland, bent low in the saddle, for several long hours. It was near dawn when he reached the cabin, and Sue Ellen came out to meet him, holding a lantern in one hand and a rifle in the other.

He pitched forward, wrapped both arms around the horse's neck to keep from hitting the hard, stone-strewn ground.

Sue Ellen cried out, leaned the rifle against the out-side wall, set the lantern on the chopping block next to the woodpile, and rushed over, braced to break his fall if she could.

"That bastard McKettrick shot me," he said, through his teeth.

She helped him down from the saddle, positioned her small, strong body under his left arm. "Dammit, Jack," she hissed, "you went ahead and did it, didn't you? It wasn't just talk. You killed Jeb McKettrick!"

The open doorway of the cabin loomed ahead; Jack set his mind on staying upright long enough to get through it and leaned heavily on Sue Ellen. "I wish I had," he said, "but there were riders coming, so I had to leave before I'd finished him."

"You wretched fool," she berated, even as they stepped over the high threshold and into the dark house, "you'll bring the whole lot of them down on us now!"

Right then, the collective wrath of the McKettrick clan was the least of Jack's concerns, though he reckoned it might get to be an issue later on. "Just get me some whiskey, Sue Ellen," he grumbled, "and shut up."

She fetched him to the bed, where he fell heavily, then scared up some rotgut from someplace and gave him a dose.

"I should have kept going, after I left the Circle C, instead of letting you talk me into staying around," Sue Ellen fussed, after she'd retrieved the lantern, shut and latched the door, and come back to the bedside to peer at his wound.

"You wanted revenge on the McKettricks as much as I did," Jack pointed out, flinching when she helped herself to his jackknife and cut a slash in his trouser leg.

"Just Holt," she snapped. "Not the whole damn Triple M outfit!"

Jack drew in a hissing breath and swore. "Take it easy, will you? That hurts!"

"Good," she retorted, and plunged what felt like a hot poker into the gash in his flesh.

"Anyways, Holt's a McKettrick, whatever he calls himself," Jack grated. "He'll be in the thick of this, you can count on that."

She hesitated; he felt it in the motions of her hands. "I don't want you to kill him," she said.

"Too late for tender sentiments," Jack answered. "Give me some more of that whiskey."

She held the flask to his lips, and he drained it to the dregs.

"I mean it, Jack," she went on, not so haughty as before. "I was furious when he sent me away, and I wanted him to be sorry for what he did, but I didn't bargain for any killing."

"You're in as deep as I am," Jack said. "No going back now."

Her eyes glittered in the bleak dimness of the cabin. "What are you planning to do next?"

"Hit 'em where it hurts," he replied. He hadn't made any definite plans on that score, as up to a few minutes ago he'd been concentrating on reaching the cabin without falling off his horse, but a few ideas were starting to come to him, like ghosts gliding back and forth at the borders of his mind, fixing to cross over.

She sounded breathless, and scared, too. "What do you mean?"

"Home is where the heart is," Jack said, but that was all he was willing to say. He'd had a hard night, and he needed his rest.

33

*C*hloe was on her way to the hotel, for breakfast with Becky, when she spotted Angus, Kade, and Rafe McKettrick standing on the board sidewalk in front of Doc Boylen's office, and a frisson of alarm fizzed in the pit of her stomach. Holding her skirts so she wouldn't trip on the hem, she crossed the road at a rapid pace.

Kade was the first to notice her, and the look of despondent fury in his eyes practically stopped her heart, never mind her feet. By process of elimination, and some fierce, dark instinct, she knew that Jeb was the object of their vigil.

Kade touched the brim of his hat in a habitual motion. "Morning, Miss Chloe," he said. The grave note in his voice skewered her on a shaft of fear.

"Where's Jeb?" she demanded, terrified of the answer.

Rafe, who had been pacing, stopped to look down at her. "Inside," he said. "Doc's operating on him right now."

Chloe's knees sagged, and she might have dropped, right there in the dirty street, if Kade hadn't been so quick to reach her side and take a firm hold on her arm. "What—?"

Kade squired her as far as the bench under Doc's shingle. She shook her head, dizzy.

"Jeb was shot last night, on the road home," Kade told her quietly.

She put her hands over her face, but only momentarily. Angus sat down beside her on the bench, took her hand between his callused ones.

"Doc says he'll make it, Chloe," he assured her, but his face was ravaged by a sleepless night, and his skin was gray. The ache she saw in his eyes matched the one tearing at her insides. "He wasn't killed. That's the important thing."

Chloe's empty stomach flung itself at the back of her throat, making her glad she hadn't eaten. In her mind's eye, she saw Jeb sitting across from her at supper the night before, talking about hunting down murderers. He'd been so coldly certain that he couldn't be on the receiving end of a bad man's bullet, and now he was lying on a surgeon's table, shot. He hadn't had to go looking for trouble—this time, it had found him on its own.

Angus patted her hand. "Get her some water," he said.

Kade fetched a canteen from one of the horses' backs, unscrewed the lid, handed it to her. She drank deeply.

"Was he—did you talk to him?" she managed, handing back the canteen with a nod of thanks.

"Doc's got him drugged up," Angus answered gruffly. "Ether, for the surgery."

"I just hope to God he's sober," Rafe fretted. Chloe's gaze shot in his direction like an arrow.

"Do you mean to tell me the doctor is *drunk?*" she marveled, in horror. She started to her feet, meaning to intercede, but Angus held so fast to her hand that she had to sit down again.

"Hell, Rafe," Kade said, "*that* was a stupid thing to say."

"Well," Rafe retorted, "you'll pardon me if I'm a little worried about my *brother!*"

"That's enough," Angus said, with raspy ease. "We're all worried about Jeb, and going for each other's throats won't help. Doc's no drunkard, Chloe. He likes to let on that he is once in a while, though." He shook his head. "No understanding some folks."

Chloe longed to march inside and stand at Doc's elbow, supervising, but she knew Angus would never allow it and, besides, she'd probably swoon at the first sight of blood anyway. A tear slipped down her cheek and, shamed, she dashed it away with the heel of one palm.

She heard the sound of an approaching horse, traveling at a gallop, and Holt appeared, dismounting and leaving the reins to dangle.

"Where's Lizzie?" Angus demanded, without preamble. "You didn't go off and leave her alone, did you?"

"She's at the Triple M, with the women," Holt answered, putting a fine point on every word. His gaze traveled, full of challenge, from Angus to Rafe to Kade, and softened a little when it came to rest on Chloe. "How's he doing?"

"Doc's hacking away at him right now," Rafe said, and earned himself another scathing glance from Kade.

"See to that horse," Angus told Holt sternly, "before the poor critter trips on those reins and breaks a leg."

Holt looked exasperated, but he did as he was told.

Rafe grinned at that little concession, albeit grimly, and Kade resettled his hat. Chloe had seen Jeb do the same thing, the same way, at least a hundred times.

With the gelding secured to the hitching rail, within easy reach of a water trough, Holt stepped onto the sidewalk. After another kindly glance at Chloe, he set his face into a scowl again and jabbed a thumb toward the door of Doc's office.

"How long's the operation supposed to take?"

Angus sighed. "Doc said it would be over when it was over. Jeb took a bullet in his right arm, and there was some damage done."

"If he'd stayed on the Circle C," Holt said, "this wouldn't have happened."

"Well," Rafe said tersely, "he didn't do that, did he?"

"If you can't mind your tongue," Angus said, watching Rafe, "you'd best go elsewhere, find yourself something worthwhile to do."

Rafe's broad shoulders sagged under the reprimand. He took off his hat, thrust a hand through his dark hair. "It's hard to just stand around here and wait, Pa," he said.

"I know," Angus answered quietly, "but arguing won't make it easier."

Folks were beginning to take note of the gathering, now that the bank and the shops were opening for business, and all three of Angus's sons stiffened, as if preparing to form a human barrier in front of Doc's office door.

Before that happened, however, there came a shuffling sound from inside, and Doc appeared on the threshold. He looked as if he'd been dragged through half of hell behind a team of demon horses, but there was no blood on him, and he managed a smile.

"Angus," he said, "it's done. Jeb'll be all right, in time. If he takes it easy—stays off those wild horses he likes to ride."

"I'll chain him to his bed if I have to," Angus said. He released Chloe's hand and stood. "I'd like to see him."

"He's still unconscious," Doc answered, watching Chloe closely as he spoke. "Make it a short visit." He nodded to Rafe, Kade, and Holt. "You boys will have to bide a while. Might as well go on down to the hotel and get yourselves some breakfast. Becky'll be pacing the floor, waiting for news."

All three of them clearly wanted to argue, but they finally relented, Rafe and Kade going on together, Holt hanging back, watching Chloe with a somber expression. She knew he was inviting her to join them, even though he didn't speak, and she shook her head in response.

He gave a slight nod and followed his brothers.

Angus vanished into the office, and Chloe would have been alone if Doc hadn't stayed and taken a seat beside her on the bench.

"You all right?" he asked gently. "You're a little green around the edges."

"If I had anything in my stomach," Chloe answered honestly, "I'd throw up."

Doc chuckled. "Me too," he said.

Now that there weren't so many people watching her, Chloe felt free to cry, and she commenced to do just that.

The doctor produced a clean handkerchief. "Now, now," he said. "If you're going to love a McKettrick, you've got to be tough."

Chloe stiffened. "Who says I love him?"

Doc smiled. "I do."

"I might *like* him a little," Chloe conceded. *Did* she love Jeb McKettrick? Certainly not, she decided. If she'd loved him, she wouldn't have arranged a divorce.

Doc took the handkerchief from her and dabbed at her face, which felt hot and fragile, like it might crumble into pieces at any given moment. "Once Angus is through paying his respects, you can go in and see Jeb. It might do him good to know you're there."

Chloe blinked. "But you said he was unconscious."

"There's a part of a person that never sleeps, no matter what," Doc told her. "You touch his hand, and tell him he's a ring-tailed waste of good skin. I guarantee you, he'll feel obliged to get better, just so he can contradict you."

Chloe laughed, right through her tears. "I may have to revise my opinion of you," she said.

Doc's wise old eyes twinkled. "I didn't know there was a need of that," he replied.

"Rafe said you might be drunk," Chloe explained, and promptly wished she could call the words back. It was the story of her life, she thought with chagrin; from everlasting to everlasting, she was forever saying things she shouldn't. *Doing* things she shouldn't. Her history was one long train wreck, with good intentions scattered on either side of the tracks.

The doctor's smile was gentle, and full of humor. "I must see to my reputation," he said. "It's a poor one, it would seem."

Angus's long shadow spilled over the sidewalk from the doorway, and Chloe looked up, full of questions. Aching with them.

"Go on in," he said gruffly.

"Thank you, Mr. McKettrick," she replied, rising.

He touched her arm, and looked as if he might say something. In the end, though, he merely nodded.

Jeb lay on the doctor's all-purpose table, his flesh pale, his hair blood-matted and rumpled, his eyes closed.

Chloe laid a hand to his cheek, bent to kiss his forehead. "Get better, you ring-tailed waste of skin," she said tenderly, hoping Doc was right—that he'd fight his way to the surface just to take his own part.

34

At first, Jeb thought he'd been buried alive, such was the weight of the pain, but when he opened his eyes, Chloe was standing next to him, gripping his hand. Her red hair was falling from its pins, and he could tell by her puffy eyes and red nose that she'd been doing some crying.

"It's about time you woke up," she said. "Becky and Sarah will be serving supper in a little while."

He let out a raspy chuckle, and she gave him some water from a china mug. The stuff tasted like ambrosia, but the touch of her hand, supporting the back of his head, was better yet. "Am I still in Doc's office?" he asked, thinking it a reasonable question.

She shook her head. "You're at the hotel. Rafe and Kade brought you here a few hours ago. They made a litter out of an old door."

He took more water, letting the image of that take shape in his mind, then allowed his head to fall back onto the pillow. "Well," he said, "at least the grub will be good. Doc's not known for his cooking."

She put the mug aside. "Does your arm hurt much?"

"I feel like the barn fell on me," he admitted. He wondered what he'd have to promise to get Doc to give him another one of those shots.

She smoothed his hair back from his face; he liked the feel of that. "You could have been killed," she said, and tears glistened in her eyes. He wondered if things would change between them now. Maybe getting shot hadn't been such a bad thing, even if it did hurt like Holy B. Jesus.

Carefully, he lifted his left arm, cupped his hand behind Chloe's head, and drew her down into a light kiss. "But I wasn't," he said hoarsely, when their lips parted. "Don't cry, Chloe. Please, don't cry."

Contrary creature that she was, she laid her forehead against his and sobbed.

35

*T*he trouble with being laid up and in pain was that it gave a man too damn much time to think. Lying there in that hotel room, Jeb counted the cracks in the ceiling and the boards in the wall. A single fly had come to keep him company, now buzzing at his head, now bumbling against the glass in the window. He tried to read some from the lofty tomes Kade had brought him, but words on those pages seemed as restless as the fly. They just wouldn't light on his brain and settle in.

Perhaps because he'd come so close to crossing over—according to Doc, he'd tried to slip away a couple of times during the operation—he kept thinking about his mother.

He remembered once, when he was six or seven, spending a night in town with a friend and taking in the fiery sermons of an itinerant preacher. He'd been terri-fied, and awakened screaming and sweating in the depths of a summer night, flailing at his covers.

"I'm bad and I'm going to hell," he'd told Georgia McKettrick, in a bullet spray of words, when she hurried into his room with a lantern and a concerned expression.

She'd sat on the edge of his narrow bed, wearing a satin wrapper and smelling of some combination of lilacs and sleep, and smoothed his hair back from his forehead with one blessedly cool hand. "Nonsense," she'd said.

"But the preacher said so."

"The preacher is full of sheep dip," his mother replied, and it seemed to him that there was more than enough affection in her smile, even some left over for the preacher. "The poor man's just confused, that's all."

About then, Angus had appeared in the doorway, leaning one shoulder against the frame. "That's how the bastards get you, son," he'd said, yawning. "By making you scared. Don't you ever let anybody or anything do that."

His ma had cast a glance in her husband's direction, evidently a sharp one, judging by the reaction to it, which was plainly visible in Angus's much-younger face. Jeb had an idea that it was the word "bastards" that got Georgia's hackles up; she didn't hold with swearing. Said it was a sign of a poor vocabulary and a mean spirit.

He'd smiled then, comforted, and he smiled now.

He was hurting. He was bored and frustrated half-out of his skull. But damned if he was scared.

A heavy knock sounded at the door of his room; he knew, by the weight of it, that the visitor was Angus or one of his brothers and not Chloe. It was the first day of school, and she was down the street, riding herd over a wild bunch.

He was still coping with the letdown when he offered a gruff, "Come in," and Angus walked in. Jeb craned his neck, looking past the old man for Doc, with one of his magic needles. Another disappointment—Angus was traveling alone.

"Afternoon," he said.

Jeb nodded a greeting. Now that he wasn't dangling a foot in the grave, the old man probably meant to give him trouble about leaving the Triple M.

Angus drew up the only chair in the room and sat down next to the bed with a heavy sigh. He eyed the sling supporting Jeb's right arm. "How's the pain?"

"Oh, the pain's doing fine," Jeb replied. "*I'm* a little worse for wear, though."

Angus chuckled, rubbed his beard-stubbled chin. He was a tougher than boiled owl, his pa, a quality Jeb both admired and resented. He'd seen that McKettrick grit carry the day, times beyond counting, and against formidable odds, but he'd also collided with it on a number of occasions and landed on his ass in the dust. "You up to talking a little, boy?" he asked.

For a moment, Jeb was small again, and fearful of devils and hellfire, but the feeling quickly subsided, finding no place to take hold. If he got to the pearly gates and found out his theology was wrong, at least he'd be able to say he'd thought things through for himself instead of taking somebody else's word. "I can manage some listening," he said. "Talking might be another matter."

Angus smiled distractedly, ran his big, work-worn hands down the thighs of his trousers. "I'll try to hold up my end, then," he said. As if he'd ever had to make an effort in that direction. "I do have a few questions for you, though."

Jeb nodded, to show he was paying attention, and waved away the fly with his good arm.

"What made you take a notion to sign on at the Circle C?" The old man was trying to be diplomatic, Jeb could see that, but he'd never really gotten the hang of it, and this time was no exception.

"The pay was better," he answered, a mite flippantly.

Angus thrust out one of his gusty sighs. "We could have talked about that," he said, picking his way through the sentence like a man crossing a wild creek, inching from stone to slippery stone. "If you'd given me the chance, I might have upped your wages."

Jeb's jaw tightened; he willed it to relax a little. "Or said I was already earning more than I was worth," he replied.

Angus surveyed him from beneath lowered and bristly brows. "It's true," he allowed, "that if there's been an improvement in your output, I haven't seen it."

This was the old Angus, the one he knew. Jeb let the corner of his mouth quirk upward in a semblance of a grin. "Maybe I've changed," he said. "Maybe I'm ready to take hold, make a place for myself."

"About time," Angus said, and shook his head, as if reprimanding himself for letting his tongue run away from him. With the old man, two words were a verbal stampede.

"It's all right, Pa," Jeb said quietly, and with a note of humor, shifting the pillows behind him in a vain effort to find some comfort. "I know what you think of me."

"Do you, now?" Angus rubbed his chin again. "You just go ahead and tell me, then."

Jeb shrugged his one responsive shoulder, cradled the slinged arm because of the pain. "I'm the youngest. Spoiled. Wild. Irresponsible. Not as strong as Rafe, or as smart as Kade."

"The hell you say," Angus shot back, in a rumbling huff. "The only thing you got right there is your being born last. I don't compare my sons one to the other. I reckon that's your own definition of Jeb McKettrick, but don't go putting my brand on it."

Jeb was at a loss, so he kept quiet.

Angus smiled, though sadly. "Here's how I see you," he began. "You're *my son*, and you've got a steel backbone and a go-to-hell attitude. You're the best rider and the fastest gun I've ever seen. You take too damn many chances, trying to prove you're nobody's little brother. And you're smart as anybody, when you take the time to think before you jump, which—it seems to me—is a relatively rare occasion."

Jeb swallowed, fumbled with the carafe on his bedside table, poured a one-handed slug of water. Angus, in typical fashion, didn't try to help, just sat there, resting his arms on his thighs, fingers loosely entwined. Even an hour ago, Jeb would have interpreted this as pure cussedness, but now—well—he'd have to do some reflecting to line it all up proper in his mind.

"I want you to come back home to the Triple M," Angus said forthrightly. "When you can ride again, and make yourself useful, we'll talk about your wages."

Something inside Jeb yearned to accept, but he resisted the pull. He had things to prove, though he wasn't exactly sure what they were, and he knew he'd never come to terms with himself if he took to walking backward.

"I've got a job, Pa. At the Circle C."

"You're not going to be much use to Holt or anybody else with your arm tied up in a dish towel," Angus pointed out. No sense slapping a coat of varnish on a perfectly good truth. Just lay the matter right out there, whether anybody liked it or not, that was the old man's way.

Jeb swallowed again, though this time, it was more of a gulp. The things he felt were tangled and spiky as barbwire, rusting in his throat.

"Holt wants me to look out for Lizzie until he can

come up with a better arrangement," he managed, after some struggle. "By the time he ropes in a housekeeper, I'll be good as new."

Angus studied him. "You're going to be a babysitter."

Jeb considered flinging the glass at his father's head, but decided against it. He'd only duck, and he was still quick enough to get out of the way, for all his age. "Call it whatever you like, Pa. Holt can't be with Lizzie *and* on the range, and he's got a ranch to run."

"You've developed quite an affection for your brother, it seems."

"I'm fond of Lizzie," Jeb insisted. "Just like you are."

The big shoulders moved in a shrug. "That's as it should be. She's a child, a baby, really, and she's a McKettrick."

"Not according to Holt, she isn't. He says her name is Cavanagh."

"Holt's just pissed off at me," Angus said, and he sounded weary. "Can't say I blame him, but damned if I know how to make it up."

Jeb reached for the glass again, took a steadying sip. Where the devil was Doc with that shot? "What do you figure he wants from you? Holt, I mean?"

Angus got to his feet. "My blessing," he said. "I reckon that's what all of you want." He shifted his weight, hooked his thumbs under his belt. His holster was empty, one of Becky's house rules. "Well, for what it's worth, you've got it," he finished, and headed for the door.

Jeb didn't want the old man to go just yet, but he was damned if he'd say so. "Even if I never come back to the Triple M?" he challenged, addressing his father's broad back.

"Even then," Angus said, without turning around. And then he went out.

"I'll be a ring-tailed waste of skin," Jeb muttered, grinning. The fly landed on his chest, but he didn't try to whack it.

36

Chloe assessed her students, one by one, now that their heads were bent over their slates, and they wouldn't see her looking.

There was Harry Sussex, her favorite, at the left end of the first long table, facing her desk. He wanted, above all else, to be like Kade McKettrick. Not a bad objective, she supposed, though her goal for him was a little different. She wanted Harry to be Harry, in all his individual glory.

Next to him was Lucas, his brother, and next to Lucas was Benjamin. To his right sat Clarence and George, respectively, and the five of them made a set of stair steps. The baby of the family, a girl named Hortense, was too small to attend school. According to Harry, she'd "pitched a fine fit" that morning when she realized she was being left behind.

At the next table were the banker's two daughters, nine-year-old Marietta and seven-year-old Eloise, well-shod and ringleted, wearing ready-made dresses, hair ribbons, and shiny shoes. They sat close together, primly intent on their slates. Chloe felt a rush of warmth for them; for all their confident appearance, they were as worried about fitting in as any of the others.

Finally, at the last table, were Jesse Banner, a big boy of nearly fourteen, a rancher's son who had traveled since dawn to be there, and Jennie Payle, whose mother was employed at the Bloody Basin Saloon, doing what Chloe did not exactly know, though of course she had her suspicions. Walter and Ellen Jessup, brother and sister, made up the last of the crew. New to Indian Rock, like Jennie, they were motherless and even poorer than the Sussex children, living out of a wagon parked back of the church. Chloe hadn't been able to learn much about their situation, beyond the fact that their father worked on the Triple M and wanted them to "git" an education. To that end, he'd left them to fend for themselves through the week, promising to return on Friday nights, after he'd gotten his pay. She worried over the Jessups; surely, they were frightened, alone in their little camp, especially when it got dark. On the other hand, they were probably used to hardship; many children were. Down South, they picked cotton and worked long hours in textile mills, and in the Pennsylvania coal country, they labored in mines.

Her misgivings aside, Chloe was deeply grateful for her students; without them, she'd spend far too much time thinking about Jeb. As it was, he crept into her mind whenever she left a space open.

She reminded herself that they'd resolved nothing, she and Jeb. She lived from her mind, he from his body. She was bold, but innately cautious, too, while he stuck his chin out at everything, daring life to thwart him. This wasn't just her own supposition, either; Doc had told her several chilling stories about his exploits. He'd patched Jeb up on a regular basis from the time he was ten years old, and declared himself a born bronc rider.

Chloe sighed. It was God's own miracle that the rascal wasn't lying under six feet of dirt over at the cemetery instead of in a bed at the Arizona Hotel, complaining that he was bored.

Of course he was bored. He probably wasn't happy unless he was barreling through the world like a runaway freight train, looking for something to collide with. Chloe sat down at her desk, cupped her chin in one hand, and wished she'd never complicated her life by making his acquaintance.

She had a lot to learn when it came to picking men.

"Teacher?" the small, earnest voice startled her, and she turned to see little Jennie standing practically at her elbow. "Are you sad? You sure do look downhearted."

Chloe felt a pang. This ragged child, with her limp blond hair and shabby dress, was concerned about *her.* "I was merely thinking," she said quietly, resisting an urge to put an arm around Jennie's thin shoulders and draw her close for a moment. She didn't want to risk hurting Jennie's pride. "I can see where you'd get that impression, though. I can look *very* somber when I'm considering a matter."

Jennie's smile was tentative, and there was relief in it. "I finished with my numbers," she said.

Chloe took the slate, examined the figures. "Excellent," she said. The problems of addition were incorrect, the subtractions, perfect in every way. A commentary, Chloe thought, on Jennie's life. Young as she was, she knew more about taking away than accumulating. "You've made a fine start." She pointed out the errors as kindly and matter-of-factly as she could. "Try again," she said.

When lunchtime came, Marietta and Eloise went home for their meal. The Sussex children played in the yard, pretending not to care about food, Jennie nibbled at a biscuit and a chunk of cheese, probably purloined from the spread at the saloon, always on hand for the customers, and Jesse Banner opened a brown paper parcel, containing a sandwich and two hard-boiled eggs. Walter and Ellen Jessup simply sat in their places, staring straight ahead and waiting for class to start again.

Emmeline, who spent a lot of her time at the hotel, being part owner, appeared out of the blue, with a large pan in her hands, just as Chloe was about to fetch crackers and fruit from the cottage and set them out for the taking. Mrs. Rafe McKettrick swept into the schoolhouse in a breeze of calico, closely followed by the Chinese cook from Becky's kitchen, bearing plates and spoons. The

Sussex children crowded in behind them, all eyes and twitching noses.

"To celebrate the first day of school," Emmeline announced, setting the pan in the middle of the front table with a flourish. "Everybody, help yourselves."

The Sussexes swarmed, while Walter Jessup peered at the contents of the pan, a noodle casserole with a creamy sauce and various vegetables mixed in, his small sister at his side.

Walter's expression was stoic. "Me and Ellen ain't eatin'," he said.

The two women exchanged glances, both of them laughing silently.

Bless you, Emmeline, Chloe thought. Not only had she been generous, providing badly needed food, she'd done so graciously, in a way that wouldn't make the children feel like charity cases.

The Chinese cook trotted out, and Emmeline dusted her hands together, as if to declare her business finished. There was a flurry of eating, and, at long last, the Jessups relented, joining in. The way they tucked away food made Chloe wonder when they'd last had a decent meal.

Having little or no appetite herself, Chloe sat on the front steps, with Emmeline perched beside her.

"That was a very kind thing you did," she said. "I appreciate it."

"We're glad to have a school," Emmeline replied, as though that settled the manner. "Not to mention a teacher. Becky's going to ask the town council for a food allowance for the children. She says if they refuse, she'll see to it herself." She smiled. "That'll shame them into doing it."

Chloe laughed, but the sound fell away in the air as she gazed toward the Arizona Hotel, where Jeb lay, recovering. He'd get over the wound, according to Doc, but he was bound to go looking for trouble as soon as he could ride. Chloe knew he half hoped Sam and his posse wouldn't find his assailant—he wanted to do that himself.

Emmeline must have read her mind, at least partially, for she patted her hand. "Jeb will be fine," she said softly.

Sudden tears stung Chloe's eyes, and she tried to blink them away. "Will he?" she asked. "What about next time?"

Emmeline frowned. " 'Next time'?"

"He's got no sense at all," Chloe fretted, wringing her hands a little. "He's such a—such a—"

"McKettrick?" Emmeline supplied.

"Yes," Chloe said. "Do they all think they're immortal?"

"Pretty much," was the quiet answer.

"How do you stand it? Don't you worry about Rafe?"

Emmeline sighed. "Of course I do," she said. "But if he wasn't hell-bent-for-election, he wouldn't be Rafe. And if he wasn't Rafe, I wouldn't love him so very much."

The children, crowded into the schoolhouse, were making a great deal of happy noise, and that lifted

Chloe's spirits a notch. They were life itself, those little ones, dancing, laughing, chasing each other on the very edge of the abyss. But they were *children*, and Jeb McKettrick would be thirty in a couple of years. What was *his* excuse for tempting Fate the way he did?

Come and get me, he seemed to say, to man and cosmos alike. *Catch me if you can.*

Respecting Chloe's silence, probably well aware of the turmoil within her, Emmeline squeezed her hand once, then stood. "Don't be afraid," she said, musing. "That's the first rule of the McKettrick clan. Better to die in a hail of gunfire than whimper behind a wall and survive." She turned to look at Chloe, and her eyes were bright with conviction. "Much as I'd hate to lose any one of them, especially Rafe, I wouldn't ask them to live any other way."

"You," said Chloe, without particular admiration, "are a very brave woman."

Emmeline smiled. "I have to be," she said, then she was gone.

37

*T*o say Jeb was bad-tempered, Chloe reflected, later that day, when school was over and she had made her pilgrimage to his room at the hotel, would be like saying Genghis Khan was warlike. He was out of bed, though Doc had specifically told him, in her hearing, to stay down. Clad in a flannel bathrobe, he was making his determined way from one side of the room to the other and back again. Each time he reached a wall, he slapped it hard with the palm of his left hand.

"I want to see those divorce papers," he said, almost the moment she stepped over the threshold. "Not ours. The first ones."

Chloe tensed, as though he'd slapped her instead of the wall. "They're gone," she said. She'd written the judge in Tombstone for verification, but such things took time.

"What do you mean, 'gone'?" he snapped.

"I mean someone took them," Chloe said, with hard-won patience. "Probably Jack."

"Jack?"

"You were shot in the arm, Jeb, not the head. Jack was my first husband, and you damn well know that. Stop taking your sorry mood out on me, or I'll leave. I've got no reason to be here anyway."

He looked taken aback at her words, even though they had been quietly spoken. For one fanciful moment, she thought he'd apologize for his surly manners, but he set his jaw instead and resumed his pacing.

" 'How was school today, Chloe'?" she prompted, and planted herself directly in his path, with her arms folded.

He glared at her in stubborn silence.

She laughed, surprising them both. "Poor Jeb," she teased. "You're used to doing what you want, when you want to do it. And now, here you are, trapped in a tiny room with nowhere to go. How do you like your own company, Mr. McKettrick?"

"I liked it better than yours," he said, but a grin was teasing the corners of his mouth.

"Too bad," she said, taking the one chair. "I've decided, quite against my better judgment, to stay a while."

He said nothing. He was pacing again. Slapping walls. And every slap was louder than the last one.

She picked up the thick book on his bedside table. "The History of Rome," she read. "My, my. You must be pretty smart."

"For a cowboy?" Jeb gibed.

"For anybody," Chloe said blithely. He'd ruffled her feathers but good, but she wasn't going to let him know it. She opened the tome at the place he'd marked with a cigarette paper. "Page three," she marveled. "Whipping right along, I see."

Whack. He'd reached another wall. "If you came here to annoy me," he huffed, "it's working. Count it as a victory, why don't you, and go away."

She closed the book with a delicate authority and set it back in its place, where it would most likely remain until it sprouted arms and legs. "Why don't you lie down?" she asked, without looking at him. "You're going to wear yourself out."

"Did those papers ever exist?"

Chloe's spine stiffened, but she kept her voice light. "Yes," she said. "And what do you care, anyway?"

"I'd just like to know that I'm not a bigamist, that's all."

"I guess you'll have to take my word."

"I don't have to do anything," he retorted, "but eat, sleep, and ride horses. Why didn't you say anything about him, Chloe? Before we went through with that charade of a wedding, I mean?"

The "charade" had been quite real, but she'd given up trying to convince him of that, so she didn't comment. "Why did you tell me that you were from Stockton?" she countered.

He was silent a while, except for the shuffling and the wall-slapping. His answer, when it finally came, left Chloe shaken. "I guess I wanted to think you were marrying me, not the Triple M and my pa's money."

She turned in her chair, met his gaze, less ferocious than before, but still full of obstinate challenge. "How could I have married you for that blasted ranch when I didn't even know it existed?"

That one stumped him, judging by his expression. "I asked first," he pointed out, with a shake of his index finger. The motion must have hurt, for he flinched and cupped his right elbow in his hand, but the pain didn't distract him from his cross-examination. "Why didn't you tell me about Jack?" he insisted.

"I was ashamed," she said, and flushed.

He stopped his restless travels, at long last, and came to sit on the edge of the bed, facing her, his eyes bleak. He waited.

"I don't seem to have any luck when it comes to men," she admitted. *I will not cry,* she vowed silently. *I will not.*

"Gosh," he said, with grudging amusement. "Thanks."

"He lied to me, just like you did, and I believed him."

"What happened?"

She sighed. "I met Jack in Sacramento. He was nicely dressed, and he had very polished manners. He began courting me—I think now that he only wanted my stepfather's money, but at the time, I believed he—he loved me. I *wanted* to believe him, get away from home, start my life. Jack went back to Tombstone, and when he sent for me, I joined him there." She paused, frowning, marveling at the naive little fool she'd been back then. Mr. Wakefield had allowed her to attend normal school and obtain her teaching credentials, but neither he nor her mother had seriously expected her to work for a living. They'd wanted her to marry within their social circle, but, given her tendency to speak her mind, the prospects hadn't been good. She'd just about resigned herself to a lifetime of such spinsterly pursuits as throwing tea parties and tatting doilies, when Jack Barrett came along.

Jeb waited passively for her to go on. Perhaps he found her account entertaining. To Chloe, the story was purest humiliation, which was why she'd kept it to herself for so long.

She swallowed. In for a penny, in for a pound. Might as well get it over with. "When I reached Tombstone, I expected Jack to meet the stage, but he didn't. I sat at the depot for two hours, waiting for him." Shame seared her insides at the memory, and she couldn't meet Jeb's gaze, though she felt it as surely as if he'd been touching her with his hands. "Finally, he turned up, gave me some excuse about being delayed in his office at the bank. We were married by a justice of the peace, that very afternoon, and we were on our way to the rooming house where he was staying when a man approached us in the street, and accused my brand-new husband of gunning down his brother for pay. Of course I thought it was a lie, I was so stupid—"

"Never that," Jeb said, watching her intently.

The approbation, small as it was, and hoarsely uttered, gave her the impetus she needed to press on.

"The—the man was drunk, and he was old, too. He drew on Jack, even fired a shot, but it went wide. He couldn't have hit the side of a barn. But Jack—Jack shot him, just the same."

Jeb brushed the side of her face with his fingers, but he didn't speak again.

"It took a man's death to make me see the truth about Jack Barrett," Chloe murmured, seeing the grisly scene again, in her mind, as dazed by the horror of it as she'd been when it happened.

"He got away with it? Barrett, I mean?"

Chloe nodded. "People had seen the old man draw on him, and he'd pulled the trigger, too. Jack said it was self-defense, but it wasn't. He didn't have to shoot anybody—he was so much younger, so much faster. He could have disarmed the fellow, with no bloodshed at all." She shivered, suddenly cold. "I should have gone to the law myself, told them what really happened, but I was scared of what Jack might do. He was furious enough when I left him." She blushed. "We were never—together, Jack and I."

Jeb's hand lingered on her cheek, was gentle there, but she couldn't tell what he was thinking. She needed some sort of response from him, no matter what it was.

"Well," she said tartly, "I've told you the whole story. Are you satisfied now?"

He left her standing in the middle of the room, went back to the bed, swung his legs up onto the mattress, and settled back into a pile of pillows. "How about a game of checkers?" he asked, as if she hadn't just poured her heart out at his feet.

She stared at him, confounded. "Is that all you're going to say?"

"I need to think things over some," he replied. "Black or red?"

It took her a moment to realize he was still talking about checkers. "You're impossible!" she accused.

"I can beat you in five moves," he said, with a slight smile.

She was competitive, especially where Jeb was concerned, and this was a challenge she couldn't ignore. "Black," she said, and drew a chair up close to the bed, watching carefully as he prepared the board.

They were still playing when the sun set, and Becky came in to light the lamps. She disappeared, only to return minutes later, followed by Sarah, each of them carrying a tray of food.

"Who's winning?" Becky asked.

"I am," Jeb said, without hesitation. Unfortunately, that was quite true, but Chloe hadn't given up hope of prevailing.

"Kade's here," Becky told them, setting Jeb's supper tray in his lap. "He and Mandy are downstairs in the dining room."

Jeb surveyed his plate, as if taking inventory, picked up a chicken leg, bit into it, and spoke with his mouth half-full. "All this attention," he said. "I may get spoiled."

For a moment, Becky looked as if she meant to tousle his hair, though she must have thought better of the inclination, for she refrained. "Yes," she said. "The sky may get blue, too."

He laughed at that, and Chloe found herself envying Becky a little. If *she'd* pointed up one of his many faults, however obvious it might be, he would have glared the hide right off her.

Becky went sailing out, Sarah following, and Chloe, starving, concentrated on her supper.

"Tell me about the kids," Jeb said.

Briefly, Chloe was confused; Jeb had a way of changing horses in the middle of the conversational stream. Then she realized he was asking about her students, and since it seemed like a safe subject, she was disposed to enter into a discussion. They hadn't spoken much, while playing checkers, and the confessions she'd made earlier, in regard to Jack, had taken a lot out of her. Anything remotely serious would have been a strain at that point.

"There are the Sussex children," she said, feeling greatly cheered. "Harry wants to be like Kade when he grows up."

Jeb made a noncommittal sound, rather like a grunt.

"I think his younger brothers are only there because Harry is," Chloe went on, warming to the topic.

No response. Why had Jeb initiated this conversation, she wondered, if he didn't intend to participate? On the other hand, whenever he spoke more than two words, they wound up snarling and clawing like a pair of alley cats. It made sense to leave well enough alone.

She liked talking about the children, found it easy. "Jennie's mother works at the Bloody Basin."

"I've met her," Jeb said, helping himself to another piece of chicken.

Chloe felt a sudden thrill of jealousy. "Oh, really?"

His grin was insufferable. "What's the matter, Chloe? Afraid I might be one of her regular customers?"

She bridled. "I don't care one way or the other, Jeb McKettrick."

He was cocksure. "You're a liar."

"If you'd like me to leave, just keep talking like that."

He made a face. "It's okay, Chloe," he said. "All we did was play poker."

"Do you honestly think that's of any interest to me whatsoever?"

He put the tray on the table next to his bed, atop the Roman history, leaned forward, and captured her gaze as surely as if he'd clasped her head in his hands and forced her to meet his eyes. "You're jealous as hell."

Her temper came to a steady simmer. "You're flattering yourself," she said stiffly. "Something you seem to be very good at, I might add."

He chuckled, reached to stroke her cheek with the side of his thumb. "I'm good at a few other things, too. Remember?"

"Am I interrupting something?" The third voice separated them as surely as a cleaver quivering in the floor between them.

Chloe whirled, watched as Kade McKettrick walked into the room, grinning a little. "You ought to make sure the door's shut," he observed, "if you're going to stare into each other's eyes and talk about what you're good at."

Chloe blushed, and so did Jeb, although she suspected he was merely irritated rather than mortally embarrassed, like she was.

"I could come back later," Kade suggested mildly, though his eyes were still alight with mischief.

"That's what I'm afraid of," Jeb retorted.

Chloe set her tray aside and stood, smoothing her skirts. "I'd better go," she said hastily. "I've got tomorrow's lessons to prepare."

"Becky asked me to tell you she has a basket ready for the Jessup kids, whoever they are," Kade remarked, watching her closely. "It's in the kitchen."

Chloe nodded, silently blessing Becky for her unceasing generosity, glanced at Jeb, and got her gaze snagged on his, as easily as that.

"I still want to see those papers," he said.

She slammed the door on her way out.

38

The Jessup wagon was lit from within, the canvas cover glowing in the gathering dusk, and two swaybacked horses grazed nearby, in the deep grass, hobbled. Chloe held her skirts in one hand and Becky's food basket in the other as she made her way over and tapped politely at the tailgate.

There was a hush inside, then the burlap curtain at the back was swept aside by a small, grubby hand, and Walter's face appeared, a pale oval of concern. Recognizing Chloe, he smiled, though cautiously.

"Good evening," she said.

Walter's gaze dropped to the basket she carried. It was covered with a red-and-white checked napkin, and emitted the savory scent of fried chicken.

"Hullo," he said, sobering. Ellen peered around his shoulder. The child needed her face washed and her hair combed, but Chloe let the thought alone, since there was no diplomatic way to broach such a subject.

She smiled and held up the basket, privately wondering what the missing Mr. Jessup expected to do with these children when winter came. "I've brought you some supper."

Walter recoiled ever so slightly. "Charity," he said, with sage contempt.

"All we got is beans," Ellen put in, looking hopefully at the basket.

"This is absolutely *not* charity." Chloe replied to Walter's statement, with conviction. "It's a present."

"What's the difference?" Walter demanded, though he did seem to be wavering slightly.

Chloe considered carefully before she replied. "You give charity when you feel sorry for a person," she said. "A present means you like somebody and want them to be your friend."

Walter weighed the matter, taking obvious care to find the balance. "All right, then," he allowed, at some length. "Long as it's a present."

"It most definitely is," Chloe said firmly, extending the offering.

Ellen licked her lips. "I am purely weary of beans," she confessed.

Chloe smiled at that, though inside, she wanted to weep because there were so many children like the Jessups, living on stubborn pride and very little else. Times were hard, and folks did what they had to to survive. "Do you ever get scared, staying here by yourselves?" she asked, treading lightly onto dangerous ground.

"No," said Walter, very firmly, but Ellen's "Yes" ran right over it.

"We got Pa's rifle," Walter said, giving Ellen a subtle elbow to the ribs.

"But he told you not to shoot it," Ellen pointed out staunchly.

"I could probably find you someone to stay with," Chloe said, still thinking of winter. It was autumn, and the bite of the next season was already in the air.

Both children shook their heads.

"Pa wouldn't like that one bit," Walter explained.

Chloe wished she could get hold of Mr. Jessup's ears and give them a good twist, but he was safe at the Triple M, sleeping with a roof over his head and eating regular meals. She'd catch up with him sooner or later.

"Well," she said, with a smiling sigh, "if you ever need help, you just come and knock on my door. I live in the cottage behind the school."

"We'll bring the basket back tomorrow," Walter said, giving the offer of sanctuary a tacit dismissal, along with Chloe herself. "Meantime, we can look after ourselves."

"When you see your father again," Chloe said, turning to go, "you tell him Miss Wakefield wants a word with him."

Walter nodded, but only after a long, solemn interval of silence. Then the burlap curtain fell back into place, and he and Ellen were reduced to shadows behind a wall of canvas.

Chloe walked slowly back toward the cottage, wondering how she'd ever manage to meet up with Mr. Jessup before the snow flew; they would be traveling in separate directions, he coming in from the Triple M on Friday, after a hard week's work, she going to the Circle C to tutor Lizzie Cavanagh at the very same time. Perhaps they might meet on the road.

Lost in thought, she took a shortcut through the cemetery, meaning to stop by John Lewis's grave on the way, and say a brief howdy-do.

Jack startled her by stepping out from behind a tree, as if he'd been spun from the darkness itself.

"Hullo, Chloe," he said, as cordially as if they'd met at a pie social, or in front of the mercantile on a sunny morning, instead of a dark churchyard, surrounded by the slumbering dead.

She put a hand to her heart, which seemed to be looking for a way out, whether through her throat or by bursting her chest open. "Jack," she gasped. "What are you doing here?"

"Came to see you."

"Well, you're wasting your time."

He merely grinned at that, effectively blocking her way when she tried to pass. He lit a cheroot and drew deeply on the smoke, the ember glowing in the chilly gloom. "I reckon you didn't expect to run into me," he observed. She looked up into his hard face, faintly pitted by an early case of smallpox, and asked herself what she'd been thinking, in the first days of their ill-fated acquaintance, when she'd counted him as handsome, and a gentleman.

"You took the divorce papers," she accused. She was full of trepidation, but she let none of it show into her voice or her manner. "I want them back."

"Chloe," he said, in a wheedling croon. He moved to touch her face, and she stepped back out of his reach. "Has he spoiled you for me, your fancy man?" he asked, sounding wounded now. Grievously wronged.

In that moment, a horrible possibility dawned upon Chloe. She had not entertained it before, thinking Jack was still in Tombstone, about his nefarious purposes, but now it was right there, in the forefront of her mind, and would not be ignored. "Did you shoot Jeb McKettrick?" she asked.

"Of course not," he scolded mildly. "Why would I do that?"

"I can think of a thousand reasons," she said, wanting to turn and run, and staying because she knew he'd bring her down in a few strides if she made the attempt. If she screamed, he would strike her, maybe even shoot her.

"Does he touch you, Chloe?" The question was hoarsely uttered, and there was pain in it, though she didn't credit it with any substance. One thing she knew about Jack Barrett: He was cold, clear through to his soul. "Does he put his hands on you?"

"That's none of your business."

He blew a smoke ring. "It's my business, all right."

"I'm his wife."

"You're *my* wife."

She shook her head. Retrieving the divorce papers was the least of her worries now; she wanted to escape, that was all. Just get away. "Let me by," she said coldly, and started past him again.

He grabbed her arm, yanked her against his chest. "I've got money now, Chloe," he said, breathing whiskey fumes into her face. The smell nauseated her, but not as much as the fear she felt. She was choking on that. "Come away with me. Right now, tonight. We'll be done with this place, start over someplace else."

She wrenched free and put a few yards between them, dodging when he tried to grab her again. "No," she said. "*No*. Do you hear me? It's over. We're not married anymore. We never *were* married, in any true sense of the word."

He pushed back his coat, revealing the .44 caliber pistol he always carried, and Chloe thought he might actually have shot her, if not for the sound of a rifle cocking nearby.

"Leave her alone, mister," said Walter Jessup. He might have been a child, but it was a man doing the talking, and from the timbre of his voice, he was in deadly earnest.

"Walter," Chloe said firmly, "give me that gun. This instant."

Walter obeyed, but reluctantly, and Chloe aimed the barrel straight at Jack Barrett's middle.

"I'm taking you to the marshal's office," she said, with resolve, audacity being all that was left to her, besides the gun, which would be of little use if she couldn't pull the trigger. "So you might as well put up your hands."

He laughed at her. "You wouldn't shoot me," he said.

The hell of it was, he was right. She might despise Jack, but he was a living, breathing human being, and when he turned his back and walked away, disappearing into the darkness, she let him go.

"You should have nailed him," Walter said.

Chloe held the rifle like a cane, barrel up, and willed the strength back into her knees. In the near distance, she heard Jack speak impatiently to his horse, heard saddle leather creak as he mounted.

"He's getting away," Walter told her, with some urgency.

"Go find the marshal," Chloe said, with a wave of one hand. "Tell him to come to the cottage. I'll talk to him there."

Though it was plainly against his wishes, Walter hurried away to do her bidding.

39

"*I* don't want Jeb to know about this," Chloe told Sam Fee, as he sat beside her on the cottage steps. She'd leaned Walter's rifle against the wall when she got back, knowing he'd come to reclaim it.

Sam, having absorbed her account of the incident in the churchyard in somber silence, along with her theory that Jack Barrett had been the one to shoot Jeb, sighed and thrust himself to his feet.

"Why would this feller want to do a thing like that?" he asked. "Shoot a man right out of the saddle, I mean?"

Chloe bit her lower lip. This was the part she wished she didn't have to tell. "Because he and I were married once," she said miserably. "Now, I'm Jeb's wife, even if we are getting divorced, and Jack hates him for it." She remembered the way her one-day husband had pushed back his coat, in order to put his .44 within easy reach, and shuddered. "He hates me, too."

Sam surveyed the darkened landscape, as though he

could see for miles. "Where do you figure this no-gooder was headed, when he left here?"

She shook her head, holding her middle with both arms. "I thought he was in Tombstone," she murmured. "All this time, *I thought he was in Tombstone.*"

"You figure he might have been the one to rob the stage, too? Murder that driver and the woman?"

"Yes. He's a professional gunslinger," Chloe said wretchedly. Her temples were throbbing, as if attempting to meet in the middle of her brain and form a single pulse there. "He said he had money. And those two people on the Circle C, the man and the boy, he probably killed them, too."

Sam laid a hand on her shoulder. They were not well acquainted, but she knew this was an unprecedented gesture for him. He was a taciturn sort of man and had never shown sentiment in her presence. "I can't promise Jeb won't find out about this," he said gravely. "He'll be mad as hell, I reckon."

A single tear slipped down Chloe's cheek, and she raised her eyes to Sam's face, entreating. "He'll go after him if you say anything," she said. "And he'll be gunned down—you know it as well as I do, Sam. Jack has killed a lot of men. Jeb won't have a chance, with his arm the way it is."

Sam was still for a long time, but then he gave one abrupt nod. "I reckon that's exactly what he'd do, go right after the feller. Trouble is, much as I'd like to think I could round this outlaw up on my own, I'm going to need help, and that means going to the McKettricks. It would be a poor posse without them."

Chloe swallowed. Nodded. "I know," she said, as Walter came around the corner of the schoolhouse, bent, most likely, on recovering his father's rifle. "Just make sure you don't talk to them in Jeb's presence. They'll tell you the same thing, Sam—Angus, Kade, Rafe—all of them—that he mustn't know about this until it's over."

"Most likely, you're right about that," he said thoughtfully. "I'll ride out to the Triple M and speak to Angus in the morning."

"Thank you," Chloe said.

Sam answered with a nod and took his leave. He ruffled Walter's hair as the two of them passed each other.

"I'll need that rifle, Teacher," Walter said, facing her.

She reached for the hateful thing, handed it over carefully. "I've got a favor to ask of you," she told him, when he would have turned away without another word. "There's something else I need to say first, though. You probably saved my life tonight, Walter, and I'm grateful. You were very brave."

His small, dirty face was expressionless, and he said nothing.

"What were you doing out there in the cemetery, anyhow?" she asked. "I should have thought you'd stay in the wagon with Ellen, eating Mrs. Fairmont's fried chicken."

"I get feelin's sometimes," he said. "A sort of pinch in

the bottom of my belly. Always means trouble, when that happens." That, plainly, was all the explanation she was going to get, since he fell into a ponderous silence as soon as the words were out of his mouth. He was waiting, she knew, to hear the favor she'd mentioned.

"It's really important," she said evenly, "that you and I don't talk to other people about tonight. Not right away."

He crooked an eyebrow. "You told the marshal," he reasoned.

She nodded. "Yes. I had to do that. But there's a man—if he hears about it, this man, I mean, he might go right out and get himself killed."

"Damn fool thing to do," Walter observed stalwartly.

Chloe's smile felt wobbly on her mouth, perhaps because its roots didn't reach into her heart. "I absolutely agree," she said. "But since we're *dealing* with a damn fool, we have to be careful."

Walter shrugged, holding the heavy rifle easily in one hand, as though it were a stick he'd picked up off the ground, to play with, or a fishing pole, instead of a deadly weapon that weighed nearly as much as he did.

"All right, then," he agreed, and turned to go. He paused, looked back at her over one shoulder. "Obliged for that fried chicken," he said brusquely. "We got plenty of beans, but Ellen favors a drumstick somethin' fierce."

If he'd been closer, and not looking as though he wanted to bolt like a deer catching a hunter's scent on the wind, Chloe might have touched his face, or even embraced him.

"I'll pass the word on to Mrs. Fairmont," she said. "She'll be glad you enjoyed it."

Walter nodded. "See you in the mornin', Teacher."

Chloe smiled, and this time, it wasn't a strain. "Good night, Walter."

40

*L*izzie peered into the cradle at the baby, there in the cozy kitchen at the Triple M, and decided she'd gotten a little better looking since the last viewing. Her face wasn't so red, or so crinkly, and her dark hair didn't stick out around her head the way it had the first couple of times she'd seen her. It looked as if somebody had spit on their fingertips, the way her mother used to do with her, and smoothed it down.

Concepcion laid a hand on Lizzie's shoulder. Over their heads, above the sturdy roof, above the clouds, the sky rumbled. "Would you like to hold her?"

Lizzie looked up at her grandfather's wife in amazement. "You'd let me do that?"

"Of course I would," Concepcion said, in a whispery voice. "As soon as she wakes up from her nap."

"Thunderation," Lizzie marveled. "Nobody ever let me hold a baby before."

Concepcion smiled. Her eyes were a warm shade of brown, like strong coffee, but sparkling, and her dark hair gleamed, neatly braided and wound into a coronet at the back of her head. She was like an angel, Lizzie thought, smelling of cinnamon and lemon and talcum powder, Concepcion was, and being around her, she didn't miss her mama quite so much. "Come and sit close to the stove, and I will make us both a cup of hot chocolate."

The men, including her papa, were closed away in the big study at the other end of the house, talking with Sam Fee, the marshal, so Lizzie and Concepcion had the kitchen to themselves, except for the baby, of course, and she didn't make much of a difference unless she was crying. When she got to squalling, though, there was no ignoring her.

"Is Katie my cousin?" she asked. It was a question she'd been trying to work out since the baby's arrival, and one she hadn't quite dared to bring up with her papa.

Concepcion set a pan on the stove, humming. She seemed happy most of the time, and even when she was frowning at one of the men, her eyes went right on smiling. "Katie," she said, "is your aunt."

Lizzie thought hard, picturing her aunt Geneva. "But Katie's *little*," she countered. "And I'm big. How can she be my aunt?"

"You certainly are big," Concepcion agreed, slicing a chunk of dark, bitter chocolate into the pan on the stove and reaching for the sugar bowl. "Katie is your papa's sister, though, and that means she's your aunt."

"That beats all," Lizzie said. She wasn't sure she liked

the idea of having an aunt who was only a baby. Did that mean she'd have to let Katie boss her around, when she got so she could talk?

Concepcion laughed. "*Sí,*" she said. Then, "Yes." As if Lizzie wouldn't know what "*sí*" meant, growing up in San Antonio the way she had.

She didn't take offense, though. She settled herself in the rocking chair, close to the stove and stiffened when lightning lit the glass in the window. "Is my uncle Jeb coming home soon?" she ventured to ask. This, too, was a question she hadn't wanted to put to her papa. Even though he came to the Triple M willingly enough, like he had today, he always set his jaw when she said the name "McKettrick." He was still put out, she supposed, over being left behind in Texas when he was no bigger than a puppy.

Concepcion stopped making hot chocolate and leaned down to kiss the top of Lizzie's head. "Yes, little one. He will be back soon."

"Somebody shot him." In her mind, Lizzie saw her aunt Geneva fall down, bleeding. Saw the stage driver fold to the ground with a terrible grace. Back of it all loomed the wicked man, with the bandanna over his face.

She shivered.

"Your uncle is very strong. He will be fine." She went back to the stove and stirred the mixture of sugar and chocolate with a wooden spoon, adding a chunk of yellow butter.

"My aunt Geneva was strong, too," Lizzie said. "And she died. Papa says she's buried in town, and he'll take me to her grave when I've had some time to heal up." She frowned, puzzled. "I *told* him I didn't get hurt."

There were tears in Concepcion's eyes, though she tried to hide them by turning her head. When that failed, she crossed herself with a hasty motion of one hand, then dabbed at her face with the corner of her apron. "There are many kinds of wounds, Lizzie," she said, with a sniffle. "You should not have to bear such a memory."

"I do cry sometimes, when I know Papa won't see."

Concepcion sniffled again. "You have had too much sadness in your life," she said, though she wasn't looking at Lizzie, but staring through the window over the sink, and stirring away. "It is not right, for a child to endure so much tragedy."

"Papa says things will get better."

A shoulder-moving sigh, another faltering smile. "Your papa is right."

The door leading into the corridor swung open. "Now there's a rare idea," Holt said, grinning a little, though he looked sad around the eyes and a little angry, too. "I'm right about something?"

Concepcion blinked, in the way of someone waking up from a daydream. "Where is your father?" she asked Holt.

"I wasn't aware that I had one."

She gave him one of those looks and tightened her

mouth. Lizzie watched with interest as Concepcion's stare found its mark. She wondered if that trick would work for her, too. Her papa needed a great deal of managing, to her way of thinking, and he was a stubborn case.

He sighed. "He's out front, seeing Sam off."

"And your brothers?"

Holt lowered his eyebrows. This time, he was the one doing the staring.

"Kade and Rafe," Concepcion said, saying the names slowly, as if he might not have heard them before. "Are they still here?"

Concepcion was worried about something, Lizzie decided, and it concerned her uncles, whom she liked very much. Which meant that Lizzie was worried, too.

"Gone to the barn," Holt said. "To saddle their horses."

Concepcion flinched. "They did not come through the kitchen," she reflected, and whatever that meant, she didn't seem pleased about it.

Holt gripped the back of Lizzie's chair and set it to a gentle rocking. "Smarter than they look," he observed.

Lizzie wished grown-ups would talk plain English. It wasn't as if she didn't know they were hiding something from her.

"I'm getting a teacher," she said, because she was scared all of a sudden, because she could feel the thunder, no longer just a faraway rumble, high in the clouds, settle in the center of her chest. She needed to talk about something cheerful. "It's Miss Wakefield, from the school in town. She's going to stay at our house from Friday to Sunday, every week."

Concepcion's gaze ricocheted past her, to land on Holt. "Does Chloe know Jeb is going to be staying there, too?"

Lizzie glanced up just in time to see a smile spread across her father's handsome face.

"It's the surprises," he said, "that make life interesting."

41

For Chloe, the rest of that week went by with all the speedy dispatch of a centipede slogging through a puddle of molasses. During the day, she taught classes. After school, she visited Jeb, weighted with her necessary but unwieldy secret and the guilt it caused her. During those times, they either argued, played checkers, or both, but there was no more mention of the missing divorce papers. She had that to be grateful for, at least.

At night, she tossed and turned, starting at every sound, afraid to close her eyes lest she open them to see Jack leaning over her. She kept the derringer close at hand, either in the pocket of her skirt or on the table beside her bed.

When Friday afternoon finally arrived, and Holt came personally to collect her, she was looking forward to a change of scene. He took her box of supplies under one arm and grasped the handle of her reticule in the opposite hand. He seemed subdued, and when they rounded the schoolhouse and Chloe saw the wagon waiting in the road, with its sole passenger, she knew why.

Jeb sat, grim and pale, in the seat.

Chloe stopped in her tracks, shot a sidelong glance at Holt. "I do not," she said, "intend to ride with Jeb McKettrick."

"Why not? According to Becky, you've been playing checkers with him all week."

"Where are you taking him?"

"Back to the Circle C. He works for me."

"You mean he and I are going to be under the same roof? *Overnight?*"

Holt smiled slightly. "A deal's a deal, Miss Wakefield," he said.

"But you didn't say—"

"Lizzie's waiting. She's real eager to get an education."

Chloe set her jaw. "That's dirty dealing, dragging Lizzie into this!"

"Lizzie's the whole reason you're coming," Holt said reasonably. "Unless, of course, you were serious when you told Jeb you and I were considering marriage."

A hot blush surged into Chloe's face. "You are enjoying this!"

"Yes," Holt said, giving her a nudge toward the wagon. "I am."

She went, but only because of Lizzie.

Jeb looked every bit as confounded as Chloe felt, and

he frowned when Holt helped her up into the seat. She would be in the middle, squished between the two of them. She squirmed a little and fixed her gaze straight ahead while trying to collect her thoughts.

Out of the side of her eye, she saw Jeb tug at the brim of his hat, noted the look of wry irritation on his face. "Afternoon, Miss Wakefield," he said, though he was watching Holt now. "I certainly didn't expect to run into you. Since you *said* you'd be busy making lesson plans all weekend."

Chloe lifted her chin, turned her head in Jeb's direction. "And you *didn't* say that you were planning to do any traveling."

With a low word to the horses, Holt slapped down the reins and set the wagon in sudden motion. When Chloe glanced at him, she caught him with another grin on his face.

"Have you ever told the truth about anything in your life?" Jeb demanded, plainly addressing her.

Color boiled up Chloe's neck, and she straightened her spine. If Jeb still thought she was a liar, even after she'd told him about her marriage to Jack, what would he say when he learned that she'd known who shot him and kept the knowledge from him?

"Have you?" she countered.

The ride to the Circle C seemed even longer than the week just past.

By the time they arrived, it was nearly dark. Lizzie ran

out to meet them, followed by Mandy McKettrick, who had apparently been recruited to look after her while Holt was gone.

"Uncle Jeb!" the little girl crowed, face alight.

"Hey, kid," Jeb answered. He's been disagreeable all the way from town, but now, all of a sudden, he was his old, charming self. Had the recipient of that smile been anyone but Lizzie, Chloe would have been furious.

She'd felt Holt stiffen beside her, at the child's exuberant greeting, though he recovered quickly, setting the brake lever and getting down from the wagon box.

Mandy smiled up at Chloe, making her feel welcome just that easily. "Lizzie's been waiting for you," she said, ignoring the men. "We've got your room all ready, and supper's cooking, too."

Chloe gave the other woman a grateful look.

Meanwhile, Jeb left the wagon on his own; nobody would have dared try to help him. He held up his left hand to Chloe, his eyes challenging her to spurn the grudging gesture.

She hesitated, then relented, seeing no graceful way to refuse, and stepped down with all the dignity she could manage.

Lizzie beamed up at her. "I can already read pretty well," she announced.

Chloe laughed and leaned over to look directly into Lizzie's eyes. "Wonderful," she said. "Then perhaps *you* can teach *me* a thing or two."

"You might start with something biblical," Jeb suggested, from beside her. " 'God hates a liar' would be appropriate."

Chloe turned a scathing gaze on him. "Or," she suggested, in a purposely sweet voice, " 'Judge not that ye be not judged.' Or, perhaps, 'Let him who is without sin cast the first stone.' "

He scowled, but before he could reply, Mandy stepped forward and linked her arm with his. "Come inside," she said, with cheerful determination, her tone indicating that she'd drag him if he didn't go peacefully. "You could do with some supper. Might improve your disposition."

"I didn't know you could cook," Jeb said, momentarily distracted.

Mandy fluttered her lashes. "There are a great many things you don't know," she replied. "But you're not entirely hopeless." With that, she pulled him up the porch steps.

Holt carried in Chloe's things, asked Lizzie to show her to her room, and went out again, probably to put away the team and wagon.

Chloe's quarters were upstairs, and comfortable, for a remote ranch house. The ceiling slanted, and there was only one window, but a needlepoint rug graced the floor, and the bedspread, though worn, was pretty. Someone, probably Mandy, had left a cracked jug on the nightstand, its narrow opening jammed with pretty grasses.

"Papa's got a lot of books," Lizzie said, sitting on the

bed with a little bounce. "So if you didn't bring any, that's all right."

"I did bring some, though," Chloe assured her. She went to the bureau, poured fresh water from a china pitcher into a mismatched bowl. She splashed her face, dried it with a flour-sack towel, then washed her hands with lavender soap. "Does your papa read a great deal?"

Lizzie shrugged. "I haven't seen him do it, 'cause he's real busy with the ranch," she said, "but he must, because he knows a lot."

Yes, Chloe thought, a little sourly, *he knows plenty. For instance, he knew Jeb was coming here, but he didn't trouble himself to mention it to me.*

She unpinned her hat, set it aside, and took off her fitted jacket. She would speak to Mr. Holt Cavanagh later, she promised herself. In the meantime, she would occupy herself with Lizzie, and with supper, and the formidable task of ignoring Jeb.

42

When Lizzie and Chloe reached the table, Holt and Jeb were already seated there, and Kade, with a fresh-air swirl of arrival surrounding him, was just hanging up his coat and hat. Chloe felt a little pang of envy as she watched him kiss Mandy, and shifted her gaze, only to have it collide hard with Jeb's.

She flushed at the impact and turned her eyes to the floor.

Kade, meanwhile, focused his attention on Jeb. "Well, now," he said. "Here's my little brother, up and around."

Through her lashes, Chloe saw Jeb bristle and figured it was the words "little brother" that got under his skin, even though they had not been spoken unkindly.

Jeb simply watched Kade, without speaking, but his thoughts were clear in his eyes, and they were not affable ones.

Kade smiled, slapped his disgruntled brother on the left shoulder. There was a rough sort of tenderness in the gesture, aimed as it was at the side that didn't hurt, though Jeb probably didn't appreciate the distinction. "We miss you down at the Triple M," Kade said. "Nobody to pick on."

Jeb grinned, though unwillingly. "You'll get along," he answered.

Mandy had busied herself serving supper, and Chloe went to help. The meal was a sizable one, a venison roast, potatoes, and three kinds of vegetables, plus biscuits and gravy, and as Chloe lifted her fork, she couldn't help thinking of the Jessup children, alone in that wagon behind the church, and of little Jennie, probably pilfering food from the saloon.

"There's a man named Jessup working on your ranch," Chloe said to Kade, when the moment seemed right. "If you're acquainted with him, I'd like you to pass on a message."

"I know him," Kade said good-naturedly. "What shall I say?"

"Tell Mr. Jessup, please, that I want to speak with him about his children," Chloe answered. "At his earliest convenience."

Kade nodded. "Done."

She reached for a biscuit, and her hand bumped into Jeb's over the basket. They both drew back as if they'd been burned, and it seemed to Chloe that everyone at the table noticed, though nothing was said. They had a way of smiling behind their eyes, these McKettricks, while their lips remained still.

After that, she stole only the occasional glance at Jeb, and with each one, he seemed to be paler. It had only been a few days since the shooting, not to mention the surgery. He should have been at the hotel, in bed, not way out here on the Circle C, showing the effects of a long and uncomfortable wagon ride. She wished he'd excuse himself—he'd hardly touched his supper anyway—and take his surly self off to wherever Holt meant for him to sleep, but she knew he wouldn't leave before everyone else, lest he miss something. Like a chance to nettle her.

"Tomorrow," Lizzie told Jeb brightly, barely able to contain her delight at his presence, "I'll show you where I mean to keep my pony, once I get one."

"Tomorrow," Holt corrected his daughter, with quiet firmness, and a sour glance at Jeb, "you will be busy studying with Miss Wakefield."

Jeb seemed to find something funny in her name, for he gave a desultory little snort and repeated, "Miss Wakefield," under his breath, but still loudly enough for everyone to hear.

Lizzie frowned in disapproval. "Polite people," she told her uncle frankly, "do not snort."

Kade, having just taken a sip of coffee, was constrained to keep the stuff in his mouth long enough to swallow. His eyes danced. "You keep your uncle Jeb on the straight and narrow path for us, will you, Lizzie?" he said, when he'd managed the crisis. "It's a big job, but I reckon you can handle it."

Jeb looked both annoyed and chagrined. "Sorry," he said, addressing the apology to Lizzie and, very pointedly, to Lizzie alone.

After that, the talk turned to cattle, and droughts, and the coming of a hard winter. Something about the caterpillars having more fur and the behavior of squirrels. Chloe was relieved that the conversation did not touch on the recent shootings, which probably would have been the main topic, if Jeb and Lizzie hadn't been there.

When the meal was over, Chloe and Lizzie set about doing the dishes, and Mandy and Kade said their goodbyes and left for the Triple M. Holt squired Jeb out of the kitchen, though he plainly didn't want to go, to show him to his room.

Chloe wished him good riddance as she swabbed a plate clean at the sink, up to her elbows in hot water and soap suds. Lizzie stood on a chair beside her, dish towel in hand, working efficiently.

"I understand you lived in Texas before you came to the Arizona Territory," Chloe said, because her mind kept straying after Jeb, and a change of subject seemed a good way of tugging on the leash. Besides, she was genuinely interested in Lizzie, already felt a bond growing between them.

Lizzie nodded. "With my mama and my aunt Geneva," she said. She was such a sturdy little thing, adult in many ways, but at the same time, delicate, a wild rose, just beginning to bud. "I didn't know I even *had* a papa back then. Sure would have come in handy."

Chloe wasn't about to venture into that territory, considering it to be private ground, but she was powerfully curious, just the same. People fascinated her, especially children. What complex creatures they were, playing out their secret, inner dramas. "Did your mother remarry?"

Lizzie shook her head. "I don't think she ever got married in the first place," she replied sagely. "Mama said the last thing she needed was a man around, making demands and getting underfoot."

Chloe smiled. She could certainly empathize with *that* philosophy; hadn't her own experiences borne it out, not once, but twice? "How did she earn a living?"

"She was a seamstress," Lizzie said matter-of-factly. "So was Aunt Geneva. We had a pretty big house in San Antonio, and sometimes they took in boarders, when the money ran low."

"No wonder your clothes are so fine," Chloe remarked. Lizzie's dress *was* well cut, and the fabric was of very high quality, although she was outgrowing it. "Your mother must have made them for you."

Again, Lizzie nodded. Looking bemused now, she stared at the darkened window over the sink, as if she were seeing something far beyond the glass, beyond even the rangelands that spread into the vast, lonely distance. "I miss Mama so much," she confessed, in a small voice. "I mostly get by all right in the daytime, but it's harder at night."

Chloe's heart seized with sympathy. Soap suds and all,

she put her arms around the little girl, held her very close for a moment. "I'm sure you do, Sweetheart," she said. "Oh, of *course* you do."

Lizzie clung to her, tightly. "You smell like her," she murmured. "Like flowers and rain."

"I don't believe anyone has ever paid me a better compliment," Chloe said, kissing the top of Lizzie's head, and it was only then that she noticed Holt standing in the inside doorway, watching with sorrow in his expressive eyes and that helplessness that is peculiar to men when faced with the deeper needs of women and children.

"Finish up there, Lizzie," he said, as though Chloe's notice had brought him to life. "You've got a lot of learning to do tomorrow."

Chloe gave the child a final squeeze. "I'll manage the dishes on my own," she said quietly. "Your papa is right. It is very important that you get some rest."

Lizzie had regained her dignity—Chloe suspected it never strayed very far, that indeed it was inherent to the child's nature—and, extracting herself from her teacher's embrace, she got down from the chair, said good night to both adults, and left the room.

Holt walked over to the stove, poured leftover coffee into a mug, and took a measured sip.

"Lizzie is a lovely child," Chloe said. "Exceedingly bright, too. Teaching her will be a delight."

Holt nodded, but his face looked grim. "Yes," he agreed, without looking at Chloe. "I owe you an apology,

Miss Wakefield," he went on, after a few more thoughtful draughts of coffee. "I should have told you ahead of time that Jeb would be here."

"Yes," Chloe agreed, scrubbing industriously at the pot Mandy had used to boil the potatoes they'd had with supper. "You should have. But you didn't, and your reasons were sound enough—you were concerned about Lizzie. For that reason, I will accept your regrets."

He gave a sheepish grin. "Thank you for understanding."

Chloe had little choice but to be gracious. She cared deeply for Lizzie's welfare, for that of all her students, but there was another factor as well. Holt could have made an issue of the deception Chloe had perpetrated, by leading Jeb to believe the two of them were thinking of marriage, and he would have been justified in doing so. For some reason, he had chosen not to, and she was grateful.

She turned the conversation in what she hoped was a safe direction. "It must have been quite a surprise to you when Lizzie showed up."

Holt shook his head, marveling. "That's for sure," he said. "If I'd known she existed, I would have brought her home long ago."

Chloe spoke softly. "And her mother?"

He'd turned solemn again. "Her mother, too."

"What was her name?" There she went again, stepping off the path of good manners and whacking her way through the underbrush. Little wonder she'd gotten into so much trouble in her life, plagued by curiosity as she was, not to mention wild impulses. Just then, it occurred to her that she disliked Jeb's reckless qualities so much because they reflected her own, and the thought left her thunderstruck.

"Her name was Olivia," Holt answered. His eyes held an infinite sadness. "She was beautiful, full of spirit. And she was good—half-again too good for me, I can tell you— and brave to the bone." He paused, shook his head again, took another sip of coffee. "I was such a fool back then. I thought we had all the time in the world, Olivia and I."

"Perhaps," she observed, with a twinkle, wanting to ease his way a little, "you're being a trifle too hard on yourself."

Holt's grin returned, and Chloe almost wished they really were going to be married. He was so solid, so intelligent and honorable. It would have been so blessedly simple to love a man like that.

"Thank you," he said, with a slight bow of his head. "Before we get off the subject of fools, though—you're aware, I suppose, that Jeb is acting like a horse's ass because he thinks the real reason you're here is to get better acquainted with me?"

The pot made a clattering sound as Chloe set it on a shelf underneath the sink. "You haven't set him straight on that, I gather?"

"No."

"Why not?" She knew why *she* hadn't told Jeb the truth, of course; he already thought she was a liar, and confessing to something like that would prove it. But Holt's motives baffled her.

"As far as I can tell, my brother has had things go his way most of his life," Holt answered mildly. "I figured a little wondering might be good for his character."

She smiled, relieved. "All the same," she admitted, "I do wish I hadn't said it in the first place. Sometimes my impulses run away with me."

Holt simply watched her for a long moment, and Chloe wondered if he was thinking the same thing she was, that she and Jeb weren't as different as she would have liked to believe. "Guess that makes you human," he said, at last. He thrust out a sigh. "If I'm going to be honest, I have to admit I enjoy being a burr under the McKettricks' saddles now and again. Nothing admirable in it, but it's the way of things."

Both Emmeline and Becky had told Chloe about the enmity between Holt and his father and brothers; but he was civil with Kade and plainly fond of Mandy, and when Jeb had been shot, he'd come to town to join the others in their vigil. Perhaps, Chloe reflected, he cared more for his family than he knew.

When Chloe didn't speak, Holt went on. "I guess it's not Jeb's fault, or Kade's or Rafe's, that the old man didn't want to be bothered with me," he said, without a trace of self-pity.

For a moment, Chloe wanted to put her arms around Holt, just as she'd done with Lizzie earlier, but of course she refrained, because embracing him wouldn't be the same. Not at *all* the same.

She bit her lip, unsure of what to say.

Holt smiled. "Now that we've discussed my family," he said, "let's talk about yours. Becky says your people live in Sacramento. What do they think of your being way out here in the wild country, all on your own?"

Chloe gave a rueful sigh. "I'm sure they wouldn't approve."

He looked troubled. "They don't know where you are?"

She straightened her shoulders. "No. Mother and Mr. Wakefield were traveling in Europe, last I heard, so it wasn't as if I could get word to them easily." She folded the dish towel, laid it aside. "Besides, they pretty much washed their hands of me when I went to Tombstone against their wishes." *When I married Jack.*

"You ought to write to them or send a telegram," Holt reasoned. "They've probably cooled off by now. Most likely, they're fretting."

Suddenly, there were tears in Chloe's eyes; she blinked them back furiously. "What would I say? That they were right, and I should have stayed home and crocheted edgings for pillowcases for the rest of my natural life? That I've made a spectacular mess of everything—again?"

"It's not hard to put myself in their place," Holt said

quietly. "If that happened with Lizzie, I'd sure as hell want to hear from her, no matter how angry I might be, or how much of a 'mess' she might have made."

Chloe folded her arms, gazed at the floor for a long time, digesting this. When she looked up at Holt again, she heard herself ask, "Do you think Jeb is resting comfortably?"

Holt's gaze was level, and she knew he was seeing more than she wanted to reveal. "His pride's smarting. He's tired, and he's in some pain, but he'll be his old devil-take-the-hindmost self again soon enough. It would take more than a bullet in the arm to bring down anybody with Angus McKettrick's blood in his veins." He paused, rubbed the back of his neck, chuffed out a sigh. "Chloe, we've been beating around the bush long enough. I think it's a mistake not to tell Jeb that Barrett confronted you in that cemetery, and that your ex-husband is most likely the one who shot him. When he finds out— and he *will* find out—he's going to be furious that you kept him in the dark."

"I *couldn't* tell him," Chloe said, with quiet, plaintive dread. "Holt, you *know* what would happen—Jeb would drag himself onto a horse and go right out after Barrett, and ten to one, he'd get himself killed in the process!"

Holt looked patently miserable, and he sighed again. "I know the reasoning; I've been over it a hundred times with Angus and the boys. It still bothers me because I know how I'd feel in his place—mad as a rooster trapped under a bucket." He regarded her solemnly for a long moment. "Jeb will be ready to strip our hides, but *you're* the one he's going to blame, Chloe. There's a good chance he'll never forgive you."

"He's already written me off," Chloe said, full of despairing conviction. "Oh, he doesn't mind a game of checkers once in a while, or a good argument, but you saw how he acted tonight. He can hardly tolerate my presence."

A rueful grin crooked one corner of Holt's mouth. "Like I said earlier, his pride's hurt. Right now, he's probably lying up there wondering if you and I are down here planning a honeymoon. Believe me, Chloe, if he'd written you off, wounded or not, he'd be sparking some other woman right now."

"And he'd be better off," Chloe said sadly. "If it hadn't been for me, Jack wouldn't have shot him." She felt the blood drain from her face and had to stiffen her knees to stay upright. "Lizzie's aunt would be alive, too."

Holt approached her then, laid his hands on her shoulders. He'd just opened his mouth to speak when the door opened, and Jeb stepped into the room.

His blue gaze skewered Chloe. "You certainly are resilient," he said coldly. "I'll give you that."

Holt took a step back, let his hands fall to his sides. "Jeb—"

"I'll sleep in the bunkhouse," Jeb said.

Holt's jaw tightened. "You can sleep in the chicken coop, for all I care," he said, "but you'll hear me out first."

Chloe looked from one man to the other, too stricken to say anything at all, which, she concluded distractedly, was probably good since she usually said the wrong thing.

Jeb leaned his uninjured shoulder against the door-frame, and Chloe knew it was because his strength was ebbing. She wanted, incomprehensibly, to go to him, try to hold him up somehow, but the contempt in his face kept her frozen in place. "All right, Mr. *Cavanagh*," he said acidly, "say your piece."

Chloe interlaced her fingers and braced herself, while Holt glared at Jeb. "Chloe has no intention of marrying me," Holt said. "She just wanted to make you jealous, that's all. But here's where you'd best do some fancy listening, little brother—if I thought she'd have me, I'd take her for a wife as soon as I could round up a preacher."

Jeb opened his mouth, closed it again.

Chloe thought she'd swoon and gripped the back of a chair to support herself.

"You'd have to wait for the divorce to come through," Jeb said evenly.

"Would I?" Holt shot back. "To hear you tell it, there never was a marriage in the first place."

Jeb had gone a shade paler, but it was rage, not shock, Chloe knew, that was inhibiting his circulation. His gaze shifted to her, searing. "Do you want him, Chloe?" he asked dangerously.

She bit her lower lip, cast an apologetic glance at Holt, and blushed hard. "No," she said, in a very small voice.

Holt pulled that McKettrick trick again, smiling behind his eyes. But there was sadness in him, too.

Jeb looked triumphant, until Chloe spoke again.

"But I wish I did."

An ominous silence fell. Then, somewhere in the front of the house, a clock chimed, sounding ten ponderous strokes that seemed to echo through the walls.

"Time I turned in," Holt said, and walked right out of the kitchen, forcing Jeb to step aside or be run over. Chloe had barely restrained herself from grabbing at Holt's sleeve as he passed.

"What the hell did you mean by that?" Jeb demanded, when he and Chloe were alone. "You *wish you wanted him?*"

Chloe folded her arms, now that she was fairly sure her legs wouldn't give out. "Exactly what I said," she replied.

Jeb's eyes were round with indignation and disbelief. "*Why?*"

"Because he's a grown man," Chloe said, blushing again. "Not some hotheaded—"

"Kid?" Jeb finished for her, in a scathing undertone. "You seemed to think I was as much a man as anybody the other night, in your bed—"

"Stop!" Chloe cried, putting her hands to her ears.

He crossed to her, grasped her right hand, and wrenched it down. "Did you wish you wanted Holt then, Chloe?" he rasped.

She closed her eyes. "No," she whispered.

Jeb wouldn't let her alone. "What's different now?

Tell me. Is it this fancy house? All this land? The money in his bank account?"

She would have slapped him, if he hadn't been wounded. "*Damn* you," she spat. "It's the fact that I can talk to him without having to defend myself at every turn! It's his common sense and it's—it's Lizzie!"

Jeb released her. "Christ," he breathed, looking astounded. "We really *were* married."

"I've been trying to tell you that all along," Chloe snapped. "And we *are* married, more's the pity—the divorce won't be final for a year."

He narrowed his eyes. "Yeah," he agreed bitterly. "More's the pity." He was about to leave the room, maybe the house, she could see it in the way he drew back, the way he held himself.

"Just tell me one thing," she said hastily. "What finally convinced you that I was telling the truth about our wedding?"

Jeb gave a mocking, humorless grin. "If you could have gotten hitched to Holt right now, tonight, you would have done it, if only to spite me."

"I don't love him," Chloe pointed out, watching as Jeb took his hat down from the peg, put it on his head, and reclaimed his gun belt from the top of the cabinet, draping it over his good shoulder.

"Never stopped you getting married before," he said, and went out the back door, leaving Chloe staring after him in furious astonishment.

*   *   *

Jeb was outraged as he made his way through the darkness, headed in the direction of the Circle C bunkhouse, but he was strangely jubilant, too. If the divorce was going to take a year, then Chloe couldn't marry Holt or anybody else, not right away, anyhow, and that meant he had twelve full months to get over his fascination with her—or prove to her that he was man enough to fit the bill. In the meantime, he still had a fighting chance to win the Triple M—all he had to do was bed Chloe a few more times, get her pregnant.

He grinned, even though he still felt like punching a hole through a wall. Right then, Chloe wouldn't have spit on him if he was on fire, but she couldn't resist him forever, he knew that. A kiss or two, a little moonlight . . .

And she wasn't in love with Holt. Exultation made him forget the pain in his shoulder, for a minute, anyway.

He stopped, turned, and looked back at the house, watching as the kitchen went dark, lantern by lantern.

Glory, hallelujah, he was married.

He frowned, thinking of Chloe's fiery temper and sharp tongue, her independent ways and her hard head.

Damnation.

He was married.

Chloe was bone-weary when she reached her room on the second floor, but she knew she wasn't going to sleep anytime soon. Her nerves were too frazzled, and her mind was stampeding in every direction.

She paced a while, then, needing something to do, took paper, a pen, and a bottle of ink from the cigar box tucked into her reticule and sat down to compose the letter Holt had shamed her into writing. When her parents returned from Europe, it would be waiting.

Dear Mother and Mr. Wakefield, it began, *you will never guess where I am, or what's happened since I saw you last. I must confess I haven't told you the whole truth about a great many things . . .*

43

*J*eb was alone in the bunkhouse the next morning, wondering how the hell he was going to impress Chloe or anybody else with less than fifty dollars in the bank, when he noticed the newspaper lying on the foot of another ranch hand's bed.

He'd been drinking coffee and feeling sorry for himself, after the other men rode out to put in a day's work, leaving him behind. Now, he helped himself to the paper, sat back down at the spool table by the stove, and determined to broaden his mind.

It was fate—couldn't have been anything else. His gaze went straight to the boxed advertisement in the upper right-hand corner of the front page. RODEO, shouted the headline, in three-quarter-inch type. And underneath that, the words that made Jeb sit up straighter in his chair.

$1000 FOR RIDING
THE MEANEST HORSE ON EARTH!

RIDERS MUST BE MALE
NO CRIPPLES
FAMILY MEN STRONGLY ADVISED
NOT TO ENTER—
THIS ANIMAL IS A BRUTE!

Jeb gave the newspaper another snap and searched the lines of print for the place and the date. Flagstaff, one week from today. The rodeo would start at 8:00 A.M. sharp; the event he was interested in, at three that afternoon.

He checked the date on the masthead, then squinted at the tattered, marked-up calendar on the wall.

He smiled, smoothed out the paper on the tabletop, and read the screaming lines again, savoring every word.

One thousand dollars. He whistled through his teeth. With a fortune like that, he could make a real start for himself, buy some cattle of his own, or even build a house.

The savage ache in his right arm reminded him that, while he definitely qualified as male, he was lacking in the "fit" department. Still, he had a full seven days to prepare. Surely he'd be better by then.

He studied the advertisement a third time, slowly, and frowned.

If his pa got wind of this, he'd find a way to stop him for sure, and if Rafe or Kade knew, they might decide to enter, just to show him up. He couldn't be sure they hadn't seen the notice themselves, of course, but worrying over that wouldn't do any good.

A prize like that was bound to draw a lot of entrants.

Well, he wouldn't worry about that, either. He hadn't been thrown from a horse since he was seventeen, and that had been a fluke. He'd keep mum about the rodeo— at least until after he'd collected the prize money.

Whistling again, he put the newspaper back where he'd found it.

Sue Ellen Caruthers packed a single bag, resigned to leaving the rest of her things behind, and hid it behind the woodpile out back of the cabin. If Jack got the slightest inkling that she didn't mean to stay, he'd kill her for sure.

It did no good to wish she'd never come to this god-forsaken place, or been stupid enough to hook up with Mr. Barrett in the first place. She would just have to make the best of any opportunity that came to hand.

She didn't have a horse, and she wasn't very good at directions, since she'd lived all her life in a city, an ordinary woman, raising eight younger brothers and sisters after her mother died, and her father crawled into a whiskey bottle.

She thought she knew which way to walk, but she wasn't absolutely sure. Nor did she have a definite destination in mind; she just wanted to get away.

She was sitting at the table, which was really only a big crate, when she heard him ride in. She braced herself, summoned up a smile.

Barrett shoved open the door, stepped over the high

threshold, and hung up his hat. He took off his gun belt next and set it on the table. He'd been hiding a package under his coat, and he tossed that down, too, causing Sue Ellen to start a little.

"What's this?" she asked, keeping her voice light.

"Open it and see." He rubbed his injured left leg, grimaced.

Sue Ellen fumbled with the string, mystified, and folded back the brown paper. Inside was a pretty doll, with dark ringlets and open-and-shut eyes. She frowned.

"For the little girl," he said, limping slightly as he made his way to the potbellied stove for coffee. "I rode all the way to Flagstaff to get it."

"Why?"

"We want to make friends with Lizzie Cavanagh, don't we?"

A chill moved up Sue Ellen's spine, bone by bone. "What are you talking about?"

He made a slurping sound as he took his coffee. "I believe you know the answer to that question," he said.

Sue Ellen turned, looked up at him. "What is Lizzie to you?"

He smiled behind the mug. "A means to an end," he said.

Sue Ellen forgot herself, just for a moment, but long enough to get into trouble. "I will not help you hurt a child," she told him flatly. Maybe she'd resented taking care of a brood of noisy waifs, but she was not heartless.

She'd even shed a few tears when her father remarried, and the new wife sent her packing.

Jack looked injured, though it was a parody, and they both knew it. "I'm not going to hurt the kid," he said. "Not unless I have to. I just want to use her for bait. Draw out the McKettricks."

"You're crazy," Sue Ellen said, her voice rising a little. "You might just as well tease a wildcat with a stick!"

He merely smiled, though the look in his eyes gave her a chill.

"I won't help you," she said. "I mean it, Jack."

He set the cup aside, easily, and, in the next instant, grabbed her by the hair, wrenching her head back. His spittle misted her face as he spoke, at the same time tightening his grip until she thought her scalp would tear loose from her skull. "Yes," he rasped, "*you will.*"

Tears of fury, frustration, and pain burned her eyes. "What do you want me to do?"

He loosed his hold on her hair, and she blinked hard against the lingering pain. "Like I said, you'll make friends with Lizzie. Give her the doll."

"I can't just go walking up to that house and ask to see the child," Sue Ellen pointed out, but carefully. "Holt sent me away, remember? Besides, Lizzie and I had words—"

"Well, you won't go there when Holt's around, now, will you? And kids have short memories. The doll will win her over."

She shivered. Waited for things to get worse. And they did.

Jack sat down on a nail keg, serving as a chair. "I've been watching the place, much as I could. There's a lot of coming and going. One of these days, little Miss Cavanagh is going to wander too far from the house, and when she does, we'll be ready."

"That's—" she'd meant to say "stupid," but that seemed a poor choice, given the violence of Jack's mood. "That's going to be difficult. There are a lot of men working on that ranch, and they'll notice us."

"We'll just have to stay out of their way, won't we?"

"How?" Sue Ellen pleaded. "They'd recognize either one of us on sight."

"I'm still working that out," Jack admitted.

Sue Ellen did not cherish a single hope that he wouldn't succeed. He'd bought the doll, after all, and ridden for hours to do it. It was a symbol of the horrible objective already brewing in his mind.

"I've kept your supper warm," she said weakly, rising to her feet. Her stomach churned, and she felt shaky.

"Good," Jack said, still absorbed in his thoughts.

She made her way to the stove, lifted the lid off a pot of pinto beans, and ladled a helping onto a tin plate. She put it before him, and let her gaze stray to the .44 he'd set down earlier.

It was a mistake, for he saw her looking and guessed her thoughts.

"I'm warning you, Sue Ellen," he said. "Don't do anything foolish. I'd just as soon kill you as look at you."

She had no doubt that he meant it, but she straightened her spine. It was that or scream and tear her hair, and that would be almost as dangerous as grabbing for the gun. "Let me go," she begged. "Let me go, and I'll never say anything to anybody. I'll never come within miles of the Arizona Territory, I promise."

He reached up, caught her chin in his hand, gripping hard enough to leave bruises. "You *promise*," he scoffed. "You aren't going anywhere, Sue Ellen, except to your grave if you take it into your head to cross me. You'd just better resign yourself to your situation, once and for all."

She waited, bearing the pain as best she could.

He released his hold on her and looked down at the plate of beans with a sneer of distaste. "Is this all we've got?" he asked.

"Yes," she said. "If you wanted something different, you should have bought food instead of that doll."

He chuckled. "Maybe I'll take another ride up to Flagstaff in the morning," he said, picking up the spoon she brought him. "Get us some decent vittles and some different clothes, too." He was thinking aloud now, not even speaking to her, really, but to himself. "You'd look a sight different, dressed like a sodbuster's wife, and I could get me some denim pants and one of those big-brimmed hats. The kind that hide a man's face."

Sue Ellen said nothing. If Jack was heading back to

Flagstaff, she'd have her chance. She could clear out, now that she'd finally summoned up the courage. Nothing in the trees and mountains scared her as much as Jack Barrett did.

"You want to go along?" he asked, sounding amiable.

She hadn't anticipated such a thing, for all her mental groping, and she had to step out of the fog, think fast. She'd come through Flagstaff on her way to Indian Rock, back when she was a mail-order bride and thought she was going to marry a McKettrick and live the high life. Flagstaff wasn't a city, by any stretch, but it was a good-sized town, with plenty of people—some of whom would surely help her.

"I'd like that," she said, very carefully.

He laughed. "Too bad," he said. "You're staying right here."

She didn't look at the gun, didn't dare, but if she could have, she'd have grabbed it and shot Jack Barrett through the heart without batting an eyelash. She'd thought she hated the McKettricks—they'd been the ones to send for her in the first place, through the matrimonial service, and it was their fault she'd gotten stranded. Oh, they offered to pay her fare back home—but she wasn't welcome there, either.

Yet she hadn't known what hatred was until this moment.

"Whatever you say," she replied, keeping her voice even.

He scooped up some beans. "Get ready for bed, Sue Ellen," he said, chewing, "and don't wear your nightgown. I've been feeling lonesome all day."

Sue Ellen's stomach rolled. God in heaven, if only she could go back to the day she'd had that silly run-in with Holt, over his daughter. Just that far. She'd be sweet as pie, to him and to the child, and he'd never send her away.

Slowly, she began to unbutton her dress.

She was in bed by the time he finished his food, waiting.

He put out the lamp, and she heard him moving about, probably hiding the gun. Heard him stripping down for the night, for her, and closed her eyes.

He took her roughly, and it hurt fit to tear her to pieces, and he shouted out a name when he spilled himself inside her, but it wasn't hers.

He called her "Chloe."

44

*H*olt's desk was strewn with open books, and Chloe and Lizzie sat side by side, with their backs to Jeb, poring over them. He watched them, his good shoulder braced against the framework of the door, imagining that Chloe was truly his wife, and Lizzie their child, and that this spacious ranch house was the one he had already begun to build, on the secret landscape of his mind.

The pain in his wounded arm jolted him out of the dream. It came and went, that ache, bone deep, following a schedule of its own, and ambushed him in unwary moments.

He thrust himself away from the doorframe, turned, and walked away.

The house was empty, except for him and, of course, Chloe and Lizzie, who might as well have been in the next town as the next room, they were so absorbed in words written by dead people. Chloe was still put out with him from the night before, anyway, and probably wouldn't have spared him a kind word even if he'd spoken first, and politely.

Holt had left for the range before dawn, and most of the ranch hands were gone, too. A couple of the older ones puttered around, doing the kind of busywork that was left to their sort on any large spread.

Restless, Jeb took his gun belt down from the top of a high cupboard, where he'd set it when he came in the house, to keep it out of Lizzie's reach, and strapped it on. This was no mean undertaking, with one useless hand, and there was sweat on his upper lip and the back of his neck by the time he'd finished it.

He went back outside, and the cool air hit him, braced him up a little.

He waved to the broken-down cowboys, one sitting on a bale of hay, mending a harness, the other picking a horse's hooves. They nodded, cordially enough, but remained intent on their work.

He found a case half-full of empty bottles in the well-house, and managed to hoist the crate off the packed-dirt floor and balance it against his left hip. The task was frustrating, and it brought out more sweat, not to mention a few good twinges to his wounded arm, but he set his teeth and managed it.

Well away from the house and corrals, he set the bottles up, one by one, balancing them along the length of a fallen tree. He walked back about thirty paces, turned, and drew the .45 across his belly.

It was an awkward motion, and slow. Even worse, when he fired, he missed.

He cursed, unlaced the holster from his thigh, and twisted the belt so the gun rested against his other hip. Tying it in place again was one mother of a job, but he was double-damned if he'd give up.

The pistol grip was backward; he'd need a southpaw's rigging to do the thing right, but for the time being, he'd have to make do. He drew again, flipping the .45 end over end, meaning to catch it in midair, like he used to do with his right hand, when he was showing off a little. The thing slipped through his fingers, landed on the ground, and discharged, belching fire and damn near blowing off his foot.

He bent, cussing under his breath, which was rapid and shallow, and replaced the spent cartridge with a new one from the supply on his belt. Tried again, with a similar result, though this time, at least, he didn't drop the gun. The shot went wide of the bottles, though, and took a nick out of a mesquite tree well to the left of his target.

He was fixing to draw again when Chloe spoke from behind him.

"What do you think you're doing?" she demanded, in a hands-on-the-hips kind of voice.

He holstered the .45, turned his head to look back at her. She was holding her skirts, probably to keep from snagging them on the thistle-strewn ground, and Lizzie stood at her side, big-eyed and sober. It troubled him that he hadn't heard them coming.

"Practicing," he said.

Chloe trundled toward him. Spoke in a terse undertone, no doubt hoping that Lizzie wouldn't hear. Fat chance of that; the kid was listening with every pore in her body.

"Have you lost your mind?" Chloe sputtered. "Only a little over a week ago, you were shot!"

Jeb had been watching Lizzie, and he took his time shifting his gaze back to Chloe's pink, earnest face. He thought how much he liked her freckles, and that made him want to smile, but he didn't give in to the urge.

"Yes, I recall it clearly," he said. "Go back inside, Teacher. You're not needed here."

She flinched visibly, almost as if he'd struck her. He felt ashamed, but he reined that in before it could show, just like the smile. "Will you listen to reason for once in your life?" she whispered.

"I am listening to reason," he replied. "My own. There's somebody out there who means to kill me, and if I can't shoot, he'll probably succeed."

He saw something flicker in her face then, something that reflected the shame he'd stifled in himself a few moments before, but it was gone so quickly that he decided he must be imagining things. The annoying part was, as mad as this woman made him, without half-trying, he wanted to put his arm around her and pull her close. Hold her there.

"You'd be safer in the house," she persisted, but with less spirit than before.

"That's probably true," he retorted dryly. "I guess I could hide in there forever, read books, maybe, or put together those little ships that unfold inside a bottle. While I'm at it, I might as well sit in my coffin to do it, since I'll already be dead."

She subsided a little. Hoisted her chin up a notch. "You are absolutely impossible," she said, not for the first time.

Lizzie pulled up alongside her, like a little boat bouncing against a dock. "Do you really know how to build ships inside of bottles?" she asked, in wonder.

The eager look in her eyes made him wish he possessed that skill, though he knew it was a temporary yearning. He grinned at her and shook his head. "Just a figure of speech, Lizzie-beth." The nickname was Angus's invention, but it was a way of showing affection, so he used it.

"Darn," she said, sighing not just with her lungs but her whole being.

Chloe was watching him, her mouth slightly open, like she wanted to say something else, but thought better of it.

"If you ladies will excuse me," he said, watching her right back, "I've got shooting to do."

"You need a different holster," Lizzie informed him.

"You *need*," Chloe interjected, leaning in close, so that he could feel her warm breath on his face, and narrowing those sapphire eyes of hers to slits, "a good kick in the behind!"

"I got that when I met you," he replied, equal to any stare-down. And then he turned his back on her, pulled in a deep, resolute breath, let it out slowly, and drew the .45 again. That time, he hit a bottle, even if it wasn't exactly the one he'd had in mind, and when he turned to thank Chloe for her inspiration, she was making her angry way back to the house, dragging Lizzie along by the hand.

He shrugged, without thinking, and the resultant flash of pain almost brought him to his knees. After sweating it out for a few moments, he went back to the bottles, and every time the brown glass splintered, he felt a little stronger, a little more like himself.

"He was out there all morning," Chloe whispered to Holt, while the two of them put together a modest supper of bread and cheese and leftovers that evening, in the kitchen. "*Shooting.*"

Jeb and Lizzie were well out of earshot, playing checkers on the front porch, which made Chloe wonder why she'd taken the trouble to lower her voice.

Holt set the coffeepot on the stove, filled with fresh water, and measured in ground beans. "I reckon he knows what he's doing," he said. "This is rough country, Chloe. A man who can't use a gun doesn't stand much of a chance."

"Nonsense," Chloe countered, slamming plates down onto the table. "My stepfather doesn't even carry a gun."

"Your stepfather lives in Sacramento," Holt said. "There's a difference. Sacramento is well settled, and Indian Rock is still a frontier town, for the most part."

Chloe considered Mr. Wakefield. He was a portly man, and probably wouldn't have been able to buckle a gun belt around his middle if he'd tried. The whimsical thought sidetracked her from the point she wanted to make, but only temporarily. "If Sacramento is more civilized than Indian Rock, it's because so few men go about armed."

Holt's eyes twinkled. "So you up and left and headed straight for the OK Corral," he teased. "That is a mystery."

Before Chloe could respond, the inside door opened and Jeb appeared, effectively putting an end to the conversation. He looked from Chloe to Holt, then back again, and there was a glint of challenge in his eyes.

He was still jealous.

Chloe wondered why this lifted her spirits the way it did. She smiled warmly at Holt, even fluttered her lashes, though just once. "Thank you for your help," she said. "It's nice to meet a man who knows his way around a kitchen."

Holt rolled his eyes.

"All he lacks is a ruffled apron," Jeb remarked, so intent on Chloe that he probably didn't see his brother's reaction.

"Where," Chloe inquired sweetly, "is Lizzie?"

Jeb didn't smile at the mention of his niece, the way he usually did. "She's upstairs. Said she wanted to put a ribbon in her hair, so she'd look nice at supper."

"I'll see if I can hurry her up a little," Holt said judiciously, and left the room.

Jeb and Chloe stared at each other for a few moments. She wasn't willing to back down, and it was a pretty good bet that he felt the same way.

"Maybe *you should* have set your sights on my brother," Jeb said. "The two of you seem to get along pretty well."

Chloe felt her cheeks go pink, but she wasn't about to retreat. "Sit down," she said stiffly, and with great effort. "Supper is almost ready."

Presently, Lizzie came in, followed by Holt. Only then did Jeb take a place at the table, but his glance told her it wasn't because she'd asked him to.

The food was good, nourishing fare, and Chloe knew she should have relished it, and been thankful, but every bite tasted like gall, and landed as a lump in her jittery stomach.

When the ordeal was over, she rose to clear the table and wash the dishes, but Holt stopped her, putting a hand on her arm. "You were hired to teach, not keep house," he told her quietly, indicating the inside door with an inclination of his head. "You need some time alone, Chloe. Go read or something."

She nodded, turned, and walked out of the kitchen, without sparing Jeb McKettrick so much as a glance. Upstairs, she closed herself in her room and paced until some of her fury at Jeb was spent, and presently, she heard Lizzie call a bemused "good night" from the corridor.

"Good night," she called back, as cheerfully as she could.

Good night, hell, she thought. With Jeb around, there was no such thing.

Unless, of course, they were making love.

45

It was still light out when Chloe returned to Indian Rock Sunday evening, having been escorted by two of the ranch hands from the Circle C, one driving the buckboard, the other riding alongside, with a rifle resting in the curve of his arm. Holt had intended to bring her back to town himself, but at the last moment, there had been some crisis involving a cow, and he'd stayed behind.

She'd looked forward to being back in the cottage, but it seemed strangely lonely, rather than peaceful, as she lit the stove, put water on to boil for tea, and busied herself unpacking her things. Because she'd left the crate of books and supplies at the Circle C for Lizzie to work with through the coming week, she'd had only the reticule to carry, so she'd excused Holt's men, with her thanks, when they offered to help.

A knock at the door jarred her out of her musings.

"Who's there?" She'd forgotten to lower the latch, so she put some bravery into the words.

"Tom Jessup," was the polite answer. "I've come about Walter and Ellen."

Chloe hurried to the window beside the door, pushed the curtain aside, and peered out. Her preconceptions of Mr. Jessup—someone brutish and probably ignorant— didn't quite match up with this large, red-faced man, sporting a balding pate and a temperate manner. He held a battered hat in his hands.

She opened the door, stepped out into the twilight.

He seemed to understand that she wasn't going to invite him in and stepped down into the grass, looking up at her with an air of such guileless expectation that she felt shamed for counting him an uncaring father.

"I'm Miss Wakefield," she said, putting out a hand.

He shook it. Nodded. His eyes were large and watery, putting Chloe in mind of an ancient and well-loved dog. "Walter and Ellen," he began shyly, "they're mindin' you all right, ain't they?"

"Yes," Chloe said quickly, eager to reassure him on that score, if no other. "They're wonderful children."

"Then I reckon this is about them livin' in the wagon," he said, and the slope of his broad shoulders seemed more defined.

"I know it's hard, Mr. Jessup," Chloe said carefully, hugging herself against a chilly night breeze. "Earning a living, I mean. But Walter and Ellen shouldn't be alone that way."

He looked so pained that Chloe almost wished she'd never brought up the subject, though of course she'd had no choice. "My wife died three years ago," he said, "and we ain't got no folks anywhere near here. Mr. Kade McKettrick, he told me I could bring the kids to the ranch, that he'd find a place for them, but that would mean they couldn't go to school, what with the distance and all. It mattered the world and all to my Annabel that they get their learnin'."

Pity struck deep in Chloe, but she masked it behind a smile. "I see the problem, Mr. Jessup," she said. "But winter's coming, and little Ellen gets frightened at night. Walter probably does, too, though he won't admit it."

Jessup looked away. Blinked. His throat worked, but no words came out.

"Suppose I found them somewhere to stay," Chloe ventured.

"That would be charity," he said, his gaze still fixed on the woodpile, as though he found something of interest there. His Adam's apple bobbed.

"No," Chloe said softly. "It would just be people, helping other people."

"I don't have money to pay."

She was hurting this man, probing deep into his pride, and she didn't like it, but she had to keep Walter and Ellen in the forefront of her mind. "I'm sure they could help with chores or something."

"Where?" Mr. Jessup asked, searching her face now. "Where would they stay? This here's a little house—you don't have room."

"I'd set up cots for them before I'd see them spend the winter in a wagon, Mr. Jessup," Chloe persisted. "But I think I can do better than that. Indian Rock isn't very big, but there are good people here. Surely someone could take them in. Please—just let me try."

He considered for such a long time that Chloe was sure he'd refuse, but when he heaved a great sigh, there was resignation in it. "All right," he said. "I don't want my little Ellen scared at night, or any other time."

She started to touch his hand, hesitated, then went ahead. "Thank you, Mr. Jessup," she said.

He nodded; it was one more humbling, his manner seemed to say, in a long line of them. " 'Night to you, ma'am," he said, and walked away, vanishing into purple shadows.

Chloe met Doc Boylen first thing the next morning, on her way to the hotel dining room, where she planned to have breakfast with Becky.

"You look thoughtful this morning, Miss Wakefield," he said, with a smile. "Must be pondering a lesson on the Roman Empire, or something even more complicated."

She smiled, though perhaps a bit wanly. "I was thinking about a couple of my students, Walter and Ellen Jessup. They're living out of a wagon, you know."

Doc nodded. "It's been the topic of considerable conversation around town," he admitted. "Becky wants to take them in, but, as her doctor, I've advised her against it. She works too hard as it is, with that weak heart of hers, and she's still getting over losing John Lewis. Mamie Sussex has the room, but she's got all she can do to keep her own kids fed, even with my help."

Chloe found herself with a new worry to chew on. "I didn't know there was anything wrong with Becky's heart," she said.

"She's not one to complain," Doc replied. He put one foot up on the side of a water trough and sighed. "Seems like there ought to be a way to provide for those kids."

"I'll do it," Chloe said, "even if I have to write to my stepfather's attorney and beg him for money." It was not a comfortable prospect, for she had never really gotten along with Mr. Wakefield or his minions, but some things were more important than pride.

"Angus McKettrick would probably help," Doc suggested. "I'll have a word with him, next time he's in town."

Chloe looked away. "I suppose it's my place to ask him," she said, with a reluctance she couldn't hide. She admired her father-in-law greatly, and got along well with him, but asking him for money, no matter how good the cause, would be far more difficult than approaching Mr. Wakefield.

"How is Jeb?" Doc asked, giving her his arm and

squiring her along the board sidewalk, toward the Arizona Hotel.

"Mean as ever," she said darkly, but then, to her own surprise, she laughed. "I have never, in my life, encountered a single person as stubborn as he is."

Doc's eyes were merry. "Look in a mirror," he said.

Chloe balked, but good-naturedly. She liked Doc, and she was grateful to him for saving Jeb after the shooting, and for her job. "I don't believe you said that," she marveled.

He chuckled, opened one of the hotel doors, and gestured for her to go through. "Go and have your breakfast," he said. "I've got rounds to make."

Chloe wanted to protest—stubbornly—that she wasn't stubborn. The idea made her laugh again. She shook her head and went inside.

There was no sign of Becky in the dining room, but Sarah Fee was there, as usual, waiting on customers. Her baby sat in a laundry basket, out of the way of traffic, gurgling and playing with her toes.

Chloe paused to greet the child, and when she turned around to look for a table, Sarah was standing right behind her, smiling broadly. Even beaming.

"Why, Sarah," Chloe said, "you seem especially happy this morning. What's the good news?"

"Sam and I are going to have another baby," the woman whispered. Her face glowed, translucent.

Chloe was thrilled, but she also felt the faint sting

of envy she'd come to expect, when met with such announcements. "That's wonderful," she said. "Congratulations."

Sarah frowned. Maybe she'd heard something in Chloe's voice, or glimpsed it in her face. "Are you troubled, Miss Wakefield?"

"Please, Sarah—call me Chloe." She took the other woman's hands, squeezed them in her own. "I'm a little worried about the Jessup children."

"The ones living out of that wagon?"

Chloe nodded.

"I think that's a shame," Sarah said, steering Chloe toward a table and practically willing her into a chair. "I told Sam it ought to be against the law, and he said it probably is."

"I suppose they could stay at the jailhouse," Chloe mused. "Even that would be better than a wagon."

Sarah's eyes widened. "With drunken cowboys in there every other night? That wouldn't be proper, Miss—Chloe. Not proper at all."

"I'm not so sure I give a whistle for what's proper," Chloe fretted. The letter she'd written to her mother, her first night on the Circle C, was in her pocket, ready to post. In her mind, she was opening it, adding a pitiful plea for funds.

"What'll you have for breakfast?" Sarah wanted to know. Chloe was hungry, and she'd need food to sustain her through a rigorous morning of teaching, but her stomach was uncertain. Whether this was because of her concern for the Jessup children, or the prospect of writing her stepfather for money, she couldn't say.

Chloe decided on a poached egg, a slice of toasted bread, and a cup of tea, and sat gazing out the window, composing and recomposing her request to her stepfather. Even if he granted it, and there was no guarantee that he would, he and her mother were probably still in Europe. Winter could conceivably come and go before they even read the letter, let alone made a decision.

Sam came in, speaking to cowboys here and there as he passed their tables, but headed all the while toward his daughter. He crouched beside the basket, and Chloe watched, touched, as he chucked the child under the chin, making her chortle with delight.

Sarah brought the egg, then went to speak to Sam. Both of them glanced in Chloe's direction periodically, throughout the discourse, and she tried to pretend she hadn't noticed.

Finally, just as she was finishing her tea, Sam stepped up to the table. "Mind if I sit down?" he asked.

School would be starting soon, and Chloe didn't have much time, especially if she was going to post her letter before class, but she smiled and nodded. "Please," she said.

Sam took a seat. "Sarah tells me you're looking for someone to take in those Jessup kids," he said.

Hope stirred inside Chloe, but she tried to push it

down. It was preposterous to think the Fees could accommodate two children—they had a daughter of their own, and another baby on the way. Their house, though sturdy and new, was small, and they probably didn't make much more money, with both of them working, than she did.

"Yes," she said. "Do you know anyone who might—?"

"Sarah and I will make room for them at our place," Sam interrupted. "At least for the winter. Maybe by spring, their pa will be able to work out some other arrangement."

Chloe put a hand to her heart, fingers splayed. "Oh, Sam, how kind. But won't it be a hardship?"

Sam glanced affectionately at his wife, who apparently felt his gaze, for she met it, though she was busy serving pancakes to a couple of ranch hands at a nearby table.

"Hardship's nothing new to Sarah and me," he said. "Those children could be a help, too, I reckon. We've got a cow and some chickens now, and frankly, what with our jobs and the baby, we can't keep up with the chores."

Tears filled Chloe's eyes. "Oh, Sam, thank you."

He cleared his throat, obviously embarrassed. "Not that we'd work them hard, or anything like that. They're just little, and I know their studies are important."

Chloe stood up, laid her napkin on the table, and went around to Sam's side. She leaned down and kissed the marshal smack on the cheek, and he turned an even deeper shade of crimson. "*Thank you*," she repeated, patting his shoulder, before she rushed over to hug Sarah.

She mailed the letter from the mercantile, profoundly grateful that she hadn't had to add a plea to it, and fairly danced back to the schoolhouse, so high were her spirits.

Jesse Banner was already there, waiting on the steps, with his big, rawboned wrists protruding from the sleeves of his shirt. He stood when he caught sight of her, and smiled shyly.

"Ring the bell, Jesse," she said. "Ring it hard. It's time for school, and this is a very happy day."

"Yes, ma'am," he replied, and followed her into the little entryway, to undertake the task. He gave the dangling rope a good yank, and the bell chimed, and Chloe imagined the sound resounding off the far hills.

She took sticks of kindling from the bin beside the stove and got a good fire going, driving back the chill, turning the frost on the windows to mist.

She was dusting off her hands when her gaze caught on the blackboard and the cramped scrawl waiting there.

I will come for you.

Chloe's good mood seeped right out of her, as if draining into the floorboards beneath her feet.

Jack. That was Jack's handwriting. Jack's message.

She hastened to the board, grabbed up the eraser, scrubbed the chalked markings away. But the words were still there, ghosts of themselves, mocking her.

"Teacher?"

She turned, knowing her face was bloodless, and saw

Jesse standing close by. He was staring, squinty-eyed, at the blackboard.

"Who wrote that?"

It wasn't the first lie she'd been forced into, Chloe thought sorrowfully, and it wouldn't be the last. "I don't know," she said, straightening her spine. "Please put some more wood in the stove, Jesse. It's going to be cold today."

46

$\mathcal{T}$here were sprigs of frost on the dirt floor of the cabin when Sue Ellen arose, before it was light out, to build up the fire and put the coffeepot on to boil. Breakfast would be more of last night's beans; there was nothing else.

She kept her motions slow, though something inside her wanted to hurry, because Jack was already stirring in the musty bed, stretching as he woke. She didn't want him to suspect what she was planning.

"I'll bring back some salt pork and the like," he said, half-yawning the words. The rope springs creaked beneath mattress as he sat up, put his bare feet on the floor.

"That would be fine," she answered mildly, busy with her tasks. The water buckets wanted refilling, and she'd need more firewood to keep the stove going. The limited supply outside, left behind by whoever had built, then abandoned the cabin, was dwindling fast.

Jack got up, went outside to relieve himself and to

check on his horse, and came back. She could feel his gaze on her, studying, weighing, measuring. It was as if he were trying to elbow his way into her mind, read her most private thoughts. Well, she had that much power, at least. She didn't have to let him in.

She forced herself to smile. "If you'd buy the staples, sugar, butter, and some flour and salt," she said brightly, taking a bucket in each hand, "I could bake you a cake."

"I do favor sweets," he allowed, but the look in his eyes was still cold, musing, probing.

"Good," she said, and went past him, to make her way to the cistern. It was covered by a panel of rotting boards, and she had to move that aside and kneel and bend from her middle to reach the water. The buckets were heavy, and she strained to draw them up full, one, then the other.

They breakfasted on beans.

"Coffee's almost gone, too," she said, when the moment seemed right.

"I'll fetch you some," Jack answered, but he sounded distracted, and testy as well. Did he suspect that she meant to escape, that very morning? If he did, he'd watch her from the woods, run her down with his horse, or even shoot her, the moment she tried to leave the clearing.

She decided she couldn't afford to retrieve her reticule from the woodpile, lest he catch her at it. She felt a plundering stab of sorrow at this realization; her mother's brooch was in that bag, along with her Bible and her favorite dress. Leaving the old behind, she would have nothing but the new, and that was an insubstantial thing, soil with no seeds planted.

Jack watched her, chewing, and suddenly, he smiled. She was terrified, since his smiles usually presaged some outburst of cruelty, until he spoke. "Maybe I'll bring you back something nice. A sort of reward."

She knew he was referring to their intercourse the night before. She'd endured it, for one reason only: Because she had no choice. Did he think she'd been trying to please him? If so, well and good. That would make him less suspicious.

"Lift up your dress, Sue Ellen," he said.

She flushed, hoping he would mistake her horror for coquettish reluctance.

He was testing her, she realized, and she had to pass through this trial, however she despised it, if she wanted to survive. She did as she was told, and even moaned a little, the way he liked, when he began touching her.

He had her on the table, rutting at her from behind like an animal, and she cursed him even as she made the sounds she knew he wanted to hear. When it was over, she opened her eyes, her palms braced against the rough wood, and pushed herself up.

He wasn't even looking at her. He was buttoning his trousers, whistling under his breath. How she yearned to get hold of that .44 of his and put a bullet through his forehead, but having learned her lesson the last time that thought had struck her, she schooled her features into a benign smile and even managed a sigh of womanly satisfaction.

"See you tonight," he said.

She didn't trust herself to speak; it would be so easy to go too far, say too much, and make him wonder at her acquiescence. So she hummed, very softly, under her breath. It was that or scream hysterically, and she knew that once she got started at that, only a fist or a bullet would stop her.

He went out, mounted his horse carefully, since his leg was still sore from the flesh wound he'd sustained trying to kill Jeb McKettrick.

Sue Ellen stood in the doorway of the cabin, smiling wistfully, as if she sorrowed at the parting, and would be waiting eagerly when he returned.

He raised a hand in farewell, wheeled the horse around, and rode off.

She waited an hour, and it was one of the hardest things she'd ever done. She dusted that filthy cabin, made up the bed, washed out the coffeepot at the cistern. She composed a letter to her father, in her mind, and followed that with a silent recitation of every Bible verse she knew.

And then she left, not walking purposefully, like she had a destination in mind, but strolling, bending now and then to pick a dandelion green. If Jack came out of the woods, she'd say she meant to cook them up with the salt pork he'd promised to bring back.

She reached the edge of the woods, stiffened in spite of her stalwart intentions, and stepped into the trees. There, she waited, behind the trunk of an ancient, twisted oak, her heart hammering so hard that she could barely breathe.

One minute passed—she counted it second by second, and then another to follow. And another.

He didn't come.

She made her way to another tree, waited again. Counted again.

No shout, no crashing of horse's hooves, beating through the brush, bearing him down upon her like the wrath of hell itself.

Exhilaration surged into her throat, and only an inborn prudence kept her from shouting in triumph.

She traveled from oak to pine for a while, then took bolder strides, stopping every few minutes to listen. As she proceeded downhill, there were fewer and fewer trees, but there were red boulders. If she heard anything, she could hide among them.

The sun was high when she came to the wide creek, and recognized it, from her time with Holt, as the border between the Circle C and the Triple M. She crouched in the shelter of a rock pile on the shore, splashed water on her face, then drank from cupped hands.

All this time, she'd been on the Circle C, probably only a few miles from Holt's house. The knowledge both comforted and grieved her. Help had been so close and yet so far.

She surveyed the creek, wondering whether she ought to cross it there, where it was deep, and the water traveling fast, or go on downstream a ways, where it might be shallower.

She looked back over one shoulder and felt a prickle on the nape of her neck. Better to cross, she decided. Even a few yards of water would be a barrier, though not much of one, to a man on horseback.

She prayed she'd meet someone—anyone—before Jack caught up with her. There would be no convincing him now that she'd only been gathering dandelion greens, and she couldn't claim she was fishing, either, since she didn't have a pole.

She shaded her eyes with one hand, looking for a fallen log, but there was none. If she wanted to get to the other side, she'd have to scramble from rock to boulder to slippery stone. She tied her skirts up around her waist, so they wouldn't drag her under by their weight if she fell in, and the first cold jolt of the water bit into her legs as she waded to the closest stone.

She'd made it to the middle when she heard the approaching horse, and panic seized her. She lost her footing, slid into the rushing water, felt herself being swept along by the current, pummeled by the force of the stream. Her face and hair doused, she was blinded, and could not see the rider, nor could she hear anything over the roar of the creek itself.

She spun wildly, helpless, going under and coming up. Her skirt came untied, and pulled her under the surface as effectively as an anchor.

And then her head struck the rock. She was going to die, she thought matter-of-factly, as the darkness took her over.

47

Tom Jessup couldn't swim, but it wasn't in him to stand by and let a woman drown. He spurred his horse into the wild water, groped for the lady's hair, and finally caught hold of it on the third try. He dragged her up, sodden and heavy, into the saddle, and reined toward shore.

On the sloping bank, he leaped down, hauling her after him, and laid her out on her back, so her head was lower than her feet. She was blue, and she didn't make a sound.

He pressed his ear to her chest, heard a faint heartbeat. But she sure wasn't breathing.

He put both hands to her stomach and pushed as hard as he dared. Water gurgled out of her nose and mouth, and she began to cough. Encouraged, Tom repeated the process.

She blinked, opened her eyes, looked at him blankly, then rolled over onto her belly and vomited.

Tom stroked her back, wishing he were a smarter man, who knew what else to do, and when she seemed to be through, he wet his handkerchief in the creek and washed her face. She was unconscious again, but she was breathing. Thank God, she was breathing.

He scanned the surrounding landscape, looking for a horse and seeing none, wondering where she'd come from, on foot. They were miles from anyplace, and if he hadn't been out looking for strays, he'd never have seen her.

Crouching beside her, he debated with himself.

He ought to take her to town, where there was a doctor, but it was too far, and if the water in her lungs didn't kill her, the ride probably would. No, he'd best head for the ranch house on the Triple M. Somebody there would know what to do.

His own clothes soaked by then, Tom hoped he wouldn't take a chill, come down with the pneumonia, and leave his kids without a father. He mounted his horse again, pulling the woman up with him as he went, and turned in a southerly direction.

She was still drooping like little Ellen's rag doll an hour later, when they rode up to the ranch house.

The two Mrs. McKettricks ran out to meet him, the older, Mexican one, and the one Tom knew as Kade's wife. They stretched up their arms, and he handed the near-drowned woman down with relief.

"She is half-dead!" cried Mrs. Angus.

"Found her in the creek," Tom said, dismounting. The two women were trying to support the third between them, but she was unconscious and couldn't stand. He scooped her up again.

"Bring her inside," said Mrs. Kade, shivering.

Tom complied. They led him upstairs, with his sodden burden, to a small room with a slanted ceiling and a man's things lying about, and had him set her in a chair rather than lay her out on the bed.

"Go downstairs and warm yourself by the stove," Mrs. Angus told Tom, with soothing certainty in her voice and manner. Somewhere nearby, a baby commenced to squalling.

He hesitated; now that he'd gotten into the habit of looking after the woman, he didn't like leaving her.

The baby cried harder.

"We've got to undress this woman," Mrs. Kade told him pointedly.

He bolted, the cries of the baby shrill against his eardrums.

Downstairs, he got as close to the kitchen stove as he could, wishing the ladies had told him to help himself to some coffee. Since they hadn't, Tom kept his hands to himself and waited.

Mr. Angus came in from outside, gave him a curious glance, then shouted, "Concepcion! What is the matter with that baby?"

"Angus McKettrick," the missus hollered back, "I am busy at the moment—see to Katherine yourself!"

The boss gave Tom another disgruntled look, then

started up the back stairs. Tom was frozen to the bone, so he decided to risk the displeasure of the household and help himself to some hot coffee after all. If it was the wrong move, he'd have to take the consequences.

He was sipping from a steaming mug when Mr. Angus came back downstairs, carrying an incongruous bundle of flannel and loud displeasure in his arms.

"You know anything about babies, cowboy?" he wanted to know.

"No, sir," Tom answered. "My Annabel always looked after ours."

"Damnation," Mr. Angus muttered, bouncing the bundle. "What the devil is going on around here?"

"Woman almost drowned," Tom said, relieved that the stolen coffee had not yet come under discussion. "I pulled her out of the creek up north."

The boss scowled. "Every time I turn around," he grumbled, "somebody's getting themselves shot, drowned, struck by lightning, or run over by cattle. Nobody's got a whit of common sense anymore!"

The baby hiccoughed, and then, blessedly, stopped its wailing.

Mrs. Angus appeared at the top of the stairs. "Angus, get that poor man some dry clothes before he takes sick."

Angus scowled again. "In case you haven't taken notice yet, Concepcion," he said dangerously, "I've got my hands full just now."

His wife rolled her brown eyes. "Put Katie in the bassinette first," she instructed, measuring out her words in a determined way, "then find the man something warm to wear."

Angus put the child into a basket and covered her awkwardly with something knitted from different colors of yarn. Meanwhile, the mistress of the house had disappeared again.

"I took some coffee," Tom confessed, being a man of conscience.

"Have all you want," Angus rumbled, and stormed upstairs.

Tom peered in at the baby. Katie, her name was. A girl, then.

Angus returned with long johns, pants, a shirt, and dry socks, shoved them at Tom. "You can change in the pantry," he said. "While you're at it, I'll add a little whiskey to that coffee of yours."

"I still got the day's work to do," Tom reminded him, though he did yearn for a dose of good whiskey. He wasn't a drinking man, but between the shock of seeing that woman tumble into the creek and the long, cold ride back to the ranch, he leaned toward self-indulgence.

"You've done enough," the boss said. "Take these clothes, dammit. I can't stand here holding them all day."

Tom did as he'd been told.

48

"This is Sue Ellen Caruthers," Mandy said, when they'd gotten the visitor out of her wet clothes, rubbed her down with towels, and maneuvered her into one of Concepcion's nightgowns. "She was one of the brides."

Concepcion nodded. "Yes, I remember," she said. "She kept house for Holt for a time."

Mandy bit her lower lip. "Holt told me she left the ranch house when Lizzie came," she said, wondering what had transpired between then and now. "We all figured she'd gone to Flagstaff or somewhere. What do you suppose she was doing out there on the range alone, when Tom found her?"

"I do not know," Concepcion sighed, tucking the covers in around her patient, then adding a quilt from the bottom drawer of Jeb's bureau.

"Should I send someone to town for Doc?" Even though Mandy and Kade occupied the main bedroom now, and Angus had signed the house over to them, she still deferred to Concepcion on most matters. The woman was a second mother to her, and her sensible ways and genuine kindness gave the lie to most people's perception of a mother-in-law.

Concepcion smoothed Sue Ellen's damp hair back from her face and pondered for a long moment. "No," she said presently, with a slight shake of her head. She touched the gash on Sue Ellen's right temple, which they'd treated, as best they could, with salve, and peered beneath each of her eyelids. "She does not have a concussion. We must let her rest, and watch her, but for now I think there is little Doc can do that we cannot. If she runs a fever, then we will ask him to come."

"I'll sit with her," Mandy said, drawing up a chair. "You'd better go see what Angus did with the baby."

Concepcion sighed and shook her head. "*Sí*," she agreed. "The man can drive a herd of cattle from Texas to the Arizona Territory, with less than a dozen men to help him, yet he does not know how to tend a little child."

Mandy thought of her own husband, and her secret, and she smiled to herself. Kade would make a good father, but he'd need some teaching if he was going to be any real help when it came to changing diapers and calming a fitful infant.

She could hardly wait to start the lessons.

49

*S*he was gone, the sneaking bitch.

Gone.

Jack swore. There was no sense in trying to track her now, as it was stone dark out, and besides, he was tired from the long trip into Flagstaff. He'd brought back a nice team and wagon, too, and boxes of groceries, and how had Sue Ellen thanked him? By running off the moment his back was turned.

He tossed his hat across the cabin and shoved a hand through his hair. She couldn't have gotten far, not on foot. Trouble was, if she met up with anybody along the way, she'd surely tell them where he was, what he'd been up to of late, and what he had planned for the McKettricks.

Damn her, anyway. When he caught up to her, and he would, he'd see that she never ran off at the mouth again. To anybody. He should have taken care of her early on, when he'd known she was going to be trouble, but he'd been lonely, wanted a woman handy, to give him ease and cook his food.

Jack seethed with impotent fury. Now he'd have to move on, find another place to hide out. Dark as it was, well-digger's-ass cold as it was, he couldn't risk staying put, not even for one night. And what was he supposed to do with the team and the wagon, the foodstuffs he'd paid good money for, and that damn doll?

His anger shifted to Chloe. This was her fault, when it got down to cases. It was all Chloe's doing. Chloe, with her fickle, whoring ways. And the task of cleaning up the mess fell to him.

He'd left that note for her, on the blackboard at the schoolhouse.

Next time, he'd be a little bolder.

Outside, he unhitched the four horses he'd bargained for, and left them to graze and find their own way in the world. He saddled his gelding, having led it behind the buckboard all the way from Flagstaff, and hoped it wouldn't go lame on him before he'd found a new place.

After stuffing what he could of the provisions into his saddlebags, along with the doll he still meant for Lizzie Cavanagh, he lit out, much diminished and more determined than ever.

His luck took a more favorable turn an hour later, when he came upon the cave, tucked away in a nest of rocks alongside a creek. There was plenty of grass, so he hobbled the gelding, took off the saddle and bridle, along with his other gear, and spread his bedroll on the ground. He couldn't risk a fire, since he wasn't sure who might be nearby to see it.

By God, he'd have Sue Ellen's gizzard for this, he vowed, as he lay down and tried in vain to get comfortable on the cold, hard ground. And when he was done with her, he'd see to Chloe and her fair-haired cowboy. No sense kidding himself any longer; after all that had happened, his lovely bride would never see things his way. She was too stubborn for that.

He'd have to kill her.

A shame and a waste, that's what it was, but sometimes a man just didn't have a choice.

It was another long week for Chloe. Walter and Ellen moved in with Sam and Sarah Fee, and Becky got the town council to provide bread, fruit, and cheese for the students' lunches, but Chloe didn't take as much pleasure in those victories as she might have. She was too uneasy about the message from Jack Barrett, left scrawled across the blackboard sometime during her first visit to the Circle C.

She hadn't told anyone besides Sam Fee about it, though Jesse Banner had seen it for himself. She'd sworn him to secrecy while the two of them scoured the last vestige of the words away with hot, soapy water, barely finishing before the other children arrived.

She counted the days until she would be back on the Circle C, and did it guiltily, feeling like a fraud. Yes, she wanted to see Lizzie. And yes, she looked forward to Holt's company, too, but it was Jeb's presence she longed for. Against all reason and sense, as surly and as unwelcoming as he was bound to be, she needed to be near him.

When Friday afternoon finally came, she was packed and ready, and waiting in front of the schoolhouse when the buckboard rolled up, driven by the same cowboy who had brought her back to town the previous Sunday. As before, he was accompanied by an armed rider.

In turn, Sam Fee had kept a protective eye on her and the cottage, but Chloe felt uneasy all the way to the ranch. The ride was bumpy, and her feet were so cold they went numb. It seemed to her that somebody was watching their progress, every mile of the way.

If this last had been a mere fancy, Chloe could have dealt with it, but she knew it wasn't. Jack Barrett was out there someplace, and God only knew what he was planning to do next.

When the lights of the Circle C finally came into view, she wanted to weep with relief.

Lizzie rushed out to greet her, closely followed by Holt, but there was no sign of Jeb. That figured. He'd decided to stay inside and be cussed, most likely. She shouldn't have been so disappointed, given his behavior the last time she'd seen him, but she was.

Upstairs, in the room where she'd stayed before, Chloe

began unpacking her things, while Lizzie watched her intently from her seat on the bed. No pretty, wild grasses had been set out this time, and the place hadn't been aired out, like before.

"Uncle Jeb's gone away," Lizzie said, with no preamble whatsoever.

Chloe stopped what she was doing and turned to face the child, a folded nightgown in her hands. "What do you mean, he's gone?" she asked.

Lizzie's expression was solemn, even stoic. "He saddled up his horse this afternoon and left," she said, with a nonchalant little shrug. It was an act, of course. Chloe saw confusion in her eyes and worry in the set of her small shoulders. "He said he'd be back, but I'm not sure he was telling the truth."

Not trusting her knees to support her, Chloe went to sit beside Lizzie, and wrapped an arm around her. "What did your papa say?"

"That he shouldn't have counted on a McKettrick," Lizzie said sadly.

Chloe propped her chin on top of Lizzie's head. "I see," she answered.

There was a rap at the door. "You'd best come and have some supper," Holt said, from the hallway.

"We'll be right there," Chloe answered, trying for Lizzie's sake, and for her own, to sound cheerful.

She heard him walking away, descending the stairs.

"Maybe Jeb went back to the Triple M," Chloe suggested.

Lizzie shook her head. "He told me he wasn't going there again, until he had something to show my grandpa."

Chloe closed her eyes. Where had he gone?

Lizzie stood, took Chloe's hand, and tugged. "Let's go," she pleaded. "If we sit here any longer, I'm going to cry."

"Me too," Chloe agreed, and allowed Lizzie to lead her out of the room, along the corridor, and down the stairs.

The kitchen was warm, in comparison to the rest of the house, and there were lamps burning on just about every available surface. Holt had made sandwiches, and he set them on a platter in the middle of the table.

Lizzie ate numbly, and when she was finished, and Holt sent her off to bed, she didn't take the trouble to object. She kissed him lightly on the cheek, did the same with Chloe, and vanished.

"Do you suppose Jeb found out somehow, and went looking for Jack?" Chloe asked, when she heard Lizzie's footsteps overhead and was sure she wouldn't be overheard.

Holt's jawline hardened. "I know where he went," he said.

Chloe set down the crusts of her sandwich, surprised. "And you just let him go?"

"I wasn't here when he rode out," Holt said. He looked as though he could bite a stove lid in half. "Not that I could have stopped him if I had been."

"Then how do you know—?"

"A couple of cowhands came to the back door while I

was waiting for you and Lizzie to come down to supper. They wanted time off, so they could go to Flagstaff—to the rodeo."

Chloe waited, confused.

Holt thrust out a sigh. "I guess my brother never mentioned his penchant for bronc-busting in your presence," he said.

Chloe felt the color drain from her face. "Bronc-busting?" she echoed stupidly. "But that's—his arm—he couldn't—"

"Oh, yes, he could," Holt interjected, shoving his plate away.

"But that would be—" she sighed dismally, as her mind collided with the truth. "Reckless," she finished, on a breath.

"Exactly."

"But why—?"

Holt looked impatient, as well as exasperated. "He wants the prize money, of course."

Chloe took that information in, but she still didn't know what to do with it. "What are we going to do?"

Holt answered with a question of his own. "How would you like to go to a rodeo, Miss Wakefield?"

50

𝒯he ride north took a lot out of Jeb, but his mind was fixed on a single purpose, and when that was the case, even his own better judgment was no deterrent. He set aside pain, he set aside fatigue, and barreled in the only direction he knew: straight ahead.

When he arrived in Flagstaff, he stayed clear of the rodeo grounds, even though they drew him, for he was seeking to avoid special notice. He headed for the first establishment his gaze fell upon—the Buckle and Spur Saloon.

Standing just inside the swinging doors, he waited for his eyes to adjust to the dimness. He'd seen a hundred places like the Buckle and Spur in his lifetime; there was tinny piano music ringing in the smoke-shrouded air, and the floor was covered in lumpy sawdust. The bar stretched the length of one wall, and the murky mirror behind it reflected softer versions of the drinkers bellied up to drown their sorrows. The women were painted, frilled, and feathered, but their kohl-lined eyes brimmed with bitterness and abiding grief—they were creatures of the half-light, appealing in shadow but tawdry on the rare occasions when they ventured into full sun.

He bought a beer, newly parsimonious with his money, now that he had definite plans for it and, having made the requisite purchase, helped himself to hard-boiled eggs and pickles from the spread provided for the customers. It was just plain foolhardy to drink on an empty stomach, and likely to cut the term of commerce short, so most such places provided vittles.

He'd taken a seat at a table, by himself, and made short work of the food, when a woman sashayed over. Once, he'd taken a not-so-secret pride in the way they gravitated to him, whether they were upright and calico-clad, or brazen and beplumed, like this one, but since Chloe, the phenomenon mostly irritated him.

"Hullo, cowboy," she said. "What happened to your arm?"

"Accident," he replied, knowing she'd keep after him until he answered.

She studied him. "Do I know you?"

He sighed, resigned to his less-than-salutary past. "Probably," he said.

She smiled a little at that, though tentatively. Obviously, she didn't have a great deal to smile about. If Jeb had been a crusader, he would have told her to grab up the scattered pieces of her soul and get out, while she could, that it would be better to scrub floors or even starve than to sell herself to any man with the money to pay, but he was no evangelist. If there was one thing he'd learned in life, and it was beginning to seem that there were fewer and fewer of those things than he'd originally thought, it was that folks had to find their own way. Sermons and signposts were mostly ineffective, until a person took them inside, and thus gave them a personal meaning.

"You can't be in town for the rodeo, not with that arm." Uninvited, she took a chair. "Buy me a beer?"

Again, Jeb sighed. "Not today," he said.

Something flickered in her eyes. "Here on business?"

"Yes."

"Anything I can do to help?"

Jeb scanned the room, though he'd already taken note of every person in it. His gaze settled again on a certain peddler, dressed in a plaid suit and wearing a bowler hat. "You know that fellow?"

She frowned, following his look to the table closest to the roulette wheel. "He's a shyster, and a hand with cards. You want to stay clear of him."

Jeb pushed back his chair, stood. The pain caught up with a wallop, and he swayed under the force it, then shook it off. Taking his beer along, he approached the peddler.

"Howdy," he said.

The fellow summed him up in a glance and revealed nothing of the total he'd reached. "Looking for a game of cards?"

"I might be." Jeb took a seat, waited for his arm to stop screaming.

The peddler was interested. "What kind of stakes you have in mind?"

"Your suit." He put out his good hand. "Frank Potter's the name. Who are you?"

"Bobby-Ray Walker," was the pensive reply. "You put me in mind of a man I met once down in Indian Rock," he added, still musing. "He was a glib talker, a fast gun, and one hell of a bronc buster."

"Never made his acquaintance."

Bobby-Ray pulled a poker deck from the inside pocket of his dusty suit coat, watching Jeb narrowly. Evidently, the adding and subtracting was still going on behind that homely face. "What am I supposed to do if you win my clothes right off my back?" the peddler asked, and he didn't sound the least bit troubled by the prospect. "Even in a cow town like this one, a man can't go around naked."

"Wear mine," Jeb said easily. "We're about the same size."

"I'd be getting the best of that deal," Bobby-Ray allowed cheerfully. "Why don't we just swap?"

Jeb shrugged, taking care not to involve the wrong shoulder. "Fine by me."

Bobby-Ray frowned. "Shame to pass up a good game of poker, though." He turned the deck end over end, in an idle, practiced motion, as he spoke.

Jeb focused his gaze on the cards and in the back of his mind, he heard Angus's voice. *Never bet on the other man's game, son. It's a sure way to lose.* "It isn't like I'd let you use your own cards," he said moderately.

"You think this deck is marked?" Bobby-Ray's little eyes gleamed with good-natured challenge.

"I know it is."

Bobby-Ray grinned, but there was an edge to it. "I remember you now. I watched you take every prize at a rodeo, down Indian Rock way, about a year ago. You relieved me of twenty dollars in a poker game at the Bloody Basin into the bargain." He paused, shuffling those cards as easily as another man would breathe. "Your name ain't Potter, either."

Jeb smiled. "And yours isn't Bobby-Ray Walker, so I guess we're even."

"Give me my twenty dollars back, and we'll swap duds," Walker said shrewdly.

"You lost that money fair and square."

"Maybe so," said Bobby-Ray, "but it's the price of shutting my mouth. I'm not sure what you're up to, but I *have* figured out that you're not looking to draw folks' attention."

Jeb had no choice but to agree. He laid a gold piece, borrowed from Holt's tobacco-tin stash, back at the Circle C, on the table. "Deal," he said.

Fifteen minutes later, he walked out of the Buckle and Spur, happily clad in the ugliest suit of clothes he'd ever had the good fortune to set eyes on. The bowler, being a little big, shadowed his features nicely, and he'd pinned the right sleeve up, so it wouldn't flop around like a flag and rile the horse he intended to ride. That critter was likely to be riled enough on its own.

Leaving his own mount at the hitching rail in front of the saloon, he strolled to the rodeo grounds. Folks took him for a hayseed, judging by their smug smiles, and that was fine by him.

The bleachers were already filling up. He approached the registration table, amid much murmured speculation, and laid out more of Holt's money for the entry fee. His conscience chafed a little, but he overrode it. He'd replace what he'd taken from his winnings, and his brother would be none the wiser.

"Rules say a man's got to be fit to ride," said the fat money taker, seated behind the table and sweating copiously even in the crisp fall air.

Jeb leaned in, aware that when his coat fell open, his .45, now fitted with a southpaw holster of his own making, was plainly visible. Not that he'd shoot anybody without it being a matter of life and death, but he wasn't responsible for any conclusions the other fellow might come to on his own. "I'm fit, all right," he drawled.

The big man blustered a little, but in the end, he scooped up the gold piece. "It's your money," he said. "You want to throw it away and get yourself stomped by the meanest horse God ever created at the same time, I reckon that's your affair."

Jeb smiled his I-knew-you'd-see-reason smile and scrawled his alias on the entry roster. His left hand was still awkward, but he'd been working with it right along, copying pages out of books and drawing the .45 whenever he got the chance. Lizzie was getting to be a pretty fair bottle thrower.

"Ride starts at three o'clock sharp," the moneyman said.

"I'll be here," Jeb replied, and walked away.

Now that he'd gotten into the game, he'd lie low for a while. Bide his time and get a look at the horse even hell wouldn't have.

51

"*Look!*" Lizzie cried, bouncing between Holt and Chloe on the hard seat of the buckboard as they rolled into Flagstaff. They'd left the ranch at dawn to get there, and the ride over cattle trails and dirt roads—where there had been roads at all—was difficult. "That man is wearing the shirt Concepcion made for Uncle Jeb, just last week."

Chloe shaded her eyes from the bright, cold sunlight and followed the direction the child indicated. Sure enough, she recognized that blue checked shirt, along with those buff trousers and the light-colored hat, with its distinctive copper band. Only the boots—and the man himself—were unfamiliar. Jeb's easy grace, that innate sense of being fully at home in his skin, with all his joints greased, was missing.

Holt steered the team alongside the sidewalk. "Where'd you get those duds, stranger?" he demanded, sounding even more like Angus than usual.

Chloe didn't speak, but she was sitting on the very edge of the seat, and both ears were wide-open.

The man looked rueful, but relaxed. "Swapped with a one-armed feller," he answered. "Fair and square."

Chloe jumped into the conversation. "Where is this 'one-armed feller' now?" The big event was scheduled for three, according to Holt's newspaper, though the rodeo itself had already started and would go on for several days. By the clock on top of the bank, they had less than an hour to find him.

The man on the sidewalk looked her over in a way she would have found wholly objectionable had the situation been less urgent. "You his wife?"

"We'll ask the questions," Holt put in coldly. "If you don't mind."

"Don't know where he went," the man said. "He shouldn't be too hard to spot, though."

"Why's that?" Holt asked, his voice as tight as the muscles lining his jaw.

The fellow shrugged. "He's wearing a mighty fine suit. And he's only got one good arm."

"Thanks," Holt said, probably deducing, as Chloe had, that they weren't going to get any more information out of him. Most likely, he didn't know much else, and even if he did, Jeb had surely made secrecy part of the deal.

They drove to the rodeo grounds, scanning the streets for Jeb as they did, but they had no luck. The town was jammed with rodeogoers, but all they saw were children, cowboys, ordinary smiths and merchants, and women clad in calico and sateen. Not a "fine suit" in the lot.

Three trips around the dusty edges of the dusty gathering served no other purpose than to take them in circles. Finally, at quarter to three, by his pocket watch, Holt parked the buckboard with a flock of others, set the brakes, and secured the reins. He got in line to buy tickets, while Chloe and Lizzie waited off to the side, watching everyone who came and went.

Still no trace of Jeb.

Holt joined them, then escorted them to their places in the crude grandstand. "Stay here," he said tersely, when they were seated. "I'll head over to the chutes, see if he's there."

Chloe watched helplessly as he walked away.

Lizzie took her hand, squeezed it, and brought her back to herself. "Might as well enjoy the show," she said, grinning that McKettrick grin. "If Uncle Jeb's made up his mind to ride in this rodeo, nobody will be able to stop him anyhow."

Chloe feared Lizzie was right, but she searched the milling throngs anyway, growing more frantic with every passing moment.

The bronc-riding event was announced by a man with a big voice and a megaphone. Only four riders had entered, he said; the horse had never been ridden, and the prize money was an unprecedented $1000 in gold.

Chloe watched, with her heart in her throat, as a chute opened on the far side of the large arena, and the fabled horse sprang out in a fury of snorting and stomping. The cowboy on his back went flying over the beast's head with the first good buck, and his chest was crushed under those deadly hooves before two other men managed to drag him out of the ring.

"Oh, dear God," Chloe whispered, searching the area around the chutes for Jeb or Holt, but there was no sign of either of them. They were lost in a cloud of churning dust and cowboys.

"This horse is a killer!" crowed the man with the megaphone, as if it were something to be celebrated.

Chloe shook her head, watched as the hell-born bronco was roped and half-dragged, half-herded, back to the pens. A garish flash of color—red and yellow, mixed up in a blur of motion—drew her eye to the next rider.

It was Jeb.

She tried to cover Lizzie's eyes, but the child squirmed free.

Even over the din, Chloe heard Jeb's shout of challenge, meant for the heavens, as well as the horse. Like as not, he didn't give a damn about the crowd.

At the edge of her vision, Chloe saw Holt climb up onto a fence to watch, but she couldn't take her gaze off Jeb, even for a moment. She was willing him to stay on that devil horse, or be thrown clear, and as clods of dirt flew from under those wicked hooves, still stained with the other cowboy's blood, her heart beat hard enough to rattle her bones.

She surged to her feet, but Lizzie caught hold of her hand and pulled her down again, with a strength Chloe might have marveled over, if she hadn't been so completely absorbed in the horrid spectacle.

The horse was an ugly creature, albino white, except for a splotch of mud brown on its heaving chest. It had wild pink eyes and narrow, spavined legs and its tail and mane were sparse. It was a monster, and the man dearest to Chloe's heart was riding on its back.

If Jeb McKettrick survives this, she thought vehemently, *I'll kill him myself.*

"Ride him!" Lizzie shouted, into the thundering, breathless silence around them.

Jeb gave another rebellious yelp and hung on with his one hand. The bowler hat sailed off and was soon ground into the bloody dirt, and Jeb's fair hair gleamed, a fire of gold in the sunlight.

After an eon, a bell clattered, and a cheer went up. Jeb had ridden the required length of time, but somebody had neglected to tell the horse that the contest was over. It went into a dizzying spin, then rocked from hind to forelegs, determined to ditch its rider or die trying.

Cool as an April evening, Jeb swung a leg over the brute's neck and jumped off. Even from that distance, Chloe could see the white flash of his grin, lighting up his dirty, triumphant face. Meanwhile, the horse whirled and went after him like an enraged bull, head down, foam flying from its mouth. He sidestepped it in a deft motion, watched calmly as the animal was roped in again, and subdued, though barely.

Chloe shot out of her seat, and this time, Lizzie couldn't restrain her. She ran to the fence, scrambled over it, her legs tangling in her skirts, and ran through the middle of the arena.

Jeb stood facing her, in his silly plaid suit, beaming like an idiot. The spectators roared, seeming to shift the very earth with the force of their exuberance, but for Chloe the sound was just a pulsing hum, distant and wholly irrelevant. Looking past Jeb's shoulder, Chloe caught a glimpse of Holt, sprinting toward them; but in that moment, he was no more real to her than the people swelling the grandstands and lining the fences.

"I won," Jeb said, evidently expecting a crown of laurels, then his eyes rolled back in his head, his knees buckled, and he would have gone down if Holt and Chloe hadn't grasped him and held him upright.

Holt draped Jeb's good arm over his shoulders and supported him. "Get Lizzie," he said to Chloe. "We're leaving."

Jeb's head lolled on his neck. "Not without my thousand dollars, we aren't," he said, and passed out again.

"Damn fool," Holt muttered, and steered his brother toward the nearest gate. Meanwhile, a third cowboy was mounting up for a suicidal attempt to take the contest for himself.

Chloe hurried back for Lizzie, who was still sitting in the bleachers. The child stared mutely into space, and her face was so pale that, for a moment, Chloe forgot all about Jeb McKettrick.

"Lizzie?" She touched the little girl's shoulder, noticed the doll in her lap.

Lizzie looked up at her, blinking. "I saw him," she said, her voice small.

"Who?" Chloe asked, sitting down, gathering Lizzie into her arms and holding her close.

"The bad man. The one who shot Aunt Geneva and the stagecoach driver," Lizzie murmured. "He wasn't wearing the bandanna over his face, like before, but I recognized him just the same. I knew his voice."

A chill struck Chloe to the marrow, and she looked around desperately for Jack, but he was nowhere in sight. "What did he say, Lizzie? What did he do?"

"He gave me this doll," Lizzie said, looking at the thing in her lap with horror, as though it were something coiled and venomous, ready to strike. She flung it down, and its china head cracked on the ground. "He wanted me to go with him, but I wouldn't. I kicked and bit—"

Chloe hugged Lizzie close again, fiercely, and she was sick with fear. Between Jeb's exploits and the rising threat from Jack Barrett, she felt light-headed and wobbly clear through. "Dear God," she whispered.

"He took hold of my arm," Lizzie went on, as if she were reading the words off some invisible scroll. "So I bit him."

Chloe kissed the top of Lizzie's head. "It's all right, sweetheart," she said. "He's gone now, and you're safe." The child was trembling, and Chloe waited for it to stop, holding on tight. "Let's go and find your papa, shall we? He'll be wondering where we are."

Tears glittered along Lizzie's lower lashes. "He's coming back. I know he is."

Chloe cupped the girl's chin in her hand. "Listen to me, Lizzie. Your papa will go to the law, and they'll find the man and arrest him. He can't hurt you."

Lizzie didn't look convinced. Maybe she knew Chloe was just as scared as she was, and whistling in the dark.

"Here's your money!" Holt growled, when the bronc-riding event was over, and two more cowboys had been injured in the effort to claim it, flinging the heavy bag of gold coins at Jeb's chest. He'd just collected the prize from the table, a few yards away. "Are you happy now?"

Jeb, sitting on the floor of Holt's buckboard, with the tailgate dangling, caught it with his left hand, hefted it in his palm, gauging its weight, and shoved the thing into the pocket of his ill-fitting plaid coat. "You're damned right I am," he said. He still felt a mite woozy, and he knew he was in for it with Chloe, but he'd *won*. He was a man of property, and for the moment that was all that mattered.

It was a short moment.

Something inside him quivered and, at the familiar

signal, he looked up. Chloe was hustling toward them, her hat askew, her dress covered in dust. Clasping Lizzie's hand tightly in her own, she gave him one skewering look and turned to Holt. He hadn't minded the look, but he wanted her attention on him, even if she *was* spitting mad.

She went so far as to take Holt's arm and pull him out of earshot, which added insult to injury, from Jeb's perspective. They spoke in hushed voices, and as he watched, the color drained out of Holt's face. He drew Lizzie to his side, hoisted her easily onto his hip, and she threw her arms around his neck and clung for dear life.

Jeb frowned. He wanted to jump down off the wagon, walk right over there, and demand to know what was going on, but he'd torn out some of the sutures in his arm during the ride, and blood was seeping through the sleeve of his coat. His knees might as well have been made of water as muscle and bone; If he tried to stand on his feet, like as not he'd pitch over in a swoon and get a mouthful of dirt for a bonus.

Chloe went on talking, waving her arms. Holt listened and shook his head, as if refuting whatever point she was trying to make, and he kept looking around, even as he held Lizzie with one arm and patted her back with the other. The kid was sobbing.

Jeb felt a rush of chagrin. Had his ride scared Lizzie that much?

No, he decided. It couldn't be that—Lizzie was a McKettrick, whatever Holt's stubborn claims to the contrary. She'd probably been cheering for him the whole time he was on that demon's back.

Suddenly, the gold felt cold as ice against his chest, even through his shirt.

Chloe hurtled toward him like a barrel rolling downhill, her face streaked with dirt and tears, and he wanted more than anything to take her in his arms and hold her, but he didn't quite dare.

"Look at you," she said, with none of the admiration he reckoned as his due. "You're filthy, and you're *bleeding*!"

Out of self-defense, he shifted his gaze to Holt, who spoke quietly to the child as he carried her toward the wagon. "What's the matter with Lizzie?" Jeb snapped to Chloe.

Chloe put her hands on her hips. "What do you care?" she shot back, in a sizzling whisper. "You never think about anyone but yourself!"

Dammit, that hurt. He'd been thinking of Chloe, and no one else, the whole of this adventure. "I wasn't—"

Just then, Holt reached the wagon, hoisted Lizzie up into the seat. She huddled there, hugging herself, but her chin was at an obstinate angle, she'd squared her shoulders, and she'd stopped crying.

"Don't ever come near me again, Jeb McKettrick!" Chloe raged. "I don't want to look at you, I don't want to hear your voice—"

Fury stung through him. "Now, wait just a damn minute—"

She whirled away from him, rounded the wagon, raising little puffs of dust as she went, and hauled herself up beside Lizzie. Holt came his way, but from the expression on his face, there were no words of praise forthcoming and none of condolence, either.

"I'd advise you to settle in and hold on tight," Holt drawled, his eyes snapping with bad temper. "It's going to be a rough ride back to the Circle C, and an even rougher one when we get there."

A handshake would not have been untoward, considering that Jeb had just ridden an unrideable horse and earned himself a thousand dollars while he was at it. At the moment, though, he was more concerned with Lizzie than his pride. "Just tell me *what happened*," he rasped.

Holt was already turning away, fixing to climb into the wagon box and take the reins. He stopped, though, and fixed Jeb with a gaze hot enough to scorch cured leather. "When I get the time," he said tersely, "I will." With that, he got aboard, released the brakes, and slapped down the reins.

The wagon shot forward so suddenly that Jeb nearly hurtled over the tailgate, now raised and latched. That would have been downright humiliating, when he'd just ridden the meanest horse in the Territory without getting thrown.

He pulled himself back into the wagon bed and held on with his one hand, all but choking on the dust that rose up around them in a smothering cloud.

They stopped in the center of town, and Jeb braced himself for an argument, having no intention of wasting time or money on an unnecessary visit to some sawbones, but instead of hauling him to a doctor, Holt got down and strode into the sheriff's office.

Chloe put her arms around Lizzie, tight, and they sat waiting in the wagon seat.

Jeb let down the tailgate and eased himself to the ground. He was still a mite unsteady, so he gripped the edge of the wagon and waited until the ground stopped swaying. When he figured he could cover the distance to the entrance, he set out to follow Holt.

He felt Chloe's gaze searing his back as he passed on her side of the wagon; but she didn't speak, and he didn't look back.

When he got inside, Holt was already shut away with the sheriff, behind closed doors, so the whole effort was for nothing.

52

For Chloe, the ride back to the Circle C was not only hard, but interminable, fashioned of stony silence as it was. Holt drove the team at a demanding pace and kept looking around, as if expecting Jack Barrett to set upon them at any time. Lizzie huddled against Chloe, both of them cosseted in the same cloak, and Jeb sat in the wagon bed, with a pile of feed sacks behind his back, the .45 resting loosely in his hand.

Chloe had tried to ignore him, but her gaze strayed in his direction every so often, and he always caught her looking.

"I thought you never wanted to see me again," he said once.

She'd sniffed at that and summarily turned her back, straightening her spine.

They reached the ranch without incident, which was something to be grateful for. Chloe tried hard to ratchet her spirits up a couple of notches, hoping the others would be cheered, too, but it didn't work.

Holt brought the wagon to a stop behind the darkened house, and a couple of elderly ranch hands came hobbling to unhitch the team. Meanwhile, he lifted Chloe down, then Lizzie. Jeb was left to manage on his own, which was fine by Chloe.

Inside, she lit the lamps while Holt built a fire in the cookstove. They were all hungry and tired, after a long and arduous day, especially Lizzie.

Despite Holt's previous insistence that she'd been hired to teach, not keep house, Chloe assembled a supper of pancakes and fried eggs, and put water on to heat while they were eating, so she and Lizzie could wash up before bed.

By the time she'd tucked Lizzie in and read her a chapter from one of Charles Dickens's novels, having convinced her that that would suffice for Saturday's lessons, Chloe was bone tired.

She went back downstairs, carrying the basin from her room, intending to ladle in some hot water. She longed for a real bath, but the preparations were beyond her current strength. She thought with yearning of the fine porcelain tub at the Arizona Hotel and promised herself the use of it when she got back to town.

She got a shock when she stepped into the kitchen. Holt had either gone to the barn or to bed, and there was Jeb, splashing in a round washtub in front of the stove, the light of one lantern rimming his hair in a flicker of gold.

She froze, unable to go forward or back.

He grinned, probably well aware that her immobility was his doing. "Join me?" he teased.

She felt color rush into her face, and the indignation that went along with it served to stiffen her knees and align her sagging backbone. She still couldn't move, though, and her gaze went straight to the neat though jagged line of stitches in the upper part of his right arm. He'd washed away the blood, but the skin looked angry, and there were gaps in the incision. He'd have a nasty scar, and he'd be lucky if he didn't get an infection.

"Not a chance," she answered, well aware that the response had been too long in coming.

"How about washing my back?"

"How about you go straight to hell?"

He laughed. "Chloe, Chloe," he scolded, stopping his one-handed scrubbing to sit back and soak. "Is that any way for a loving wife to talk to her husband?"

She didn't trust her legs to carry her any farther than the chair at the head of the table, the one where Holt generally sat. She dropped into it, resting her forehead in one hand and shaking her head.

"What happened today, Chloe?" His voice was serious now, and earnest. "To Lizzie, I mean. I asked Holt, but he wouldn't tell me a damn thing."

Chloe felt a tear tickle its way down her cheek. "A man tried to carry her off," she whispered, too tired to fight him anymore.

He rose out of the tub with a whoosh of water. "*What?*"

Chloe kept her gaze on the tabletop, watching a tear spread on the oilcloth. "She said it was the same man who robbed the stagecoach and shot those people." *It was Jack Barrett,* she added miserably, in the silence of her mind. *It's me he wants, and he'll stop at nothing and no one until he succeeds.*

Jeb was right beside her, looming over her, dripping wet and most definitely naked. Chloe squeezed her eyes shut.

"Why didn't anybody tell me that?" he demanded.

She shook her head. "Leave it alone, Jeb. Please."

He grasped her chin, made her look at him. "Who was it, Chloe? And don't say you don't know, because I can see it in your face—you *do* know."

Chloe swallowed. "It was Jack Barrett," she said, with a sense of impending doom. "My former husband."

53

"*Jack Barrett*," Jeb said, through his teeth.

Chloe's gaze was locked with his, and his grip on her chin was firm; she couldn't have looked away, even if she'd tried. "Yes. I'm sure he was the one who shot you."

His face hardened, and something quickened in his eyes. "And you weren't going to tell me?"

Everything within her seemed to wilt. She shook her head miserably. "Because we—I—knew you'd go after him, and I was afraid he'd kill you."

He absorbed that, his breathing shallow and rapid, hissing in and out. "You've seen him, haven't you?" he guessed. He was so firmly planted in himself, body and mind, that his powers of perception sometimes amazed Chloe.

There was no going back; she'd reaped the whirlwind, where Jeb was concerned, and even though she still believed with all her heart that if she'd done the wrong thing, it had been for the right reasons, she knew no power on earth would convince him of that.

"Once," she admitted. "I saw him once."

"When?" The word zinged through the narrow space between them, deadly as a bullet.

Chloe flinched, and her eyes stung mightily; she hated letting him see that she was crying, hated even more that he'd been the one to cause this assault on her pride. "Soon after you were shot," she admitted. "I was walking back from the Jessups' wagon—I went to see Ellen and Walter—and Jack was waiting for me when I took a shortcut through the cemetery."

"*And you're just telling me this now?*"

Her temper, at once her curse and her salvation, swelled, raising her with it, propelling her to her feet. He stepped back, and she was woefully conscious of his naked state, though he seemed heedless, in his fury.

"You were flat on your back, recovering from a bullet wound! What could you have done?"

He ignored the question. "Did my brothers know?"

"Yes."

His blue eyes glittered, stone-cold. "By *God*, none of you had no right to make the choice for me!"

"We were trying to protect you!"

"I don't need protecting, Chloe. I can do a fair job of that myself, *if* I know what the hell I'm up against in the first place!"

She snatched a towel off a chair back, shoved it at him. "A fair job? Oh, I saw that for myself, this very day," she said scornfully. "You're a reckless fool, and if you want to kill yourself, go right ahead, but don't expect me to help you do it!"

He wrapped the towel around his hips, one-handed, deft even in his anger. "I did that for you!" he yelled. "I wanted to—oh, *hell,* just forget it. There's no reasoning with you anyhow!"

"You dare speak to me of *reason?!*" she shouted.

The kitchen door swung open. "Would you two mind lowering your voices?" Holt snapped. "The roof is about to come off this place, you're raising so much hell. I won't have my daughter any more upset than she already is."

Chloe sat down again, hard. In her outrage and injury, she'd forgotten all about Lizzie's presence, and she was ashamed of that.

"I'm gone," Jeb said, and turned his back on them both. A great deal of scuffling about followed, while he got back into his clothes, then his sling. Holt tried to help him once, but Jeb shoved him away.

"Dammit, Jeb," Holt growled, "it's dark out, and you're in no condition—"

"Shut up, Holt," Jeb warned. "You knew about Barrett all along, and that means you're as big a liar as she is!"

Holt gave a gusty sigh. "Chloe's not a liar," he said. "She just has the bad judgment to love your sorry hide, that's all."

"I do *not* love Jeb McKettrick," Chloe felt compelled to point out.

Holt gave her a look. "You're not helping," he said.

"It's probably the first time she's ever told the truth in her life," Jeb seethed. He snatched his gun belt down off a shelf and strapped it on with an effort that was painful to watch.

Holt took a step in his brother's direction. "Jeb—"

"Leave me the hell alone," Jeb said, grabbing his coat and hat. A moment later, the back door slammed behind him.

Holt let out his breath, and there was a curse riding on it.

"You're not just going to let him go!" Chloe marveled.

"How do you suggest I stop him? I guess I could lasso and hog-tie him; but, short of that, I can't think of a way."

Chloe doubled up one fist and slammed it down on the tabletop.

"I told you it wasn't a good idea to keep this from him," Holt said, with another weary sigh. He went to the stove and poured himself a mug of leftover coffee.

"Where do you think he means to go?" Chloe asked, in a small voice.

Holt stood looking out the window, though it was doubtful he could see much, with the moon in hiding. "Back to the Triple M, I suppose. I'll let him get a start, then ride after him. If he ran into Jack Barrett along the way and got himself shot to death, I'd never forgive myself."

Chloe stood, smoothing her skirts with damp palms. "I'll go with you."

At last, Holt turned to face her. "You'll stay right here," he said. "With Lizzie. Lock the doors and keep a gun handy."

Chloe collapsed into her chair again. Much as she hated it, he was right. She couldn't leave Lizzie alone and unprotected, especially now. Jack might be watching the place, waiting for a chance to finish what he'd started at the rodeo. If he wasn't already tracking Jeb.

"I should have stayed in Tombstone," she lamented, more to herself than Holt.

He laid a loaded .45 on the table in front of her. "Right now, I'd have to agree," he said evenly. "Do you know how to use this, Chloe?"

A horse thundered past the house.

She nodded. The pistol was heavier than her derringer, and it had a better range, but the principle was the same.

"I'll post some guards outside," he told her. And then he was putting on his coat and hat, getting ready to leave. "Latch the door."

"Be careful," she said.

Chloe waited until he'd gone, then forced herself across the room to lower the latch. She checked the front door, to make certain it was locked as well, and went back to the kitchen to retrieve the .45 Holt had left for her. Its metal barrel was cold as well water.

A shudder went through her. The last time she'd faced

Jack, she'd had Walter's rifle, but hadn't been able to use it. If he came to the Circle C, though, and took so much as a step toward Lizzie, she'd drop him in his tracks.

She tried not to think about Jeb, out there in the darkness, or Holt either, as she went back upstairs, a lantern in one hand and an instrument of death in the other.

54

*J*eb braced his gun hand on the pommel of his saddle and rode out into the middle of the trail to await the rider he knew was a hundred yards or so behind him. It was stone dark, but his eyes had adjusted to the gloom, and he knew every inch of this ground anyway, like he knew the terrain of his own soul.

Startled to find him in the middle of the road, Holt reined in. "Shit," he said. "You scared the hell out of me."

"You must have been one pitiful Ranger," Jeb observed, thrusting the pistol back into its holster. "I could have shot you six different times before you even knew I was here."

"Well, you didn't," Holt said, his horse fitful alongside Jeb's.

Jeb's mood was not cordial. "What are you doing here?"

"Trying to make sure you don't get yourself killed."

"I can do that on my own."

"Get yourself killed? I have no doubts on that score."

"That isn't what I meant, and you damn well know it."

Holt sighed. "If I ever had any faith in your good sense, I lost it when you entered the rodeo."

Jeb grinned in spite of the ache in the center of his chest. Chloe had left her mark on him, and it would be a long time scarring over. "I owe you some money," he confessed. "You should find a better hiding place for that tobacco tin. Easy pickings."

"Maybe I'll just take it out of your hide, a strip at a time."

"You're welcome to try."

"I like an even fight, and right now, you're a cripple." Leather creaked as Holt shifted in the saddle. "Let's go, cowboy. It's too cold and too dark to sit out here jawing in the middle of the trail."

Jeb turned his horse toward the Triple M. He didn't particularly want to go there just now, but town was too far away. Short of shooting Holt, he didn't see how he could stop him from riding along, so he resigned himself to unwanted company. "You shouldn't have left Chloe and Lizzie alone."

"In case it's escaped you," Holt said, "Chloe can take care of herself and Lizzie in the bargain. You're the one who hasn't got the wits to stay out of the way of a bullet."

Jeb offered no argument, though he figured he could have come up with plenty of good ones. Given a little time.

They rode at an easy trot and reached the Triple M an hour later.

It was late, but there was light glowing at the kitchen window, and that troubled Jeb. He'd intended to put away his horse and find a place in the bunkhouse, but he knew he wouldn't sleep until he made sure nothing was wrong. Holt evidently felt the same way, because he dismounted and left his horse standing in the dooryard, just as Jeb did.

Angus was in his place at the head of the table, wearing blue long johns and drinking coffee from a mug. He narrowed his eyes when Jeb came through the door, with Holt right behind him.

"Fine time for calling on your neighbors," the old man grunted, but the look in his eyes revealed a more complicated state of mind. He was curious, and worried, and maybe a little pleased, too.

"I'm not a neighbor," Jeb said. "I live here. Are you all right?"

"Just going over a few things in my mind. The older a man gets, the less sleep he needs." Angus sized him up. "Don't go bursting into your room. That Sue Ellen Caruthers woman is in there, and she's under the weather."

Holt stepped past Jeb, jostling him a little. "Who?"

Angus's gaze flickered over his eldest son now, surmising. "You heard me the first time, boy," he said. "One of the hands fished that poor gal out of the creek day before yesterday. She damn near drowned. Wakes up now and then; but if she can talk, she's decided against it for now."

Jeb watched his father and Holt as he hung up his coat and hat in their customary places. He'd put his horse away in a few minutes, then bed down in the spare room, though he didn't reckon he'd get any more sleep than the old man.

Holt dragged back a chair, still wearing his outside gear. He seemed to have forgotten everything at the mention of his former housekeeper's name. Jeb supposed he'd wind up looking after two horses, instead of one. "What the hell happened?" Holt demanded of the old man. "How did she wind up in the creek?"

"Don't rightly know," Angus said, pondering. "We figured she was long gone, after you sent her packing. Never expected to see her again."

Jeb took up a position that allowed him to see both men's faces. There was something more going on here than a discussion of the leftover mail-order bride Holt had hired to look after his house. She'd set her cap for Kade, poor girl, but he'd only had eyes for Mandy.

Holt's jaw was hard as steel. "She told me she was going back East," he said.

"Well, I guess she lied," Angus answered. His gaze drilled into Holt's face. "Take off your hat," he said. "It's the middle of the night, and everybody but me is asleep, but since you're here, you might as well make yourself at home."

Holt scowled, but he took off the hat. For a moment, Jeb thought he was going to fling it across the room, but in the end he just set it on the bench beside him.

Glad of the distraction this little interchange offered, Jeb sat down in Concepcion's chair and settled back for the show.

Angus lowered his bristly brows at him, saying nothing. Jeb shifted his weight, well aware that he was expected to make himself scarce, but he didn't budge. "Is Miss Caruthers going to be all right?" he asked, making his voice and expression as ingenuous as he could. If he left that room, he'd have to think about Chloe, and he wasn't up to that yet.

Angus didn't like relenting, but he did. "She's scared as hell. We've been able to figure out that much."

"I want to see her," Holt said, starting to rise.

Angus laid a hand on his forearm and stopped his progress. "You'll scare the spit out of her," he said. "Anyway, Concepcion says she'll be fine, once she's had some time to rest up." His gaze swayed back to Jeb like a cattle gate to the latch. "You here for a visit, or to stay?"

"I'm staying," Jeb said. "Not that I want to."

"What about Lizzie?" Angus wanted to know. It was plain the question was meant for both his sons. "She up at that place alone?"

"She's with Chloe."

Jeb felt the name like a well-aimed creek rock.

Holt cleared his throat, shifted in his chair. "I'd like to bring Lizzie here for a while," he said carefully.

"She's welcome anytime," Angus replied. "But you

haven't exactly been eager to let her be a part of this family. What's this about, Holt?"

Holt stiffened visibly at the gentle note in Angus's voice. "I'm heading back to Texas," he said out of the blue. "I'll sell you the Circle C, if you want it."

Angus had lusted after that land for as long as Jeb could remember, but now that it was actually within his grasp, he brushed the idea aside with a wave of his hand. "Where the hell did *that* come from?" he demanded, shooting to his feet and looming at the end of the table like a geyser of steam straight from hell. "You never said a word to me about going back to Texas. Now all of a sudden you just *announce* it?"

"I don't have to explain my decisions to you, old man."

Angus slammed his fist down on the table, causing the sugar bowl to make a leap. "This time you damn well do!" he roared.

Holt clenched his jaw. "I did what I came here to do. Got a look at you and your sons and this ranch. Now I'm ready to head back where I belong."

"You're a liar as well as a coward!" Angus bellowed. Upstairs, the baby took to squalling. "You're starting to give a good God damn about this family, and you can't stand that. It scares you to death!"

Holt kept his temper, even looked a little ashamed, but the glitter in his eyes said he wasn't about to give ground. "I'll come for Lizzie in the spring."

"The way I came to fetch you?" Angus challenged, breathing so hard that Jeb thought his shirt buttons might pop off.

Holt glared. "No, old man. I'm actually going to do it."

Angus reflected for a long time, and with every passing moment he seemed to get older. His back and shoulders had always been straight, but now they stooped. "If you've made up your mind," he said finally, "I'll give you a fair price."

Holt only nodded. He wouldn't look at Angus again, though, or even at Jeb. "Good," he said without conviction.

"You're sure you want to do this?" Angus ventured. Jeb hoped the old man's ticker wouldn't give out, because beneath that crusty exterior it was breaking for certain.

"I'm sure," Holt said, but he didn't look or sound that way. By Jeb's reckoning, the old man had stuck a little too close to the bone for Holt's liking.

An insight struck Jeb then, one he couldn't share with his father.

This was about Chloe. *But here's where you'd best do some fancy listening, little brother,* Holt had said when Jeb had stepped into the Circle C kitchen and caught him holding her. *If I thought she'd have me, I'd take her for a wife as soon as I could round up a preacher.*

At the time Jeb had figured it for a gibe. Now he reckoned different. He should have known Holt wouldn't speak lightly of something like that.

Jeb ached inside, just to think of Holt bolting for Texas, but under the circumstances he was all for it.

Angus's weary gaze groped for and found Jeb. "Good night, boy," he said pointedly. "See to the horses, if you haven't already done it."

Jeb was almost too thunderstruck to speak. "I've only got one good arm, you know," he said lamely.

Angus didn't look away. "Doesn't seem to keep you from doing whatever the hell else you want to do."

Jeb went back to the door, reclaimed his hat and coat from the pegs beside it, and whistled for the horses, but he was just going through the motions. His mind was on the Circle C, with Chloe.

Did she feel the same way Holt did?

55

*C*hloe had tried in vain to sleep, but she was up, red-eyed and despairing, when Holt rode in at dawn. She set the coffee on to brew while he was putting his horse away in the barn, and when he knocked at the back door, she raised the latch and opened it.

His expression was so bleak that she raised a hand to her throat in alarm.

"Did something happen to Jeb?" she asked, stepping back.

"He's fine." Holt's every motion was fraught with weariness as he hung up his hat and coat and took off his gun belt. "You don't look like you got any more rest than I did."

Chloe set aside her own concerns, laid a hand on his arm. "Holt, what's the matter? You look wretched."

He turned to her. "I sold the Circle C." He sounded surprised, even as he spoke the words, like it was something he hadn't expected to do.

Chloe's mouth fell open.

He brushed past her, went to the stove, poured himself a cup of coffee, even though the grounds hadn't had time to settle. "It's part of the Triple M now," he said. "All of it. Including this house."

Chloe shook her head, unable to take it in. She wasn't well acquainted with Holt, but she knew how he felt about the ranch by the way he ran it, and she was baffled. "Wh-what about Lizzie?" she asked.

He glanced at the ceiling, as though he could see through the boards, catch sight of his young daughter, asleep in her bed. "She'll stay with the McKettricks until I get us a place in Texas," he said.

Chloe had to sit down. "*Why?* Why would you leave here?"

Holt took a sip from his coffee cup, avoided her gaze. "Because Texas is home."

"*This* is home," Chloe said, though she didn't have the right. "Oh, Holt, Lizzie is going to be devastated. She just found you, just began to settle in."

"She loves her grandfather. She'll be fine at the Triple M."

"She loves *you*. If you leave, she's going to believe you're not coming back, no matter what you tell her beforehand."

"It's done," Holt said, in a tone that brooked no further discussion. His expression was grim, his eyes haunted. "Go ahead with the lessons, and don't mention any of this to her. I want to break the news myself."

Chloe shook her head.

Holt left the room without another word, and he stayed clear of Chloe the rest of the day.

She went over Lizzie's schoolwork with her, but they were both distracted and fitful, and they didn't accomplish much.

"I think something's the matter with my papa," Lizzie said late that afternoon, watching dolefully as Chloe packed her reticule to go back to town. She wondered if she'd ever set foot in this house again and felt sad to think of it standing empty, without Holt and Lizzie.

"He's got some things on his mind," Chloe said carefully. Holt had made his wishes clear, where Lizzie and the sale of the Circle C were concerned, but it was hard to be cheerful.

Lizzie looked sad. "He liked having Uncle Jeb here, I think."

"Yes," Chloe agreed. *So did I.*

"Is Uncle Jeb mad at my papa?"

"I don't think so, sweetheart. And I know for sure that he's not mad at you, either, so don't be worrying."

"He sure sounded like he was mad at somebody last night." Lizzie's gaze was level. Chloe's last hope that the child hadn't heard the argument between her and Jeb was dashed. "So did you."

Chloe went to sit beside Lizzie on the bed, slipped an arm around her. When Lizzie rested her head against Chloe's shoulder, the cracks in her heart gave way.

"You mustn't fret, Lizzie," she said, very softly.

A little shudder went through Lizzie. Realizing it was a sob, Chloe held her closer and rested her chin atop the small head. "Uncle Jeb only rode that bad horse for you," Lizzie said, and wept in earnest. "He was going to build you a house with the money he won."

Chloe's own eyes were wet. "Did he say that?" she whispered.

Lizzie nodded against her shoulder. "We talked a lot. I threw bottles up in the air, so he could shoot them." Another shudder went through the child. "Why can't anything ever stay like it is? Why do people always go away?"

Chloe didn't know how to answer. She was asking the same questions, inside, where nobody else could hear.

There was a sound from the hall, and she looked up, saw Holt in the doorway. She couldn't remember the last time she'd seen so much pain in a man's eyes as she saw in his in that moment.

"The buckboard's out front," he said to Chloe. "If you're ready, you'd better go while there's still some daylight."

Chloe sniffled, nodded her head. "I'm ready." She extracted herself gently from Lizzie's embrace, kissed the child's forehead. "Work hard on your lessons," she said, nearly choking on the words, and her attempt to say them without breaking down completely.

"I will," Lizzie promised. She glanced at her father

and, probably wanting to please him, dashed away her tears with the backs of her hands.

Holt carried the reticule downstairs, put it in the back of the buckboard, helped Chloe up into the seat. The driver had a rifle close at hand, she noticed, and this time there were two men on horseback to accompany them instead of just one.

"Good-bye, Chloe," Holt said, and that was when Chloe knew how soon he meant to leave for Texas. She wouldn't be coming back to the Circle C, not to teach Lizzie, anyway.

He handed her an envelope.

She glanced over at Lizzie, who stood shivering on the porch, and saw the realization of what was happening strike the child like a blow. Chloe tried to smile, to wave, but she couldn't lift her hand, and her mouth refused to work.

Holt stepped back from the wagon and signaled to the driver, and in the next instant the team was in motion, with a great clatter of hooves and rattling harness fittings.

Nearly blinded by tears, Chloe knew she shouldn't look back, but she did.

Lizzie ran after the wagon, waving her arms and weeping. "Chloe!" she shrieked, squirming free when Holt tried to restrain her. "Chloe, come back!"

"Stop!" Chloe cried to the driver. "Stop this wagon!"

He drew back on the reins, yelled "whoa" to the horses.

Chloe scrambled over the side and raced back to gather Lizzie into her arms. Holt was right behind Lizzie, but he stood back now, looking helpless. His throat worked as he swallowed.

"Hush, baby," Chloe said, holding Lizzie fiercely. "Please don't cry."

"He's sending you away forever!" Lizzie wailed. "I know he is!" She whirled in Chloe's embrace to look at Holt. "I hate you!" she screamed. "I hate you!"

Holt lowered his head.

Chloe cupped Lizzie's wet face in her palms. "You mustn't say that, Lizzie," she said. She was crying, too. "Your papa loves you very much. He's trying to do what's best for you."

"Don't go," Lizzie whimpered. "Uncle Jeb went away, and now you're going, too."

"You can visit me in town," Chloe said, because it was all she had to offer. She was watching Holt, holding Lizzie. "We'll always be friends, Lizzie. I promise you that."

Lizzie seemed to deflate. "But you have to go?"

Chloe swallowed, nodded. "Yes," she said.

A tremor went through Lizzie, and she broke out of Chloe's arms, turned on Holt, grabbing up handfuls of dirt and small stones, flinging them at him in a shower of despondent fury. "You're not my father!" she shrieked. "I hate you! I want my grandpa!" With that, she raced into the house, stumbling as she went, and slammed the door behind her.

Holt had endured it all in silence. With a nod, he indicated that Chloe should get back into the wagon.

Having no choice, Chloe obeyed.

 Sue Ellen Caruthers sat in a rocking chair on the front porch of the Triple M ranch house, bundled in a quilt and watching the autumn sunlight dance on the creek. Across the water, Rafe McKettrick was driving stakes into the ground, fixing to put up a picket fence around the sturdy house he'd built for himself and Emmeline.

 Just that morning, Sue Ellen had taken breakfast at the kitchen table for the first time, instead of from a tray in bed, and she'd watched Kade—the man she'd come west to marry—with Mandy. The two of them joked a lot, and even bickered a little; but when Kade looked at his wife, the whole of his heart was in his eyes.

 Sue Ellen ached inside. For a while, she'd hoped to win Holt's affections, cooking and cleaning for him, dusting all those oft-read books he had, taking any chance to please him and making the most of it. Even before the child, Lizzie, came, though, she'd known she was practically invisible to him.

And then there was Jack Barrett. She'd entered into that alliance in a spirit of vengeance and shouldn't have hoped for anything better than she got. She had things to make up for, where that choice was concerned.

The front door opened, and she knew by the good smells of lavender and cinnamon and starched cotton that Concepcion was there.

"Feeling better?" the other woman asked gently. Sue Ellen hadn't said a word since she'd awakened, hadn't been able to, but Concepcion never gave up. She just kept on reaching out, trying her best to initiate a conversation.

Tears burned in Sue Ellen's eyes, and she shook her head.

Concepcion pulled up a second chair and sat down, facing her. The crisp breeze ruffled tendrils of her ebony hair, made them dance around her brown-Madonna face. "I suppose it was hard for you, seeing Kade and Mandy together this morning at breakfast."

Sue Ellen kept her gaze on Rafe, watched numbly as Emmeline came out of their fine house to speak to him. He picked her up in his arms, kissed her soundly, and spun her around in a dance of purest joy, and the sound of her laughter floated across the sparkling creek.

What was it like to be that happy? Sue Ellen despaired of ever knowing.

Concepcion took her hand, squeezed it. "I was alone, once, like you are now," she said, very quietly. "My Manuel was murdered. It was a horrible thing, and I did not think I could endure it. The first Mrs. McKettrick—her name was Georgia—took me in. My life changed that day, though I did not know it yet."

Sue Ellen met the other woman's eyes, curious and quietly moved. If she could have spoken then, she would have, but words, however clear in her thoughts, were garbled when she tried to voice them.

Concepcion squeezed her hand again, and the dark eyes turned sad, reflective. "When Georgia died, I wanted to die, too. The world seemed too cruel a place to live in. But she had made me promise to stay and look after Angus and her boys if anything ever happened to her, so I had to do it. It was hard, and Angus was so broken that I thought he would never mend; but in time, things changed. Things will change for you, too, Sue Ellen. If you hold on, you will see."

Sue Ellen swallowed. She had to warn these people about Jack Barrett, but it seemed impossible. Then, through her confusion, a single shaft of reason shone. On the strength of that, she made a writing motion with one hand.

Concepcion understood immediately, and hurried into the house. She was back in a few moments, with a ledger book and a stub of a pencil.

The effort of writing was laborious for Sue Ellen, and eminently frustrating. The letters were lopsided and child-like, and like her private attempts to speak, they didn't come out right, but Sue Ellen got her message down.

JACK BARRT TRI TAK HTS GIRL.

Concepcion's eyes widened as she read the words over, once and then again. She crossed herself and dashed back into the house, shouting for the men.

Kade came out, crouched in front of Sue Ellen's chair, nodded to the ledger book and pencil she was still holding. "Where, Sue Ellen?" he asked quietly. "Where is he?"

CABN WOODS CC, she wrote, agonizing over every letter.

He nodded. "Thank you," he said. Then he turned, this man who might have been hers, and shouted across the water for Rafe to come. Rafe nodded and ran toward his barn, with Emmeline right behind him, holding her skirts so she wouldn't fall.

A tear slipped down Sue Ellen's cheek, but Kade never noticed. She hadn't expected him to, but it still hurt that he didn't.

Time had passed, she didn't know how much, when someone took her hand. Startled, she turned and saw Mandy standing beside her. Her smile was gentle, and her eyes saw too much. "You'd better come into the house now," she said. "Rest up and have some tea. I'll help you back to bed, and bring you a tray if you're hungry."

Sue Ellen felt raw inside, as though everything vital in her had been scraped clean away; but she nodded, and let Mandy help her to her feet.

*　　*　　*

Lizzie's eyes were puffy from crying, and her stomach felt peculiar, all jumpy and fretful. She'd listened woodenly to her papa's explanations at supper—Chloe hadn't done anything wrong, he'd said. He'd sent her away because the ranch was sold, and she, Lizzie, was going to live at the Triple M, with her grandpa and Concepcion, while he found them a new ranch in Texas.

She didn't want to go back to Texas. It would hurt too much to see those old places again, without her mother in them.

So she'd pretended to go right to sleep after Papa tucked her into bed, and waited with her eyes closed until she heard him come back up the stairs, a long time later, and go into his room down the hall. Then she'd gotten up, put on her clothes and her sturdiest shoes, and sneaked out.

There was a light under his bedroom door, and she almost ruined everything by going over and knocking. Telling Holt Cavanagh straight out that she wasn't going to Texas or anyplace else.

She knew what he'd say, though, the same thing Chloe had said. That he was doing what was best for her. Well, the best thing *wasn't* going back to Texas. The best thing was staying right there, where they had a family. She felt a deep need to get to her grandpa as soon as possible. When Angus McKettrick heard tell of this foolishness, he'd straighten everything out.

She let herself out of the house, and the cold wind

buffeted her. It was powerful dark, too, and she knew the bad man might be out there someplace, the one who'd killed Aunt Geneva and the stagecoach driver, then tried to steal her at the rodeo. She'd remembered his eyes when she looked into them; they were cruel, those eyes, with no soul behind them. Even if she lived to be older than her grandpa, and that was old, she would never forget the evidence of that cruelty, her aunt and the driver falling down dead, with his bullets in them.

Again, Lizzie hesitated. Her papa's temper would be sorely tried when he discovered she was missing, and though he'd never whupped her, he probably would this time if he caught up to her before she got to her grandpa.

She heard her grandfather's booming voice in the back of her mind. *If you ever run up against something you can't handle, Lizzie-beth, you just come to me, and I'll fix it directly.* If he'd said those words to her once, he'd said them a dozen times, and Lizzie believed them with the whole of her spirit.

So she started walking toward the Triple M.

She walked, and she walked. Her feet started to hurt, and she was scared the whole time, though she felt better when the sun came up and warmed her as it climbed higher into the sky.

She heard the horses coming, and almost ran to hide, trying to decide which side of the road to go toward, then her uncles came around the bend, all three of them. They were clearly surprised to see her.

It was Rafe who swung down and scooped her up.

"Lizzie-beth," he gasped, "what the Sam Hill are you doing out here by yourself?"

"I ran away," she said, without a shred of remorse.

"Well, that was a damn fool thing to do," Rafe replied, but he smiled a little, with his eyes, if not his mouth. "Is everything all right up home?"

Lizzie shook her head. She hoped Rafe wouldn't set her down too soon, because it felt good to be held in those strong arms, even if she wasn't a baby, like little Katie. "Papa says we're going to Texas," she said.

Rafe walked back to where Jeb and Kade sat, like giants on the backs of their big horses, looking on with serious faces. Lizzie hoped they weren't put out with her for leaving home.

"I only wanted to talk to Grandpa," she said, in her own defense.

Rafe handed her up to Kade, probably because Jeb's arm was still such a mess.

"I think we'd better have a word with your father, first," Kade told her.

They didn't have to travel far to do that. They met her papa less than a mile up the road. He was riding hard, and he looked more scared than mad, though he narrowed his eyes when he saw her and swung down off his horse while it was still moving.

"Lizzie McKettrick!" he yelled, storming toward her. "I ought to tan your hide!" He was so furious that he didn't seem to notice he'd called her by a different name.

"There'll be none of that," Kade said, and his arms tightened around her, just a little, though he held the reins easy, like he'd been born with them in his hands. "Calm down, Holt."

"Calm down?" her papa hollered, flinging his hat right to the ground and stepping on it once, in a purely ornery way. Lizzie began to wish he'd look scared again, and she didn't hold out much hope that he'd be over his fit anytime soon. "Damn it all to hell, Lizzie, if you ever run off like that again—"

"I wanted to see Grandpa," she explained, chin high. "And you'd better not whup me, either, because he might just whup *you*."

Her uncles chuckled at that, but none of them spoke.

Her papa let out his breath, and his big shoulders seemed to sag a little. "Lizzie, what the devil were you thinking? If you wanted to see that old buzzard, I would have taken you there myself. But to set out on your own—"

Lizzie stiffened her spine, the way she'd seen Chloe do. There wasn't another woman in the world, now that her mama was gone, that she admired more than Chloe. "You'd have said you had work to do, and I should be a good girl and study my lessons," she replied.

Jeb shifted in his saddle. "We ought to take Lizzie back to the Triple M, Holt," he said. "She'll be safer there, with plenty of women to look out for her."

Lizzie's papa bent to pick up his hat and tried to

straighten it out, but it was ruined for good. He gave her a look that would have meant a trip to the woodshed for sure, she figured, if her uncles hadn't been there to see that he kept his temper.

"You're right," her papa said. She could plainly see that he didn't like admitting even that much, though, not one bit. "I take it you were on your way to the Circle C when you ran across my hellion of a daughter?"

"We were," Rafe told him. "We've wasted enough time. We've got to find Jack Barrett."

He considered that, then mounted up. His hat was a loss, so he threw it aside, and it landed in the branches of a juniper tree.

They rode back to the Triple M at a hard gallop, and by the end of it, Lizzie not only wondered if she really wanted a pony after all; she felt like she'd already been spanked.

He met them in the dooryard, her grandpa, but he didn't look inclined to talk. He was dressed to ride, he had his old horse, Zeus, right handy, and he was wearing a gun belt, just like the rest of the men.

He spared her a smile, though, and she hoped nobody would mention that she'd run away from home. Face-to-face with him, and thinking sensibly again, now that the fit of sorrow had passed, she knew he wouldn't like what she'd done any better than her papa had.

"You go inside, Lizzie-beth," Angus said, and even though he was talking to her, he was looking up at his four sons. "Tell Concepcion to give you the present I was keeping back for Christmas."

Kade leaned to set her on her feet. She glanced back at her papa, who still looked as if he could bite a rusted horseshoe clean in half, then studied her grandfather.

"I'm not going to Texas," she said, in case anybody thought different, and headed for the house. "Not ever."

57

Chloe tried her best, but she couldn't concentrate on the lessons that Monday morning, even though her students were all there, bright-faced and eager.

She resolved to keep her mind on good things. Walter and Ellen Jessup must have settled in nicely with the Fees, for they were scrubbed and brushed, each sporting a new set of clothes, which probably represented quite a sacrifice for Sam and Sarah. Jennie Payle had all her arithmetic problems right, and when it came time for the first recess, she didn't hold back, like before, but ran and played with the Sussex boys, and even laughed out loud once or twice.

Still, Chloe felt uneasy, and her thoughts kept straying to Jeb, who'd made it clear that he would never trust her again, and to Lizzie, who would be left behind when her stubborn father took himself back to Texas.

She got through the day by rote, and when three o'clock came, she dismissed the children, washed down the blackboard, made sure the fire was out in the stove, and went straight to the churchyard to sit with John a while, hoping that would settle her nerves.

Becky was already there, wrapped in a cloak against the chilly wind and wearing a bonnet. Her back was straight, and her head was not bowed, but there were tears on her face.

Chloe stopped, feeling like an intruder, and would have slipped away, hoping to go unnoticed, if Becky hadn't seen her right away.

The older woman smiled.

"Did you love him?" Chloe heard herself ask in an anxious whisper. She was thinking about love a lot these days—and nights—thanks to Jeb McKettrick.

Becky sighed. "With all my heart and soul," she said.

Chloe's eyes burned, and her throat felt tight. She had to squeeze out her answer. "You must miss him terribly."

"Every minute," Becky confirmed. "If I could trade all the rest of my life for one hour with him, I'd do it."

Chloe swallowed hard. No more words would come, and she couldn't think of any anyway.

"Love is a rare and precious commodity, Chloe," Becky said quietly, and her eyes were wise, seeing deep, even through a veil of tears. "Not everybody gets the chance, and only a fool lets pride stand in the way when that chance comes."

Chloe said nothing, but she managed to shake her head.

"Do you love Jeb, Chloe?" Becky asked. Her voice was

kind, but relentless, too. She would settle for nothing but the truth, and she'd know if she was shortchanged in the transaction.

"Yes," Chloe managed.

"Then stop this foolishness, right now," Becky said. "Take the first chance you get to settle things between you. The shooting should have convinced you that we never know, any of us, how much time there is."

Chloe sniffled, shook her head again. "It isn't that easy," she whispered. "He thinks I'm a liar, and he wants nothing to do with me, ever. He told me that straight out."

"And you believed him?" Becky chuckled, as if mystified. "He's stubborn, that's in his blood. Jeb's a McKettrick, after all. But I've been watching him since Kade brought him back from Tombstone last spring, and since you got here, too. Before you came to Indian Rock, he could have had his pick of half a dozen women, what with all the brides Kade and Rafe ordered up; but he didn't do any more than dance with them."

"He thought we were married," Chloe said, despairing.

"Did he?" Becky inquired, raising an eyebrow.

Chloe stiffened. No, Jeb *hadn't* thought they were married. He'd believed exactly the opposite, that he'd been duped, that she was Jack Barrett's wife, body and soul, and up to some kind of treachery. Why, then, had he been faithful to a woman he regarded as someone else's?

"Jumping Jupiter," Chloe said, going weak under the weight of that revelation.

"Exactly," Becky replied. "Is Jeb still on the Circle C?"

Chloe shook her head, reminded that he'd left Holt's ranch in a cold rage. Reminded that Lizzie had lost her home and perhaps her father, too.

"It's too hard," she said.

Becky looked her over. "That's not John Lewis's daughter talking," she said. "There must have been a mistake somewhere along the line. No child of his could ever be a coward."

Color throbbed in Chloe's face. She was on the verge of protesting that she wasn't a coward, that she was *indeed* John Lewis's daughter, when Becky smiled. Humming softly under her breath, she bent to lay a wildflower, surely one of the last to be found in the high country, at the base of his headstone.

Chloe took a step toward Becky, then a step toward the schoolhouse. Damned if she knew which way to go, literally or figuratively.

"You're right, Becky," she said. "I have been a coward. There's a man who means to kill Jeb, and I'm scared it'll happen. I've never been so afraid of anything in my life."

Becky lifted her chin. "If you pull back now," she said, "you'll be letting that man win, and you'll have to live with the consequences."

With that, she turned and walked away, leaving Chloe alone with her thoughts and the bite of a northerly wind, promising winter.

*   *   *

The cabin was empty, though there were signs of recent habitation. Angus and the others found stores of food, an abandoned buckboard, and a coffee mug on the spool table inside. Mold was already forming on the dregs.

"He won't be back here," Angus said to Holt. Jeb and Kade were outside, beating the brush for Jack Barrett, and Rafe had spotted stray horses, probably Barrett's team, and gone to round them up, check for brands. If the animals were marked, they might be able to find the original owner and get some information out of him.

When Sue Ellen had written those two words on the ledger page, they'd known this was the place she meant because it was the only empty homestead standing for miles around. If such ruins were found on Triple M land, Rafe generally burned them to the ground, but this one was within the borders of the Circle C.

Holt cursed. "I'm one hell of a Ranger," he muttered. "Lucky to find my ass with my hat, let alone the bastard who tried to kidnap my daughter."

"If we have to turn over every rock in the Territory," Angus said, with conviction, "we'll do it, but we'll find him."

Holt met his eyes, something he'd been careful not to do, Angus had noticed, for the better part of the day. "We?" he asked.

"Whether you like it or not, Holt," Angus said, "you're

a McKettrick, and we're your family. You're stuck with us, good times and bad."

Holt sighed, worn down by his worry over Lizzie, and Angus felt sorry for him, though he was too smart to show it. "What is it that I want from you?" his son muttered, shaking his head as if to clear it.

"You want my blessing," Angus said. His thoughts were following another trail, though. During the long night just past, it had come to him—Holt had taken a shine to Chloe, his brother's woman. *That* was why he was so all-fired eager to head for Texas.

Holt made a disgusted sound. "I couldn't care less what you think about me, old man."

"I suppose that's why you traveled all the way from Texas to be a burr under my hide," Angus said with a mildness he didn't feel. In truth, he wanted to take his boy by the shoulders, make him look him in the eyes, make him see, somehow, that he loved him as much as Rafe and Kade and Jeb. Tell him that what he felt for Chloe would pass, when he found a woman of his own. "Lot of places you could have picked to settle, but you chose Indian Rock."

At the edge of his vision, Angus saw Kade step into the doorway, take a measure of the situation, and duck out again. There might be hope for those three rascals yet, but getting them all going in the right direction was like trying to herd a bunch of scalded cats through a mouse hole.

"Here's the fact of the matter, Holt," Angus went on when his firstborn didn't speak. "Take it or leave it. You are my son, and I love you. I have never said that straight out to anybody but Lizzie, your mother, Georgia, and Concepcion. You're a fine man, and I'm proud of you, even if your head is harder than a plate of Arizona bedrock." He chuckled, though he hadn't felt so much like weeping since Georgia passed. "Guess you came by that honestly."

Holt stared at him, confounded. Maybe, Angus thought, he'd gotten through all that granite at last, but he didn't want to be hasty in his hopes. The fall might just kill him if he let them rise too high, and his foothold was tenuous.

"Chloe—" Holt began after a good long time.

"You'll get over that."

The boy looked taken aback. Maybe he thought his old man didn't recall what it was like to be young. "Jeb," he said, "is my brother. Chloe is his wife. How do I—?"

"You let some time pass, that's all. Maybe you tell Jeb how you feel, and maybe you don't, but running away won't solve anything, Holt. Nobody knows that better than I do."

There was a long pause while Holt worked out the knots in his thinking. Finally, with an expulsion of breath—relief, Angus thought—he nodded, and there was an easing in the way he held himself.

Another silence fell, even longer than the first. Angus waited it out.

"What about the ranch?" Holt finally asked.

"Which one?" Angus asked, stalling. Scared to hope he'd gotten through.

"The one I just sold you. Maybe I want to buy it back."

Tread carefully, you old coot, Angus told himself. *There are pot-holes aplenty along this trail.* He shifted his weight, wedged his thumbs under his gun belt. "It's too late for that," he said. "You signed a bill of sale, and I wrote you a bank draft. Anyhow, it doubles the size of the Triple M."

"What the hell do you expect me to do without any land?"

"I reckon you should have thought of that before you made the deal," Angus said, praying he wasn't overplaying his hand. "And I never said you wouldn't have land."

Holt shoved a hand through his hair, exasperated. No wonder he was so muddle-headed, going around without a hat. Even in the fall of the year, the high country sun could fry a man's brain. "What the *hell* are you trying to say?"

Angus cocked a thumb toward the dooryard. "That you're as much my son as any of those yahoos out there," he said. "And that means it's only fair to include you in the deal I made with them. Get yourself a wife, and you'll run the Triple M, since you've already met one of the conditions by giving me a grandchild." He paused, laughed out loud at the images that came to mind—Rafe, Kade, and Jeb would be scrambling for sure. "Goddamn, that would piss them off," he finished, with a nod toward the cabin door.

A slow, incredulous grin spread across Holt's face. Folks said Holt looked like him, but Angus saw a lot of the boy's mother in him, and sometimes it wrenched his heart. "Maybe I'll send for a mail-order bride," he said.

"That would take a while," Angus allowed.

Holt was clearly mulling things over again.

"There's one other stipulation," Angus said, wondering why he didn't have better sense than to do a jig on thin ice.

Holt's gaze was fierce. "Like what?"

"You'll have to take your right name back. You're a McKettrick, and calling yourself Cavanagh is a lie. Nothing good ever came of jimmying with the truth."

Holt didn't answer, and Angus didn't press. He'd given the lad plenty to chew on as it was.

"Guess we'd better get back on that polecat's trail," Angus said with resignation. "We're burning daylight here, and God only knows what devilment Barrett is up to by now."

"I'm not moving into your house, old man," Holt said as they both made for the door, and darn near got wedged in the narrow space, shoulder to shoulder.

"You can stay where you are," Angus told him. "Just remember, that place is part of the Triple M now, and it's going to stay that way, no matter which of you boys ends up calling the shots."

Holt held his ground for a few moments, then sighed and stepped back to let Angus pass through the doorway.

Smiling, he stepped into the sun.

Rafe, Kade, and Jeb were standing side by side in the knee-high grass, and they didn't look cheerful. Especially Jeb.

Might as well get it over with, Angus decided. "Holt's in the contest now," he said bluntly. "If he lands a wife, the whole shootin' match will be his."

The silence was ominous, and Jeb, not surprisingly, was the first to break it. "I'll be a son of a bitch!" he rasped, and whirled to mount his horse. He might have had two good hands, he did it so easily.

Rafe and Kade stayed where they were, glaring at Holt.

"You can ride out," Angus told them, "or you can help us track down this Barrett feller. It's up to you."

Rafe swore, and Kade looked like he might go for Holt's throat, if not Angus's own. Jeb simmered atop his horse like a kettle about to boil over.

Angus waited, as immobile as a canyon wall, holding his breath.

Rafe and Kade climbed into their saddles, and for a moment the three of them looked as though they might take the option he'd offered, and light out for home, or even parts unknown.

"Are you coming, old man?" Rafe finally demanded. "We've got a hard ride ahead."

Angus ducked his head so they wouldn't see his smile, and got on his horse. There might be a fight down the road, but he had four sons behind him, however mulish their natures.

Jack Barrett didn't stand a chance.

58

𝒞hloe was in a grand dither, after her conversation with Becky next to John Lewis's grave, and try as she might, she couldn't settle herself down. Driven to take some kind of action, she went to the telegraph office and wired the judge in Tombstone, requesting written confirmation of her divorce from Jack Barrett. She couldn't wait for a response to the letter she'd sent earlier.

Taking action should have resolved some of her turmoil, but it didn't. Jeb was far away, and she couldn't just go to him and tell him how she felt, much as she wanted to do exactly that. The distance was too great, and too dangerous, with Jack out there, watching. Waiting for his chance.

She would have to bide her time, whether she liked it or not.

She went back to the cottage behind the schoolhouse, built up the fire, and set water on for tea. She paced, and just when she thought things couldn't get any more trying, her gaze fell on the wall calendar, the one she'd brought with her from Tombstone.

Awareness struck her like a bucketful of cold water.

She rushed over, flipped back the pages, noting the small x's she'd made at precise intervals of twenty-eight days, then flipped them forward again.

"Dear God," she whispered, torn between an elemental jubilation and absolute horror. It seemed she had one thing more to tell Jeb McKettrick, and it would put paid to matters, in his mind anyway, for all time and eternity.

He would want their baby, there was no question about that.

But would he want her?

Chloe went to the window, looked out at the twilight through a sheen of tears, seeing the place where Jeb had stood that momentous night, the night they had conceived their child, serenading her.

She heard the door open behind her, and smiled, even though her heart was in pieces, as she turned.

But it wasn't Jeb standing just inside her cozy little cottage, come by some sweet miracle of fate to hear the news. No, it was Jack Barrett.

"Hullo, Chloe," he said, leaning back against the door. He was holding his .44 on her. "Don't scream, or I swear to God I'll shoot you."

Chloe might have screamed anyway, if it hadn't been for the baby tucked away inside her, silently trusting in her good sense.

Jack pushed away from the door, hung up his hat beside her calico bonnet, like any husband coming home after a long day and expecting a welcome. Except, of course, for the .44, still aimed squarely at her center.

"What do you want?" she asked, though she knew. Even as terror seized her, a new strength flowed beneath it, buoying her up, clearing her mind, sifting the confusion roiling there into a soft sediment at the base of her spirit. Strange, she thought, that in the face of death, she should come smack up against the true nature of its opposite. Life. Rich, vibrant, contrary life.

How very much she loved it, and what a fickle steward she had been.

"You," he said. "I want you. I would purely hate to kill you, Chloe, but I will, if you don't listen to reason."

"I'm listening," she said, standing absolutely still, grateful that he had stopped at the table instead of coming to her.

The teakettle boiled over, the water sizzling on top of the tiny stove. Chloe thought she heard the sound of approaching horses, beyond the hiss, but decided it was wishful thinking when Jack didn't react.

"You'd best see to that kettle," he said. He'd laid the .44 on the table, but his hand rested lightly upon it, and his finger was still curled around the trigger.

Chloe forced some starch into her knees, walked over, and, using a dish towel, lifted the pot off the heat. Men's voices. She heard them clearly, from the direction of the schoolyard, and closed her eyes.

No, Jeb, she thought, with desperate calm. *Don't come any closer.*

She turned, saw Jack smiling, and knew he'd heard what she had. He stood, at his leisure, the .44 ready in his hand.

"Well, now," Jack said, grimly pleased. "It seems the McKettricks are better trackers than I thought. When I couldn't get my hands on the little girl—almost had her, too, but they came riding 'round the bend just as I was about to make my move—they must have figured I'd come here next."

"I won't let you hurt him, Jack," Chloe said. Inside, she was screaming, hopelessly, *Run, Jeb! Run!* She knew he wouldn't, though. He didn't know how.

Jack chuckled, shook his head, as if marveling at her stupidity. "This won't be over until they're all dead, Chloe," he said, with deadly reason. "It's Jeb I want, but as long as there's a one of those McKettricks left, I'll be looking over my shoulder. That's not the way I want to live out my days."

Chloe watched him turn, and when he did, she threw the kettleful of boiling water at him. It struck him square in the back, and he screamed with pain and fury, but he was still on his feet. He crossed to her in two strides, grabbed her hard by the hair, and half dragged, half hurled her toward the door. He yanked it open with his free hand and stepped out onto the stoop, the barrel of the .44 digging into her left temple.

The McKettricks were there, all of them, including Holt.

Chloe's gaze locked with Jeb's, and she begged him, with her eyes, to back down. He refused, as clearly as if he'd spoken aloud. He stepped forward, and when Kade reached out to stop him, Angus laid a hand on his arm and shook his head.

"Put the guns down," Jack said. "All of you."

They complied, after a moment's hesitation. Angus, Holt, Kade, and Rafe laid their pistols on the ground, though Jeb kept his. His right arm was still in its sling, Chloe noted with despair, and his holstered gun lay awkwardly against his left side.

"Kick them out of reach," Jack prompted, giving Chloe's hair a yank that sent fresh pain shooting through her scalp.

The McKettricks did as they'd been told—except for Jeb.

Don't do this, Chloe pleaded silently, her gaze never straying from Jeb's face.

He was ignoring her, wholly focused on Jack.

"You shouldn't have messed with my woman," Jack said, with false benevolence. He shook his head. "That was a bad mistake, young McKettrick. A very bad mistake."

"Let her go," Jeb said evenly. His voice was quiet, but the undertone was deadly. A chill wind blew through Chloe's spirit, set her to shivering.

That was when Jack hurled her off the porch, into the grass. She heard the shots in the second before she landed, two of them, one right after the other, and whirled on her hands and knees to look.

Jeb was standing, his pistol still smoking in his hand.

Jack lay sprawled against the cottage door, his face completely gone.

Chloe screamed, scrambled to her feet, dashed across the space between them, and flung herself at Jeb, felt his good arm close blessedly around her. "I'm sorry, Chloe," he whispered, against her temple. "Christ, I'm so sorry."

She clung to him, sobbing, only dimly aware of Angus and the others moving around them, picking up their discarded guns, shoving them into their holsters.

"I love you, Chloe," Jeb said.

She looked up at him, searching his face, his eyes. "Do you mean that?"

"Like I've never meant anything before," he answered.

Another tremor went through her. "Oh, God, I thought sure he'd kill you," she cried. "I was so scared!"

"Everything's all right now," he assured her, but a question took shape in those blue, blue eyes. "Isn't it?"

"I love you, Jeb," Chloe said. "Heaven help me, I love you so much—"

He smiled. "That's all I needed to hear," he said.

Sam Fee and a bevy of other men rushed into the yard, and Angus spoke to them, explaining quietly. Jack's body was gathered up, taken over to Doc's office.

"I sent a wire to the judge in Tombstone," Chloe felt compelled to say, when only she and Jeb were left, there in the gathering darkness. "He'll confirm what I told you, about the divorce from Jack—"

Jeb laid a finger to her lips, stemming the rush of words. "I don't need proof, Chloe," he said. "You're my wife. That's all that's important now."

She let her forehead rest against his chest, gathering her scattered emotions. "There's going to be a baby," she told him.

He cupped her chin in his hand, raised her face for his kiss. "Even better," he said. He nodded toward the door of the cottage, with its speckles of blood. "Let's go inside, Chloe, and shut out the world for a while."

Life roared through her, sweet and infinitely complicated, making its claim.

She nodded, and Jeb took her hand and led her over the threshold.

"Hold me," she said, when the door had been closed and latched behind them.

He kissed her deeply. "I plan to do a lot more than that," he said.

 $\mathcal{T}$om Jessup stood with his hat in his hands, on the front porch of the Triple M ranch house, where Sue Ellen had a habit of sitting for long spells, wrapped in a heavy cloak and watching the creek waters frolic past.

She met his kindly eyes. "Thank you," she said. The words got tangled, coming out, but she'd been practicing them right along, and she knew by the look on Tom's face that he got their meaning. He'd come to call often in the three weeks since she'd escaped Jack Barrett and nearly drowned herself, and each time he'd visited, Sue Ellen had liked him a little more.

"It's turning cold," he said, with a good-natured shiver. "It'll be winter soon, I reckon."

Sue Ellen nodded. She'd be going away, as soon as she was well enough to ride a stagecoach, and even though she should have been happy to leave it all behind, she found she was sad instead.

"Mr. Kade, he's given me the use of that cabin," Tom

said, with considerable effort. "I don't reckon you'd ever want to go back there, on any account."

Sue Ellen stared at him, confounded and faintly hopeful.

"It's a good place," Tom went on, struggling in the throes of some dear misery. He was hands down the shyest man Sue Ellen had ever met, and poor as a church mouse, but she'd have been dead, if not for him. "Just needs some fixing up, that's all."

Sue Ellen didn't move.

"I can't give you fine clothes and the like," Tom proceeded, blushing furiously, and fairly crushing his hat in his big hands, "and I know a woman wants pretty things." He fell silent, struggling again, then cleared his throat and pressed ahead. "What I'm trying to say, here, Sue Ellen, is that I've been half-crazy with loneliness, ever since my Annabel passed. I'd like nothin' better than to marry up with you."

What Sue Ellen felt for Tom Jessup was gratitude, not love, but she was a wiser woman than she'd been when she took up with Mr. Barrett. She freed one hand from the tightly wrapped cloak and extended it to Tom, and he took it hesitantly, and with such wonder that it might have been a treasure.

"I have two young'uns," he said, and flushed again.

She nodded, smiled. She knew a thing or two about raising children, having brought up her brothers and sisters.

"You sayin' yes?" Tom asked, and gulped.

Sue Ellen nodded again. Life had given her a second chance, just as Concepcion had promised it would, and she wasn't about to turn it down. Going back to that cabin would be a hard thing, but there was a rightness about it, too, a sense of making over old things into new. She'd plant a garden, hang curtains at the windows, and learn to love Tom Jessup and his children.

"Hallelujah!" Tom shouted, and threw his hat in the air.

Holt McKettrick—he wore the name self-consciously, like a suit of foreign clothes—had no intention of getting married, even to get control of the sprawling Triple M. For the time being, he meant to concentrate on getting over his infatuation with Chloe. He and Jeb hadn't discussed it, never would, probably, but there was an understanding between them just the same. He'd been willing to leave behind everything that mattered to him, to do the right thing, and Jeb knew that.

On the other hand, he didn't mind letting his younger brothers think he was looking to take a wife. It was a pleasure to watch them scramble.

Thinking these thoughts, he whistled under his breath as he walked into the barn at the Triple M, looking for Lizzie. Found her just where he'd expected—with Old Blue and the puppies, in the back stall.

She looked up at him with both excitement and trepidation in her eyes. "You going to Texas?" she asked, and he could tell she was holding her breath.

He hunkered down beside her. "Nope," he said, surveying the pups. They were big now, less interested in their patient mother than in exploring every corner of the stall. "Which one of these ugly customers did you finally settle on?"

Her small face glowed with relief. "That one," she said, pointing to a fat little female with a ring around one eye. "Can we take her home?"

"If she's ready to leave her mama," Holt allowed, and then wished he'd chosen different words. The subject of Olivia still lay between them; he'd never been able to find a way through all the regret, all the wishing he'd done things differently, when he'd had the chance.

"She's big," Lizzie said, with confidence, gathering the puppy to her and holding it close. It squirmed and licked Lizzie's face, and she laughed with a delight that soothed a lot of bruises inside Holt.

"Lizzie," he said hoarsely.

Her gaze shot to his face, wondering.

He laid a hand on her back. "I'm so sorry," he said.

"For what?" she asked, her brow crumpled.

"For leaving your mother," he said. "For not being there when you needed me."

She leaned forward and placed a wet, impulsive kiss on his cheek. "That's all right," she said, with an air of finality.

Surely a prize like the forgiveness of an innocent child

could not be won so easily. Holt looked away, blinked. Looked back. "I'll do my best to make it up to you, Lizzie. All of it."

"I wouldn't mind a new mother," Lizzie speculated. "Not that anybody could replace Mama."

Holt smoothed her hair. "When you're ready," he said, "I'd like you to tell me everything you remember about her."

She smiled, nodded, then looked happily speculative. "You could send away for a wife, like Uncle Rafe did," she said.

Holt laughed. "Don't tell your uncle Rafe," he answered, in a confidential whisper, "but I don't think I'm brave enough to do that."

Lizzie looked disappointed, but only briefly. "All right, then," she said, with resignation, "we'll just have to get along on our own until you find her, I guess."

He recalled what Angus had said in that godforsaken cabin the day Jeb had put a finish to Jack Barrett, words that hadn't come easily to the old man, and didn't come easily to him, either. He'd had next to no practice at saying them. "I love you, Lizzie."

She put the puppy down, threw her arms around his neck, and nearly toppled him. "Concepcion said you'd say that," she said, into his shirt collar, "if I just waited."

He kissed the top of her head, then stood, hoisting her onto his hip.

"I'm a pretty big girl to be carried," she told him solemnly.

He laughed again. "I think I can manage. Let's go inside, Lizzie. Your aunt Mandy has been baking pies. Turns out she's a pretty fair hand at it, and all of a sudden, I'm starved."

60

*T*hroughout the winter, Jeb had lived in town with Chloe, in the cottage behind the schoolhouse. He rode to the ranch every morning, just after dawn, and returned around suppertime, except when a blizzard made the trail impassable, and even that didn't generally stop him. Each night, she made supper and told him about her day at school, but he was not so forthcoming about his own efforts. She knew from Emmeline and Mandy, both of whom were as obviously pregnant as she was, that he didn't spend much time working with his brothers, but they would tell her nothing more, and she was mystified.

The last day of school came and went, and Doc Boylen told her, as kindly as possible, that the town council would be hiring a replacement for the fall term. It was virtually unheard of for a married woman to teach, and one about to bear a child was simply beyond their capacity to accept.

Chloe was standing in the center of the schoolhouse, saying good-bye to it all, when she heard a wagon roll up outside.

She went to the open doorway and saw Jeb grinning at her from the buckboard, the reins resting lightly in his gloved hands. "Time to go home, Mrs. McKettrick," he said.

She looked around the schoolhouse, just once more, and closed the door. Jeb had already loaded her belongings into the back of the wagon, and now he got down, took her in his two good arms, and kissed her, right there on the main street of town.

He lifted his gaze from her face to the building behind her. "I guess you'll miss this place," he said.

She sighed. "Yes," she admitted.

He kissed her forehead. "One thing I've learned," he said. "Never look back. Everything good is up ahead."

She blinked away her tears, tears of happiness and nostalgia, mixed together. "You didn't have to learn that," she told him. "You were born knowing it."

He smiled. "We'd best get home while it's still light."

She nodded, and he lifted her carefully into the wagon, a harder job than it had once been, now that she was within a month of delivering their child.

When they reached the turnoff that led toward the Triple M, Jeb surprised Chloe by steering the team in another direction.

"Where are we going?" she asked.

"You'll see," he told her.

They climbed and climbed, through stands of junipers,

then pines. "This used to be Rafe's place," Jeb said, relenting a little in the face of Chloe's consuming curiosity. "He got mad at Emmeline and put a torch to it."

Chloe frowned, trying in vain to reconcile that Rafe with the one she knew. Except for the matter of the ranch, which continued to plague the three younger McKettrick brothers, each of whom was hoping his wife would be the first to give birth to an heir, he seemed an equitable man. He worked tirelessly, and there was nothing he wouldn't do for his Emmeline.

A small log structure stood, alone and brave, on top of the rise.

Chloe's heartbeat quickened. Was this to be their home, hers and Jeb's and the baby's? Angus had been building on to the ranch house, whenever the winter weather permitted, and she'd assumed they'd live there, with the others.

Jeb set the brake, laid down the reins, jumped to the ground, and walked around to hold his arms up for Chloe.

He gave an exaggerated grunt while lifting her down, as though the weight of her was a strain on his muscles, and she laughed and swatted at him in playful objection.

"Is this where you've been working all winter long?" she asked.

He nodded and, holding her hand, pulled her toward the cabin.

"It's a little isolated," he told her, with cheerful resignation, "but the way Pa and Holt are hiring ranch hands, I reckon this will be the middle of town before long."

"I don't mind living out here," Chloe said. "Not as long as I'm with you."

He pushed open the door, gestured grandly for her to precede him over the threshold. She was a little disappointed that he wasn't going to carry her, but she *was* heavy, and unwieldy into the bargain.

With a sigh, she stepped inside.

Her breath caught in her throat.

There was a blackboard on one wall, with a desk placed just to one side, and facing a lot of smaller ones.

She turned, looked up into Jeb's face.

"It's a school," she whispered.

He grinned. "Yup," he said.

"You built me a *school*."

"I surely did." He gathered her close, bent his head to kiss her, lingeringly.

She wept, full of amazement and pure happiness. "Oh, Jeb."

He stroked her cheek with the backs of his knuckles. The hope in his eyes touched her heart, moved her even more deeply than the kiss had done. "Do you like it?"

He'd worked through the winter on that little country schoolhouse, built it with his bare hands, and probably alone, between ferocious snowstorms. And all this while, he'd kept it a secret, this incomprehensible gift. It was so much more than a building—it was an affirmation that she had something to offer the world, something important.

"I love it," she said. *And I love you. Dear God in heaven, how I love you, Jeb McKettrick.*

His tension eased visibly. "The Jessups live just over the hill," he said, with a quiet eagerness that brushed against her spirit like an angel's feather. "Now that Tom and Sue Ellen are married, Tom's kids will be living with them, instead of Sam and Sarah. So you'll have at least two pupils when the new term starts." He looked worried. "Of course, it's a long way from the main house—"

She rested a hand on either side of his face. "We'll manage, Jeb," she said.

"You'll need to bring the baby along with you," Jeb went on, still fretting a little. Then he smiled again. "I reckon we ought to build a house, right here, so you don't have so far to travel."

She slipped her arms around his neck. "You are a remarkable man," she told him.

He left her to build a small fire in the shiny new stove, which stood in the far corner of the room. Evidently, they were staying a while.

Chloe went to the blackboard, picked up a piece of new chalk from the narrow tray beneath it, and wrote in large, flowing letters, I LOVE JEB MCKETTRICK.

He laughed, but his eyes were serious. He approached, laid a hand to either side of what had once been her waist. "Thank you," he murmured.

"For what?"

"For a thousand things. For being a redheaded hussy and putting up with me. For carrying my child."

Chloe arched an eyebrow. "A 'redheaded hussy,' am I?"

He laughed. Kissed her lightly. "That and more," he said.

61

Indian Rock
JULY 4, 1887

A few eager types were already setting off fire-crackers, even though it was barely dawn, but Holt figured the best explosions of the day would seem like mere whimpers, compared to the blast that was bound to go off once his brothers awakened from last night's celebratory drunk to find themselves locked up in Sam Fee's jail.

He sighed and settled back in Sam's chair, feet on the desk, hands cupped behind his head, grinning. They'd made it so damn easy. They'd brought their well-ripened wives to town the day before, guessing by certain signs that the babies would be coming soon, and settled them in at the Arizona Hotel, under Becky's assiduous care. Doc had examined the mothers-to-be, in strictest privacy, of course, and announced that there was plenty of time.

The scribbled note from Emmeline was still tucked away in Holt's shirt pocket. *Mandy, Chloe, and I are counting on you to keep our husbands away until we've all delivered our children, no matter how long it takes. Concepcion will keep Angus corralled until she receives word from one of us. Please employ any means of restraint necessary, short of murder. In gratitude, E.*

Holt intended to keep that little missive on his person until such time as he could tuck it between the pages of the McKettrick Bible. It was, to his mind, a piece of family history.

Behind him, a cot creaked. There was a moment of quivering realization, seeming to fill the whole jailhouse, then Rafe's voice, bellowing. "What the hell—?!"

At last, Holt thought, setting his feet on the floor and swiveling the chair to meet Rafe's furious glare. He'd been waiting for this moment ever since he'd invited the boys to the Bloody Basin, the night before, for a few toasts to impending fatherhood. Ranch hands from the Triple M had helped him steer the inebriated yahoos here, when the whiskey supply was all but exhausted, and lock them up.

It would be a pure miracle if any of them recalled the journey.

Now, on the inevitable morning after, Rafe was upright again, holding the bars of the cell he and Kade shared, his grip so tight that the knuckles stood out. Kade stirred in the other cot, and Jeb in the next cell.

"Morning," Holt said affably. "Sleep well?"

Kade stood up, groaned, and sat down again, clasping his head in both hands. Jeb muttered something unintelligible and hoisted himself to his feet, looking around, first in bafflement, then with rising irritation.

"Open this door, you ring-tailed polecat!" Rafe shouted.

Kade flinched. "Don't yell," he pleaded.

Holt folded his arms, but made no move to rise out of his chair. He tried to look regretful. "I wish I could turn you loose," he told Rafe, "but I've got strict orders from the McKettrick women to keep the three of you penned up, and I wouldn't dare disobey."

The change in Rafe's face was downright comical to watch, ranging from anger to bewilderment to horrified comprehension, all in the space of a few seconds. "But Emmeline's about to—"

"Give birth," Holt finished for him, lightly. He sighed, delighting in the way Jeb and Kade came to their senses, as swiftly as if they'd been yanked up hard against those iron bars.

"So is Mandy," Kade said, bleakly outraged.

"So is Chloe!" Jeb barked, his statement tumbling roughshod over Kade's.

Holt shook his head, struggling not to smile. "Remarkable, isn't it? All of them coming to term on the same day? What are the chances of that?" He paused, pretended to consider the marvel. "Unless, of course, they all got pregnant at the same time." He made a show of counting on his fingers. "Takes us back to the night Katie was born, or thereabouts. You must have been inspired."

"Damn you, Holt," Jeb rasped, "let me out of here! I've got to get to Chloe!"

"I surely will," Holt assured him. "When it's over."

Kade glowered. "Who put you up to this? The women?"

"None other."

"Why?" Rafe ground out, looking exasperated now, giving the bars a hard rattle just to expend some of that bull strength of his.

"It would be my guess that they don't want you to know which baby was born first," Holt answered, in moderate tones.

"How are we supposed to figure out who gets the ranch?" Kade demanded. He looked as if he might just try to chew his way out of that cell.

Holt arched an eyebrow. "You're supposed to be the smart one, aren't you?" he countered easily. "They've taken matters into their own hands, Emmeline, Mandy, and Chloe, with some help from Becky and Doc Boylen, not to mention Concepcion. I figure they want the ranch divided four ways, and they're not going to tell which baby was born first until their demands are met."

Kade sat down hard on the cot. Jeb kicked the wall. Rafe spat a curse.

"Where's Pa?" Kade asked, recovering first. "He'll straighten this out."

"Concepcion's probably got him hog-tied someplace," Holt said.

Jeb strained to see the clock on the sidewall. "The babies—?"

Holt went to the stove, poured himself some coffee, drank with noisy satisfaction. "While you boys were over at the Bloody Basin last night, swilling whiskey, bragging, and making bets with each other, the ladies were getting down to business. I figure we'll hear something soon."

Rafe was pale with frustration, barely controlled annoyance, and fatherly concern. "It was *your* idea to pay a visit to the Bloody Basin," he pointed out. "I seem to recall that you bought the drinks."

Holt allowed himself a smile, took another sip of coffee, and did not bother to defend himself.

"Did you put something in that whiskey?" Jeb wanted to know, and there was an accusatory note in his voice.

Kade's attention was on the coffee. He was powerfully fond of the stuff. "You *bastard*," he growled.

Holt laid his free hand to his chest, splayed, in the manner of a man sorely wounded. "I'm as legitimate as you are. Just ask our dear old daddy."

"You doctored those drinks!" Rafe roared. He was a single-minded sort, ofttimes to his advantage, but more often, to his detriment.

"I didn't have to," Holt said. "The way you three were throwing them back, all I had to do was watch and wait. And make sure the bartender got paid, of course." He speculated a moment. "Your credit isn't too good at the Bloody Basin, it seems."

They were digesting that, his trio of recalcitrant brothers, when the jailhouse door burst open and young Harry Sussex blew in, wild-eyed. No doubt, he'd been dispatched by either Becky or Doc.

"They're here!" he shouted. "The babies are here—all three of them!"

All hell broke loose in the cells, but Holt took his time getting the keys out of Sam's desk drawer, opening Jeb's cell first, then Kade and Rafe's.

They fairly trampled him and Harry, getting to the door. From the sidewalk, Holt watched with interest as the three of them raced toward the Arizona Hotel, Jeb in the lead, Rafe and Kade gaining fast.

Harry tugged at his sleeve. "Mr. Holt?"

Holt looked down at him, questioning. Fished a nickel out of his pants pocket to reward the boy for his efforts.

"All girls," Harry said, grinning.

Holt laughed out loud. It was a new day on the Triple M.

Epilogue

*A*ngus McKettrick stood beside Georgia's grave, high on the ridge overlooking the ranch they'd built together. A few yards away, Concepcion sat on a blanket spread in the grass, nursing little Katie. The sight of her stung Angus's eyes and set the back of his nose to burning. For one man to have so much, well, it was past understanding.

He took off his hat, touched the stone angel guarding Georgia's resting place with the rough tips of his fingers.

"I came to tell you that you don't need to worry none about any of our boys," he said quietly. He heard the baby laugh, a sweet sound of celebration, a call to travel on, in good spirits, toward whatever lay in store.

"They're all three married now, with babes of their own," Angus went on. "Rafe and Emmeline, they called their girl Georgia, after you. Kade and Mandy's is Rebecca, and Jeb and Chloe drew a little red-haired bit of a thing. Named her Anne. Said it was as close as they could get to Angus. I just thank God that baby wasn't a boy."

He felt Concepcion's gaze on him, turned his head to acknowledge her.

She smiled, nodded ever so slightly.

"Holt's come home, too, where he belongs. I know you always wanted that, just like I did. You'd like him, Georgia. He's strong, maybe because he mostly raised himself once Ellie died and I left him, and he's good to that little daughter of his. Lizzie, she's called. She's a pistol, I'll tell you. I wish you could have met her."

A soft breeze ruffled his white hair, thinning now that the years were catching up, and he would have sworn he felt Georgia touch the center of his heart. He used to get the same feeling sometimes, when they were alone and she smiled at him in a private way.

"I reckon you're wondering about the ranch," he said, turning his hat in his hands. "Well, I divided it among them, four ways. Equal shares, right down the line. Emmeline and Mandy and Chloe, they wouldn't have it any other way. Birthed those babies of theirs upstairs at the Arizona Hotel, on Independence Day, mind you, and not a dern one of them will say who crossed the finish line first. Swore Doc and Becky to secrecy, too." He chuckled, shook his head, put his hat back on. "It devils me considerable, wondering how it all would have turned out if they hadn't pitched a petticoat rebellion."

He looked out over the land again, miles of red dirt and sparse grass, land soaked with his own sweat. He loved every grain of it, every rock, rabbit hole, and cactus. It was his legacy, and he was proud to pass it on.

Finally, after some wide traveling, his gaze settled back on Concepcion. She had finished feeding the baby and undertook to fasten her bodice up again, her fingers brown and slender and graceful.

"Finished?" she asked, her eyes tender.

He smiled, loving her, not more than Georgia or Ellie, but not less, either. In a new and different way, that was all.

"Just beginning," he answered.

Not sure what to read next?

Visit Pocket Books online at

www.simonsays.com

Reading suggestions for
you and your reading group
New release news
Author appearances
Online chats with your favorite writers
Special offers
Order books online
And much, much more!

Fantasy.
Temptation.
Adventure.

Visit PocketAfterDark.com, an all-new website just for Urban Fantasy and Romance Readers!

- Exclusive access to the hottest urban fantasy and romance titles!

- Read and share reviews on the latest books!

- Live chats with your favorite romance authors!

- Vote in online polls!

 www.PocketAfterDark.com

26119

Get a Lesson in Love

with bestselling historical fiction from Pocket Books!

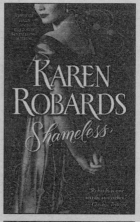

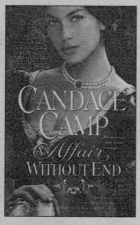

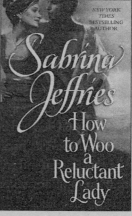